I'd Rather Burn

The Legend of Mortem | Book One

J.L. Weir

Trigger Warnings

I'd Rather Burn contains content which may trigger some readers. If you are bothered by torture, kidnapping, self-harm, or mentions of rape, please consider carefully before reading this book.

CHAPTER 1

They wandered through the decrepit, decaying corridors, beneath the desert sands, the air thick with dust and the stifled whispers of forgotten secrets. The shelves lined with ancient tomes, their leather bindings cracked and peeling, stood like silent sentinels against the ravages of time.

"No one touch these until I've bound them. If we pick them up as is, they'll be as useful as the desert sand when they crumble," Arcadia stated.

They slipped through the dark corridors, allowing their keen sense of sight to guide them. Following the vague amount of intel they were given, they stumbled upon a hidden chamber, untouched for centuries. Crumbling stone statues, their features worn away by time's relentless hand, watched silently from the corners, peering out from beneath layers of dust covered cobwebs.

Lazier pushed aside a thick, cobweb, revealing another shelf lined with crumbling tomes and a pile of rolled up scrolls, their faded words inked across ancient parchment. "I found the scrolls," he called out.

The entire group gathered around and awaited Arcadia to bind them. "It's done, but be gentle when you open the tomes or unroll the scrolls."

Everyone gently, flipped through the tomes and unrolled the scrolls. Nothing out of the ordinary stood out, and after a few hours of sifting through them, a few words in particular, written across the pages with what appeared to be black scroll ink, stood out.

"What is this?" Markus questioned aloud. "Something about an original—it trails off."

Arcadia carefully took it and looked around and nodded toward a large table. "Clear it off."

Markus moved aside some objects which had been strewn about and wiped the layers of dust from the center. They then unrolled the scroll and did their best to decipher the ancient writing.

"It's Galatian," Arcadia stated as he blew the dust off the scroll.

"What does it say?" Markus questioned, unable to fully decipher the ancient writing.

After a few minutes, Arcadia spoke up. "It's talking about a powerful female bedlam. The last descendant of lineage who had once commanded some type of—" he paused, "something—power?" He then ran his fingers down the undecipherable paragraphs. As he scanned further down the parchment, he read another passage. "She's being hunted by those who covet her powers for—" His words trailed off once again as he studied the enigmatic symbols. "I can't make this part out."

While the rest of the group carefully placed the tomes and scrolls into crates, the sound of Arcadia's voice echoing throughout the chamber, made Markus feel as if the hunted female's presence was encompassing him. "You feel that?" he whispered as he glanced around.

"Don't let your imagination take hold." Arcadia chuckled.

His body was solid and heavy as he lay on top of hers; he felt familiar, but not human. He slid his hand up her thigh and pushed her knee to the side, settling himself further between her legs. Every touch of his brought about a lingering, erotic desire. The heat of his tongue left hers as he pulled back and gazed into her eyes. There was a devoid look of desperation behind his coal black pupils; he looked as lost as she felt.

A chill swirled around them, and his burning, amber eyes slowly faded into the darkness. The warmth of their intertwined bodies gave way to a cool detachment. She desperately tried to hang onto him and as they grasped each other's forearms, he whiffed into a smoky haze; the blackness devouring his silhouette. He was becoming an obscure, fuzzy memory, and she stood alone in a blackened wasteland filled with demonic whispers.

A vague voice called her name. Each time she heard the voice call out, it grew further and further out of her grasp. The ground beneath her feet gave way with each step. The decaying vegetation, barely visible, was vanishing into the dismal landscape. She felt as if she was trying to run through a murky bog; with each step denied, she was pulled back to the gluttonous ground. The suction under her feet made it difficult to pick up one foot at a time, rendering her helpless to gain any momentum. The more effort she exerted, the more her body fought against her. The only sound was that of her own footsteps, neither slow nor quick. She looked down and saw nothing but the gliding, featureless fog. There was a familiar stench that wafted through the air, searing her nostrils; the smell of rotting flesh. She did not know where she was, lost in a place that seemed old and otherworldly. It was a place of death and decay. Nebulous waves of mist drifted aimlessly, engulfing her and the vastness of the obscure wasteland.

Once again, she heard the faintest of voices calling out in subdued, muffled tones, echoing from all directions. She tried to run but could not. Something else was also there, whispering words in a language she did not comprehend. She could feel it watching her from off in the distance. Whatever it was, it was there to take her life, and all she possessed.

The neon alarm went off at eight a.m., frightening Jadis awake. She fumbled for her phone, trying to stop the obnoxious beeping. She rolled onto her back, feeling haunted by an inner anxiety. *I need to wake up and wipe the nightmare from my mind. It's just a dream,* she told herself, as she reached for her dogs. Just knowing their health had been declining for some time now, she was thankful they were there at all. Moca, ten, had passed away in her sleep a few weeks ago. She knew Sativa and Tyrian, who were now eleven years old, would also leave her sooner than later because of their failing health.

The sunlight gleamed through the crack in her curtains and the familiar sounds of the jubilant birds singing outside her window brought her a sense of peace and calm. Sativa and Tyrian were now nose-to-nose with her with wagging tales and wet kisses, eagerly awaiting breakfast.

After feeding them and grabbing a couple pieces of toast for herself, they made their way outside. Trees towered above her, standing tall and strong. The landscape was dense and the smell of fresh pine was pure and clean. The only sounds penetrating the silence were the rustling of the leaves, the multitude of songbirds, and the occasional chirping of a chipmunk seeking handouts.

Jadis currently lived in the mountainous terrain known as Sagvon and owned both the home and surrounding acreage, having been passed down by her ancestors for generations; a luxury few mortals could ascertain. Those fortunate enough to possess land were individuals with esteemed connections or holding prestigious positions under the jurisdiction of either Bureau of Antinoc or an appointed, Nosferatu Lord. She lived a solitary life, except for her sisters, Skye and Ivory, who also owned homes on the same land, not too far from her. They were only a year apart in age; Jadis was a year older than Ivory and two years older than Skye. Jadis lived in the shadows, ever present yet indistinct, while her sisters enjoyed all the comforts and conveniences of the modern part of the world. However, their lives were neither ordinary nor mundane, and they had a past, a long and complicated one.

Over the last six months, a strange and eerie presence appeared in the surrounding woods. Nightmares and terrible visions continued to plague Jadis. The stench, the eyes, the death; it always began with her being stalked, subdued, and finally, silenced. It always defeated her in the end and she could never decipher enough to discover what it was. It was unquestionably nerve racking even though she had yet to encounter the haunting phantom.

The same pungent scent of rotting flesh, always drowned out the aroma of the fresh pine and fragrant flowers with its presence. Her dogs also sensed it; their acute sense of smell could detect the faintest of odors. Whenever there was a shift in the energy, the hair on the napes of their neck raised and they would release a guttural growl and quick barks of warning toward their invisible intruder. The wave of elaborate warning calls from the surrounding wildlife never went unnoticed. As the calls of warning ceased, a hushed, eerie silence would fall over the area and the wildlife would move away from the approaching threat, slowly retreating into the forest.

Two days ago, Sativa and Tyrian had passed and for the first time, she felt alone and isolated. She longed for the sounds of their exuberant, rough housing. The house was now muted and still. Only echoes of all twelve feet trotting behind her remained. Shortly thereafter, she decided to stay with her sister Ivory for a while. She had an uneasy feeling she couldn't shake, and she knew something was amiss. She began packing a bag with every intention of putting some distance between herself and the negative energy. After having her dogs by her side as her loyal protectors and companions, her paranoia set in and it became difficult staying there alone, especially at night.

She was heading to bed when out of the corner of her eye she caught a dark veil slowly creeping toward her expansive living room window. Her heart lurched, and she stopped mid-stride. Whatever she did not want to believe existed, the thing from her nightmares, stood on her porch. It was glaring back at her, and there was a cruelty wrapped within its oddly shaped, slate grey eyes. She stood frozen in place; suddenly it vanished, and she knew she had to get the hell out—fast. It should not exist, and yet, there it was.

She grabbed the partially packed bag, ran into the garage, and lunged into the driver's seat, slamming the door shut. She was not about to confront the creature by herself.

She anxiously waited for the door to open, being guided by the starting of her car's engine; her hands clenched around the steering wheel. Her heart stumbled over its own rhythm as she sat with tunnel vision, awaiting what felt like an eternity. However, she knew her car was nothing more than an illusion of security.

She was fully expecting to see whatever it was, standing on the other side of the neon blue door. It slowly rose, revealing the darkness a bit at a time, and to her relief, there wasn't anything there. She then heard what sounded like something enormous, running head first into her house which shook the wall of the garage adjacent to the porch; that was then followed a bloodcurdling, hellish screech off in the distance. She knew a sound like that did not come from anything living in the forest. Her foot hit the gas like a lead weight as she sped out of the garage in reverse. She cranked the wheel, threw the car into drive, and took off down the old dirt road. Kicking up a cloud of dust and debris from beneath her spinning tires, she headed straight for the highway below.

The screeching of her tires, crunching metal and a waterfall of glass shattered the intense silence. Her hands were still wrapped around the steering wheel when she felt a wave of warm liquid running down her face. She lay motionless in the front seat, barely conscious and disoriented. Shock and fear filled her mind, and the pain from her body being jerked around inside the car was excruciating. She reached up to see where the blood was coming from and felt a large gash in her forehead, and began coughing from the smell of smoke, and dust filling her lungs, making it difficult to breathe. She could hear the raging water from the river below, close to where her car had tumbled down the embankment, lodging itself amongst the pine trees. She found herself trapped within the mangled wreckage. The windshield had imploded, and the steering wheel and dashboard were compacted together. She tried to slip out, but she struggled to pull the door handle. Even though her mind was panic stricken, she had a terrifying epiphany. The word *'tracker'* popped into her head, shattering the last of her fragile reality.

As she struggled to open the door, she heard a warm voice call out to her.

"Hey there, I've got you. You're going to be okay," he said calmly.

The stranger pulled her from the wreckage with such ease; it was as if she wasn't trapped at all. She wasn't sure how he was carrying her through the rocky, mountainous terrain. As disillusioned as she was, she couldn't help but fix her eyes on his.

The stranger had the most mysterious eyes, his coal black pupils were surrounded by a swirling amber hue. Although he was very gentle with her, she couldn't deny how powerful he seemed to be. She felt both oddly at ease and on alert at the same time. She thought it was strange she couldn't hear the crunching of the ground or snapping of the brush under the weight of his steps.

All she felt, other than the pain was the rain's relentless, chaotic drops hitting her face. She was trying to reach out mentally to see who was helping her and where he was taking her, but with each attempt, the throbbing pain in her head took over; it was only moments before her vision blurred and everything faded.

Jadis awoke the next morning in someone else's bed. It was large and extravagant, with a solid wood frame which had been hand-carved and engraved with impeccable detail. Shapely raised panels in the headboard and footboard were also intricately detailed.

She didn't recognize the writing carved into the leaves of all four posts on which it stood. She laid in between the silken sheets, feeling the irresistibly soft duvet against her skin. Her head rested on a plush velvet pillow, the warmth of the bed enveloping her.

The remaining furniture was as unique as the bed, dark and rustic, complemented with vibrant cushions and throws. The hues of the room were burnt oranges and reds, giving off a calm, warm feeling. Original oil paintings and antique mirrors hung on the walls. As old as the room seemed to be, someone had impeccably restored it.

She reached up and felt the dressing covering the wound on her forehead. There was still a buzzing in her brain, but the throbbing wasn't as bad as she had remembered last night. She felt hungover, not from drinking but from the nightmares of the accident, along with the physical trauma her body had suffered.

Slowly and reluctantly, she sat up and looked down at herself. She was no longer wearing the clothes she had worn yesterday. Instead, she was wearing someone else's cotton t-shirt, her underwear, and nothing else. Feeling self-conscious, she couldn't help but wonder who had gotten her out of her clothes. She also wanted to know where she was, and who it was that seemed to carry her so effortlessly across the rugged terrain.

There was a soft knock at the door, snapping her out of her train of thought. She grabbed the corner of the duvet and pulled it up.

"Come in," she said, sounding quieter than she had intended.

The door slowly opened, and the mystery man walked in. For whatever reason, how he paused in the doorway momentarily and stared at her made her feel even more self-conscious. His sandy blonde hair was cut close to his scalp around his ears; the top pulled back into a perfectly messy, untamed hair do, and tousled on top of his head. He was tall, at least 6' 3" and in perfect physical shape. He was wearing a tight navy blue t-shirt hugging every muscle, and a pair of loose-fitting jeans hanging on his hips.

It's definitely him. He's the one who pulled me from the car last night. She could smell the familiarity and sense his energy.

As he walked into the room, her beauty took him a-back. He had only seen her from a distance prior to last night, and now he was face to face with her. *She's exquisite,* he thought. She had strikingly soft features, perfect rose-colored lips, and her hair was the color of aged mahogany. The soft, wavy strands tumbled gently down the sides of her face, spilling over her shoulders. *Her eyes are something else all-together.*

"Good morning, how are you feeling?" he asked, breaking the awkward silence, not to mention his fixation.

"Much better, thank you. I assume you're the one who pulled me from my car last night?"

"Yes." He shut the door and walked over to the other side of the bed and pulled open the large, cream-colored drapes, allowing the mid-morning light to shine in through the expansive, floor to ceiling windows.

"I'm Aiden Cirillo and you're Jadis Arwen?"

"Yes, how do you know my name?"

He pointed to where her purse was sitting on top of the large antique bureau on the opposite side of the room from where he was standing.

"We looked last night to see if there was someone to call, but you only had your registered form in there."

She had left in such a hurry last night and out of necessity and her panicking; she grabbed her partially packed duffle bag and took off so abruptly she left everything not within arm's reach behind.

He made a slight motion of his hand toward the other side of the room. "It's on the floor next to the dresser."

Jadis stared at him blankly. *What the hell?* She said to herself. *Not only did he read my mind, there is something strangely familiar about him.* It was as if his smell and his energy had been around her prior to last night when he pulled her from the wreckage.

He noticed the curiosity cross her face. "Yes, I read your thoughts. It's a talent I possess. I apologize. I didn't mean to intrude. Sometimes I forget to turn it off," he explained with a warm smile.

"No worries." She waved her hand in a gesture to let him know it was not a big deal. However, all her senses piqued immediately. She knew she was not in the presence of a mortal and the sooner she got out of there, the better. She also had no desire to bring the horrific visions she had been having into his home.

"Did you say we?" she questioned.

"Yes, I live here with my brothers."

"So last night—this," she pulled at the t-shirt, "did you—?"

He chuckled. "As much as I would have liked to be the one to undress you, it was my brother's wife Madolyn who cleaned you up and helped you into one of my shirts."

With his sudden and unexpected admission, she blushed. She tried to hide it, but she knew the rosiness of her face, would undoubtedly give her away.

"Oh—okay," was all she muttered; her words lost in the warmth of her cheeks.

Aiden took a seat at the window. "You need to eat something. Why don't you get dressed? I'll wait."

She slipped out from under the sheets and pulled the t-shirt down as far as she could, trying her best to be discrete. She could feel his eyes on her as she walked over, collected her bag, and headed to the lavish bathroom adjoining the room. She closed the door behind her and her immediate thought was the need to call her sisters. More importantly, she needed to shield her mind from him.

She sat down on the luxurious alpaca rug. It was dark grey, soft underfoot, and warmer than the onyx marble floor. Jadis and her sisters were well versed in the dark arts and it had served them well, and on more than one occasion. She mentally prepared herself for a quick spell to bind him out. She took a deep breath and began an incantation. Once completed, she finished getting dressed. She put on a pair of torn jeans and a maroon button-up, satin shirt, which hung just below her waistline. She walked out of the bathroom and Aiden was patiently waiting for her.

His smile was warm and friendly. "You look amazing," he offered politely.

She walked over and sat on the end of the bed. "Thank you for everything you've done for me; pulling me from the wreck, bringing me here—I can't thank you enough."

"There's no need to thank me. Let's get you something to eat," he suggested.

"I appreciate the offer, but I'd rather have you call me a car—shit!" She stopped mid-sentence, feeling panic-stricken. *Screw my phone. Where are their ashes?* She leapt from the end of the bed and darted across the room to grab her purse. She dropped to her knees and scavenged through the random items. Although, Jadis kept a phone with her, she only did so to blend in. Her sisters, however, reveled in the technological advancements made by the Nosferatu engineers.

"We didn't find your phone. We looked, but it must have been lost in the wreck. By the way, the ashes are in there."

The ashes? Okay, twice now, as if it were nothing. Welp, apparently I'm going to have to go in stronger to block him out. She thought, as she cast him out of her mind using a darker incantation; not only was she perplexed why the first hadn't worked; she was more concerned that she felt as if her powers were waning. Something was also telling her him not finding her phone was bullshit, but she would not call him out on it while she was alone in the bedroom with him. She also felt a strange, supernatural aura about the place. She glanced around the room, feeling like she was sitting in the middle of a sleeping hornet's nest.

I can't penetrate its energy. I won't be calling anyone, not even psychically, she thought.

She looked over at him as he was getting up. "Aiden, would you call me a ride so I can go see my car and head into town to get a rental? I have somewhere I need to be."

"Let's discuss it over breakfast. Based on that gash, you suffered quite a blow to your head during the accident. Going anywhere right now is not the best idea."

"Okay," she replied softly, having a daunting feeling she wasn't leaving at all. She reminded herself to keep her wits about her. She also needed to figure out what was keeping from her from using the energy around her but would put her questions aside for the moment.

"You ready?" he asked, interrupting her train of thought.

"I am."

They headed out of the bedroom with Aiden leading the way. The hallway was beautiful. All the ornamental handrails had been impeccably carved and made from the finest dark oak. Antique Persian rugs covered the floors, allowing for a glimpse of the outer dark wood edges. At the end of the hall-way was a grandiose staircase which became wider the further down they went. Beautiful old tapestries and original works of art hung from the walls throughout the mansion. Statues of various sizes depicting people and animals, both real and mystical, sat on top of the pedestals at the base of the stairs and throughout the foyer. One statue in particular caught her eye. At about 8' tall, it was beautifully carved and appeared to be made of solid marble. It was an erotic depiction of a man and a woman standing naked, locked in a passionate embrace.

The artwork looks like it should be in a museum or a King's castle, but not in someone's personal residence. They have obviously been building the collection for a lifetime, or were perhaps the fortunate heirs to an inheritance older than the house itself?

"You like it?" A smile tugged at the corner of his mouth.

She motioned her hand toward the statue. "Yes, It's stunning. Is it yours?"

"Yes." He chuckled to himself as he looked at the statue with fond memories. "The statue was a gift, but the rest belongs to our family, most of which has been passed down for generations."

She knew he was being honest about the beauty that surrounded them, however; he was withholding other, more important information for sure. *He sounds genuine enough, but a wolf in sheep's clothing is still a wolf,* she thought.

They made it to the kitchen where other members of his family, or so she assumed, were making breakfast. A young woman looked up from the stove and walked over to her with a radiant smile.

"Hi, how are you feeling today? You look much better than you did last night. I'm Madolyn Cirillo, but call me Maddie. That's Eden Cirillo, my spouse and Aiden's brother."

Madolyn gently took Jadis's hand and led her around the large island sitting in the center of the kitchen and pulled out one of the bar stools.

Jadis thought it was odd they way she winked at Eden when she said he was *her spouse*; it was if she was lying for some reason.

"Take a seat and I'll get you something to eat," Maddie offered.

Eden nodded his head toward Jadis, and she responded in the same manner. She subtly studied Maddie, trying to get a feel for her. She was beautiful and had long, curly, brown hair, and iridescent blue eyes. She was on the taller side, maybe 5' 7" with the build and grace of a dancer.

Her soft, knee high, floral patterned, cotton dress flowed loosely around her tender figure as she walked back around to the stove and finished the eggs. Eden, however was leaning against the counter next to Maddie with his arms crossed, staring at her.

Jadis stared back at him. He was looking at her with a strange, questioning expression and she could feel him trying to pull her thoughts. She was thankful she had done the additional binding spell after the first one had failed against Aiden.

Eden was as big and as strikingly handsome as Aiden. One could easily see the resemblance between the two. However, Eden seemed to be the one in charge and was more intimidating based on first impressions.

"Good morning," Eden said. "You were in quite an accident last night. How do you feel?"

"Good, and I want to thank you all for your help. Madolyn, I appreciate you getting me cleaned up. However, I can't recall anything that happened after the wreck," she replied, hoping Maddie would give her some insight into why she couldn't remember any of it.

"It's Maddie, and please, don't mention it," she said dismissively as she handed her a plate of fresh cut fruit and scrambled eggs. She set a glass of freshly squeezed orange juice down as well.

"Eat something, it will do you some good." Maddie smiled.

It's obvious she will not acknowledge my non-question, Jadis thought.

Maddie took her plate, leaned up against Eden, and he wrapped his arms around her waist. He then pulled her hair to the side and kissed her neck, while she playfully slapped his arm.

"Stop, Eden. We have company." She giggled. "Just ignore him, he's incorrigible."

If this is the hornet's nest, at least Maddie isn't intimidating, Jadis thought. Although she appeared to be mortal, her energy, however, was strange and noticeably different from Aiden's and Eden's, but she couldn't quite put her finger on it.

Aiden took a seat next to Jadis, and they engaged in a light, superficial conversation, which mostly comprised Maddie and Eden teasing each other. *The two appear to be truly in love,* Jadis thought.

Maddie watched how Jadis mostly pushed the eggs around the plate with her fork. "Can I get you anything else?"

"No, this is great, really. I'm just feeling the effects of the accident," Jadis replied. However, she was more tuned into what Aiden and Eden were discussing.

Eden and Aiden briefly mentioned a command center in the house, while vaguely discussing some business and a recent reconnaissance mission; though they shared very little.

"That was a hell of a blow to your head," Maddie said.

"Oh, I felt it." Jadis chuckled.

Aiden stood up, and Eden turned to Maddie and kissed her forehead.

"Will you excuse us? Aiden and I have some business we need to attend to."

"You think you'll be okay here with Maddie?" Aiden asked politely, but based on the undertone in his words he wasn't asking.

"Of course." She looked over at Maddie, who smiled sweetly.

"Go. Jadis and I will be fine."

"Don't worry," Aiden stated, answering her silence, "Our brother, Lars, already had your car towed here. It's in the garage if you'd like to go see it."

"Yes, I would."

"I'll take you to have a look. It will give us some time to get better acquainted," Maddie offered.

As Aiden and Eden walked away, disappearing around the corner, a foreboding feeling crept over Jadis, and she knew she was their *business*, so to speak. Being here wasn't exactly the escape she was hoping for last night.

Jadis and Maddie made their way to the garage where her car sat. It was obvious it wasn't going anywhere, anytime soon, if at all.

"Jesus, it's worse than I thought it would be," Maddie stated, as she looked over the mangled car.

Dammit! Now what? I have no phone and I'm miles from civilization without another home in sight. I have the daunting, mountainous terrain standing between myself and my freedom, not to mention whatever showed up on my porch last night is still out there, lurking somewhere in the shadows. Why else would it be lurking in the forest, outside my home and appearing on my porch if not to kill me? She held her sore wrist as she recollected the events that had started this whole mess. She let go of her wrist and rubbed her face, feeling uncomfortable, confused, and did not know how to deal with her current predicament.

"Hey, Maddie, do you have a phone I can borrow?"

"Sure, but I don't have it on me. I left it in the command center. What do you need?"

"I was hoping to call for a ride. I have somewhere I need to be."

"Is there a friend or family member you need to call? I can let Eden know."

Although she didn't say it, Jadis knew she was fishing for information based on the look of curiosity she shot her way. *She is certainly trying to discern the truth.*

"Sort of," was all she said, being afraid to reveal the unimaginable reality. *I certainly can't tell Maddie I was running from the monstrosity that appeared on my porch conjured straight out of a nightmare. She will think I either have a concussion or I'm bat shit crazy. Not to mention, whatever I reveal to her will obviously be relayed to Eden.*

"We can grab my phone as soon as Eden and Aiden are back. It shouldn't be much longer."

Jadis simply nodded. What other choice did she have but to wait?

CHAPTER 2

A s Jadis stood there with Maddie, her mind wandered back to her nightmares.

She and her and her sisters were being hunted. They were frantically running through the woods. Whatever it was, was closing the distance between them. Her pulse raced as she kept throwing herself forward with even greater abandon. She felt the cold air burning her lungs and the will of her muscles being forced to go far beyond what sprinting could ever demand. Her body and her brain were in full survival mode. It didn't just want them; it needed them, but she did not know why. Her visions were always clouded and abysmal, just a fragmented reenactment. It seemed her sisters were just as uncertain. One thing was obvious; a creature of death was stalking them. Somehow, they were a threat to its very existence. Not only that, but during the same time period, there was also something else lurking around her. It, too, had been hiding in the shadows. She had the same placid feeling every day for months; it was also tracking her. Only it seemed to provide a barrier of protection between herself and the ominous creature.

The situation both scared and intrigued her. As far as she was aware, there was nothing that could remain hidden from her and her sisters, except for the creatures depicted in ancient tales from centuries ago. However, none of this could change her current reality.

"Jadis?" Maddie asked, interrupting her train of thought once again. "You look lost. Is there anything I can do?"

"No, I'm just looking at the wreckage and thinking about how lucky I am Aiden found me when he did." She still wondered what he might have been doing out there so late. "Maddie, do you know how Aiden found me?"

Maddie looked at her as if she were carefully contemplating her words. "Yes, he was handling some family business. As he was about to head back down the canyon, he spotted your car's headlights just down the embankment. He ran toward the lights, found you, pulled you from the wreckage, and brought you here."

"Strange, I don't remember being driven in a car. It felt like he carried me here." She chuckled, again fishing for information she was undoubtedly not going to get.

"He couldn't exactly do that," Maddie said kindly. "You probably just remember him carrying you back up the embankment to his car. Aiden said you passed out shortly after he pulled you from the wreckage."

Maddie's explanation made sense in her mind. But as logical as her answer was, Jadis knew she was lying. *Maddie is covering for them, no doubt about it.*

"Come," Maddie said, making a slight motion with her hand. "Let's go out back and sit on the veranda for a while."

Jadis willingly followed her, assuming once they were outside, she might gain a hold of her energy and make arrangements to leave. She hoped whatever was slowly binding her energetically would be isolated to the mansion.

As Maddie took her for a stroll around the grounds, she had to stop to take in the sights, as it was truly impressive. According to Maddie, the mansion was built in the mountains over six hundred years ago. It was nestled amongst the trees and lush terrain, blending in with both the mountains and the fragile alpine scenery. It backed up to the red-colored, rocky cliffs, having its own private lake on one side, stretching as far as the eye could see, and a large koi pond on the other. It was surrounded by aspen and pine trees. Native plants grew untouched by humankind, providing food and shelter for the abundance of wildlife. As Jadis stood momentarily watching the red-tailed hawks soar above the towering rock formations, she tried to reach out to her sisters, to no avail. It became apparent the energy blocking her powers was not isolated to the mansion. She also felt a supernatural aura surrounding Aiden and Eden. As the thought crossed her mind, the word *Nosferatu* popped into her head. As menacing as the thought was, she decided it would be best if she played along; at least until she could come up with an alternative plan to get out. Thankfully, she could grasp enough of the surrounding energy to make sure the second incantation stuck, blocking them from her mind—permanently. It wasn't much but she would take what she could get.

Maddie and Jadis sat outside for a few hours, chatting about the lives of all who lived there, along with how much work they had done to add the modern conveniences and technological advancements.

Maddie and Jadis were quietly sitting back in their chairs when the sounds of soft footsteps approaching interrupted the comfortable silence.

"Chloe," Maddie said, happily.

Chloe took a seat and smiled. "It's nice to meet you. I'm Chloe, Maddie's sister."

Jadis smiled back. "It's nice to meet you as well."

Like the others, Chloe was also attractive. She was slightly shorter than her sister, Maddie, with chestnut-colored, shoulder-length hair. She appeared to be of Greckian descent, with chiseled yet gentle facial features. She joined their conversation, and had quite a sense of humor, which Jadis found to be a welcomed relief.

It must have been a couple of hours before Aiden and Eden returned. Another male, who was a slightly larger version of Eden, also joined them.

"I presume you're Jadis?" the stranger offered.

"Yes."

"It's nice to meet you. I'm Bain, the Head of security," he stated before taking a seat opposite Chloe.

"It's nice to meet you as well," she replied.

Eden sat next to Maddie, reached for her hand, and gently kissed her knuckles. *As intimidating as he seems to be, he is certainly gentle and loving with Maddie,* Jadis thought.

"How is everything?" Eden asked.

"Great, we're just getting acquainted," Maddie replied.

Shortly after Eden, Aiden, and Bain joined the girls, two of their maître d's served lunch. The gourmet soup, salad, and sandwiches were exactly what she needed after only picking at her breakfast.

Jadis felt Aiden's eyes on her, and she subtly looked in his direction. "You look good, relaxed," he offered.

"I feel much better. Maddie and Chloe have been great company; a much-needed distraction from everything that's happened over the past couple months—" She stopped herself mid-sentence. *Dammit! I always fucking talk too much when I'm nervous.* She immediately noticed the curiosity flashing across everyone's faces.

Eden, however, was more than curious, and that uneasy feeling welled up inside her once again. *His subtle keenness to seek information is unnerving.* Jadis also noticed how he casually side-eyed Aiden before focusing his attention back on her. "What's happened over the last couple months, if you don't mind my asking?"

"I lost someone very close to me and it's been difficult." It was all she could think to say. Since Aiden had seen the ashes, she hoped he would choose to accept her reply without following up with additional questions.

"We're sorry to hear that," Maddie offered sincerely.

However, by the looks of the brothers' faces—they weren't buying it, but damned if she was going to open up. And then she felt it once again. Eden was trying to burn a hole in her thoughts. *Good luck, try as you might, but you are not getting into my head.* Jadis pursed her lips together, fighting the urge to chuckle a loud.

"Last night you were going somewhere, and fast based on the skid marks your car left. Why were you in such a hurry?" Eden questioned.

Jadis shrugged her shoulders. "I was heading to town and lost control of my car in the rain, is all."

"Eden, enough," Maddie demanded. "Leave the poor girl alone, she's been through a lot and doesn't need you prodding."

Jadis smiled at Maddie, appreciating her intervening.

Chloe also chimed, "We've been out here for a while now, why don't we all take a break and give Jadis some time to herself?"

Nothing more was said as they rose from their seats. Aiden escorted Jadis back to the guest room and after they'd walked in together, Aiden closed the door behind them and she could tell he was heavy in thought. *This can't be good.* Her pulse quickened, and she anxiously awaited what he had to say.

Aiden took a seat in a chair across the room while Jadis sat on the edge of the bed, facing him. Initially, he didn't speak, as if he was trying to find the right words.

After sitting there for a few very uncomfortable minutes of silence, Jadis spoke up. "So, are you going to sit there in silence the rest of the evening, or would you like to tell me what's on your mind?"

"Sorry, I was just thinking," he mumbled, running his hand over his mouth.

"Obviously. What are you thinking about?"

"How to tell you."

"Tell me what? Something to the tune of, Jadis, you're not leaving?"

"Yes," Aiden replied bluntly.

"Had it not been for Maddie and Chloe, I would have left while you were in the meeting with your brothers, but I suspect you and Eden had them monitoring me."

He chuckled in response. "Honestly, I was prepared for you to try to leave. I didn't think you would still be here. I thought I was going to have to chase your ass down." He winked.

"Why would you *chase me down*? More importantly, why do you care if I leave?"

"It's not safe out there for you, that's all. We've all decided it's best for you to stay with us for the time being." Aiden's once warm voice now had an audible edge of sternness.

"Why is it not safe? What aren't you telling me, Aiden? I want to know now or I'm walking out that door, and I promise you won't be able to stop me. And who the hell decided what's best for me?"

"I can and I will stop you, but I don't want this to turn into a fight. We want to protect you. My brothers and I have decided it's best for you to stay. So stay you will."

"We'll see about that. By the way, do you want to fill me in on who or *what* you all really are?" she asked coldly.

"What do you mean, *what are we*?"

"I know you're not mortal. I also know you carried me here last night. You didn't drive me, as Maddie claimed you did."

"You are perceptive. We knew you were special, but you're definitely stronger than we gave you credit for."

"Is that why you all have been trying to read my thoughts?"

"And you blocked us, didn't you?" Aiden replied, cocking his head to the side.

"Hell yes, I did. What did you expect?"

She was now standing against the bedpost with her arms crossed, ready to make a run for it the first chance she got.

Aiden stood up; his eyes fixed on hers. *Great,* she thought. *I'm now in a standoff of wills with a vampire.*

Aiden put his hands up in front of himself as a sort of gesture of peace. "Look, I don't want to fight with you. I'm also not trying to stoke your temper or make you feel like a prisoner. We want you to be comfortable, but there is a lot you don't know. Or perhaps you do, and you're not saying it? You were running from something last night that terrified you. Isn't that how you wrecked your car?"

She was standing there when it dawned on her. "It's you! It's been you all these months tracking me in the woods by my cabin, hasn't it? You've been stalking me!"

He laughed a loud. "*Stalking you*? No, Jadis, you have it all wrong. I was watching over you. We both know it was something else *stalking you*. My brothers and I just don't know why it chose you."

"You attacked it on my porch! That's what I heard."

"Yes. I didn't have time to catch up to you while I was killing your *stalker*. By the time I headed for you, the accident had already happened. And yes, I carried you here. Vampires don't need to drive." He smirked.

"Dammit, Aiden! Why weren't you honest when I first asked?" she snapped.

"It's not like you didn't figure it out, so what does it matter? You knew it when you did your '*thing*' this morning and again while walking around with Maddie, blocking us out of your head. Hell, you should have seen how much you surprised Eden and Bain with the little witchery of yours." Aiden laughed.

"Not sure what you find so funny. Do you see me laughing? Not to mention, I am leaving!"

"Fine, after dinner, you may go, if you can." He grinned, and raised an eyebrow as if challenging her.

"You're not scaring me, Aiden," she replied, along with a sneer.

"Keep threatening to leave and I'll lock your ass in this room."

"Lock me in?" Jadis pushed herself form the bedpost with her butt and laughed. "You have no idea."

She pressed her fingers against her palm, pulled what energy she could, and the blow to his chest sent him sliding a couple of feet back before he caught himself as gracefully and agilely as any feline.

He bounded toward her. She shrieked aloud and ducked around him. She hadn't been looking to get into a fight with him, alone in a bedroom, in his house, full of other vampires.

Jadis thought it would give her the opportunity to escape, but as she turned to run for the door, he had a hold of her arm and spun her around to face him before she'd taken two steps.

As she tried to wrench her arm from his grip, the bedroom door flew open, and there stood Eden and Maddie, both of whom looked shocked at the unexpected sight before them; Aiden and Jadis were clearly struggling with each other physically.

"Let her go, Aiden," Eden demanded calmly.

Aiden reluctantly released her arm, and the two of them stood in silence, looking at the intruders.

"I can see your talk didn't go so well?" Eden said.

Aiden continued to glare at Jadis. "No, and she is full of surprises."

"My God, Aiden!" Maddie said harshly. "What the hell are you doing?"

She walked over to Jadis, took her hand, and led her to the other side of the room.

"Jadis, are you okay?"

"I'm fine, Aiden's just being an ass." She could see a smirk, similar to that of Aiden's, cross Eden's face. She stepped back from Maddie, feeling betrayed by her as well.

"Eden, none of this is funny!" Maddie snapped.

"Did you know about all of this?" Jadis asked Maddie.

"I only knew part of it. Chloe and I wanted to tell you what little we knew, but it wasn't our place. We never thought for a minute you and Aiden would end up getting into an altercation," she said, glaring at both Eden and Aiden.

"Now, I'm leaving and none of you are going to stop me. I appreciate everything you have done for me, especially you, Maddie. You have been truly kind, but I can't stay here." She walked to the other side of the bed, and as she reached for her bag, she felt a powerful presence behind her. She spun around, only to find herself face to chest with Eden.

"Sorry Jadis, you're not leaving. We have no choice but to keep you here. If you think the *tracker*, as you call it, appearing on your porch was deadly—you have no idea what else is out there."

"Baby, calm down. If you're trying to keep her here by making her feel safe with us, you're doing a pretty shitty job." Maddie stepped between them, put her hand on Eden's chest, and gently pushed him back.

Maddie to the rescue once again, Jadis thought.

Maddie placed her hand on her lower back and escorted her away from Eden. "Come sit with me and Chloe. I think we could both use a drink. We'll fill you in on what little we know."

"Forgive me for sounding rude, but it doesn't seem like I have a choice in the matter," Jadis snarked, genuinely frustrated.

Maddie looked at Eden and angrily squinted her eyes, as she and Jadis walked out of the room.

Once they'd stepped into the hallway, Jadis heard the two of them chuckling. *Things certainly could have ended up much worse,* she thought.

Maddie and Jadis made their way back out to the veranda, and Chloe stood up and pulled a chair out for her.

"I heard what happened with Aiden and Eden, and I'm so sorry. We desperately wanted to tell you they weren't letting you leave. Please understand, we couldn't."

"It doesn't appear you tried very hard," Jadis replied.

Maddie let out a heavy sigh. "You're right, Jadis, we didn't."

"Try not to be too hard on Aiden. He can be an ass, but his heart is always in the right place. He just struggles to show it sometimes. Well—maybe I'm being a bit too easy on him now." Chloe chuckled. "Today he definitely went about it in the wrong way."

"Yes, he did," agreed Maddie. "We are not making light of what happened or excusing his behavior. It's just classic Aiden is all."

"Chloe, how did you know what happened before we made it out here?" Jadis questioned.

Chloe and Maddie glanced at each other briefly, but before Maddie could answer, Jadis interjected. "I'll know if you're lying to me."

Chloe filled the highball glasses and handed them to Maddie and Jadis simultaneously.

Jadis spun her glass on the table. "So what's going on?" she asked, not wanting to wait any longer.

"I don't want to scare you, but we know you are being hunted," Maddie admitted.

"Hunted? Why and by who, or should I say what?"

"Again, we don't know. Eden and Aiden haven't said much to us either," Chloe offered softly.

Jadis knew they were trying not to upset or frighten her, but it didn't change how she felt about leaving. "If Aiden killed that thing, why am I still in danger?"

"You are aware of the old tales of Pagnan, aren't you?" Maddie asked.

"Yes, go on," Jadis said.

"It seems as if the tales are no longer tales. Something from Ipheanor has arisen and has been hunting females—well, females with certain abilities," Maddie explained.

Jadis sat back, feeling as if her world was turning on its axis. "I don't have any *abilities* which would be useful to some fucking creature."

"Well, clearly something has been hunting you," Maddie replied.

Jadis wiped the condensation from her glass, knowing damn well she had *certain abilities* others didn't. "What do they want with their *abilities*?"

"Again, we don't know. They tend to keep a lot of shit to themselves," Chloe replied as she took a drink.

"The two of you—are you a part of this?"

"No, not exactly. We do trust Eden and Aiden and if they say you are in danger, then we have no reason to believe otherwise," Maddie answered.

Jadis thought about what they were and were not saying. *Play along,* she told herself, *play along.*

"Is there anything else we can say to help you feel more comfortable?" Maddie asked. "No," Jadis replied, deciding to put the conversation to bed, since she was clearly not going to get the answers she wanted. She certainly didn't mind learning more about them, realizing it might give her an advantage. As nice as the girls were being, Aiden's explanation for keeping her there still seemed ambiguous. She especially felt the need to get away from Eden. He had proven that he was not to be underestimated, much less challenged. She also didn't believe Bain was their *Head of Security*. His essence had hit her like a runaway freight train the moment she'd encountered him, and she knew there was much more to him than they were letting on.

Jadis gazed into the horizon, admiring the warm wash of colors spilling over the mountain's peaks from the setting sun. Keeping her alcohol consumption to a minimum, making sure not to let it affect her the way it had Maddie and Chloe, who were now slightly tipsy, she planned her escape. Sitting there, she felt a little tinge of guilt when she thought about them. Had the situation been different, she thought the three of them would have been great friends, but she knew she couldn't stay with vampires; they were also danger to her for many reasons. Their intentions may have been genuine, but it she couldn't dismiss the words of warning her mother drummed into her brain. She was more to them than a damsel in distress. In fact, she was a lot more.

Out of her peripheral vision, she had noticed a nice-sized window at the end of the upstairs hallway earlier. *Remain calm, do nothing to raise their suspicions. Only the Gods know how they will respond,* she thought.

She had no idea the extent to which they would go to keep her there, and the mere thought scared the hell out of her. *If they discover who I am, I'm fucked—as are my sisters.*

"Jadis?" Maddie said, snapping her back to reality.

"Sorry, I'm tired. It's been a long day."

"It has been. We should head inside. You could use a good night's sleep. We can talk more in the morning," Maddie offered.

Chloe pushed her chair back. "I agree, we will talk with Aiden and Eden as well; I promise we'll make the situation better."

"I would appreciate it." *Too bad I won't be here in the morning.*

They headed upstairs, and Jadis was more than happy to have seen no one else on their way up as Chloe escorted her to her room.

"Jadis, I'm down the hall. If you need anything, knock on the third door on the left."

"Thank you, Chloe."

She closed the door behind her and sat on the bed nervously, waiting for the right time to make her move. Looking out the window, she noticed it had begun to rain. *Great. Just what I don't need. Then again, it will help to hide my scent and my tracks, theoretically speaking.*

Jadis pulled a small backpack out of her duffle bag and filled it with a few of her belongings. The rest of the items were disposable. She could not run through the terrain carrying a large duffle bag.

Stay calm, she told herself as she lay on her back listening to the rain pinging against the windows. She waited a few anxious, heart-pounding hours before deciding it was safe to make her escape.

It must have been about midnight when she put on the backpack, took a few deep breaths, and silently opened the bedroom door. She snuck to the window and, thankfully, it opened. She wasn't sure if she had managed to unlock it while sitting outside with the girls.

She stepped out onto the brick ledge and closed the window behind her. She then hopped into the tree, climbed down, and as soon as her feet touched the ground, she ran as fast as she could.

She felt like she was running for her life through the rain and the cold. The rugged landscape was tough to traverse, and the rain made it challenging to see where she was going. She jumped rocks, dodged boulders, and weaved her way through an endless array of trees blocking her path, using little more than her senses to guide her. She slipped and fell more than once, but she didn't let herself feel the pain.

Nothing is going to slow me down, keep running, she coaxed herself. All she had to do was run as fast and as far as she could. She did her best to ignore the stinging sensation from the branches as they clawed against her face and hands as she shoved them aside.

An eerie feeling crept up her spine; she was being followed, and she prayed to the Gods it wasn't another *tracker* Eden warned her about. Her body and brain were now on overload as she pushed herself forward.

"Jadis?" a voice called out.

Oh shit! How did Aiden already find out I was gone? The thought barely crossed her mind when it dawned on her. *Bain! So that's why they call him the Head of Security.* She should have known he was the one who had weaved the binding spell.

She was now in survival mode; she fell again when her feet slipped outwards in front of her on the soggy leaves and dead pine needles as she ran downhill. This time she felt a shooting pain moving from her ankle to her knee. The cold night air shocking her lungs each time she tried to inhale more deeply, but she knew she could not stop.

Even the healing spell which would camouflage the pain for a short period would take at least a minute. With Aiden calling her name and closing in behind her, she didn't have a minute to spare. She gathered herself off the ground, having come to terms with the fact that her body would pay the price later.

She tried to run again, but she noticed Aiden's silhouette blocking her path. For a brief second, all she heard was silence.

As she looked in Aiden's direction, she noticed a second silhouette appearing beside him.

Fuck! Aiden and a yet-unidentifiable companion were coming toward her. She tried to run to the right, only to find Aiden blocking her way while the other moved to her left.

"Headed somewhere, Jadis?" Aiden's eyes were now slit like, aglow in the dark, and his white canines gleamed from beneath his parted lips. Jadis looked in every direction, desperately looking for a way around them.

"Don't bother," Aiden said. "You can't outrun us, no matter what you are or what your powers may be."

"I have to say, your magic is pretty impressive," added the unfamiliar voice.

Despite the situation, he sounded more amused than angry.

"If you want to run, run. I'll even give you a five-minute head start," the stranger added, along with a chuckle.

"Jadis, meet Lars, another brother of ours. You won't find a better tracker, and not the kind you've met already," Aiden joked. "He lives with us as well. Sorry I didn't get a chance to introduce the two of you earlier."

"Lars? Is this the same Lars who brought my car to the house?" *Of course, he's a tracker. What is it with all these trackers?*

"Yes. Would you like a more formal introduction?" Aiden replied as he moved closer.

"What? An *introduction*? I don't have to put up with your bullshit, and I'm not going back with you!"

"She is feisty," Lars retorted.

"I warned you, but this isn't a time for playing around. It's time to get her ass back to the house and out of these woods," Aiden said.

"Don't be in such a rush, Aiden. I haven't had this much fun tracking in a very long time. What's another thirty minutes?"

Jadis stepped back as Aiden approached and she tried to duck around a tree, but he reached out and grabbed her forearm. She tried to pull away, but she couldn't break his grasp. She swirled her free hand, and he grabbed it as well. *Yep, that hurt. In fact, it all kind of hurt.* Her body was still sore because of the accident and falling on her ass multiple times certainly didn't help.

"Not tonight, my dear. One punch in the chest is enough. I'm a quick learner." Aiden winked.

Lars moved behind her, and she felt a prick on her left shoulder. In an instant, everything started swirling. Her thoughts became jumbled, and her body failed her. Worst of all, her powers felt non-existent, and they were nowhere near the mansion's grounds.

"What the hell was—" Jadis began.

"Don't worry," Aiden interjected. "It's a little something Bain concocted."

"You drugged me?" She fought the effects as best she could but was unable to counteract it; had it not been for Aiden holding her she would have dropped to her knees. Unfortunately for her, it was too powerful.

"She's still awake? Very impressive," Lars stated.

"I'm a bit surprised myself," Aiden replied.

"Answer me! What was—is it," she demanded less forcibly than intended. She tried to pull away again, but it was pointless.

"Let's go, darling, this has been fun though," Aiden said, as he tossed her over his shoulder.

Jadis was in and out of a daze, trying to stay semi-conscious. "Aiden, put me down," she mumbled.

She tried to get off his shoulder however, her efforts were useless. She just wanted to stay conscious more than anything else.

"How do we tell Bain his shit is weak?" Lars chuckled.

"I swear I'm going—"

"*Going* to what?" Aiden asked, interrupting her.

At that moment, she didn't know herself. Her body hurt, her head was throbbing from being upside down, she was shivering from the cold, and the rain was dripping off her hair, which hung down Aiden's backside. *Give it up, you're not getting down. All you have to do is stay awake,* she told herself.

They made it back to the mansion in no time and Jadis was still over Aiden's shoulder when they were greeted by not only Eden, but Bain as well.

This is humiliating. She felt like she was being carried back to daddy after sneaking out.

"I see you caught our little runaway," Bain joked. "The serum seems to have worked?"

"You want to tell him, or should I?" Lars joked.

"Aiden put me the fuck down!"

Bain's eyes widened, and he was taken aback. "She's still awake?" he asked in amazement.

"Yes, apparently you're not as powerful as you think you are," Lars declared.

Aiden and Lars laughed all the more at the look that crossed Bain's face.

"Yes, I'm awake, now dammit, Aiden, put me down!"

The one person she expected to be the angriest was Eden. His silence, however, was more unnerving than his words. At least when he was talking, she sort of knew where she stood.

"Damn," Bain stated.

"We can talk more tomorrow. Right now, I need to get her ass upstairs and out of these wet clothes before she freezes to death." Aiden turned to Lars, who tossed him her backpack as he carried her back upstairs.

"Aiden, remember what I said to you earlier," Eden said assertively.

"I got it."

What he told him earlier? What is that supposed to mean?

Just as Aiden turned to carry her back upstairs, Bain touched her head. By the time Aiden gently set her down in a padded armchair, she had regained full control of her body.

"I'm sure you'd like to take a hot shower after your midnight run in the rain. If you need help getting to the bathroom with that ankle, I'll help you."

"No. And, I'd prefer it if you didn't speak to me." She was confused from the injection and the last thing she needed was to be getting undressed in the bathroom, alone with him.

As she limped to the bathroom, she heard him chuckle, and angrily shut the door. She gazed into the mirror, her disheveled appearance reflecting back at her. An exasperated sigh escaped her mouth as she defiantly swept her tousled locks away. She then turned on the shower and hobbled in. The hot water felt amazing as it flowed over her scrapes and scratches, and soothed her sore muscles. She washed her tangled hair, letting the thick bubbles run down her body, and stood under the hot water for quite a-while as she tried to gather her senses. Once her skin had pruned, she got out of the shower, brushed out her hair, and dried it with the towel the best she could.

"Thanks, Maddie," she stated sarcastically, as she grabbed the shorts and t-shirt that had been placed neatly on the counter. She then headed back into the bedroom.

"You've got to be kidding me? Don't you have something else to do, somewhere better to be?" she questioned.

"No. And since you can't be trusted, it looks like we are going to be bunkmates."

"*Bunkmates*? If you think I'm sleeping with you, you have another thing coming."

"Well, there's always the chair or the floor if you'd feel more comfortable," Aiden said in jest.

"I'm not sleeping on the floor or in the chair and you will leave this room!" She swirled her hand, and nothing happened. *What the hell?* She tried again and still nothing happened. "What did Bain do to me?"

"He just put out the fire under your ass for the time being. Now I assume you're tired, but I can do this all night. We're creatures of the night, remember?" Aiden quipped, with that same flippant smile.

"This is not funny, now get out!" she demanded, pointing toward the door.

"No."

His amusement only pissed her off more. "Fine!" She limped over to the bed and threw a pillow at his face. "You sleep on the floor." Of course, he caught it in mid-air.

"Thanks for the pillow." He plopped onto the bed on his back and tossed the pillow under his head. He then crossed his legs, casually re-adjusted one arm beneath the pillow, and rested his other arm over his stomach. He was now wearing a pair of clean, grey joggers. However, he hadn't bothered to put a shirt on. His chest and arms were fully covered in old world, intricate tattoos which unfortunately caught her attention. As angry as she was, she found herself admiring their beauty.

"Are you going to stand there all night, or are you going to get some sleep? I'm not leaving." He turned his head and stared at her. His words pulling her attention back to the matter at hand.

At this point, she didn't care anymore. She no longer had the energy to fight and argue with him. Not to mention she needed to get off her swollen ankle, the pain was excruciating.

She slipped under the covers and put a row of pillows behind her back, making sure he stayed on his side. It was a futile attempt to separate them, but nonetheless, it made her feel better. *All I need to do is to wake up and find I've rolled over and slept on his perfect chest.*

Thankfully, Aiden's words pulled her thoughts away from his body. "Really? A row of pillows? What are they supposed to accomplish? I've got to give it to you. As much of a pain in the ass as you're becoming, you are entertaining." He chuckled.

"I'm a pain in your ass? I think it's quite the opposite. I'm not the kidnapper here."

"If I had kidnapped you, you would be shackled in a cell not lying in a bed."

"Can I leave?"

"No," he replied.

"Then you're a kidnapper."

"Think what you want, prisoner," he joked.

"You're not amusing."

Just as she dozed off, there was a knock at the door. "What now?" She yelled, not being in the mood for any more introductions or surprises.

Aiden didn't answer. He rolled off the bed and answered the door as if he'd been expecting someone all along. Jadis heard the hushed conversation, but she couldn't make out anything being said. When the chatter ended, Aiden shut the door and walked over to her, carrying something. He knelt down at the side of the bed.

"Give me your ankle," he requested softly.

"What?" she asked.

"How was that not clear?" he asked as he raised an eyebrow.

"Why do you want my ankle?"

"You sprained it, didn't you?"

"Yes, but I don't need you touching it. You're the reason it's sprained in the first place."

"Me? How am I responsible for you slipping and falling on your ass? I don't remember pushing you."

"Aiden, I'm in no mood. Go away," she mumbled.

"Your ankle needs attention. So, you can either choose to let me help you, or I can pull those covers off and take it. The choice is yours."

"I seriously hate you. You know that, right?"

"Two seconds. How's this going to play out?"

"Oh my God. Here!"

She flipped the covers over, slipped her ankle out to him, and grimaced from the pain.

He laid her foot on his knee and wrapped it tightly with a compression bandage.

"You smell like jasmine," he said.

"You smell like an idiot," she snapped back. Although, if she was being honest with herself, he smelled amazing. Even the slightest scent of him evoked a longing she didn't care to admit.

He chuckled at her quip. "It's pretty swollen. This is going to be uncomfortable for a while. If you'd like, I can take the pain away for you."

"No."

"I'm assuming under normal circumstances you could heal yourself?"

"It's none of your business what I can or can't do."

There is a lot she is capable of, he thought. "I'm finished." He slid her foot under the covers before pulling the covers back over the edge of the bed for her. "Here, take these."

"If it's more of Bain's fuckery, forget it."

Aiden laughed a loud. "They are nothing more than a few pain meds."

Jadis took them out of his hand, felt them for a moment, and he was telling the truth. He handed her a glass of water, and she swallowed them. That was the last thing she remembered.

CHAPTER 3

The following morning, Aiden was still on the bed next to her and appeared to be asleep. The golden rays of the early morning sun gleamed through the creamy satin curtains. She listened intently to the familiar sounds of the chipmunks chirping and scurrying about, while the birds filled the air with a melody of warbles and songs. As she moved her ankle, the pain radiated up her calf. *Yep, it still hurts like hell.*

"I put a couple more pills on the nightstand for you."

"What are you, a nurse now?" she asked sarcastically.

"Still tempered, I see." He chuckled. "You know we did what we had to for your own safety."

"Yeah, you keep saying that." She picked them up and headed to the bathroom.

"Need help?"

"Nope." She turned to walk, but instead hobbled away.

"You are a stubborn one. No doubt about it," he said.

"Like you're not? If I'm stubborn, you're tantamount to a whim of iron. I'm being held captive, so I think that gives me the right to protest."

"Maybe, but you don't have the right to put yourself in danger. You're too important."

She was now only halfway to the bathroom when she stopped and turned to face him. He was up on one elbow, head in hand, watching her limp across the bedroom.

"What do you mean, *too important*? You are full of secrets, aren't you? Care to fill me in?"

"Yes, eventually."

"*Eventually*? Why am I not the least bit surprised that's your answer?"

Jadis turned away and continued to the bathroom. *I'm over arguing with him.* Her entire body hurt, and she was physically and emotionally exhausted. When she wandered back out, he was still lying on the bed.

She slipped back under the luxurious sheets without saying a word and pulled the duvet up. Between the tracker on her porch, the car accident, being chased by vampires, and the multiple injuries she'd sustained, everything had taken its toll, and the little concoction Bain had conjured was still lingering in her system. *I will work on that as soon as I am able; Bain will not outdo me,* she told herself before falling back asleep.

The following afternoon, Jadis rolled over and noticed Aiden wasn't in bed. She glanced across the room, hoping he had left. However, there he was, sitting in the chair next to the expansive windows that were opened. She could feel the warm breeze, carrying with it the fragrance of fresh pine.

"The windows open, after all?" she questioned smugly.

With a flick of his wrist, they slammed shut.

"What the hell, Aiden? It was nice to smell something besides you."

"I don't trust you."

"Open it back up."

"No," he said, looking amused as usual.

Why does he enjoy baiting so much? "Dammit, Aiden. It's not like I can jump out the window in my current condition. My ankle is sprained, if you hadn't noticed, and my powers have been bound. What more do you need from me?"

"Say please."

"You're kidding me, right?"

"Nope. All you have to do is say please, and I'll open the window."

"You are the most annoying thing I have ever met."

"First, I'm *annoying*, and then I'm a *thing*, however, do I manage?"

"First off, I don't know how to answer that. Second, you're not funny at all, and I'm in no mood for your screwing around. I'm feeling better for the first time in three days, so just open the damn window."

"Say please."

"No." She did her best to sound serious, but it didn't work and she chuckled at the stupidity of the entire conversation. It was becoming a game of wills, but she would rather take Aiden's joking and annoying-ness than the seriousness of Eden.

He flicked his wrist and opened them back up. "Is that better?"

"Yes. That wasn't so hard, was it?" She limped over to take in a breath of the warm scented air, and he moved to her side.

"Not planning on jumping, are we?" He winked.

She chuckled and rolled her eyes. "You're an idiot."

"Why don't you get dressed? You could use something to eat. It's been a couple days now since you've eaten anything of substance."

"I'm not leaving this room. I can't face everyone down there after everything that's happened. I can't imagine what Maddie and Chloe think about me right now."

"I think you'll be pleasantly surprised."

"You carried me back like a child, how is that not embarrassing?"

"You have nothing to be embarrassed about and the girls understand more than you realize. They have been worried about you. They've been requesting updates constantly, to the point they're annoying me."

"It's a crazy thought something besides you is *annoying*," she quipped.

"Touché." He chuckled. "They're excited to see you. We have a lot to discuss and fill you in on. You not only need to know, but you deserve to know why you are here. We'll also talk about what was on your porch the other night and answer any other questions you have. We want you to feel at ease and straighten things out. Now, get dressed."

Jadis remained in the bathroom for about forty-five minutes, mostly procrastinating. She didn't want to see anyone, much less the crowd that had been waiting for her for two days. When she came out, Aiden was dressed and ready to go. He was leaning up against the window, arms crossed, looking like they were heading out on a date. *He may be annoying, but hell, he is gorgeous.*

"Are you finally ready?"

"Not really. Would you bring something up here?"

"No." He walked over, took her hand, and pulled her toward the door.

Jadis looked up at him, "I feel like I'm about to be thrust before a firing squad."

Aiden smiled and continued to lead her downstairs. As much as she didn't want to admit it, holding his hand was reassuring, and she needed all the reassurance she could get right now. She took a deep breath and reluctantly followed along.

"Relax," he said, as he squeezed her hand. "It's going to be fine."

They made their way to the grand staircase, and Aiden picked her up in his arms. He set her back down at the bottom of the stairs, allowing her to limp the rest of the way with some sense of dignity.

Her heart was thumping against her breast and as much as she wanted the truth, she wasn't sure she was prepared for it.

As they walked down the long hallway leading to the kitchen, the door that had been closed the first day she was there was now open. The room buzzed with a myriad of state-of-the-art surveillance systems, sleek computers, and an assortment of other gadgets one might deem essential if they were trying to dominate the world. She assumed it was the command center they mentioned. *From what I can gather with such a quick glance, it's impressive as hell.*

They walked into the kitchen and there was Eden, Lars, and Bain talking amongst themselves. The large French doors were open, allowing the conversation occurring outside to echo into the kitchen. She also heard a couple of other male voices she didn't recognize.

Through the window, she could see Maddie and Chloe eating breakfast at the same table where they had been when she decided to try to escape a couple of nights ago.

"Well, look what the cat dragged in," Lars announced.

Leave it to Lars to say something to embarrass me. Damn, as if I needed more attention on myself, she thought.

Jadis ignored Lars and stayed halfway behind Aiden, still holding his hand as they continued walking further into the kitchen. Aiden stopped and stood next to Eden.

Perfect, she thought. *He could have at least stood next to Lars, who wasn't so serious and at least had a sense of humor.*

"Cat got your tongue? You sure had a lot to say a couple nights ago." Lars winked.

She failed to reply to Lars based solely on the intimidating stares of Eden and Bain.

Bain looked at Eden with a half-cocked smile. "Think she's going to run off again?

Everyone chuckled except for Eden, who always seemed too serious.

"She's agreed to stay for the time being," Aiden replied.

Jadis looked up at him and rolled her eyes.

"You all stop it right now," Maddie demanded as she rushed into the kitchen. "Jadis, come outside."

"I didn't leave on account of you and Chloe," Jadis blurted out.

Maddie ran her hand down her arm. "We know. Come."

Jadis glanced up at the unknown males as they crossed paths on the veranda. *Damn, if someone is looking to start a fight, this is definitely not the place.*

"That's Dimitri, and Niko. They're part of our security team," Chloe added, having noticed the way Jadis watched them leave. "How are you feeling?" she asked, as she set a platter of food in front of her, and a clean plate.

"Better, thank you." She smiled.

"It's time we had a real conversation," Maddie stated.

Aiden, Eden, Lars, and Bain emerged from the kitchen and sat quietly while Maddie and Chloe explained who and what they were.

"So you are brujas," Jadis said.

"Yes, we would have told you, but Eden asked us to keep it quiet for the time being." Maddie smiled warmly, but Jadis caught her squinting her eyes at Eden.

Of course he did, Jadis thought.

"You are powerful. Bain had sealed the house and grounds in order to control your powers, which completely bound ours," Maddie said, sounding impressed.

Chloe chimed in, "Even if Eden had given us permission to reveal this, we couldn't show you anything to prove it. And we didn't want you to think we were lying to keep you here. Many words can be spoken, but without any validity, they are meaningless."

"I had a feeling the two of you weren't mortal, but I couldn't quite put my finger on it." Jadis paused momentarily before speaking to Eden. "I know there's more."

There was another long pause, per usual. When Eden finally spoke, she took a deep breath, not sure she was ready to hear what he had to say.

"We did some checking and electronically you're a ghost. It's as if you don't exist at all," Eden stated bluntly.

"Who the hell gave you permission to do a background check on me?"

"We needed to confirm your identity." Eden answered. "You have a legal document with your name on it, but there are no records with the Bureau of Antinoc, not to mention you don't so much as have a registered number."

"If you were mortal, or an original, there would be some sort of electronic trail," Bain interjected.

"Only sired originals who have something to hide conceal their true identities," Eden added.

Damn, Eden is methodical and calculating. I better tell him something, other than the truth, that is. "You had no right to do that. And as for me being on original, you definitely have it wrong. We all know what happens when someone crosses the Bureau of Antinoc. I choose to remain off grid, is all."

Eden tilted his head to the side and looked at her as if he didn't believe a word of it, but Aiden gently rested his hand on her forearm. "Jadis, we have more to explain. You need to hear the rest."

Jadis looked at Eden. "Go on."

"It's a long and detailed story. I'll try to make it easy for you by simplifying things and getting right to the point. The reason you are here is we think you are being sought after by something more powerful and more ancient than you realize. We, along with a few other clans, have been doing some reconnaissance based on recent and not so recent events taking place in the Valley of the Old Gods. One of our clans has come across some interesting scrolls, leading us to believe something, from Ipheanor, is about to awaken."

"What something? Awaken? And what does it have to do with me? How am I connected to the Valley of the Old Gods or Ipheanor? I've never been to either place."

"We're not sure. I offered to find you and keep an eye on you. You weren't mentioned directly, but the clues leading us to you are in the details. We assumed you were an original descendent based on the translated information," Aiden explained.

She looked at Maddie and Chloe. "I don't believe you didn't know something about this?"

Eden piped in, "I told them not to say anything until we had gathered more information. We needed to know for sure you are the bruja we've been searching for. If the scrolls are correct, then we are not the only ones looking for you, and I'm not talking about the *tracker*, more specifically the Baskale, Aiden, killed."

Jadis felt like she was being sucked into a black hole, her mind was spiraling down into the blackened abyss that were her night terrors and visions as her eyes darted amongst the group. "Baskale? It's not possible, they were eradicated centuries ago."

"Apparently not," Eden stated.

"You keep saying you're not an original but something is telling me otherwise. That's part of the reason I put a binding spell on you. We needed to make sure if there is another in the area it won't sense you. It can feel your powers which is what drew the creature to your cabin the other night. Baskales were—are nothing more indentured minions. We don't assume they have the ability to arise again without something else controlling them," Bain explained.

"Well holy shit. This was not what I was expecting to hear." Thinking she was being held captive by a bunch of vampires for their entertainment sounded much better than what she was now being told.

She looked directly at Eden again. "You still haven't fully answered my question. Why me?"

"We're not sure? As you say, you're not an original," Aiden answered sarcastically.

As Jadis glared at Aiden, Eden piped in. "In any case, I need to know you're going to stay put, or I'll make other, less comfortable arrangements."

Jadis opened her mouth to snap back when Maddie chimed in, "In other words, we would like to invite you to stay with us for the duration to ensure your safety. You are not a captive, nor are you a prisoner." She squeezed Eden's thigh and looked at him with a keep-your-mouth-shut kind of look, and he obliged.

"You can hang with us," Chloe added, dismissing the vampires with slight a wave of her hand. "They aren't so bad once you get to know them, but for now it will just be us girls."

Aiden looked at Jadis and patted her thigh. "I promise—once we figure it out, we will get you safely back to your cabin if that's where you want to be. There is just one other thing, you and I will continue to be bunkmates." Aiden stated it as if the decision had already been made regardless of how she felt about it.

"Oie vey," Maddie mumbled under breath.

"We can do this the easy way or the hard way," Eden threatened.

Always the charmer, Jadis thought, ignoring Eden and looking at Aiden. "Since you asked so nicely, I will stay for the time being, but on one condition."

Eden raised an eyebrow. "What's that?"

"We will not be *bunkmates*."

Aiden tilted his highball glass at her. "Sorry darling, that arrangement is non-negotiable."

"Says who?" she demanded.

Aiden casually flicked a piece of lint off his cotton trousers. "Back to this again, are we?"

The tension between Jadis and Aiden intensified as she once again issued a challenge.

"*Back to what*?" she questioned as she turned to face him directly. "You are such an ass and you're not sharing the bed either! You *take it or leave it*."

Eden looked at Maddie, stopping her from interfering. She was shocked to find out Aiden was sharing the bed with her. She had known he was in the same room with Jadis, sleeping in the same bed was a whole different story. Maddie glared at Eden but as usual he brushed it off.

Aiden laughed a loud, "*Take it or leave it*? What makes you think you have any say in the matter?"

Everyone got up from the table, wanting to get some distance between themselves and the fight brewing between Jadis and Aiden. They all walked away and sat at the other end of the veranda.

Damn, he's controlling. Hell, they all are! Jadis thought.

"Good luck, brother," Lars said as he placed a couple hard pats on Aiden's shoulder before following the others.

Jadis felt an energetic surge and realized she had some of her power back. *Bain must be giving me a reprieve?* she thought, as she glanced at him. She didn't know if he wanted a more entertaining show to enjoy or if he was testing her abilities. At this moment, it didn't matter. Before dealing with Aiden, she took the opportunity to spin Bain's energy around to her advantage. *You won't bind me now,* she thought.

As Aiden rose to his feet, he remained oblivious to the swirling motion of her fingers as she pushed her chair back and stood. The veranda fell into a collective gasp when Aiden was propelled about three feet backward by the forceful blow to his chest. The gasps quickly turned into ripples of laughter.

Aiden's eyes swirled with excitement, and his canines slid from his gums. He tilted his head from side to side as if adjusting his neck. "You want to play do you?"

Jadis quickly regretted her actions and took a step back.

"I forgot to tell you there was a slight shift in the energy," Bain announced.

Aiden shot a quick look in Bain's direction, and if looks could kill, Bain would have been pinned to the wall. He then stepped toward Jadis, and she stepped back.

"Aiden, if you come any closer, I'll make the next one count!"

"*Make it count* then," he snarled.

The moment he lunged, Jadis yelped, darted into the kitchen, and knocked a barstool onto the floor behind her.

Aiden easily leap over it and grabbed her.

The moment the crowd sitting outside heard a crash Maddie and Chloe fell into a heap of laughter, which was followed by Lars and Bain who couldn't contain their amusement either.

"Holy shit," Bain said through his laughter.

"She is going to put him over the edge," Maddie added.

Chloe placed her hand over her stomach. "I haven't laughed this hard in a long time."

Lars crossed one leg over the other and leaned back. "Aiden's ego has been hit twice now by my count. I don't know about the rest of you, but I'm thoroughly enjoying it."

"Looking at her I never imagined she'd be willing to go toe to toe with him," Bain said.

Eden rubbed his temples, not finding any of it amusing. "I don't know if I'm prepared to handle those two."

Maddie pushed his shoulder. "Go, you need to do something before they kill each other."

Eden finished his drink, set the highball glass on the table, and stood. "Fuck me."

"Let go!" Jadis spun around, and Aiden tossed her over his shoulder, and headed for the stairs.

"We are not finishing this with an audience," he growled.

Jadis wrestled back enough to get off his shoulder, but he flipped her around and was carrying her in his arms now.

"Try all you want you're not getting down."

"Aiden, put me down right now. You can't do this every time you get upset. You bring this shit on yourself!"

"And you, my dear, *bring this shit on yourself!*" he replied.

Just as they reached the landing, Eden was standing in front of them. "Put her down, Aiden."

"Move, Eden," he stated.

"Listen to your brother—put me the hell down!"

Aiden tried to walk around Eden, but he put a strong hand on his shoulder. "Aiden, put her down now, I won't ask you again."

As soon as Aiden plopped her down, she shoved him in his chest. "Never do that again!"

The authoritative look on Eden's face was replaced by a look of bewilderment. "Jadis, you realize he's vampyre?"

"I don't give a damn if he's the Lamashtu himself. He has no right to throw me over his shoulder anytime he sees fit!"

Aiden grabbed her arm. "What makes you think you can challenge me?"

"Just be glad Bain has your back." She sneered.

"*Bain has my back*? So that's how this is going to be? You, me, a little game of chess? If that's the case I believe you have been checkmated."

"*Checkmated?* How about stalker and stalkee?" Jadis noticed his shit-eating grin appearing again.

"Stalker? I believe I saved your life. You seem to forget that part, I was protecting you. There was never any stalking involved!"

"Bullshit! You were in the woods watching me for months. How do you not call that stalking?"

"What did you want me to do? Should I have knocked on your door and introduced myself? 'Hello, I'm Aiden. I'm a vampire and there's a big, bad monster in the woods wanting to kill you,'" he replied sarcastically.

"You think you are so funny," she stated, as he continued laughing. "Well, it's not as bad as—"

Eden promptly interrupted her. "Enough! My God, if the two of you are going to go at it like this, I'm going to have to babysit you both. Better yet, I'll lock your asses in the room together for the duration. I should put Lars on the job, and maybe this would all end? Hell, that seems to be the best idea yet," Eden snapped.

Lars materialized at the base of the stairs. "The hell if you will." He chuckled. "I'm enjoying the show, but I'm not about to get involved. Aiden volunteered after all, she's all his to deal with now."

"That's it!" Eden grabbed Jadis's arm and pulled her back toward the kitchen. "Go!" he ordered, pointing Aiden in the same direction. "I swear, if vampires could get headaches, the two of you would give me a fucking migraine," he mumbled.

Nothing like being scolded by daddy, she thought.

When they made it back outside with her arm gripped in Eden's hand and Aiden following behind, everyone began laughing under their breath. However, Eden, Aiden, and Jadis didn't think any of it was funny. There they stood, the comedic trio, so thrilled to be the source of everyone's entertainment.

"Eden, let her go," Maddie said through her laughter.

Eden let go of Jadis's arm and walked over to Maddie, having grabbed his glass off the table on his way.

"Aiden, here, I figure you can use a stiff one." Bain chuckled, as he handed him a drink.

Aiden looked at Jadis. "I think Jadis could use *a stiff one.*" He lifted his glass at her with a half-cocked smile and she flipped him off in response.

Chloe grabbed Jadis's hand. "Come, let's go to lie by the pool. I think you need a break from all of this," she offered, trying to calm her laughter.

"Try to tame the beast," Aiden vented, as he waived his glass at Chloe.

Maddie walked over to Eden, stroked the side of his cheek, and whispered in his ear, "You asked for this."

She let out a yelp, when he smacked her ass as she followed Chloe and Jadis to the pool.

"How do either of you put up with them, much less live here?" Jadis asked.

Maddie leaned into Jadis nudging her shoulder in a friendly manner. "Trust us, it hasn't been this much fun in a long time. And yes, we realize it's often at your expense, but we can't help ourselves. Aiden has met his match, no one has gotten under his skin the way you have and likely will continue to do."

Jadis couldn't help herself and began chuckling with Maddie and Chloe. "I don't suppose there's somewhere else I could sleep without Aiden joining me?"

"You could always bunk with Bain or Lars," Chloe teased.

"Oh, hell no."

The three of them enjoyed the rest of the day, getting to know one another on a much more personal level. Now that so much was out in the open, Jadis didn't care to hear any more about the Baskale, the Valley of the Old Gods, or Ipheanor. Maddie and Chloe had also apologized again, for the way Eden forced them into silence. Even though she tried to stay engaged in their conversation, she couldn't dismiss her own precarious visions. Deep down she knew what they were saying was the truth even though she didn't want to admit it, and she couldn't ignore the kindness and sincerity of Maddie and Chloe. The rest of the afternoon was peaceful while they laid out by the pool.

"Not sure about you but I'm hungry," Maddie stated.

"I believe I am as well," Jadis replied.

Chloe stood up and wrapped the floral sarong around her waist. "Shall we?"

Jadis, Chloe, and Maddie headed for the expansive hand carved patio table, taking their usual seats next to each other, leaving Jadis next to Aiden. *At least he isn't being an ass, but I'm not ready to head to bed with him in tow.*

Dinner was pleasant, the conversation was lighthearted, and carried on for a few hours before Maddie and Chloe called it a night.

CHAPTER 4

J adis walked out of the bathroom after showering, and Aiden was sitting on top of the duvet leaning against the headboard with a tablet in his lap and a highball glass in his hand. She set her folded clothes on the armchair and as she turned to walk to the bed, she noticed the covers had been folded down. She slipped under the satin sheets and leaned against the headboard.

"Business?" she questioned.

"Yes, would you like a drink?" Aiden smiled.

"Sure."

He reached over to the nightstand and picked up another glass, which he had already filled, and handed it to her.

"Thank you. What is your so-called business about?"

"A little pain in the ass." He chuckled.

"That's rich coming from you, running another background check?"

"I think I've got what I need already," he joked.

Jadis watched the speed in which he flipped through the images; he typed so quickly it was as if his fingers were robotic.

"Are you going to watch me work all night?"

"Do you always work so late?"

"When necessary."

"What do you do for fun?" Jadis asked.

"Chase down runaways," he replied with a wink.

"A sense of humor, who would have thought," she chuckled.

"What do you do for fun?"

"Run from kidnappers and cyber stalkers."

Aiden laughed aloud and closed the tablet.

As he leaned over to set it on the nightstand along with his empty glass, she caught herself transfixed by the way his muscles rippled with each movement. The moment he leaned back against the headboard she diverted her eyes, leaned over, and put her empty glass down trying to distract herself.

He slid under the covers and pushed the pillows toward her. "So how long are you going to take up half the bed with these?"

Jadis casually reached for a pillow and smacked him across the face. "Until I decide otherwise."

"And she's playful, *who would have thought*?" He grabbed a pillow of his own and smacked her back.

They were both laughing while they wrestled for the rest of the pillows, trying to pummel each other with them. They lunged for the last pillow and found themselves tangled up together with his body on top of hers. She placed her hands on his chest to hold him back.

"I give!" She laughed.

"Give what?" He chuckled, as he pinned her arms above her head.

Their laughter calmed, and they found themselves staring into each other's eyes; his face inches from hers. The newfound tension seemed to have sucked the air from the room and the position they found themselves in was now awkward.

His eyes changed; a lifelike, swirling mixture of ice blue and sea-green hues glowed softly against his raven-colored pupils. His canines slid from his gums, and she felt herself losing all restraint.

Aiden stared down at her, contemplating his next move very carefully. He remained motionless and could feel his energy shifting as if opposing forces were pulling him in two different directions.

They held each other's gaze momentarily, their eyes communicating the sudden onset of desire neither of them were expecting.

He released her arms and slid off of her body. "I assume the pillow barrier is no longer an issue?"

She tried her best to sound nonchalant as she re-adjusted herself under the covers. "Apparently not." She chuckled as nervously as he had.

"Maybe tomorrow we can go for a hike if you'd like?" Aiden asked, trying to be casual and break the awkward tension.

"I'd love to."

"Then you should get some sleep."

"Yeah, probably."

So close, yet so far, she thought. For reasons unbeknownst to her, she longed for his touch. *Go to sleep, you're the idiot,* she told herself.

After a few minutes of deafening silence Aiden spoke, "Jadis?"

"Aiden?"

"If you need another pillow, I have a shoulder you can use."

What the hell? she thought. *Is that an offer or an 'offer?'* After careful consideration, she rolled over and laid her head on his shoulder and he wrapped his arm around her.

A month had passed, and Jadis and Aiden were still bunkmates. The only difference now was that they slept wrapped in each other's arms. They had been getting along well, aside from an occasional jab or a few heated arguments. Jadis had also called her sisters when Aiden allowed her to use his phone and let them know she was fine. They offered to come and pick her up, but she chose to stay with Aiden.

Once Jadis remained there on her own, Bain released the sorcery binding her powers.

Like every other night, Jadis was asleep in Aiden's arms when he suddenly jumped out of bed, scaring her half to death.

"What the hell?" She heard him exclaim.

Jadis sat up and Aiden was standing at the edge of the bed staring at her and appeared to be really disturbed.

"Aiden, what's wrong?" she asked softly. "Aiden—is everything okay?"

He ignored her question and kept staring at her, his expression cold and blank. He was desperately trying to understand what he had just seen and was hoping it wasn't real or some sort of premonition. *What the hell was that?* He thought to himself. *Is she going to die because of me? Am I the one putting her life at risk when I only desire to protect her? Is this real?* He couldn't bear the thought of him being an accomplice to her death. *How could this be?* Aiden wanted more than to protect her, and now it seemed as if death was surrounding her because of him. All he could do in that moment was leave.

It wasn't as if they'd had sex. Other than being bunkmates, nothing had happened between them. Sure, she had thought about it, and on more than one occasion and she knew he had as well. For him to storm out of the bedroom like that and was shocking; Jadis sat there feeling utterly confused, scared, and alone.

The following evening, Jadis was sitting in the chair, staring out at the window. No matter how many times Maddie and Chloe tried, she refused to leave the bedroom. Jadis jumped to her feet when the door softly opened and Aiden walked in. "Aiden?"

"I'm so sorry, Jadis. I didn't mean to leave you alone all that time. I mean—it's just—I think it's better for you to go to a safe house. I've made arrangements for you, and Lars will be your escort. You will be welcomed and well cared for."

Jadis blankly stared at him in disbelief and did her best to pull his thoughts. She had never seen him looking so solemn. *Even his words match his expression. They, too, are cold and empty.*

"Aiden, I'm sorry. What did I do wrong? I know we fight, but this—"

He stopped her mid-sentence. "Don't." He held his hand up. "Jadis, it's not you, it's me. As long as you are with me, your life is in danger."

"What are you saying, Aiden? Nothing is going to happen. Is this all because of your nightmare?"

Aiden's expression became that of anger. Jadis psychically felt his anguish, and then his vision flooded her mind. *She was laying lifeless in his arms.* However, it wasn't Aiden holding her. In that moment, she couldn't have been more confused, not to mention terrified.

Aiden picked up her empty duffle bag and sat it on the bed. Even though he didn't speak, Jadis assumed it was a hint for her to pack her belongings. As the tears pooled in her eyes, she headed for the bathroom, closed the door, and changed. She needed to be ready for whatever was about to happen. When she regained the courage and composure to open the bathroom door, Aiden was gone, her duffle bag had been filled with her belongings, and was sitting on the end of the bed next to her backpack.

Jadis ran. It was all she could do to keep from falling apart. She grabbed her backpack and headed down the long corridor to the top of the staircase, which now felt like it was a mile long. Her sadness turned to anger; she couldn't come to terms with how easily he could turn on her. *How can he be so cold, so heartless? He has weaponized his emotional indifference. How can he dismiss me with such ease? Casting me out like a cheap whore!*

She made her way to the front of the house and she could hear their muffled voices coming from the command center just down the hall.

She snuck to the door, hiding from view, and the conversation became clear. *They are all talking about death—my death.* She glanced over just in time to see Aiden had noticed her. He immediately headed in her direction. She summoned every ounce of power she had and slammed the door in his face. She swirled her hands and conjured a spell that would seal them in.

She had no idea where she was going, but needed to get the hell out of there and away from all of them. She had been studying Bain's abilities as much as he had been studying hers. *Right now, I am more cunning, maybe, but not more powerful, and my time is limited.* She headed down the hall to the front door and it flew open before slamming shut behind her. She stopped on the expansive front stoop, needing to catch her breath. After all, it took a lot of energy to seal in a handful of vampires, and a bad ass wizard. She knew the seal wouldn't hold for more than a couple of hours, at best, but at least it would give her enough time to get a good distance from the mansion.

Lars stood as still as an opaque statue under the cool glow of the moonlit night. He was still listening telepathically to his brother's conversations occurring back in the command center when he saw Jadis run out of the front door.

He wanted to let Aiden know he had his eyes on his girl, *"She's pissed, brother."*

"Stop her and now!" Aiden demanded.

Lars watched as Jadis angrily pulled the hair tie holding her ponytail in place before shoving it into her back pocket. Her wavy, mahogany locks tumbled down and around her shoulders as she headed toward a car parked down the road.

Aiden felt a sudden pang of jealousy, knowing Lars was watching her with an uninvited desire as he psychically relayed the vision of Jadis leaving. *"Lars, god dammit, stop her."*

"Relax, Aiden. You sort of deserve this for letting that ass go. I won't let anything happen to her. I'll stay on her, but this is too enticing." He chuckled like a kid stealing his brother's prized possession. *"I want to see where she's going. I'll keep her safe."*

"Dammit, Lars—stop messing around," Aiden demanded again.

"Sorry, brother, let me know when your time-out is over. I'll bring her back."

Jadis hurried down the sidewalk winding its way between the trees and lush gardens. She wiped away the tears, not wanting the driver to see her crying. She had called for a ride telepathically, instead of facing whatever it was Aiden had planned for her. The driver was heading up the canyon to pick up other passengers and she simply influenced him to come to her instead; he would be none the wiser.

Aiden might not give a damn about me, but he will not get away with this. He will soon see exactly what I'm capable of.

"You want to play a game of chess? You've just been checkmated," Jadis snarked telepathically.

"Jadis, stop this is not a game," Aiden replied.

"No can do." She shut him out of her mind to let him know how it felt.

"No can do? Jadis, answer me!"

She ignored Aiden and slowed to a casual walk; all the while, her heart drummed in her ears. She took a few deep breaths to calm her racing nerves. She was praying the spell would hold as she hopped into the waiting car.

"Where to, Miss?" the driver asked.

"Head down the mountain until I figure it out, please."

He looked at her in the rearview mirror and smiled, "When you *figure it out*, let me know."

"Skye, Ivory, are you listening?"

"What's up, Jadis?" Skye responded.

"I need to see you."

"Everything okay?" Ivory asked.

"Not really. Aiden decided it was best for me to leave. Where are you guys at?"

"Why would he want you to leave?" Ivory asked.

"I'll explain later." She didn't have the ability in that moment to explain the situation without crying. *"Where are you?"*

"We're going out for the night. Meet us at Temple," Skye stated.

"I'll be there."

"It'll be okay, Jadis." Ivory replied sweetly.

"Temple, in Ebonshield, please," Jadis said to the driver.

"Of course. It'll be about an hour's drive."

"No problem." *An hour will give me a chance to calm down and pull myself together before meeting up with my sisters.*

The road exiting the mansion took them down the mountain following a series of sharp switchbacks. It twisted and turned before dropping about thousand feet to the city below. The drive itself was beautiful. Granite walls rose above the road on one side, and the river ran down the canyon about five hundred feet on the other side. The drive could be dangerous on a dry day, which was part of the reason she had wrecked her car that night, amidst the darkness, falling rain, and mostly, her panicked need to escape.

While sitting in the back seat of the SUV, her mind wandered. She thought about the events that had occurred over the past month; losing her dogs, the accident, being pulled from the wreckage, the Baskale being killed by Aiden. Worst of which were the feelings she had developed for him.

About an hour later, the driver pulled to a stop in front of the club. Jadis paid the driver, stepped out of the car and walked past the line of patrons waiting to get into the hottest bar in the modern part of the city. As she walked up to the entrance, the bouncer stepped in front of the door, blocking her way in.

"Long time no see," he said.

"It's been awhile," Jadis replied as she moved in to hug him.

"Where have you been? You okay?" he inquired.

"I'm okay, and it's a long story." She waved her hand in dismissal. "I'll explain it to you over a drink sometime."

"Sounds good. I assume Ivory and Skye will be joining you?"

"Yes, they should be here shortly."

"I'll make sure they get in. It's a packed bar tonight."

"I'm sure you will. Are you going to make sure they get in, or you *get it in*?" she joked.

"Funny girl." He gave her a pat on the ass and opened the door for her.

Staldan and Skye had hooked up a year ago and were nothing more than friends with benefits, as some would say.

Inside the club, it was busy as always. The sounds of laughter, the smell of alcohol, and the pounding music permeated air. Jadis walked to the bar and leaned over toward the bartender.

"What can I get you, gorgeous?" he asked with a wink and a smile.

"Whiskey, please, and make it a double if you don't mind."

"Not at all."

All I have to do is make it through the night. I will deal with this shit later. She tried to convince herself that maybe, tomorrow it wouldn't feel this bad. She pushed her glass toward the bartender. "Another please," she asked.

The entire situation with Aiden had brought back old memories. Even though it seemed like it had been a hundred plus years ago, there was a longing that wouldn't go away, no matter how hard she tried to push it down from the surface. All this bullshit with Aiden had brought it to a level she could no longer ignore. She thought back to a time when she had found a moment of beauty in a cruel world, and it had been taken from her long before meeting Aiden. As devastating as it was, she had become her own flame in the dark. *My biggest mistake was letting Aiden become my sense of security, not to mention a bit more—or so I hoped.*

Lars made it into the club without being noticed and took a seat out of sight. He was far enough away to watch, but not close enough for Jadis to feel him there. They all knew she had the power, but none of them were sure how far it extended. After all she had accomplished, it was truly anyone's guess.

Lars also found it amusing Jadis had his brothers on lockdown, and the fact it was in their own command center made it even more entertaining. *She has surely shown Aiden what's up,* he thought, as he watched Jadis slightly bent over the bar, ordering her drink. *She is a sight to behold.* Her allure was strong enough to cause his body to react, and he struggled to maintain his composure. Aiden was a witness to the entire event as well, along with his brothers, as Lars continued to project the entire scene to them, as ordered.

"Lars, take it down a notch," Eden demanded. *"Your reaction isn't helping the situation right now."*

Lars dismissed the statement, not bothering to reply.

The fury in Aiden was smoldering behind his narrowed eyes. Certainly, the image Lars was projecting wasn't helping.

Each time her glass was empty, the bartender was there to fill it; his eyes dropping momentarily to her low-cut neckline. Jadis's perfect round breasts showed through the top of her flowing, flowered tank top, giving just enough of a glimpse to leave onlookers longing to see more. Her top was tucked ever so slightly into the front of her jeans that hugged her curved hips and muscular legs. Her black leather boots hugged her calves, showing off the curves of her lower legs as well.

Jadis leaned against the bar watching the boisterous crowd, which comprised Nosferatu, Wizards, and mortals who were willing blood hosts. Most of whom were looking to become a potential mate or bed partner in order to elevate their social standing. The upper level booths were occupied by the wealthy, and attended to by vetted, impeccably dressed girls who were carefully selected. The bar was opulent; tapestries and various other décor hung on the walls, and the white marble floors reflected the colorful spinning lights hanging above the dance floor.

She turned toward the door and noticed her sisters strutting their way through the packed crowd. *Damn, they are a sight for sore eyes.*

Skye wore a tight, form-fitting floral wrap dress and pink stilettos. Her long, flowing, raven-black hair bounced around her shoulders as she walked.

Ivory was wearing tight-fitting leather leggings, a loose-fitting grey top, and dark grey stilettos. Her thick, red locks moved like ripples of satin as she strutted toward her.

She hadn't seen them since before the night Aiden had taken her home, or rather to the place she had been stupid enough to believe was might have eventually become her home.

They ran up with a squeal and embraced Jadis tightly, and she clung to them.

"The bastard let you go?" Ivory questioned, not that it was a rhetorical question.

"I'm an idiot to believe in happy endings and false promises," Jadis replied.

"Jadis, are you in love with him?" Skye questioned.

"No! I mean I'm definitely interested, but I'm not *in love*."

"You haven't been *interested* in a male in god knows how long," Ivory replied.

"Just because I'm not jumping from one bed to another doesn't mean I don't want to be with someone."

"I get that," Ivory replied. "We're here now. Let's get a drink and forget about it for the night. We'll figure out what to do in the morning, okay?" Skye offered as she gently cupped her cheek.

"I can't believe he did this." Jadis sighed.

"It's probably not what you think. From all you have told us, it seems you two are pretty tight," Ivory stated warmly.

"Apparently not," she mumbled. *Shit! They don't know the half of it.*

"We'll have three shots of Lagavulin, please." Skye said to the bartender with a wink and a seductive smile.

"How about we hit the dance floor? Standing here thinking about it all night will not help," Ivory suggested.

"Whatever," Jadis replied, deciding to fill them in later.

The three of them soon found themselves the middle of the dance floor. Music blaring in the background while the crowd moved to the beat. Having had her share of drinks by now, Jadis had put the regret she'd felt, and the ache in her heart from Aiden's betrayal aside. If only for a few hours, it was a welcome relief to be free from all of it. She needed this as badly as she needed to breathe. *I should be feeling only that—freedom.* Yet even in her tipsy state, she could feel an energy watching their every move from somewhere at the back of the club. Being what she and her sisters were, it wasn't at all unusual for them to be drawing the stares from men, especially the Nosferatu males. However, the energy she felt this time felt different, somehow familiar. She did her best to dismiss what she was feeling as she glanced through the crowd. *What does it matter right now, anyway?*

"What have I done?" Aiden questioned, not realizing he was speaking a loud.

Eden and Bain looked at him, a bit shocked at how distraught he appeared.

There's more to his feelings than he's letting on, Eden thought. "Calm, brother," Eden spoke with the gentleness of a cat's purr. "We all make mistakes. Hell, I've made my fair share too, especially where Maddie is concerned. We were all supposed to protect her. That responsibility was on all of us. We will get her back here, and you can make amends with her in whatever way it takes. She will not die on our watch," Eden stated.

"Damn, Aiden," interjected Lars. "You've fallen for her—that's a mistake, a big, big mistake."

"I'm not falling for her! I care about her and want to make sure nothing happens to her. That's it—that's all it is," Aiden snapped, trying to convince himself as much as he was his brothers.

"You just keep telling yourself that, brother," Lars replied as he continued to watch Jadis and her friends dance amongst each other.

Their bodies gracefully twirled around one another; each alluring twist perfectly synchronized. He knew the sight would only fuel the fire burning inside Aiden. Jadis was breathtaking, sensual, and her movements flowed with mesmerizing grace.

Lars found her friends to be just as remarkable, and he felt something peculiar about them as well. They seemed to revel in the same energy, but there was more to Jadis than that of her friends.

Aiden had enough of watching the scene from a distance. *"Lars, you need to grab her now and head back."*

"Nope, sorry, brother. Your fuck up is my temporary enjoyment. Besides, what am I supposed to do with her when I get her back while you're all locked in? Do you want me to stand around and physically restrain her? I suggest you get that place unlocked post haste. Until then, I'm going to sit back and enjoy myself while you take a little time out."

"Lars, cool your shit," Eden demanded.

Aiden anxiously paced back and forth, waiting on Bain to get them the hell out of there.

"We'll get her back, Aiden," Eden stated again.

A chair flew across the room and slammed into the wall on the opposite side from where Aiden was standing. Bain and Eden ducked and covered their faces as the splintered pieces of wood ricocheted off the wall.

"What the hell, Aiden?" Bain snapped.

"We have company," Lars announced telepthicaly. The tone of his voice conveyed more than his words.

"What now?" Aiden huffed, turning his attention back to the picture Lars was projecting.

Lars watched Silas and his brothers walk into the club, and head straight for their private booth, overlooking the entire bar. His primary focus now was knowing they would pick up on Jadis and her friend's energy immediately.

Eden answered Lars's concern, *"What the hell are Silas, Syth, and Agaeus doing there?"*

"Shit," Aiden groaned.

"Your guess is as good as mine," Lars replied.

Lars' plan to grab Jadis off the dance floor and take her home had run into a bit of an obstacle. He was keeping an eye on three girls, rather than just Jadis. The greater concern, of course, was Silas and his brothers, who were some of the most dangerous of their kind. Not to mention the nefarious reputations preceding them.

"Do you think they know?" Aiden asked, looking at no one in particular.

"The fun is over. This shit just got real," Eden said. "Why else would they be in town? They have to know something?"

Lars spoke up again. *"Getting the girls away from those three is not going to be easy,"* he admitted.

"You need to make a move. You can't sit there contemplating it all night," Eden scolded.

Lars turned his attention back to Silas and his brothers, knowing Eden was correct; he needed to make a move—and now.

Silas, Agaeus, and Syth hadn't even taken their seats in the booth before they had their eyes on three girls who were in the center of the dance floor. They casually glanced at each other, curious about the unexpected energy they felt radiating from them.

"Well shit, they are an unexpected sight tonight," Agaeus said, as he leaned against the solid oak railing, intently watching the girls.

"Do you feel it?" Silas asked.

"Sure do," Syth agreed.

Silas rested his forearms on the railing and looked around. "Guess who else is here?" he stated.

Syth looked in the same direction. "Lars? What's he doing here?"

"Not sure, seeing how he's alone," Agaeus answered.

"Lars," Silas called telepathically.

Lars acknowledged him with a simple nod, looking less than thrilled. *"Silas, what are you doing here?"*

"I could ask you the same thing," Silas replied as he tipped his glass at him.

Lars returned the gesture. *"Having a drink? what else?"*

"You sure about that?" Silas realized Lars had also been watching the girls, which only piqued his curiosity.

Silas and his brothers decided to take a seat, dismissing Lars as well as the business they were there to discuss. Silas was more focused on whatever it was about the girls that were so enticing. He was determined to find out what the sudden allure was.

"I say we send the girls a few drinks," Syth suggested. Silas nodded in agreement.

The bartender interrupted the girls with a tray of highball glasses. Jadis, Skye, and Ivory politely accepted the drinks they hadn't ordered. The bartender smiled and pointed to the booth above the dance floor. They looked up and raised their glasses to the three males sitting in the VIP section, looking directly at them. The males casually nodded in response, and one of them winked at Skye.

Damn, Skye thought, as she winked back with a coy smile.

They finished their drinks and went about their business on the dance floor. Skye and Ivory had developed some new ideas after noticing how stunning the three men were; their menacing energy too enticing for them to ignore.

The males were strikingly similar. They shared the same rugged features, searing eyes, and impossible physiques.

Skye looked at Ivory and smiled deviously. *"I think this might be exactly what Jadis needs to take her mind off everything,"* she said telepathically.

"I'm all in." Ivory chuckled. *"Hell, if anyone has a chance, it is one of the men sitting in the booth."*

"That's the last thing I need right now," Jadis snapped, having heard the telepathic conversation.

Skye laughed as she grabbed Jadis's arm and spun her around, forcing her to laugh along with her. They chose to ignore the males for the time being, at least until they could pull Jadis out of her funk.

After about thirty minutes, Silas set his glass on the table and stood up. "I say we join them."

"No need to tell me twice. The red head is calling my name," Agaeus replied.

"The one with the raven black hair has my name written all over her," Syth said.

"The one with mahogany hair, she's mine," Silas stated as they easily moved through the crowded dance floor.

"Mind if I cut in?" Syth asked as he grabbed hold of his girl's hand.

"I don't mind at all." Skye smiled.

Agaeus grabbed his girl and spun her around. "Looks like my brother took one of your dance partners." He winked.

"Looks like it," Ivory replied.

Silas took a more subtle approach, having felt the anger simmering beneath the surface of his girl. He knew there was also something else, more than hurt and anger. There was just something; something deeper, something powerful, and yet somehow, she felt familiar. Jadis looked around and realized she had lost her sisters. She felt the awkwardness creep up and became fully self-conscious as she stood on the dance floor alone. Suddenly, the warmest, smoothest voice spoke from behind.

"I think you lost your girls."

Jadis abruptly turned around, only to be staring at the lower half of his chest. Her gaze drifted up his body, and little by little, the partially, unbuttoned black silk shirt revealed a bit more of his solid chest. She stepped back to look up at him and he was casually standing there with his hands in his pockets. *Damn he's tall and downright gorgeous.*

The stranger's voice was velvety smooth and there was an enticing richness in his tone. There was also something else to it she picked up on immediately. It was alarming, and deep down, Jadis knew she needed to be wary of not only him, but his friends as well. *Nosferatu, here we go again.*

Despite the feelings, she was determined to not let it stop her from enjoying the distraction of her gorgeous new dance partner. He was as smooth as any seasoned professional, his movements effortless and slightly erotic.

Jadis, Skye, and Ivory were enjoying their new company, when Jadis happened to glance across the room again and caught a glimpse of him; the one she had felt watching her and her sisters earlier. *Oh my God, it is him. Dammit, Lars!*

As she looked in his direction, a frozen expression crossed his face, realizing he had been spotted.

"More bad news, brothers. She's seen me," Lars admitted telepathically.

"Seen you?" Aiden hissed. *"How the fuck can she see you? Don't tell me you were stupid enough to sit in the club like a goddamn mortal?"*

"I'm not an idiot. I've been cloaked since your girl ran out of the mansion doors earlier this evening," Lars snapped back. *"The only one who's noticed me until now is Silas and his brothers."*

Eden spoke up, *"Are you sure she's seeing you?"*

"Yes, she's looking right at me and based on the glare in her eyes, she is not happy."

"Holy shit," mumbled Bain from across the room.

CHAPTER 5

Once Jadis realized Lars was in the club watching them, she telepathically messaged her sisters letting them know she needed to leave. She didn't want anything to do with any of them, much less Aiden. *How dare he put a tail on me after what he did? If he cares at all, it would be his ass coming after me. Then again, he is sort of locked up.*

Jadis looked up at her dance partner. "I appreciate the dance, but we need to leave."

"So soon? We were just starting to enjoy ourselves," he replied.

"Come with us if you want to join a real party," Ivory's partner offered.

The way Jadis's sisters looked at each other made it obvious they had every intention of joining them. As much as she wanted and needed the distraction, she felt an unsettling sense of caution.

"We have a car out back. You're safe with us. We have no ill intentions. My brothers are looking to have fun, and from what I can tell, so are your girls. If you want to leave, I will personally see you home," he offered.

Home? she thought. *I don't have a home anymore. Home? Shit, I can't even go back to my cabin. He'll have to drop my ass off at a hotel.* She reluctantly followed her sisters, with her new friend following closely behind.

"A limo? Really?" Ivory chuckled as her partner held the door open for her.

This is going to be interesting, Jadis thought. *I never thought I'd see the inside of one of these.*

"Only the best." Skye's friend winked.

Jadis and her sisters knew Lars was following them, so to cover their tracks, they covertly enveloped themselves in a shroud between realities so they couldn't be detected in any way. Even Lars wouldn't be able to find them, no matter how hard he tried, at least not without Bain's sorcery. As long as the three of them stuck together, they could easily disappear.

Lars found himself standing in the dark alley behind the club, feeling as if he had stepped into a void. He looked to his right, and then to his left, and Jadis was gone, as were her friends. *Fuck me!* He now had to face the wrath of his brothers, who were also staring into the empty alley. *At least they're still locked up.* He was hoping it would buy him some time to try to locate Jadis and her friends before coming face to face with Aiden. She was not only Aiden's problem, but his as well. Their tenacity, capabilities, and evasiveness have been underestimated by them all.

Skye and Ivory were happily carrying on a conversation with their new friends. Jadis, however, quietly sat with a drink in her hand, about a seat-length away from her new acquaintance, unable to escape her tormenting thoughts. She gazed at her drink as she swirled it in her hand, only half-aware of the claustrophobic comfort of the limo. *Who are these three?* she wondered. What she did know for certain was that they weren't to be taken lightly.

Silas was studying his girl's striking features; her long mahogany hair, her thin, beautiful neckline, and those full, blush-colored lips. The soul of her eyes was ageless, nothing short of stunning, yet they were all too familiar. *Definitely not mortal,* Silas said to himself.

Jadis felt his inquisitiveness, and caught his gaze, unwavering and unabashed. The longer the drive lingered on, the more awkward she felt. Her sisters' laughter, along with their subtle jabs for her to snap out of it, pulled her from her self-imposed trance.

She turned to the gorgeous man sitting beside her. *What have I gotten into now? Whatever it may be, it seems harmless. None of them have been disrespectful or given us any reason to doubt their intentions aren't genuine. They seem to be refined, polite, and courteous. It's not as if I have any better place to be.* Jadis decided she wasn't going to put a damper on the party for another minute.

She was still looking at him when he shot a demure grin her way that could light up the bleakest of nights. She smiled back and began to chuckle. Just the thought of Aiden and his brothers being locked down, as well as having ditched Lars, forced her to smile. Not to mention they left Lars standing in an empty alley, which brought forth a burst of laughter; her trepidation succumbing to her amusement.

It may have been the liquor talking, but she decided it was time to let Aiden and his brothers know how far her reach could extend.

She peered into the command center and there was an ornate, antique mirror, about 8' tall, maybe 4' wide and at least two hundred years old, hanging on the far wall. *That will work.*

Aiden looked over, having felt a strange energy, and noticed a swirling vortex of smoke coming from the mirror, which had also captured Eden and Bain's attention. An ominous silence hung heavy in the air as they stared in confusion at the swirling image.

"What the hell?" Eden stated, as he, Bain and Aiden stood in a hushed line in front of the mirror; confusion on all their faces.

Then they saw it, from the shadows came a form. They could see the distorted image of Jadis and her two friends in the back seat of the limousine with Silas and his brothers.

"She didn't just disappear, she fucking left with Silas." Aiden almost sent an agonizing blow to the mirror.

"Aiden, stop!" Eden and Bain yelled simultaneously.

They lunged in unison to stop him from destroying the only connection they currently had to her.

"If she's trying to send you a message, you about demolished the only link we have had to her since they slipped away from Lars," Eden chided.

"If anything happens to her on account of me, I won't be able to live with myself!"

"We're not going to lose her, Aiden. She has the power to appear in the mirror and the ability to dodge Lars. Jadis is more cunning and devious than we have given her credit for. I'm pretty sure she could conquer the dark," Eden stated.

"Think about it, Aiden. She's obviously not helpless, nor is she naïve. She's made that pretty clear over the past month," Bain added.

"They are no match for Silas and his brothers. You know that as well as I do. No one is powerful enough to stop their mind bending abilities.

If Silas figures out who she is, she's as good as gone to us. He'll never let her go." Aiden was speaking the truth.

"You don't know that for certain, Aiden. What could he want with her or her friends? What purpose can they serve? I can't see why her energy alone would be reason enough for him to keep her locked away," Eden reasoned.

"The only problem with your theory, brother, is that there is more to it than just my vision," Aiden grumbled, as he rubbed his forehead.

"What else have you not told us?" Eden questioned.

"Silas and his brothers think they have discovered a Segan sealed away and need a way to open the cave's vortex. Only an original with unearthly energies can unseal it. What if it is her? All the clues are pointing in her direction," Aiden replied.

"Unseal the vortex? And you know this how?" Bain demanded.

"When were you going to fill us in on this little tidbit?" Eden was clearly annoyed with the realization Aiden hadn't exactly been forthcoming earlier with his sudden admission.

"I was planning on bringing it up, but I was waiting for a bit more intel. I needed more than just muddled rumors. But if it's true then we know for sure Ipheanor is awakening."

That's fucking great. We now have more questions than we have answers for, Eden thought.

"Is it them?" Bain questioned.

"I honestly don't know. It was a rumor going around in Silas's clan my friend Arcadia revealed to me. Arcadia and I have been trying to decipher rumor from fact. There are too many inconsistencies in the rumors alone. At the time it was just chatter, but now I'm not so sure," Aiden explained.

Bain sat in his chair, contemplating what they were being told. "And Jadis? After tonight, you think she is the key to opening the vortex?"

"Maybe, and the two girls are her sisters, not her friends," Aiden admitted.

"Christ, Aiden. Is there anything else you'd like to fill us in on?" Bain asked.

"How do you know they are he sisters?" Eden asked. "Maddie said she had called a friend."

"She told me she has two sisters named Skye and Ivory. And to gain her trust, I told her what was discussed in the bedroom would remain between us."

"Lars?" Eden called.

"I heard it all. Aiden, you could have at least mentioned this while I was in the fucking club. If her sisters are anything like Jadis, no fucking wonder they disappeared so easily."

The limo pulled to a stop, and the driver stepped around and opened the door. Skye and Ivory were escorted out of the parked limo first. Once Jadis's friend stepped out, he held his hand out to her.

The girls looked down and noticed they were standing on a red carpet that had been laid out on the tarmac, leading them to a private jet standing in wait.

"Are you kidding me?" Jadis asked, looking at her new friend before casually glancing at her sisters, who also looked shocked.

"This is not what we were expecting. We thought we were headed to a party at another club or a private residence, not to a private jet?" she questioned. It wasn't just any jet either, but a Carena Cartiage.

"What's the matter?" he asked. "I'm sure you've seen a plane or two before?"

"Never up close, and this is not just a transport plane. I thought we were going to a party?" Jadis replied.

"We are going to a party. It just so happens it's in Mikalar."

"*Mikalar*? You didn't mention that in the club."

"You didn't ask," he replied. "Are you coming, or are you going to stand there all night?"

"We don't know the three of you and we are just going to hop on your plane?" Jadis said.

"Well then, let me formally introduce us. I'm Silas Montiago. These are my brothers, Agaeus and Syth Montiago. It's my pleasure to meet you, Jadis—Jadis?" Silas offered as demure as one could get.

She chuckled. "Arwen, Jadis Arwen and these are my sisters, Skye and Ivory Arwen."

"Well then, now that you know who we are, shall we?" Silas held out his bent arm along with a questioning eyebrow.

Jadis looked at Skye and Ivory, who were already walking arm in arm with Syth and Agaeus. *I guess that's my answer. If I want to get far away from Aiden and his brothers, this is certainly the way to do it.*

"Come," Silas said, as he proceeded to lead her onto the plane.

The crew, including the captain, were standing inside, ready to greet their passengers.

The captain, who was the last in line standing by the cockpit door, greeted Silas and his brothers personally. "Good evening, Silas."

Jadis watched the way in which the pilot gave each of them a quick hug, along with a pat on the shoulder. *There is more to their relationship than merely boss and employee, not to mention he greeted Silas using his first name.* The pilot appeared to be only about three hundred and thirty years old, and he had the same rugged features. Even the scar running from the corner of his eye and down the entirety of his cheek couldn't tarnish his rugged good looks.

"Good evening, Zach," Silas replied. "I'd like you to meet Jadis, Skye, and Ivory—Arwen." Silas added the last name with a wink in Jadis's direction.

"Welcome aboard, ladies. Take a seat and enjoy the flight. We will be in Mikalar in less than three hours."

Jadis looked around and thought about how beautiful it was. There was plenty of space, and the cozy, white leather armchairs were perfectly lined along each side of the jet. It was luxurious; the cabin seemed more like a lounge than something one would find in an airplane. *It is truly impressive. Everything is state-of-the art.* Custom wood veneer lined the walls on the inside, and the floor was covered with shining stonework.

They took a seat on the plush leather chairs and the stewardess immediately saw to their every need. They landed two hours and fifteen minutes later.

The stewardess opened the door and dropped the stairs. Jadis stood at the top of the stairs and straight ahead was a dock leading guests onto a beautiful yacht, complete with a helicopter pad sitting on the very top.

Once again, the girls stood awestruck as they stared silently at the yacht. Though not at all the party pad they had expected, they certainly weren't disappointed. The lights were gently shining through the galley windows, and the white ship gleamed under the silvery rays of the moon.

It's beautiful, Jadis thought.

"Not as beautiful as you." Silas winked.

The sudden compliment made Jadis's cheeks flush, as well as the realization he read her mind for the second time. *Oh boy, here we go again.*

"You're kidding me, right? First a jet plane and now a yacht? You didn't mention the yacht."

"You didn't ask," Silas replied. "Come, the party's just getting started," he said with a smirk.

"Is this it? Any more surprises? Is the yacht taking us somewhere else you've not yet mentioned?" Jadis asked.

"No. This is the party. We are going to sail around Mikalar, and no, we aren't going anywhere else—since you asked," Silas replied with a captivating smile.

They were led by the brothers onto the yacht, that appeared to have been waiting for their arrival. Jadis took in every beautiful, hand-carved detail, as well as the exotic rooms and long passageways throughout the ship. Though it was beautiful, she didn't do it for pleasure. She had to ensure she'd know where to go in the event they needed to make a quick exit. Her sisters were too smitten to take notice of anything other than the men leading them up to the top deck. As they walked up the stairs, they were escorted to a private table with a padded, wrap-around bench, complete with its own bartender. The commotion coming from the crowd below on the lower deck was somewhat mesmerizing, and the steel bass drums had Jadis captivated. She finally felt she was able to relax, even if it was for only a few hours. *How can anything all that serious possibly happen with all these people aboard and a party raging below?*

Their conversations were light-hearted and pleasant, and Jadis found herself truly enjoying their company. *Silas is sophisticated and polite, but keen. In fact, he's too keen. Another Eden,* Jadis thought. However, she felt as drawn to him as the sun is the dawn. She couldn't discern the unknown familiarity.

"Come," Silas stood up, grabbed Jadis's hand, and pulled her onto the dance floor, spinning her around in the process and bringing about a heap of laughter. She and Silas slipped through the crowd and joined his brothers and her sisters. All the while the sounds coming from the boisterous crown and the music were getting lost in the echo of the sea.

The emotions from the events that had taken place earlier faded. The gorgeous stranger was exactly what she needed as he spun her around the floor again and again. As the music slowed, she realized she was dancing with her back to him. The slow music twirled like thread around them as she leaned the back of her head against his chest and let him sway with her body. She wanted to exist only in this moment, as Silas continued to hold her tight.

Silas wrapped his arm around her waist and settled his face on the side of hers. She couldn't stop thinking about how good he felt, too damn good and way too soon. He began humming an all-familiar tune in her ear that caused goosebumps to scurry up her arms. She had heard it before but couldn't remember when or where.

The longer Silas held her and moved with her body, the more he felt he needed to be with her one way or another.

She was alluring and her energy enticing. She was a silent voice whispering to him from within. There was something haunting about the girls, but especially Jadis. He had time. No one was going anywhere if he didn't want them to, at least not until he understood the raw, undeniable tug she had on him. After all, they were on his yacht in the middle of the ocean.

The party went on into the early morning hours. It was about three in the morning when Jadis decided she'd had enough.

"Silas, this has been amazing, but I'm exhausted," she said, careful with her words, not wanting him to see it as an invitation.

Skye and Ivory decided the same, only their departure ended with an invitation. The four of them quietly disappeared in the darkness, leaving Jadis alone with Silas.

Silas had since cleared the deck of the partiers as he leaned against the rail with Jadis. *A beautiful sight she is.*

Jadis stared off into the ocean, watching the moonlight gently ripple with the movement of the soft waves. She felt Silas place his arm around her lower back before he leaned in for a kiss. She tried to resist, but he held her steady. She could feel the warmth of his skin on hers as he peered deep into her eyes with an expressionless curiosity.

Jadis held his gaze. His eyes were deep, raw, and black. There was depth within them, ancient and archaic. *Strange?* She couldn't visualize anything behind the blackness. She could usually penetrate any barrier and see beyond the physical realm, but she could not see him. His amber-lit eyes, glowing in the darkness, were fixed on hers. He kissed her again, and to her surprise, she responded without hesitation.

His tongue met hers and together they danced a slow, seductive waltz. She didn't try to resist. She wanted to take in the musky, dangerous taste that was Silas. His canines fell from his gums, and she could feel the sharpness scrape across her tongue. Unfortunately, her body responded to his, against her better judgment.

"You taste so familiar and you smell like jasmine. Your scent takes me back to a time long ago." Silas moved his lips across her neck and softly whispered in her ear, "I still remember the lingering scent, resting in the dew of delicate jasmine buds." He looked down and stared at her, bewildered. "Who are you? What are you? Who dishonored you so bad you're standing here with me?" he asked, genuinely curious.

Not prepared to answer any questions, she pulled back slightly and looked up at him. She must have had as many questions about him as he did about her. She found herself longing for his touch, but for now, she knew it was time to go to bed, alone, before her body betrayed her to this mysterious stranger. *However, there is one more thing I need to do; stick it to Aiden.*

Bain had unlocked the command center hours ago, but even so, they were left scrambling to find any clue of where Jadis and her sisters were. Lars was not only infuriated with Jadis after she'd craftily disappeared back at the club, but couldn't help but to be impressed as well.

"Now what? We've been pissing around here for hours," Aiden sighed. *I let the queen's diamond slip from my fingers, shattering at my feet.* He hadn't looked in Lars' direction since he had returned. He knew he wouldn't be able to control the rage bubbling to the surface.

"We'll find them," Eden replied nonchalantly.

Aiden was pacing back and forth when he noticed the mirror swirling, just as it had before. "Jadis," he announced.

They moved before the mirror and stood silently, watching as the fog swirl, warp and twist. The image was out of focus at first, like a poor photograph, before slowly morphing into a surreal image. There was Jadis, leaning against the rails of what appeared to be a ship, and she wasn't alone. Silas was there with her in the dark, with his eyes fixed on hers.

Just as quickly as it had taken shape, the image dissipated into a cloud of haze. Aiden stood breathless, frozen in place as the haze dissipated around him, carrying with it the subtle scent he was so familiar with.

Lars truly felt bad for Aiden. *Jadis is taunting him, allowing him momentary glimpses, hoping to afflict as much agony on him as he had her, and it's working.*

Eden patted his shoulder. "Calm Aiden."

"We'll get her back, brother," Bain interjected, reassuringly.

Aiden filled his glass, knowing there was no calming down, at least not until she was back with him.

Eden and his brothers had been out looking for Jadis all night; they returned home in the early morning hours empty handed. Once they broke her cloaking spell, it was too late and their calls to Silas went unanswered. They knew full well he had any wiped any trace of them, seeing how nothing they did to locate her worked. The only hints they'd received came from the images in the mirror, from Jadis herself.

Aiden had remained in that same spot in front of the mirror on and off since having returned, hoping there would be more to lead him to her whereabouts. More than that, he had to know if things had gone any further. *It couldn't have. Jadis isn't like that, and she knows better. She wouldn't be so careless.* If he knew anything, he knew she would never jump into someone's bed, let alone the bed of a stranger. He hoped she had kept her senses, despite any feelings of betrayal she had toward him.

Jadis woke up the next morning in a hungover haze, disoriented, and once again finding herself in a bed that wasn't her own. Her memories were as fuzzy as her mind, and her brain struggled to recover from the alcohol fueled abuse she put herself through last night. She lay between the luxurious satin, burgundy sheets, thankful she was alone.

She thought about the lingering kiss she and Silas had shared under the light of the moon before heading for bed, alone, feeling as though she had betrayed Aiden. *My sisters, on the other hand, are probably still wrapped up in the naked bodies of Silas's brothers.*

There was a soft knock at the door. "Come in," she said.

Silas strode in, wearing a confident smile. He appeared to be nothing less than lethal, powerful, and as gorgeous as she had remembered. He was wearing a pair of casual, cream-colored lounge pants hanging loosely off his toned hips. The golden-brown, cotton, unbuttoned shirt bore his muscular chest and rippled abs. Jadis's eyes began wandering further down than she had intended. Before realizing she should change her focus, she could feel the warmth of her cheeks.

His tattoos are fascinating, she thought, from what little she could see. It appeared he had full sleeves covering both of his arms, and his chest was also covered with intricately patterned tattoos.

Silas stood there, allowing her to take in the sight, enjoying every minute of her fixation.

"Morning, mon chéri. You slept well I hope?" he asked politely.

"Yes, thank you," she barely got the words out. She'd been tongue tied before, but never like that. She tilted her head and pushed her hair back, trying to hide her embarrassment, only to realize she had nothing on but a pair of lace panties and the same shirt she wore last night, however it was completely unbuttoned. She pulled the silk sheets up and discreetly tried to cover herself. She didn't want to draw any more attention to her half naked body than she felt she already had.

Silas sauntered across the room and sat in a chair directly across from the bed. He sat casually, bending one leg, with his thighs slightly parted.

The outline of what lay behind those slacks piqued her curiosity, and something else.

"Your girls are fine," he offered, startling Jadis out of her current state of curiosity. Her eyes shot upward to meet his. "If you were wondering," he added. He was smiling like he knew that wasn't what she was thinking about at all.

"You must be hungry. Would you like something to eat?"

"I'm not sure—maybe. I think I would like to take a shower first if you don't mind."

"Of course, you'll find everything you need in the bathroom. I also brought these for you." He walked over to the side of the bed, pulled a couple of pills from his pocket, and placed them in her hand.

Jadis smiled up at him. "How did you know?"

"I've had my fair share of drinking my problems away. Even though my drinking differs from yours," he joked. "A hangover is a hangover, regardless of the drink. I know one when I see it, albeit a stunning one."

Silas is a charmer, she thought, as he reached over, filled a glass of water from the crystal pitcher sitting on the nightstand, and handed it to her.

"I'll leave you to shower. Let me know if you need anything. I'll be back shortly." He winked.

Jadis stepped out of the cool shower that had helped to pull her thoughts away from what she wanted to do with Silas, and what she wanted him to do to her.

She was feeling conflicted about Aiden and how she felt about him. It was as if her thoughts and the uncontrollable pull she felt regarding Silas were a betrayal. She stood on the plush, black Alpaca rug outside the glass shower doors, and realized she didn't have clothes with her. *Shit! What am I going to do, wrap myself in one of his sheets or a towel for the rest of the day? Throw on my jeans to sit on a yacht in the sun?* She looked at the sink to find a fresh toothbrush, toothpaste, and a hairbrush. *At least I can put myself together in that regard, not that it does the rest of my body any good. Thank God I had the sense to at least grab my backpack, even though there isn't a lot in it.* She had expected to stay at her sisters' house, and she'd counted on being able to share their clothes, along with whatever else she needed.

She wrapped the towel around her body and dried off her hair with another. After getting as ready as much as she could, she walked out of the bathroom only to find a beautiful, pink lace bikini and matching floral sarong laying across the bed, along with a pair of black sandals. *What the hell?* She walked over and picked up the matching set, admiring how beautiful it was.

She put the bikini on and it fit like a glove. Again, a quick flash of caution crossed her mind, making her lose her train of thought. She jumped at the sudden knock on the door.

Silas walked into the stateroom and stopped in his tracks as he stared at the beautiful girl in the pink lace bikini standing in front of him. He looked her over in admiration, appreciating the style of her old-world tattoos. Lativin language and hieroglyphics ran up and down her right arm, from wrist to shoulder, tracing her toned bicep. The subtle hint of one tattoo, barely visible, peeking out from under the bikini bottoms at the base of her stomach, caught his eye. As little of it as there was, he knew he had seen it before. The questions continued to grow in his mind.

"Aren't you a sight to see? You look different in the daylight, Jadis. You are stunning."

Heat rose to her cheeks as she looked down at the floor, fumbling for the sandals for no other reason than to fend off his compliments. *I am nothing, apparently, nothing worth keeping anyway. He will probably throw me out as soon as he gets what he wants.*

"A penny for your thoughts?" he asked, interrupting her self-pity.

Jadis looked up and couldn't help but to smile.

"Let's go. You need to eat," Silas offered.

She knew he had read her mind and was being polite. *Time to shut that shit off—again.*

Silas took her hand and led her out to the deck, where she heard the laughter of Skye, Ivory, Syth, and Agaeus.

Silas and Jadis walked over to the table and sat down at what looked like a feast. Fruit, eggs, and pastries covered the table. Silas handed her a glass filled with fresh-squeezed orange juice and the finest champagne. *Nothing like the hair of the dog,* Jadis thought. It tasted amazing, and the fruit was some of the sweetest she'd ever eaten. As she enjoyed the moment, she realized things felt different with Silas this morning; she was comfortable and at ease.

"You girls enjoy some alone time. My brothers and I have some business to attend to, if you don't mind," Silas said it politely enough, however, he was telling, rather than asking.

"Of course." Jadis waved her hand with a gentle dismissal and a smile. "Take as long as you need. And Silas, thank you. The breakfast is amazing."

He bent over, planted his mouth on hers, and slipped her a little tongue. Her sisters stared with wide eyes before bursting out in a heap of laughter as soon as the brothers were out of range.

"You did not!" Ivory laughed.

"No, I didn't. Unlike the two of you, I slept alone."

"Well, from our experience last night, that was most definitely your loss. You have no idea what you're missing," Skye joked.

"You seriously have no idea." Ivory held her hands out about the length of her waist, and they laughed like a couple of love struck schoolgirls.

"For fucks sake, you're ridiculous." Jadis laughed.

"Listen, we need to talk alone," Jadis said, calming her laughter. Skye and Ivory perked up and became somewhat serious.

"Alone, alone?" Ivory asked.

"Yes," Jadis replied.

They stood, and walked down to the lowest point of the yacht where the deck hung out just above the crystal clear, blue waters. They sat side by side with their arms crossed in each other's and dangled their feet into the warm ocean water before speaking telepathically.

"I see you both have new bikinis as well," Skye said.

Ivory chuckled. "Yes, and it's a perfect fit."

Jadis smiled but remained serious. "*Do you feel anything from them at all?*" she asked telepathically.

"*What do you mean? I mean—I felt a lot.*" Ivory chuckled.

Jadis rolled her eyes in response. "*Be serious! You know who we are and what we are, right?*" she questioned.

"*Well, of course. That's a stupid question,*" Skye chided.

"*No, listen. I looked beyond his eyes last night, and all I saw was blackness.*"

"*That's not possible,*" Skye replied. "*You can see anyone you want.*"

"*Not Silas.*"

"*What the hell?*" A look of worry flashed across Ivory's face.

"*I don't know. I'm conflicted because I also feel strangely comfortable around him this morning.*"

"You're over questioning things, as usual," Skye said.

They stared at each other, trying to come up with a logical explanation for Jadis's inability to read Silas.

Ivory was always the one to rationalize things, *"Look, yesterday was crazy. Maybe you're emotionally drained. We had a lot to drink on top of it."*

"That's not it. He is something else, and he feels we are too."

"That's not possible. You're being paranoid." Ivory was simply trying to make herself feel better. They sat in silence for a few moments, each contemplating what it meant.

"Whatever. I think we should stay another night. I'm enjoying myself," Ivory said.

"I agree," Skye added.

"You know they aren't your average Nosferatu, right?" Jadis asked in a mocking tone.

"No, really?" Ivory replied.

"That was clear last night," Skye joked.

"Can the two of you at least agree they can't find out who we are?" Jadis requested.

"Yes, Jadis," Ivory agreed. *"I have to say, there is something very familiar about Agaeus, but I can't figure it out."*

"I felt it with Syth as well," Skye admitted.

They sat in silence again, knowing something was most definitely amiss.

Jadis looked down at the water, knowing she was holding back everything she had been told while staying with Aiden. *Now is not the time or place,* Jadis thought.

"Maybe we should stay as long as they let us and figure this shit out?" Ivory suggested, not wanting to abandon her new lover—just yet.

Skye and Jadis shrugged their shoulders and looked at one another in agreement.

Silas, Syth, and Agaeus were in Silas's soundproof office having a similar conversation.

"I couldn't bend her will last night," Silas admitted.

"What the hell are you talking about, Silas?" Agaeus asked, half amused.

"Why would you need to mind-bend that female?" Syth chimed in. "You mean for the first time you met a girl that didn't jump into bed with you and let you fuck her dry?"

Syth and Agaeus began laughing. Silas, however, remained collected and unamused. "Listen, assholes, it's not like that. There is something more to her. As much as I wanted to screw her, I couldn't bring myself to do it. I could taste it when I kissed her. They are more than they are letting on and we need to find out who they are, what they are. I should also mention she has a very familiar tattoo."

"Okay—you have our attention. What do you think *they are*?" Agaeus asked.

"The Three Keys?" Silas looked as confused as he sounded.

"Oh, come on, Silas! Now you're letting your mind run wild. You should be able to handle your alcohol better than that." Agaeus laughed.

"The Three Keys!" they announced in unison, looking at each other before looking back at Silas.

"You have lost your fucking mind," Agaeus said.

"Enough!" Silas quickly stood, determined for his brothers to take the possibility seriously.

"Shit's getting serious in here now," Syth joked.

Silas cocked his head and looked at him.

"Okay, okay, explain," Syth said as he held up his hands and calmed down with Silas's silent words of warning.

They discussed the situation in greater detail before coming to a decision regarding the girls.

"Are we all on the same page now?" Silas asked, giving more of an order than asking a question.

"Yes, brother," Syth and Agaeus agreed.

"At some point, the two of you need to try to mind-bend Skye and Ivory while I try to do the same again with Jadis and let's see what happens. If my suspicions are correct, they aren't bendable, so to speak."

"Skye is actually quite bendable." Syth laughed.

Agaeus laughed as well, until Silas looked at them again.

"Don't worry, we'll give it a shot," they agreed, taking head to Silas's unamused look.

"No time to waste," Silas said.

They walked back to the deck to find Jadis, Skye, and Ivory enjoying each other's company where they had left them an hour ago. The girls were laughing, talking, and enjoying the early morning sun shimmering off the clear ocean water.

"The three of you are a beautiful sight," Agaeus said, as they each took a seat on the white leather bench next to the girls.

Syth and Agaeus took their places beside Skye and Ivory, while Silas sat down next to Jadis.

The moment his thigh touched hers, it sent an unwelcome bolt of desire through Jadis's body. He laid his arm behind her neck, resting it on the bench beneath her hair.

A bit too close for comfort, she thought. She wasn't ready to be joining anyone in an emotional game of one-night lovers. However, looking him, she found it challenging not to entertain the thought; his earthy, musky scent certainly wasn't helping.

Silas pulled his arm off the bench and casually laid his hand across her thigh, before gently lifting her leg and resting it across his thigh.

She exhaled a bit too loudly, and she heard Silas chuckle under his breath.

They discussed potential plans for the day, maybe going for a swim in the ocean, taking the jet skis out, or exploring the island. However, Jadis knew Syth and Agaeus were being polite. They were hoping to continue the innate connection that had begun in the early morning hours with Skye and Ivory.

They had been out there for a couple of hours when a tall man dressed in casual attire approached the table. His demeanor was that of a professional bodyguard. Unlike the rest of the ship's crew, he was obviously not the hired help. He was fully armed, and all business. He pulled a satellite phone from his pocket and walked toward Silas.

"Mil—" he began, before clearing his throat. "Sir, here's the phone you asked for."

The brothers glanced at each other, and with a silent nod of their heads, Silas stood up.

"Jadis, I need to make a call. Will you excuse me?"

"Of course," she replied, welcoming the distraction more than she cared to admit. It was just what she needed in order to get a bit of distance between herself and the vampire she continued to grow more attracted to by the minute. This would also give her sisters a chance to see what they could find out about Syth and Agaeus.

"I'm going to sit on the deck by the water for a bit," Jadis stated. *It will give me time to get my shit together before I let my guard down around that sexy as hell vampire.*

Jadis sat quietly with her feet dangling in the warm water, pondering the events of the last twenty-four hours. And once again, she felt like she was betraying Aiden.

She looked over and noticed a jet ski tied to the boat when a voice from behind startled her. Before Jadis saw him move, he had grabbed her forearm to keep her from tumbling into the water when she jumped at the sound of his voice.

"I didn't mean to startle you. I was coming down here to get the jet skis ready for the day."

"Zach? You're the pilot."

"Yes. Would you like to go for a ride?"

Jadis smiled. "I would love to." *Perfect,* she thought. She could see the island off in the distance, just a short jaunt from where the yacht was anchored.

"The island is safe and only a minute's ride," Zach offered, along with the key.

Jadis turned toward him with nothing more than a thought and he held up a bottle of champagne and a cold, sealed container of freshly squeezed orange juice. He placed into the compartment along with a couple of plush beach towels.

The thought of him reading her mind so easily after trying to shut them out was another subtle warning. She was used to it with Aiden and his family, but this felt different. It was almost invasive. *Is he trying to force me to do something?* She wasn't sure, but she could still feel him trying to intrude. She hopped onto the jet ski and took off across the water, heading for the island. She began feeling a sense of relief as the distance between herself and the yacht grew. She could hardly wait to feel the hot sand beneath her feet, the warm breeze blowing over her body, as well as the sounds of the jungle. She slowly pulled up to the island, turned the jet ski off, and let it drift onto the sand.

She hopped off, grabbed the towels, the drinks, and got comfortable on the beach. She laid back, reveling in the sun's warmth, and focused on soaking up its perfect energy. *A recharge is exactly what my body needs.*

CHAPTER 6

The satellite phone rang in the mansion's control room. Aiden looked at Eden, wondering who the hell would call them on the secured line.

"Silas?" Eden was only guessing as he picked up the phone.

"Cousin, you've made quite a few calls recently."

Eden nodded; it was Silas on the other end of the line. "Silas, where is Jadis?"

"You get straight to the point, don't you?"

"We don't have time for games. We want her back."

Aiden held out his hand, and Eden handed him the phone. "Where the hell do you have her?" Aiden demanded.

Silas chuckling articulated much more than mere words.

"Am I amusing you?" Aiden asked.

"Yes, and how you ask leads me to believe she's more to you than an assignment."

Eden waved his hand and broadcasted the conversation so everyone in the room could listen in. Bain was already at his desk, attempting to locate a signal using the satellite equipment he had access to. His area looked more like a control center for the Bureau of Antinoc than a desk in the corner of an office.

"I don't find the situation funny." Aiden said, as he tossed the phone onto the desk.

"What's *funny* is your girl, you know, Jadis, the one you threw out yesterday, has hidden herself from you. That's what's funny, Aiden. Not even Lars can find her." His voice cracked with laughter over the phone.

His sense of humor was always dark; he has no room for sentimentality, Aiden thought. "Silas, if you lay one hand on her, I'll put you to the grave, cousin or not. And we all know you have a little something to do with her being hidden."

"Relax Aiden. I have bigger plans for Jadis. She's more than she's letting on, as are her sisters. I have a feeling all of you know who, more specifically what, Jadis is."

Aiden and his brothers looked at each other but said nothing more about the topic.

Eden spoke telepathically so Silas wouldn't hear. *"Their curiosity is heightened, given that Silas is calling. That alone is putting Jadis in a very dangerous position. She and her sisters are alone with Silas and his brothers and we have no idea where they are."*

"Better yet, Jadis and her sisters are now up against a clan of six hundred ninty year-old, mind-bending Breed Assassins and they have no knowledge of it. If Silas figures it out, Jadis and her sisters are in more trouble than they can manage alone," Bain replied.

"How long do I need to wait for you to finish your private conversation?" Silas questioned.

"Still listening. What exactly do you want?" Eden asked.

"It's more of a friendly call than anything else," Silas acknowledged.

Silas has always been an aristocratic vampire with an empire of knowledge. He's accustomed to being and staying in the know, not figuring out Jadis is truly bothering him, Aiden thought.

"Why are you really calling, Silas? You don't make friendly or casual calls. Jadis was entrusted to us and we want her back. This isn't a lost and found number, so what are you not saying?" Eden asked.

"I want nothing more than to let you know I am keeping her. I've decided she might be the key to a certain puzzle we've been working on." Silas sat back in his chair, flipping his hand dismissively, as if they could see him. "Aiden, I know you and Arcadia are close and have spoken. The rumors are all true. Jadis and her sisters could be the key to saving us all."

"So it's true," Aiden thought.

"They have arisen, and they did send the Baskale after Jadis," Eden said telepathically to his brothers.

"At least Silas is loyal. He's letting us know there's a fight on the horizon involving us all. He also mentioned the keys, which could be one of the most important pieces to the puzzle. If they can open the vortex, we can take control of it." Bain replied.

"If it is Jadis and her sisters, they are in his possession and he's not letting them go without a fight; not until he knows for sure," Aiden added.

"That's the gist of it," Silas stated, interrupting the private conversation. *There is something else drawing me to her, like a moth to a flame,* Silas thought. "The only problem is I find myself attracted to her in more ways than one." He chuckled.

Eden knew it wasn't really an admission. *He wants to stick it to Aiden as much as he could. After all, kindness isn't who he is. He can be as cold as a cadaver, an Assassin to the core.*

"She's not a pawn in a war you can use for your own benefit," Aiden replied calmly, not wanting to let Silas get under his skin.

"I just wanted to call and thank you, Aiden, for sending her packing. Better yet, for sending her right into my club and into my arms."

A guttural snarl crept up from Aiden's chest. "Leave her be." Aiden warned threateningly.

"I believe you packed her bag. Am I wrong? From what I can gather, I have twenty-four days before the Full Blood Moon. I intend on keeping Jadis for myself. Maybe I'll even take her as my mate." The phone went dead as Silas hung up with another crack of laughter.

"With Silas's unexpected jab, time is of the essence more than ever. We know he maintains a cool detachment to his targets. Relationships to Silas are merely a means to an end, regardless of the end," Eden stated.

"Shit! This is an erroneous situation all the way around," Bain rumbled. He leaned back quietly, thinking to himself. *Not only do we need to get Jadis back for the sake of Aiden's sanity, but if they truly are the keys that could put a stop to the thousand-year-old war springing to life, Aiden's vision may come to fruition.*

"We need to find her before Silas and his brothers confirm their suspicions," Eden stated to no one in particular.

"The girls are going to end up in the direct line of fire—worse yet, Silas could easily convince Jadis to become his mate," Aiden seethed.

Silas walked back out to the deck, looking for his brothers and their newfound playmates. They were all on the top deck, deep in conversation. He glanced around for Jadis, but he didn't see her anywhere on the boat. He cocked his head and could feel her lying in the sun on the island, and he was all too eager to join her. He needed to have one more conversation first.

He walked down the three sets of stairs to where Zach was still messing around with his prized speed boat.

Zach stepped off the boat as soon as he saw him. "How did your call go? I'm assuming, being the ass you are, you really pissed Aiden off?" He chuckled.

"Yes," Silas replied. "I certainly did. The poor bastard didn't know what hit him. What about Jadis? How did your conversation go with her?" Silas asked, wanting to confirm his suspicions.

"It's just as you suspected. I tried to bend her will, but she didn't respond at all. She was down here alone, staring off into the distance. I was behind her, watching. I tried to get her to turn around and go back up to the deck, but like I said, she didn't respond whatsoever." Zach admitted with a confused look on his face.

"Nothing?" Silas asked, as he rubbed his hand across his cheek.

"Nope. She didn't even acknowledge I was there until I spoke up and startled her. She jumped so hard she almost fell off the edge."

"Syth, Agaeus?" Silas called telepathically.

"Nothing," they answered in unison.

Silas was becoming more intrigued by the minute. *Who the hell are we dealing with? How could they possibly be immune to our mind-bending abilities?* "It's impossible. No one, not even Nosferatu, can block us."

"I know, I don't get it either?" Zach admitted. "Had I not seen it for myself and failed, I wouldn't have believed it." It was an embarrassing admission, as well as a big knock to his pride. He was as curious as Syth, Agaeus, and Silas were. None of them had the answer, but they were sure as hell going to find out.

"Do not, for one minute, dismiss what happened. They may be what we have been suspecting, as impossible as it seems. I think they are the 'three keys'."

Silas approached the beach in an obscure haze while Jadis was dozing off in the sun. The gentle rays were warming her delicate yet muscular body, giving it a sun-kissed glow.

Jadis felt the air ripple toward her, like a subtle wave gently washing ashore. She slowly sat up looking toward the water.

"Hello, Silas."

Silas appeared as if out of nowhere and walked out of the water before her. The sun gleamed off his solid, muscular chest, and all of his tattoos were in full view. *How exquisite,* she thought. However, even the colorful, intricate tattoos couldn't hide the battle scars his body bore. His arms and shoulders were strong, glistening in the sun as the droplets of water ran down them. Her eyes followed the droplets running down from his chest and over his perfect abs, narrowing into a V leading down to his groin. For the second time, she was staring where she shouldn't. Her body reacted in a way she wasn't fully expecting at that moment. She was taking in the sight of Silas in all his perfection. *Damn.*

Silas continued sauntering toward her, baring a radiant smile. She watched as he placed both hands on his forehead and pushed his hair back, letting the water fall down his back. *Yep, I'm going to have that. All of it. I can't help myself; he is hot as hell.*

Silas felt Jadis's body responding to him, and his groin rose faster than he cared to admit. It took him a moment to take control of his body, not wanting to offend her by walking right up with a full-blown hard on.

She's stunning, sitting there in the sun. He took in all of her; every curve, every toned muscle, and the way her hair moved around her face with the gentle breeze. Not to mention how her eyes swirled like pools of water around her black irises. *Their essence is like that of a leopard's eye and it appears as if they take on a life of their own.* He was mesmerized at the sight of her when he suddenly realized she saw him before he'd even materialized before her. *Great, more questions.*

Jadis stood up and laid out the other towel she had bought up with her, knowing at some point he would join her. She filled their glasses and held one out to Silas. "How's business?"

"Great," he replied. They took a seat on the oversized towels and he politely accepted the drink. He leaned back, crossed his legs, and rested on one elbow so he could face her. He took a sip and set his glass down in the sand before reaching over and moving the hair off her cheek. He rubbed the satiny mahogany strands through his fingers. *Things would be better if you were naked beneath me with those long legs wrapped around my waist.* Silas let go of her hair, picked his glass up, and finished his drink. He was trying to calm his desire to take her right then, not to mention control the growing muscle between his legs once again.

After a momentary pause, he spoke up, "I was able to put a couple pieces of a puzzle together we've been working on for quite some time. It's some business which has been stumping us, but it seems we got lucky in more ways than one." He didn't give Jadis a chance to respond before quickly changing topics. "I have to say, you look stunning. It seems the nap did you some good."

"Yes, it's beautiful here. It's exactly what I needed." Even as the words came out of her mouth, she could hear the subtle warnings coming from the creatures in the canopy behind them. She knew he was dangerous to her in more ways than one, some of which made her blush just thinking about it, and others that made her blood run cold. For now, she could care less. She was simply enjoying his company.

Jadis felt his warmth of his breath when he leaned over, ran his face up her arm and neck, and kissed her shoulder. She decided they were getting a bit too close. She knew, just by looking at him, he was picking up on her every thought, feeling, and desire. She stood up and grabbed her sarong, wrapping it perfectly around her waist to cover up as much as she could. She needed to do something, anything, to cool the ache between her legs. She glanced over and Silas was watching her every move, so she turned and walked into the jungle.

"Hey there," he called. She looked back, and he was holding up her sandals. "You might need these for a jungle walk?"

"No, thank you, barefoot is better." She turned back around and continued walking up the path. She needed to feel the earth beneath her bare feet, knowing she'd absorb as much of the energy as she could. She had a daunting feeling she was going to need it. *A bruja needs to feel the energy of the woods, or a jungle rather, when grounding is needed. Now is one of those times,* she thought, chucking to herself.

"Want to fill me in?" Silas asked as he joined her.

Jadis looked at Silas; well up at him anyway. Had she looked straight at him she would have been staring right into those perfect pecs, and that was the last place her eyes needed to be.

"Yesterday seems like a lifetime ago. Now, here I am with you in the jungle on a path to nowhere. It feels pretty amazing."

"You feel amazing." He winked, reached for her hand, and interlocked their fingers as they walked further into the jungle.

Jadis stopped and listened intently. "Can you hear them?" she asked, resting her palm on his chest.

"Hear who?" he asked, as cupped his hand over hers and held it in place.

"The jungle—it's talking to us." She smiled.

"Us? You mean you, Jadis, not me."

"If you listen, you can hear them talk to you as well."

"So what are they saying?"

The flirtatiousness in his voice brought about an unwanted shiver, not to mention what that goddamn smile of his did to her, along with that sultry, silken voice.

She poked his chest with her finger and laughed. "They're telling me to stay away from you, vampire."

"*Vampire? Stay away from me?*'" He was now circling her on the path like a leopard stalks its prey on silent paws. "You're able to joke after all?"

She shrugged her shoulders and chuckled. "I guess so."

"Your smile is beautiful. You should try it more often," he said coyly.

He was still circling her as the jungle noises heightened to a feverish pitch. She tried to walk again, but with every step she took, he was in front of her, blocking the path ahead. The next thing she knew, the jungle went silent and his mouth fell to hers.

He parted her lips and his tongue claimed hers. His arm was wrapped around her lower back while his fingers rested on her hip. His grabbed a fist full of her hair with his other hand and gently pulled her head back. He held her tightly, and she could feel every muscle in his chest resting firmly against her breasts.

As he pulled he head back, his eyes met hers. They were glowing amber slits now, not human and not kind. He was in the midst of 'turning', and she needed to stop him before she let him take it too far. His canines were fully extended, his desire for her all too obvious; she wasn't sure if he could stop himself at this point.

He pulled away ever so slightly and brushed his lips against her ear and whispered, "Tell me what you want, Jadis."

She choked on her words, "Silas, wait—we—we can't do this right now. I'm not ready," she muttered, mostly trying to convince herself. Although the temptation became harder to resist every moment she spent in his presence.

"Not ready for what, mon chéri? It's just a kiss."

Jadis watched as his canines receded, his eyes cooled, and the familiar, coy smile returned to his face.

They continued walking into the jungle in silent contemplation, even though she didn't know where they were headed. She was feeling a pull; a gentle, cleansing pull. Up ahead was a large, rocky cliff jutting out above the jungle floor. She let go of his hand, reached down, and bunched the sarong in her fist so it wouldn't get caught on the rocks she was about to leap onto.

"What are you doing?" he asked.

Silas looked amused as he stood there trying to figure out what a barefooted girl was going to do on a rocky ledge. "You'll see." She winked.

Jadis took one step, and then another, and another, leaping from one rock to the next. She stopped briefly and looked back at him. "What are you thinking about?"

"You leaping up there barefoot." He laughed.

He stood, amused, trying to figure what she was up to. He was in awe, heavy in thought, in ways he didn't care to admit. *She is beautiful, graceful, and elegant, amongst other things.* He couldn't figure out why she was devoid to him. He could pull her immediate thoughts, but was unable to bend her will, unable to penetrate the barrier she had surrounded herself with.

"You coming or what?" she asked, before turning her back to him and continuing on.

He took one leap and was right behind her. He had his arm around her waist in order to keep her from plunging off the cliff, having startled her.

"You all really need to stop sneaking up on me. Zach scared me so bad this morning I almost fell off the deck." She chuckled.

They continued up the rocky ledge until they reached the top. They gazed over the jungle canopy and the vastness of the ocean. "The view is stunning," she stated.

"Yes, it is," he replied, only he was looking at her, not the view.

Jadis didn't know what to focus her attention on. The vampire standing beside her, or the view ahead. The only thing she knew for sure was this was the perfect view to let Aiden and his brothers know she would not be returning.

Silas stood, curious about what she was doing. Nonetheless, he wanted to see exactly what she was up to. She wasn't just looking into the distance and admiring the view. He felt the vibrations shift in the surrounding air, along with the tightness in his own chest. Once again, he tried to get into her head without letting her know he was there.

A blurry image appeared and lingered off in the distance about five feet in front of her.

In an obscure haze, Silas moved behind her to let her do her 'thing', whatever it may be. The warmth of the aura now surrounding him was a powerful, archaic magic. *Jadis is more than a mediocre bruja. She is powerful, dangerous even—an original?* He wondered.

Jadis knew Silas had a hundred questions. *Maybe I should let Silas in? They all seem to want to know, so what do I have to lose? I might suffer the wrath of my sisters once I'm back on the boat, but oh well. It's time to bring all to light. Hell, it's not like Silas hasn't been reading my mind to some extent already. Here goes nothing.*

Aiden felt another energetic shift around him again, and the smoke in the mirror swirled, followed by another blurry image, which gradually took form. There she was, looking as beautiful as ever, standing on top of a rocky ledge. He couldn't make out the view any further than where Jadis stood, and the tops of the palm trees below were barely visible. She was standing in a beautiful, pink lace bikini and matching floral sarong, which she held bunched in her hand, just high enough to show a hint of her tanned, muscular thigh. Her hair flowed gently in the breeze, with the light of the sun shining on the mahogany strands, strengthening the waves. Aiden caught the faint aroma of the sun on her skin as it seeped in from the swirling, hazy mirror.

"Well, that's new," Lars said, breaking Aiden's transfixed stare. "I've seen her at the pool a handful of times, but her bikini was black leopard print." Aiden shot him a threatening look Lars dismissed. "Sorry brother, but a sight like that? Who wouldn't stop and have a look?"

"That's enough!" Eden demanded firmly. "We need to look at everything in that image to see if we can make out any trace of a location."

"I'm on it already," Bain replied. He didn't rely on the high-tech equipment on his desk, rather his six hundred seventy years of practiced sorcery.

Aiden lowered his forehead toward the mirror and placed his hands on either side, taking in the faint scent of jasmine that was so intimate to him. He opened his eyes, only to find hers fixed on his. *She is looking right at me.*

"Bain, are you doing this?" Aiden questioned.

"No, it's Jadis."

"Bain, can you grab anything at all out of this? Anything?" Eden asked.

"Not yet. I'm trying everything I can, but right now you all need to shut the hell up and let me concentrate."

They watched intently as another image warped and twist behind her. Something? No, not something, but someone—Silas.

As they stared at the image, it was apparent Jadis could also see them.

"Jadis, where are you?" Aiden asked softly, not wanting to anger her any more than he already had.

"Aiden, I wanted to thank you for setting me free. You throwing me out was for the best, you know."

"What? No. Jadis, hear me out," Aiden pleaded, as her voice rolled like thunder throughout the command room.

"I am tired of masking who I truly am, and I'll no longer hide in the shadows. I was going to tell you, but before I'd had the chance, you had already made the decision for me to leave. You left me alone, and you sided with the enemy that was your vision. You discarded me."

Eden, Bain, and Lars backed away from the mirror to allow him some privacy. However, Aiden didn't give a shit who was looking or listening. This was his chance to make amends.

"Jadis, I need you to understand. You left so suddenly I didn't have the chance to explain myself or my actions. In the vision, there was a hooded vale of death hovering over you. I panicked. I couldn't escape the image of you lying lifeless in my arms. I left you alone in the room to go to my brothers for guidance—"

She abruptly interrupted him, "The point is, you left me."

"Jadis, listen. Please don't do this. Come home. You are in more danger than you realize. Silas is not who you think he is."

"Maybe it was for the best. From your weakness, I found my strength again."

"Jadis, give me five minutes. We can fix this if you come home. Silas and his brothers are using you and your sisters. Whatever you do, do not agree to anything he asks of you. It will give him complete control over you."

"*Using me?*" She laughed. "Let me say this slowly, so it sinks in. The world around me will cower on its knees at my feet should I demand it. No one *uses me.*"

"Jadis, I don't think you're weak. On the contrary, I think you're the most perceptive, capable being I have ever met," Aiden replied.

"I see exactly what's in front of me; a man so full of jealousy at the thought of anyone else touching his things, he would say or do just about anything. You don't like anyone touching your things. Remember, Aiden? You told me that yourself."

"You're not a *thing*, Jadis. You were entrusted to us long before the night I pulled you from the wreckage."

"*Entrusted?* Of course that's all I was to you—nothing but business. I should have left the next morning. Staying with you was a grave mistake, as was trusting you."

"Jadis, I urge you—please listen. I get it. I know how much I hurt you. At the first test of trust and loyalty, I failed. I had no honor—"

She interrupted him again, "And what a tattered cloak of *honor* it is."

"Tell me where you are, and I'll be there. We can fix this. I never intended to hurt you. It was a knee-jerk reaction and I can't apologize enough."

"You're right about one thing; you can't apologize enough. I have been abandoned before but this—this time you really hurt me."

The venom in her words seared through Aiden like a viper's kiss as the fog faded. "Jadis? Dammit, answer me!" Aiden demanded.

Unfortunately for him, Jadis refused to reply.

Silas had been seized with curiosity and questions since Jadis had wandered into his life. Now it seemed as if all of his suspicions were coming to fruition as he stood silently watching the altercation unfold before him.

The altercation became indistinct as Silas's mind wandered back in time. One hundred fifty years ago, he and his brothers were hunting for fresh blood. The path they had taken was primitive, rising in steep, uneven, rocky slopes and snaking around ancient trees. The roots of the trees were crisscrossed, gnarled, and uneven. The air was rich with the scent of the freshly fallen rain, and gentle streaks of lightning pierced the night sky. The only movement was the occasional deer being startled in the distance, or a squirrel dashing up a nearby trunk. As they traversed their way further into the forest, the shadows before them waned. They stood silent, watching, waiting as the forms took shape. They appeared before them, three stunning visions, who were to be appreciated in so many ways. Their muscular frames, long flowing locks of hair: one head of red, one as black as simmering coal. The third, who seemed to be more elusive than the other two, cautiously approached him. He dared not move and held a steady gaze as a smile flashed from beneath her wavy mahogany locks of hair, captivating him. Her eyes were that of ember green with brown hues, and it appeared as if the storm clouds were swirling around her onyx black irises. The rumors were true. They were stunning and mythical; he and

his brothers had instantly been bewitched. They had no idea their hunting would lead them to three of the original coven's descendants.

Minutes became hours, and hours became days. It was like nothing they had ever experienced before or likely ever would again. He and his brothers fell hard, vowing never to leave. They spent the rest of their time together getting to know each other on a much more personal level. They also spent a lot of their time intertwined with each other whenever the desire surfaced. It was strange, frightening even. In one brief moment, they went from being strangers to being completely infatuated with one another in a few short weeks.

The perfect mate, he had thought. But he awoke one evening, only for her to have vanished back into the shadows. Silas, Syth, and Agaeus searched all night for the girls, but they found themselves standing alone in the rain after they failed to locate them. Silas knelt down and picked up a delicate jasmine bud; he could still smell her scent within the drops of dew.

They had tried for months to track them down, but the girls were becoming nothing more than fading memories. Silas left an offering for her, having decided the hunt was futile. He went back for years, occasionally, before giving up for good; she was lost to him.

Silas focused his attention back to the image and watched as Aiden, and his brothers dissipated. He felt as if the air had left his lungs, and he couldn't ignore the hammering in his heart. His mind throbbed as the same waning shadow was now standing before him. *No,* he thought. *It can't be—it can't be? She can't be?* The realization crept over him like an icy chill. Silas stood frozen as his thoughts continued to run wild. *Jadis—Skye—Ivory? Why the hell can't I remember something so simple? It's not possible! She should be at least three hundred thirty two years old, yet she hasn't aged a day.* In that moment, her motives were laid bare. *This her subtle way of telling me exactly who she is.*

Silas immediately reached out to his brothers to fill them in on what had happened. He could feel the shock taking over Syth and Agaeus, silencing the whispers of doubt.

Silas knew his brothers were beginning to 'turn'. After all these years, he knew they had always kept a small glimmer of hope in finding the brujas they had fallen in love with so many years ago.

"Easy, brothers," Silas said. *"You can't let them out of your sight, so make sure your brains do the thinking for you, understand?"*

"We weren't the ones who fucked it up to begin with!" An angry realization came from Syth before the silence that followed.

Silas knew his brothers had only one thing on their minds now. *"Syth—Agaeus—answer me! I need to know the two of you can keep your shit together,"* Silas demanded.

"We've got it," Syth replied, as he looked at Agaeus.

They nodded to each other in unison. *"Not anything or anyone will touch them. Rest assured, we will be damned if we ever let them slip through our fingers again,"* Agaeus stated.

"Do it," Silas ordered.

"You know he's in Theros," Syth replied.

"I don't give a shit if Dante is fucking The High Priestess of Theros. I want his ass here before the sun touches the horizon."

"Understood," Agaeus replied.

Silas immediately turned his attention back to Jadis, watching her with the intensity of a spider watching a fly stuck in a web as she leapt from the ledge.

Jadis jumped off the rocky ledge in an arching back dive, leaving Aiden to his regret and Silas to his silent confusion. The warm air blew through her hair and passed along her sun-soaked body. She loved feeling herself falling through the jungle canopy, hoping it would wash away a lifetime of pain, regret, and isolation. She took in a breath of air and held it as she splashed into the cool, blue, crystal-clear lagoon nestled amidst the jagged rock formations.

The soothing water rushed over her body, taking with it the darkness and the dismal reminders of her self-imposed solitude. After moving quickly toward the bottom, she arched her back and headed to the surface. She opened her eyes, letting droplets fall from her lashes, only to find herself face to face with Silas.

Silas stared at her, as if he was seeing her for the first time. He didn't utter a word. Looking at him now, there seemed to be something different. *He's changed somehow, so much so it scares me.*

Jadis knew everything Silas had witnessed would take a moment or two to sink in. She swam toward the small, sandy beach on the other side of the lagoon, hidden well within the jungle itself, leaving Silas to his thoughts.

She walked out of the water and onto the warm, soft, pink sand. The lagoon was surrounded by lush, green ferns swaying in every direction. The thick tangle of the jungle brush hung from the volcanic rocks, revealing colors, smells, and a multitude of flowers delicately blooming on the plethora of plants. She listened intently to the sounds of the jungle, the birds, the insects, and the reptiles. She took it all in, soaking up all of its healing energy.

She removed the now-drenched floral sarong from her body and hung it loosely on a palm branch, allowing the gentle mid-day breeze to dry it. She wrung out of her hair doing all she could to ignore the burning stare coming from a most dangerous vampire who stood motionless in the water. She cautiously side-eyed Silas, and watched as he pushed his hair back from his forehead with both hands and interlaced his fingers behind his head.

Silas was doing all he could to come to grips with the sudden awareness his life had been built on shifting sands. *Jadis looked like a goddess,* he thought as he watched her dive into the warm, blue lagoon, her body moving effortlessly through the crystal-clear water.

He watched intently as she removed the floral sarong, bearing her tight, round ass, her toned thighs, and shapely calves. *She is a sight to behold.* He simply couldn't take his eyes off her.

"You going to stand there all-day staring, vampire?" she asked, breaking the silence and snapping him out of his trance.

As she turned to face him, her slender stomach gleamed as the excess water trickled down her body. He took it all in once again; her gently tousled hair, her round breasts, and that tiny pink bikini. The cool breeze raised her hardened nipples. His body was now fully aroused as he stalked toward her, determined to claim what was to be his and only his.

Silas walked out of the water toward her with nothing but one thing on his mind—claiming his long lost love. He moved in so close to her, he could feel her breasts resting firmly against his body, just below his chest. He slid his face up her neck, before gently gliding up her cheek and the side of her head, and inhaled deeply.

"So, my dear girl, you've been missing for a hundred fifty years, by my count. I'll be damned if I'll let you hide from me ever again."

Jadis looked up and into his glowing embers and a slow growl welled up from his chest, his body seething with desire. He had completely 'turned'. As much as she tried, she couldn't move. Something held her there. She realized she was holding her breath in anticipation of what was about to happen. She stood in awe at the sight of the vampire who now took on an entirely new look and essence. *Shit! Silas is menacing, dangerous, and in love.* She felt his groin rising up in the loosely fitting board shorts. *Silas isn't hiding any of his desire or his wanton need to take me right here, right now.*

He placed both of his hands on either side of her hips and pulled her closer.

All the blood drained from her face. There was no denying it. She wasn't going to bother trying. He was all too serious and intimidating. There was something carnal about him now.

She rested her hands on his forearms and trembled. He wrapped one of his arms around her waist, resting his hand on the top of her ass cheek, slid it further down, and squeezed her ass. He bent down and took her mouth to his and kissed her as if he had waited a lifetime, and she didn't stop him. Their tongues met, twirling, tasting, and her body ignited.

It feels so right, as if it is meant to be, she thought. The memory of that rainy night in the cabin all came rushing back to her like a tidal wave crashing against a rocky cliff on a stormy night. Her mind was spinning along with her entire world. *Nothing seemed real, so why did he feel so right? Feel so perfectly amazing as they touched in every way? What the hell is happening?* One word, *mate,* kept moving through her mind. *It is him, without a doubt. The vampire I was forced to give up is right here. Shit!*

Silas felt her confusion. He stopped kissing her and lifted her chin up to meet his heated gaze. We have some catching up to do, mon chéri. I've been looking for you in more ways than one for far too long."

Jadis pulled away from him, trying to put a bit of distance between them to straighten out her thoughts. She was about to screw her vampire right here, right now, and she felt like an amnesiac as the memories flooded her mind. A familiar desire from long ago rose up. *He still felt the same. His desire has not diminished at all, but has instead grown more powerful over the years,* she thought.

Silas let go for a moment and watched as she walked toward a large volcanic rock nestled at the edge of the water.

She placed her hand on the rock and reached out to the earth for help. The air began to wane, casting shapes and mystical forms that swirled around both her hand and the rock on which she had placed it. *Why couldn't I remember any of this until now?*

Silas walked over and gently placed his hand on her shoulder and turned her to face him. As soon as Silas turned her around, his mouth was on hers. She felt her energy waning. *How? Why? It feels as though he is controlling it.*

Silas picked her up and carried her away from the rock. She wrapped her legs around his waist and could feel his groin growing harder and larger by the second.

Of all the things she was thinking, all she knew at that moment was she wanted him. He laid her down on the sandy beach next to the lagoon. His mouth fell to hers and ignited all her senses.

Jadis wrapped her arms around his neck and gave in. *Nothing will stop me this time,* she told herself.

The weight of his heavy body consumed her. He stopped kissing her momentarily and looked into her eyes. She could see he had as many questions running through his mind as she did. He slid his hand up her thigh and pulled it over his hip, keeping himself firmly planted between her legs.

"In the woods that rainy night, it was you, wasn't it?" he asked.

"Until the memories flooded my mind a few minutes ago, I had no idea, but yes, it was," she answered truthfully. "My sisters and I found you and your brothers that night. We took you in, wanting you, desiring you beyond words." She rubbed her face. Everything spinning in her head right now was too much to contend with.

Silas gently pulled her hands away from her face. "Yes, I remember," he replied, his tone serious. "Do you remember why you and your sisters left us standing in the rain, disappearing back into the shadows?"

"It wasn't us who did that, exactly—we weren't given a choice. Apparently, we weren't allowed to be mated before the time was right, and she heard your thoughts."

"She?" Silas asked, looking puzzled. "There wasn't anyone else there that night."

"There was, and she took you and your brothers away from us before wiping our minds. She left us nothing more than vague memories, most of which only come and go in our dreams. My sisters and I have always known something was missing, but we had no idea the extent of it. They are probably as shocked as I am right now."

"Hecate?" Silas was only guessing at this point.

"Yes, she is our mother."

"Then the rumors are true. The three of you are her direct descendants?" The answers to his questions became clear.

"Yes. At least that much we know." She rolled her eyes at the thought of Hecate pulling this shit right now.

Silas couldn't believe he was looking at her again. The vision of her face, the same as the one he had planted in his memory so many years ago, remained the same as the memories came flooding back to him as well.

"I loved you, Jadis. I looked for you for a hundred years, hoping, longing to find you. The offering I left by the tree I had first spotted you standing under—"

Before he could finish, she opened her hand and the eight hundred year-old Scarnian coin he had left appeared in her palm.

"You found it?" He was shocked. He had known it had been taken, but didn't know she was the one who had found it.

"Yes, under the tree a few months later. I didn't know what it meant at the time, but I knew it was mine, so I kept it."

Her words echoed in his mind like the silent raindrops falling over them that rainy night. He picked it up out of the palm of her hand, remembering the exact moment they were separated by a force greater than any of them. He rubbed it between his fingers, studying it. The coin was exactly as he had remembered; made of pure silver with rough edges, the Emperor Loranazio depicted on one side and three stallions on the other.

"Jadis, she no longer has the power to separate us. You have grown strong, fierce, and powerful. You are mine and you have to know I would never do you wrong."

"I know, Silas, I believe you."

He bent down, parted her lips, and took what—no who, he had been longing for all these years. The heat radiated from her mouth into his, made his body crave her all the more. The thumping of her heartbeat against his chest was bringing about a dangerous, hungry desire; one he wasn't sure he could control.

His canines extended and he let up long enough to nip her bottom lip. He then ran the tip of his tongue over the tiny crimson droplet before making his way down her neck. He stopped just under her jawline, lingering there, feeling the nervous beat of her pulse beneath his lips, the blood coursing through her veins.

She felt his desire to drink from her, and as he was about to bite down, she gently turned her head and kissed him. She shoved her tongue into his mouth, breaking him free of his fixation. She reached up, grabbed him by the nape of his neck, and began kissing her way up his jawline. She playfully nipped the lobe of his ear and felt a strange sensation; she wondered what his blood would taste like? She suddenly had an overwhelming desire to drink from him.

Silas felt it all and was suddenly in a dangerous game of tug-of-war between his sexual desire and his need to feed from her. The logical part of his mind was telling him it wasn't the time, but his body had other ideas. As much as he wanted to bite down, to feel the rush of her blood over his tongue, filling his mouth as he drank his fill, he had no choice but to control himself. He let out a raspy, desperate moan.

He removed her small bikini top barely covering her breasts and tossed it aside. His naked chest pressed against her breasts felt amazing; after all these years; she felt exactly as he had remembered. His hand wandered up her waist, his thumb rubbing up and over her hardened nipple. He bent down and suckled it, teasing it with his tongue. He then trailed his lips and tongue down from her breast to her stomach and back up again. She moaned in response, and he felt her desperation for more.

"Silas," she moaned.

He slid his hand under her bikini bottoms, and she let out another moan. She gripped his ass and pulled him closer.

"Silas, I can't take much more. I need you now," she begged in a raspy whisper.

He moved his hand between her legs and stroked her desire with his fingers. Jadis didn't think she could wait any longer, and the throbbing feeling rose to the surface.

"Silas, I want you inside me," she moaned.

"Not yet—I'm not done. Right now, I'm going to enjoy every inch of your body. I want you begging," he groaned.

Jadis tried to pull him in by moving her hips beneath his hardened muscle. He looked down at her, taking in all her aching need for him.

She slid her hand over his chest and shoulders, feeling every curve. Her other hand gently glided up from his ass and over his back, feeling his muscles soften and flex as he moved.

She arched her back in response to his touch, and the rumble rising out of his chest caused her entire body to vibrate and her moans to intensify. He growled, and it sounded dangerous, deadly even, and only served to heighten her frenzied state of mind.

She traced the tips of his canines poking out from behind his perfect lips with her tongue and pierced the tip of it. She slid her tongue along his, letting him taste the warm droplets.

"Be careful, my dear. You might get what you ask for," he responded, savoring the sweet taste of her blood.

She ignored the warning. *Consequences be damned!*

"Silas," she moaned, arching her back off the sand as her need for him intensified. She lifted her head and trailed her tongue over his neck, and he let out another guttural groan.

He removed the lace bikini bottoms and tossed them aside, along with his board shorts which no longer hid the full extent and size of his arousal; her arousal only ratcheted up his.

She reached down and wrapped her fist around his shaft and began gently rubbing up and down, nearly undoing him. He was throbbing with desire as he sank down in between her thighs and spread her legs. She let go, and he slid his erection into the heat of her core.

She let out a groan, and it took more than a minute for her body to accommodate him, accepting it one painful inch at a time. She wrapped both her legs around him, and he began gently rocking back and forth, allowing her body to accept him.

"Shit," she groaned. "Wait—I need to." She placed her palm on his hip to hold him back a bit, to give her body a moment to adjust.

He gently pulled her hand away and pinned it above her head in a vice like grip. "I've waited long enough, my love," he growled. He could no longer hold back, her pain filled moans only intensified his need to claim her. He thrust himself in and out with the force and need of a hundred and fifty-year-old hard on.

"Fuck me. I want to crawl right inside you. I can't get deep enough," he whispered, with another raspy groan.

Her free arm remained wrapped around his neck, and her fingernails dug into his shoulder as their bodies moved together in unison.

"You have no idea how good you feel," she whispered.

She took it all in; he was rough and holding nothing back. With one hard thrust after another, she felt her orgasm peak from deep down and her body melted. The release sent her head back into the sand with more than a moan.

"Oh, goddamn," she cried out.

His body responded to her words, and his climax ripped through him. He lifted his head and let out a roar that sent the jungle scurrying for cover.

Silas rested his forehead on hers and had yet to pull out. He was gently rocking back and forth, his erection still pulsing inside her flushed, throbbing core.

He slowly pulled out and rolled onto to his side, pulling her in tightly next to him. He wrapped his arms around her and held on like he was afraid to let go.

Jadis laid her head on his shoulder, her leg bent, laying across his crotch while his hand held her thigh. She didn't want to move. She wanted to stay in his arms like this forever.

He had been reading her thoughts, reveling in each one. "Don't worry, my love. We have a lifetime. You are mine, and I am never letting you go again." He turned his head and kissed her lips. "In less than a month we will make it official."

With his unexpected admission, Jadis smiled, her heart swelling. "You really mean it?" she asked, not sure she could believe it.

"Yes, Jadis. You will be mated to me under the Full Blood Moon, and nothing will stop us this time."

"Promise me, Silas—that it will happen. You were taken from me once, and I can't bear the thought of losing you again. I would rather die than go on without you. All those years, I knew something was missing. I felt empty, lonely, isolated. I never want to feel like that again."

"I felt it too, love. I never stopped thinking about you after that night. I told myself to forget you, but as much as I tried, I couldn't do it. However, Hecate managed to steal some rather important information." He chuckled.

"And what would that be?" she asked, amused.

"Your name." He laughed.

After a few moments of laughter, the words popped right out of her mouth, "I love you."

His smile radiated. "Jadis, I have always loved you. I've loved you from the moment I laid eyes on you; the moment I saw you standing by the tree in the rain; the moment I first tasted you and came inside you," he admitted with a quick wink and a soft chuckle. His mouth fell on hers once again. "Perfect," he purred.

"Yes, you are perfect." She smiled at him and suddenly remembered their earlier conversation. "What was it you were going to tell me earlier?"

A deep growl rose from his chest. "Later. I don't think I'm done with you yet."

He rolled her onto her back and pushed her thighs apart with his knees. He was once again hard with desire, and she was ready to accept him—all of him. Every glorious, painful inch.

Silas and Jadis felt total contentment lying in each other's arms, watching the sun set beyond the lagoon. The rays weaved their way through the tall palms and bamboo. It was bold, brilliant, and rich with color. The black, volcanic rocks jutted up behind the lagoon and shimmered with the sun's setting colors. Hues of reds, blues, and oranges reflected off the water, stretching the length of the horizon. Silas's voice broke the silence with his beautiful, velvety rumble, she found to be both menacing and comforting.

"We need to head back to the ship. I don't want you out here after dark." He kissed her again while simultaneously handing her the bikini. Reluctantly, she put it back on.

"And what makes you think I'm safer on your yacht than I am in the jungle?" she teased. "There's nothing here that's a threat to me, except perhaps you. I believe you are on the top of the food chain, vampire," she added with a wink.

Silas's laugh rumbled, vibrating her body. "*Top of the food chain*? I've been called many a name, but the *top of the food chain*? That's a first."

He had both her hands cupped in his. Jadis backed away, half teasing and half serious, giddy from the last few hours of a much-needed reunification. Silas didn't let go, instead he picked her up, flung her over his shoulder, and began walking. *This shit seems pretty familiar,* she chuckled to herself. *It must be a thing vampires have.*

"*A thing we have?*" he repeated with a chuckle. "It's time to go, mon chéri." He slapped her ass as he carried her back to the beach.

"I can walk, you know," she said, giggling through the sting.

"Yes, but I like this better," he responded.

"Well, I don't. Silas, put me down." She was trying to sound angry, but her laughter betrayed her.

"Never! And if you ever try to get away from me again, I promise you I will throw your ass over my shoulder and carry you back home every single time. You are mine now."

Home? Home with Silas? That hadn't even been a thought in her mind until right at that moment.

"Yes, *home*—our home. I'm thinking of a house I think you're going to enjoy," he offered.

"Well, the last time a vampire said I was home, he threw me out," she said, as she smacked his ass.

"Yes, and right into my arms. It couldn't have worked out better. By the way, smack me like that again, and you'll find out pretty quickly what I will do to you."

He flung her around, so she was face to face with him. He grabbed a fist full of hair and pulled her in for a long, hard kiss. "The last few hours will be nothing," he mumbled into her mouth. "Don't think I won't remember that smack later," he added with one raised eyebrow.

Jadis couldn't help but laugh, even though her heart pounded at the threat. She had found her vampire, and she was in his arms now. It was obvious he wasn't letting her go, and she didn't want him to. She kept her legs wrapped around his waist and wound her arms around his neck.

Home? she thought again. Thinking it sounded amazing and too good to be true.

"It's not *too good to be true*, my love. I don't make empty promises, and I will spend the rest of our lives showing you just how true it is."

He put her down as soon as they reached the edge of the beach and held her tight, stroking her hair as he placed a few strands behind her ears. He ran his fingers along her jaw, his thumb across her bottom lip, and lifted her chin.

"I know this is all happening fast, but I've chased your ghost for far too long. I need you to understand, to feel my love. We will be mated under the Full Blood Moon, yes?"

"Yes!" she declared, along with a nervous sigh of relief escaping her mouth.

Silas spoke, again having felt her emotions, "Do not question my loyalty. You are no longer just a shadow in my memories. You, mon chéri, are my everything."

CHAPTER 7

They arrived back at the yacht and the rest of their group were sitting together, enjoying the setting sun. Syth had asked their chef to cook something up once Silas had let them know they were heading back.

Damn, the smell wafting up from the galley below is amazing, Jadis thought. She hadn't realized how hungry she was until the smells hit her.

Silas interrupted her thoughts once again. "I must have worked up your appetite today." He winked, not caring who was listening.

As a flush of red rushed into Jadis's cheeks, Silas chuckled, grabbed her, and plopped down on the bench opposite his brothers, curling her up in his lap.

She couldn't get enough of those amazing, full lips or the taste of his tongue owning hers. Silas pulled back and nipped her neck. "Soon, mon chéri I'll have that as well."

The look on Skye and Ivory's faces forced Jadis to chuckle, feeling a bit embarrassed.

"Silas, are you okay?" Syth asked.

"Yes, brother, why do you ask? I am far better than okay," he replied, looking right at Jadis.

"We've just never seen you like this." Syth motioned his hand toward the two of them.

"Like what?" Silas asked.

Syth and Agaeus glanced at each other momentarily. "I don't know? Like—you look happy."

"You actually have a smile," Agaeus joked.

He was looking at Jadis with a wicked, half-cocked grin as he answered. "I do more than smile, brother."

While waiting for dinner, their conversations were deep and much more intimate now that they had been reunited.

The server placed warm rolls with squares of cold butter down on the table. The salad was mixed with fresh greens, finely cut tomatoes, cucumber, and lightly mixed oil in a spice-laden dressing. Jadis and her sisters feasted on roasted carrots, potatoes, and green beans basted in olive oil. The spices were exotic, and their aroma filled the surrounding air. The rich, dark soup stood out against the pure white bowls. A gentle whiff of steam rose from the soup as Jadis lifted the silver spoon to her mouth.

Jadis and her sisters dined, while Silas and his brothers enjoyed their company while sipping their drinks.

Dinner was interrupted when Zach walked up to the table with the satellite phone in his hand. "I hate to interrupt Silas, but you have a call."

A grim look crossed Silas's face, and in an instant, he'd gone from light-hearted, playful, and loving, to undeniably serious.

"Don't worry, baby, it's just business. Everything's fine," he offered.

He bent over and kissed her before motioning to his brothers to stand up and follow him. "I'll be back shortly. Don't go anywhere, you will be sorry if I have to find you." He ran his hand across her cheek and walked away.

Jadis and her sisters had some catching up to do of their own. "So, tell us, Jadis. We want all the dirty details," Skye said.

"You—Silas? What the hell is that all about? Did you have sex with him? Was it as good as we were telling you?" Ivory rambled.

They were shooting questions at her, one after the other sounding as if they were teasing, but really, they were begging for all the dirty details.

"It's not like the two of you have any room to talk. You've been screwing Syth and Agaeus since the first night you met." Jadis chuckled.

"Jadis, it's only been two days, so you basically slept with Silas the night you met too," Skye pointed out with a wink.

"Whatever." Jadis gave a dismissive wave and picked up her drink in an attempt to dodge more of their incessant questions.

"You both know who they are right?" Jadis asked.

"Yes, Syth and Agaeus showed us in more ways than one." Ivory chuckled. "Silas filled them in telepathically, while he was watching your altercation with Aiden."

"And just when were the two of you going to fill me in on who they were?" Jadis furrowed her eyebrows at them both.

Skye spoke in more of a teasing tone. "Well, you seemed a bit distracted, and it's not like you didn't figure it out. Not to mention our memories probably hit us as hard as yours did, and I would assume about the same time."

Jadis rolled her eyes and let out a heavy sigh. "Mother's at it again."

"That she is," Skye agreed.

"After all these years apart, it was incredible. We knew you would figure it out once you jumped off the ledge. Things between you and Silas were going to get serious fast, and we didn't want to interrupt. We felt like a couple of creepers watching the two of you. We cut ourselves off when you made the leap," Ivory explained.

"And?" Jadis questioned, motioning for Skye to continue.

"Yes, they're planning on taking us as their mates. The Full Blood Moon is in twenty-three days, to be exact," offered Skye.

"You both agreed?" Jadis asked, even though she already knew.

"Yes," they answered in unison.

"Are the two of you are ready to let go of the single life and stick to one male, or one vampire, rather? I'm not convinced either of you are ready to settle down."

"We would never had agreed had it not been our missing vampires." Skye was elated to have Syth back.

The three of them had the same feelings, the same distant memory, though shrouded in fog.

"They said they looked for us here and there for like hundred and something years. Apparently, Silas left an offering for you. Did you ever find it?" Ivory questioned.

"I did." Jadis opened her hand, and there in her palm appeared the coin.

"Holy shit, it was your coin after all," Skye said in disbelief.

Ivory studied the coin. "You always said one day it would bring you love."

Jadis was heavy in thought, remembering the night she had found it.

"Just curious. Did you sleep with Aiden?" Ivory asked.

"No," Jadis replied.

"We know how Hecate feels about you being around vampires. Did she try to intervene between you and Silas?" Ivory asked.

A sudden look of dread crossed Ivory and Skye's faces, and the air became heavy around them.

Jadis's heart beat a little faster. "No, and it felt like she released me to him somehow? I also think our mother hasn't been telling us the truth," Jadis replied, feeling as confused as Skye and Ivory looked.

"No, she hasn't," Skye agreed.

"Hecate always kept you on a tight leash regarding their kind," Ivory added.

Jadis looked at the coin, just as she had been doing for the last one hundred years. "Yes, she has."

"What's changed?" Ivory asked.

"We have always been told we held the key that could be the end to an event looming on the horizon. She's also cryptically told me their kind would want me for reasons she refused to reveal," Jadis revealed.

Whatever event it may be, they did not know. Unbeknownst to them, an ancient secret, long buried, was about to claw its way to the surface, and they were in the direct line of fire.

"Like you said, Hecate hasn't been honest with us, but stop holding back. What are you not saying, Jadis?" Ivory demanded.

"Aiden and his brothers think we are tied to the situation, and Silas thinks we are, what he refers to as the three keys," she admitted.

"What the hell?" Skye looked shocked as ever.

"How did you find this out?" Ivory asked.

"From Silas, of course. I took the time to pull his thoughts after he leapt off the cliff with me. He was in a moment of shock and wasn't sure what to think. It was the only opportunity I was going to get to prod his mind, so I took it."

Ivory spun the highball glass on the table and glanced between Jadis and Skye. "Do you think that's what their so-called business is about, us being the three key's?"

"I would assume so. I'm pretty sure they're not talking about real estate," Jadis joked before getting serious. "There is something else I haven't told you," she admitted.

"What?" Skye asked firmly.

"I don't know how to explain it," Jadis admitted.

"Start with the basics. How about that?" Ivory demanded.

"Remember when I told you I was feeling like something was stalking me?"

"Yes, go on," Skye said.

"Long story short. There was something, some kind of creature, that showed up on my porch the night I wrecked my car. Aiden killed it and took me home."

Skye and Ivory sat back, trying to come to terms with what Jadis was telling them.

"*A creature*? Explain," Skye said.

"Aiden, Eden, and Bain said it was a Baskale," Jadis admitted.

"You're just now telling us you've been being stalked by something which only exists in century old tales?"

"Yes."

"That's fucked up, Jadis, I think that's something you should have told us!" Ivory scolded.

"I didn't want to scare you."

"Well shit. I assume there is more to the story?" Ivory asked.

"Yes, but there's not much more to it after everything you found out today. Somehow we are connected to that thing," Jadis replied.

"Okay, so there's an ancient creature rising from Ipheanor? And now Hecate has released you to Silas? This is fucked up," Skye added.

"I assume she released you to Silas, for no other reason than you are being hunted like our ancestors were," Ivory stated.

"You're right and we need answers. They'll be in their meeting for a while. We should sneak out and head straight to the island and speak to Hecate. I'm not one to be out on the open water in the dead of night, so if we're going to do this, we need to do it before I change my mind," Jadis suggested.

"Let's go," Skye agreed, as she and Ivory rose to their feet.

They began walking toward the steps leading down to the dock where the jet skis were tied, when Jadis bumped into something blocking the way. She yelped and jumped back.

"Silas? What the hell? You scared me half to death."

His eyes were glowing embers, hot and angry. He had 'turned' and an animalistic sound rose from deep down. "Going somewhere, mon chéri?"

"Yes." Jadis put her hands up and rested her palms against his chest, trying to calm the beast standing before her. Silas was making her so nervous she was fumbling for words. "We just—we figured you'd be—you know, in your meeting for a while."

Silas cocked his head. "And you *thought* you could leave?"

"Well, yes, just for a little while. We need answers, so we were heading out to the island—" she tried to explain, but Silas wasn't having it and cut her off mid-sentence.

"Did I not make myself clear earlier? You're not going anywhere without me. What made you think you could wander off?" The look on Silas's face caused an immediate spike in her adrenaline. Jadis no longer recognized the vampire standing before her.

Silas stood, silent and unwavering. The intensity in which he studied her caused her heart to pound against her breast. She also felt a slight pull in her mind, as if he was trying to turn her around, however she stood rooted in place, motionless, not knowing what to say or do.

With a low growl, Silas looked at his brothers, who were blocking Skye's and Ivory's paths as well.

"Bendable?" Silas asked telepathically.

Syth and Agaeus nodded their heads no.

Skye, Ivory, and Jadis looked at each other. *"Bendable?"* they repeated amongst themselves.

"So, they have been trying to mind bend us, and they can't," Jadis said, in a telepathic tone only her sisters could hear.

"Clearly, they want to play games, so let's play," Ivory replied.

Trying to conceal their shit-eating grins, they twisted their hands counter clockwise, using their discretion. The surrounding air swirled, and a cool, grey mist crept in, consuming them. It appeared as of Silas and his brothers were still having a private conversation, so the sisters took the opportunity.

"Let's lock them down and run. We need the answers we've been searching for," Jadis stated.

"Let's go," Ivory agreed.

With a quick snap of their wrists, the three of them took off, running for the lower deck.

"They will be locked on the boat until we get back, so let's get the hell out of here before they figure out what we did. Run!" Jadis yelled, shoving Skye and Ivory down the stairs.

They hopped onto the jet ski and made it to the island in a few minutes. Their hearts thumped and their pulses raced. Jadis wasn't sure if it was the adrenaline rush from locking down three Mind-Bending Nosferatu or the anticipation of getting the answers they weren't sure they were prepared for.

They looked at one another before looking back at the boat and started laughing.

"How long do you think we have?" Ivory asked.

"I kept Aiden and his brothers locked up for about five hours." Jadis chuckled nervously.

"We'd better hurry, in case they find us sooner than later," Skye warned.

They turned toward the path leading into the darkened jungle before them.

"I should have mentioned I'm protective," Silas snarled.

Jadis hadn't noticed Silas standing there. "Holy shit!" She let out a scream, as did Skye and Ivory. Frightened to the core, Jadis jumped and fell backward over a rock, but Silas caught her before she hit the ground. *How the fuck did they manage to follow us so quickly?* Jadis wondered.

"How the hell did you get off the boat?" Ivory demanded, who was face to face with Agaeus.

Skye looked in Syth's direction, adding, "Well?"

"The ass you know as Aiden gave us a heads up," Silas answered, his eyes fixed on Jadis'.

Jadis wasn't sure if Silas was angry, impressed, or both. His eyes were cold, cat-like slits glowing in the dark.

"I don't think you understood earlier when I told you not to leave. Apparently, I'm going to have to teach you a lesson when I get your frightened little ass back on the boat," Silas warned.

"No, Silas. I'm serious. I'm not going this time. No games either, we need answers."

"*No games*?" He stroked her cheek with his fingers, before grabbing her by the arm pulling her into him. "Mon chéri, I believe you and your sisters are the ones full of *games* tonight. Did you really think you could lock us on the boat?"

Jadis was about to protest, but try as she might, the words became lodged in her throat. Silas was menacing, his eyes scrutinizing, and he scared her. She looked around, and Skye and Ivory were already gone. Jadis was furious with her sisters for leaving her there alone with him.

"They didn't have a choice," he replied, sounding menacingly calm.

"Stop that!"

"*Stop* what?" he asked, cocking his head to the side and looking at her like he was trying to play stupid.

"Reading my thoughts like that. It's intrusive," she snapped.

"Get used to it. You are mine. I will not stop, nor will I apologize for doing whatever I need to keep you. I will know exactly what you are thinking and what you are up to at all times. Quite the sneaky little mouse, aren't we?"

He pulled her body tightly against his, placed one arm around her waist and stroked her face with his other hand, tracing her jawline with his fingers. He then drug his thumb across her bottom lip before moving his fingers further down her neck and around to the back of her head. He grabbed a fist full of her hair and pulled her head back.

Jadis wrapped one arm around his neck and the other behind his back. She looked up at the menacing vampire who was all hers. Her body was hot, and her brain was spinning between fear and desire. She was scared, nervous, but mostly turned on.

He planted his sculpted lips on hers, forcing her mouth open. She could feel his erection pressing against her stomach, and her body responded. As the warmth in her core grew, she moaned into his mouth.

He kissed her neck and scraped her tender flesh with his canines. *Holy hell,* she thought. *He's going to drink from me right now!* Her anxious heart skipping a beat.

"Not tonight, baby. We have other business to attend to first." Silas flipped her around and put his foot on top of the rock she'd nearly fallen over earlier.

"Silas, stop!" Jadis spun around and tried to fight her way out of his grip, but he flung her over his bent knee and smacked her ass.

"Holy shit! Silas, what the hell are you doing? Let me go!"

"I think you need a good spanking after the shit you pulled tonight."

He is enjoying this all too much. "Stop it!" she yelled, both seriously and playfully.

Jadis laughed at the absurdity of the situation, as well as the position he had her in. He smacked her again, this time leaving a sting on her ass cheek.

A low rumble rose from his throat, and he spoke in a deep, dark tone, "We should head back. I'd like to finish this in our bedroom." He threw her over his shoulder again and walked away.

Silas burst through the stateroom door and tossed Jadis onto the bed on her back. Her body bounced on the satin duvet, provoking a nervous yelp. The plush pillows lining the hand-carved wooden headboard bounced around her head and tumbled onto the floor.

Silas grabbed her ankle and pulled her toward the edge of the bed.

"Well, now." He stood at the edge of the bed, looking down at her. "What am I going to do with you?" He grinned with a devilish half-cocked smile with the corner of his mouth turned up.

Jadis laid there, feeling exposed, even though she was still dressed. She was so nervous she didn't know what to do or say. *Should I move, not move—*

Silas interrupted her thoughts, "Don't worry your pretty little head. I know exactly what you should do. Taking those clothes off is a start."

He lifted his shirt up over his head and tossed it across the stateroom and onto the chair, revealing his perfect rock-hard body. As he crawled over the top of her, he lifted her off the bed with one arm and repositioned her body beneath his. He unbuttoned her shorts and pulled them off in one smooth motion, tossing them down, along with her silk panties.

"There now, that's better," he growled.

He lifted her shirt up toward her chest and laid a gentle kiss on her navel before trailing his tongue along her hips.

Jadis squirmed beneath him as he pushed her shirt further up and continued to kiss and lick his way up her stomach. He lifted her arms over her head removing her shirt and bra, and tossed them onto the floor.

She lowered her arms and placed her hands on either side of his back, feeling her way around his powerful body. She slid her hand further down and over his ass before and pulled him closer.

"My God, you taste so sweet. Your body feels so perfect beneath mine," he said as he gently rocked against her core.

She moaned beneath him, reached down to wrap her hand around his hard shaft, and slid it up and down his length. He groaned with each firm stroke of her touch.

"Jadis, you are everything I need. I still can't believe I had to wait—all these years—to be with you—inside of you," he whispered, momentarily pausing between words with each stroke of her hand.

"Too long, too damn long, Silas," she whispered as she playfully nipped at his neck.

He pushed her legs apart, clutched her thigh in his hand, and forcefully slid himself into the slick heat of her core. And she let out a heavy, moan filled gasp.

Jadis felt the scraping of his canines along her neck and knew he was transfixed with the blood coursing through her veins. "Silas," she whispered.

Her voice pulled his attention from the thumping pulse, and he stopped himself, knowing the consequences of taking her blood too soon. *Not yet,* he told himself. He pulled his canines away from her vein. He was hungry. He hadn't fed since the night he had been reunited with her. *When I take it all the way with her, it had better be at the right time;* he told himself. As much as he wanted to taste her, he knew he would have to wait for the Full Blood Moon. After all, she was not mortal and the consequences to Jadis, if he took her too soon, were dangerous—deadly.

Jadis felt the same familiar feeling swelling up inside, rising with each hard thrust of his hips as he shoved himself deeper. Her body ceased all control, and she couldn't hold back any longer. *He is so big—so hard.* However, the pain from his size was as much of a turn on as the pulsing muscle itself. Another forceful shove brought her climax to the threshold, as well as his own.

Silas released a deadly growl as he came inside her with another hard thrust. Once he finished, he laid his head on the side of hers and kissed her neck. They lay intertwined together, letting their breathing return to normal.

He remained inside her, rocking back and forth for a few minutes before finally pulling out. After which he rolled over, pulling her close.

She laid her head on his chest, and he gently stroked her arm. *Exactly where I belong. Everything feels right again. There is no better feeling in the world than that of Silas.*

He laid there, deep in thought, thinking about how close he had come to feeding from her. Being that Jadis is an original, if he bonded with or took her as his mate at the wrong time, it could potentially pull her into the shadows between realms. The powers of Hecate flowed within her veins and if he fucked up, she could be lost to him for good.

Silas sat up on one elbow and looked down at her and she stared at the glowing ember of his eyes, that now appeared sated and calm.

"A penny for your thoughts?" she asked as she cupped his face in her palm.

"Baby, you are mine, and you're here in my bed. I never thought it would happen." He smiled. "We have much to discuss."

"Yes, we do."

"Well, now is not the time, nor the place. I want to enjoy this moment with you in my arms, wrapped around my body. Let's leave business until tomorrow. Right now, I have other things on my mind."

He rolled over the top of her, his heavy body crushing hers. Jadis wrapped her leg around his waist and her arms around his body as he tantalized her tongue with his.

After having overseen Jadis's care, if only for a month or so, Aiden and his brothers were not about to let Silas keep her without at least hearing from her personally. They were afraid he was going to use her to help defeat the creatures from Ipheanor, which would put Jadis and her sisters at the forefront of the upcoming war; they were't going to let it happen.

Eden and Aiden knew Silas and his brothers would do everything within their power to keep Jadis and her sisters to themselves. So much so, according to Bain, Silas had summoned for his brother Dante, who was also a powerful Master Wizard. It wasn't as if Aiden and his brothers could simply show up and leave with the girls in their possession, especially after witnessing Silas's newfound revelation. According to Arcadia, Jadis was indeed the one he had been searching for all this time.

They followed a trail Skye and Ivory had left for them during Jadis and Aiden's altercation. The girls opened their veil just enough for Bain to catch a glimpse of the dock from where they had initially boarded the yacht. As soon as they got to the dock, it was completely vacant; the yacht was gone, as expected.

"Can you find any trace of where they headed?" Aiden questioned.

Bain spoke up, "No, it appears to have been cleansed, energetically speaking."

Aiden lifted his head and took a deep breath. "I can still smell a faint, lingering trace of her," he rumbled. "Dante—he covered their tracks." Aiden stated.

"You got it," Eden replied.

"At least we know where they set sail from, which is a lot more than we knew before the little argument with your fair maiden," Lars said in jest, along with a smirk.

"I'm in no mood for your shit," Aiden snapped back.

Eden bent down, resting his elbows on his knees. He placed one hand on the cement, feeling the vibrations from the dock, trying to feel for any trace of the girls. He picked up a rock from the ledge, stood up, and threw it out into the open ocean. "Shit—shit—shit," he mumbled. "I hope you're ready for plan B."

"How about filling us in since none of us knew you had a plan B, brother," Aiden snarled.

"Silas has them well hidden. Once I figure what plan B is, I'll let you know," Eden replied.

"Bain, you and Dante are very close. Maybe you could reach out to him?" Aiden suggested.

"Dante does as his brother says, especially if it's an order. He wouldn't betray Silas if his life depended on it, not even for me," Bain replied.

Jadis was still lying in Silas's arms, heavy in thought. She couldn't leave things as they were. She needed to make amends. "Silas?" she said, softly.

"What is it, darling?"

"I need to make a call." As soon as those words left her mouth, she felt a pang of regret for having spoken.

"A call?" Silas was now propped up on one elbow, looking at her with one raised eyebrow.

"Yes," she said, treading very lightly.

"Who do you need to call?" Silas was asking, even though he already knew the answer.

"Aiden—" she could barely get his name out of her mouth, not knowing how Silas would react.

"No."

He said it so calmly she thought he was kidding. "What do you mean, *no*?" Not that his answer was unexpected, but she was a bit taken-a-back by the coldness in his tone and his lack of emotion.

"I mean no. Why do you need to speak to him when he already knows you're with me?"

"That's not it, Silas. It's the way things were left. I need to talk with him," she reiterated, knowing any attempt to reason with Silas would get her nowhere. *Good luck,* she thought to herself.

"*Good luck* is right. It's not happening."

"Silas, we are not doing this again. You can either let me call him, or I'll do it another way. Do you understand what I'm saying?" she replied.

Silas stared her dead in the eyes. "Is that a threat, mon chéri?"

"Yes, actually. I can call now while you are here, or I can call later since you have to leave on business. The choice is yours, vampire." She had to admit the way she'd said it did sound kind of threatening.

"I can stop you altogether. Don't think for a minute I can't." He chuckled.

Well, that sounds as if he has already done something, she thought. "I'm calling Aiden whether you like it or not, but if you want to be in on the conversation, give me your phone."

"Nope," he stated, as he casually placed one arm behind his head.

She decided to take a different approach. Demanding Silas do anything was obviously a no-win situation.

"What are you afraid of? Are you afraid he's going to steal me from you? You're jealous!" She started to laugh, but realized right away laughing at him was not probably not the best approach. The way he was staring at her with hardened eyes confirmed it.

Silas laughed aloud. "*Steal you*? How can Aiden steal you from me when he can't even find you?"

He acted so nonchalant, Jadis started to think she had backed herself into a corner. "Silas!" she said more adamantly. "I'm calling Aiden. I need to mend fences, so to speak. Their family was good to me. Maddie and Chloe are my friends, and I want to talk with them as well."

"Nice try," he replied, looking amused.

"Silas, come on. I have to do this." She got up, sat on top of him, and straddled his hips.

"You're like a dog with a bone once you get an idea in that pretty little head of yours, aren't you?" He placed both hands on either side of her ass and squeezed. "I like you in this position." He winked and thrust his hips upwards between her spread legs.

"If you mean I'm not taking no for an answer, then yes." It was hard for her to be serious with him in her current position. She didn't mean for it to take a sexual turn, but everything with Silas seemed to be sexual.

"Silas, please," she said softly.

He reached over and picked his phone up off the nightstand and spun it in his hand.

She reached for it, but he quickly pulled it back and wrapped it in his fist. "Silas—stop." She chuckled.

"You want to call Aiden, huh?"

"Was I not clear the first ten times I asked?"

"How about you *clearly* tell me just how close the two of you are?"

"What exactly do you mean?"

"You slept in his bed for weeks—yes?"

"You cannot be serious right now?"

"I'm very serious," he replied.

"Stop joking around and give me the phone."

He kept flipping it in his hand just out of her reach, waiting for a response. "Well?"

"Not that it's any of your business, but no, we did not sleep—*sleep* together."

"I know," he said.

"Then why ask?"

"Just so you know, anything having to do with you is my business."

"You are seriously ridiculous."

"Here." He held out his phone to her, and she grabbed a hold of it, but he didn't let it go. He looked into her eyes, his face serious as he reminded her, "You're mine, and nothing else matters. Don't forget it. Now make your call."

Apparently, I'll be calling Aiden with Silas between my legs. As soon as she went to make the call, it suddenly dawned on her.

"I'm curious. How does your cell phone work when my sisters' don't?" She waved the phone back and forth in front of his face.

"Do you want to make that call or not? I can throw your ass on your back right now if you want to keep it up." He pulled her down harder onto his crotch and moved her hips back and forth. "Forget the call." He smiled deviously.

Jadis did her best to ignore his sexual innuendos. "I see you have him on speed dial. Care to explain?"

"Just for business purposes. Are you calling or not? Tick tock—tick tock." He chuckled, looking fully amused with himself.

"*Business,* my ass." She hit the speed dial before the argument could end with him taking the phone back.

"Don't say a word," she said as she playfully slapped his stomach.

Aiden's phone rang, and he quickly pulled it from his back pocket. "Silas," he rumbled.

"Hi Aiden." Jadis's heart was pounding. *Hell, I've got Silas underneath me listening to every word. Not to mention, I'm not exactly in a position to be making a serious call.*

"Jadis? Are you okay? Why are you calling me from Silas's phone?"

"I'm fine, Aiden. I'm using Silas's phone because my sisters' don't seem to work," she said as she glared down at Silas. "I wanted to call you and apologize."

"You don't have to apologize for anything. This is all my fault. Tell me where you are, and I'll be there in five minutes. We can sort this all out."

Silas interrupted the conversation, just to piss Aiden off, "You only have a few minutes, so you'd better get to it."

She slapped him on the chest, and he grabbed her hand and raised his eyebrows.

"Do you want to play?" he asked, toying with her.

"You're unbelievable," she mouthed back.

"Silas, what the hell are you doing there? Why are you talking, much less listening to any part of this conversation? Jadis is a big girl, she doesn't need you sitting over her shoulder."

"I'm not exactly sitting over her shoulder, Aiden—would you like a view?"

"Oh, my God, you two, I'm sitting right here," she snapped.

"Jadis, tell me where you are." Aiden was trying his best not to let Silas get under his skin.

"Unfortunately, I can't. I honestly don't know where we are, other than being in the middle of the ocean, but that's not why I called. I called because I hate the way we left things. You saved my life, and you took care of me. You pulled me from the accident, and I was a bitch. I am so sorry. You definitely didn't deserve that," she said with all sincerity.

"Jadis, you were not a bitch at all. I know I deserved everything you dished out, and probably more. And if we're being honest, I was kind of an ass." He chuckled.

"Well, that's true," she agreed, joining him in laughter. At the same time, she could feel the seething anger of Silas rising.

"I want to tell you how much I appreciate you and your family. Will you tell them for me, especially Maddie and Chloe?"

"This sounds more like a goodbye than anything else. If you are in trouble, just say it." Aiden truly sounded worried.

"I promise you I'm not in trouble, quite the opposite actually, I'm happy."

Jadis could feel Silas's hands move to the back of her ass, as if making sure nothing could touch her, even though he was right there.

"Then what are you saying?" Aiden sounded confused now.

"I had to talk to you, to tell you I'm sorry. I don't hate you at all. I appreciate everything your family has done for me, especially you. I need you to know that." She knew the statement would likely make Silas angry, but she didn't care. She had to do what she felt was right, and she really didn't hate Aiden in any way.

"None of that is important, but Silas is not what he seems, and you need to know that."

"I know exactly who he is. He is the vampire from that night in the woods. I also know he is a Mind-Bender." The phone went silent, and she waited for Aiden to respond.

"Aiden?"

"Yes, I'm here, darling. Everything is fine. I think you should come home with me for a few days and think about your decision. You should put some distance between yourself and Silas. I'm not going to try to change your mind, but you should be clear this is your will and not his being forced upon you."

Aiden must have been told Silas was taking me as his mate, and I'm pretty sure it came from Silas himself. "It's my decision, Aiden. I stopped that mind-bending shit on night one."

Aiden let out a hearty laugh. "How am I not surprised? I bet Silas was even more surprised."

"Yes, in fact he was." As they laughed, she could feel the rumble of warning rising from Silas's chest.

"Well, it still might be a good idea for you to come here for at least a short time. Everyone would love to see you—I would love to see you."

"Not happening," Silas replied. "I'm not sure how many times I need to tell you she's not leaving my side."

Jadis slapped Silas's chest once again. "Be quiet!" As usual, he grabbed her hand.

"That one hurt? I heard it through the phone," Aiden said in jest.

"Maybe it's Silas who needs a break?" Bain joked, causing everyone on the dock to chuckle.

"Jesus, you two are like a couple of birds ruffling their feathers," she said.

"Well, I've been called worse—I believe, by you?"

Hell, he wasn't wrong. I had called Aiden a lot of things. "Yes—you have."

"I take the bird thing, it's better than being an ass," Aiden retorted.

That cracked Jadis up, but heightened Silas's annoyance.

"I can't deny it."

"It's great to hear your voice," Aiden admitted.

"Yours too, Aiden. I guess I'll say goodbye for now, but I'll call you again."

"Anytime you need anything, reach out. Regardless of how you do it, I'll be listening."

"I understand—"

"Call's over." Silas snagged the phone out of her hand and hung it up before she could finish her sentence.

"Are you kidding me right now?" She tried to get up, but he held her there.

"Let me be clear, there will be no calling Aiden regardless of how you do it, understand?" he threatened.

Jadis simply rolled her eyes in response.

CHAPTER 8

Eden placed a hand on Aiden's shoulder. "You look like a thousand pounds has been lifted off your shoulders."

"It feels like it." Aiden smiled for the first time in days.

"Is Jadis good?" Lars asked, not really needing to, since he had also heard conversation.

"Hell, she's better than good. Did you hear her tell Silas to shut up? Better yet, did you hear her slap him?" Aiden laughed.

"We sure as hell did," everyone answered in one way or another.

"I have never heard anyone tell Silas to shut up, much less dare to slap him. I don't know anyone who would have the guts to do it, much less live afterwards," Eden said.

Lars was still chuckling. "Only Jadis. I almost feel sorry for the poor bastard. Maybe he's the one we should be worried about."

Bain looked at Aiden and gave him a slight nod. "At least we know she's safe, and that's what matters most. Silas wouldn't let anything happen to her. She is his mate to be, after all. He won't let anything within a mile of her, and he certainly won't put her in harm's way."

"She made the call, she told him to shut up, and she smacked him twice by my count. It seems as if Jadis is in control of that situation. How, I will never understand. I didn't think there was anyone on this planet who could control Silas, much less someone who's 5' 6" and one hundred thirty pounds soaking wet," Bain stated.

Eden patted Aiden's shoulder a couple more times. "Good to have you back, brother. Our girl is safe for now. However, we still need to see her face-to-face just to be on the safe side."

"My thoughts exactly. Agreeing to become his mate gave him a lot of power over her," Aiden said.

"Back to business, brothers. However, I would love to be a fly on the wall right about now," Eden joked.

"I think we all would," Lars agreed.

"You know who is blocking her abilities?" Bain stated, offering up the obvious.

Aiden looked at Bain. "Yes, but I think Dante's met his match. You sure as hell did."

"I can't argue with that." Bain chucked as he raised an eyebrow. He then walked toward the edge of the dock and stared into the vastness of the open ocean. *She has no idea what she's agreed to,* he thought.

Jadis was sitting on top of Silas with her arms crossed, waiting for the scolding she had no doubt was coming. *Hell, Silas is intimidating, especially when he is hell bent on putting me in my place.*

"That was the one and only call, understand? I shouldn't have indulged you in the first place," Silas said seriously.

"Excuse me?" The moment the words escaped her mouth, she realized she probably shouldn't keep pushing her luck.

"*Pushing your luck* is right."

"You're not going to tell me what I can and cannot do. Let's get that straight right now!"

"You will do as I say. You are going to be my mate," he stated, clearly staking his claim.

"The hell I will! And if you keep this up, I might need to rethink this whole situation." Jadis flipped her leg over, got off him, and stood up from the bed. Silas, however, was standing in front of her in an instant.

"You are really trying my patience," he stated firmly.

"And you, mine! If I am going to be your mate, that does not mean you own me or control me. I also don't have to do what you say when you say it."

Jadis knew she might have crossed the line based solely on his hardened expression. He had likely never had anyone speak to him in such a manner. His eyes turned cold and angry, and his canines slid from his gums. He didn't answer her, he just started walking toward her, backing her into the bed. The back of her knees hit against it, and she fell onto her ass.

Silas picked her up, scooted her to the middle of the bed, and laid her on her back. He hovered directly above her, without touching any part of her or the bed.

"I think you need a little reminder of who's in charge here."

"I guess it depends on the reminder." She put both of her hands on his chest, trying to calm the beast hovering above her. Unsure of what else to do, she nervously grabbed the back of his head and pulled his mouth to hers.

He forced her legs apart and stroked her sex with his fingers. *There is nothing else that compares to the way he touches me, wraps his arms around me, and feels between my legs, she thought.*

Jadis rolled him over and straddled him. And he grabbed both sides of her hips and pulled her down onto his erection.

She moaned as she slowly slid herself down onto his shaft, taking it all in.

He groaned beneath her and thrust his hips upward.

She rocked back and forth on his crotch with the palm of her hands resting on his chest. "Shit," she moaned, as her body began to climax. The ripples of pleasure taking over as her sex rubbed against his crotch. The release broke and her body quivered with the heated sensation.

Jadis lowered her head to his chest and continued to rock her hips back and forth, reveling in the feeling.

He flipped her onto her back and re-adjusted her body beneath his. He pushed her knee to the side and drove his shaft into her core with a forceful shove.

"You're so wet—so hot," he whispered. The way her tight core squeezed his shaft, throbbing with her release, almost put him over the edge.

"Goddamn, you feel so good," she moaned.

Silas was relentless. He didn't stop, and he wasn't gentle either. Every hard shove was him claiming her as his, and she felt it.

The feeling rose again, and her core pulsated around his shaft with another release, which brought his orgasm crashing to the surface. He let out a guttural moan as he released inside her.

After a few moments, he rolled over and pulled her into his body. He held her in his arms and stroked her hair.

She traced his endless tattoos with her fingers, admiring the age and authenticity of each one. *The majority of them have to be hundreds of years old; done before the use of modern equipment.* Each tattoo told a different story; it was like reading into the depths of his soul as each one spoke of his life. They depicted pain, joy, struggle, war, and triumph, all perfectly intertwined with his battle scars.

Silas lay there so still and quiet she knew there was something weighing heavily on his mind. She rested her chin on his chest so he could look into his eyes.

"Care to share, vampire?"

"You're right, my love. You don't deserve to be controlled. That's not how it will be, unless of course you give me good reason." He winked. "You have to understand you will be my mate and my equal in every way. You are amazingly powerful in your own right, and that deserves respect. I would do anything for you, give anything to you, and protect you with my life. However, the one thing I will not do is take your freedom, at least not in the way you are thinking."

He rolled on top of her and took her mouth to his. He pulled away ever so slightly. "I love you, mon chéri, and you are mine."

"Yes, I am yours. I always will be," she agreed softly.

She rolled over and placed her back to his front, wrapped his arms in between her breasts, and held onto him tighter as a sense of dread crept up her spine.

"Shhh—calm your thoughts. There's no need to worry, darling. I will never let anything happen to you. I have no intentions of putting you in harm's way," he said honestly.

He stroked her face and playfully slapped her ass. Once again, he rolled over the top of her, squishing her into the mattress, which brought out a chuckle as she tried to breathe. "Silas, get off!" She laughed.

"Are you hungry?"

"I guess," she answered, knowing that once they had gotten out of bed and started the day, it would be all business.

"I only need one more thing before we get up." He winked.

"And what is that?"

He looked down at her with a cool, devious smile. "I think I'm going to have my breakfast in bed."

"Didn't you just eat?" she joked, feeling sorer than she had before.

"Yes, but I'm still hungry."

She grabbed the back of his head and pulled his mouth to hers. Once Silas finished his breakfast, he rolled over onto his back and pulled naked body on top of his.

She lay there with her head on his chest as he held her with one arm across her lower back, his other hand cupping her ass.

Silas laid a gentle kiss on the top of her head. "We should head up for breakfast this time." He chuckled. "You need to eat some real food."

"Maybe, but I think I'd rather stay here like this. Besides, I'm not sure I can walk." She joked, poking him in the forehead with her finger.

"You need me to carry you?"

"Oh, hell no. You'd probably enjoy that way too much."

Silas rolled over the top of her and got out of bed. He grabbed a pair of casual pants and a tank top. She watched him dress, thinking what a sight he was to see, no matter what he was doing.

After watching him dress, Jadis realized other than the pink bikini he had laid out for her, and a few outfits Silas and his brothers had provided her and her sisters, she didn't have anything else to wear. Once again, she felt him intruding on her thoughts.

"I have something for you, by the way." He smiled.

Jadis grabbed the sheet and wrapped it around her body, bunching it up just above her breasts. She sat on the edge of the bed and rubbed her toes against the white Persian rug covering most of the solid marble floor.

Silas walked over to the double closet doors at the other end of the stateroom and opened them up; the closet was filled with beautiful clothes. Jadis jumped up, walked over to the closet, and ran her hand over the top of them. She looked up at Silas, a bit shocked.

"Where did you get all of these?" she asked, delighted.

"I have my ways, darling. I can't let you walk around naked or in the same few outfits you've been wearing now, could I?"

He stood behind her, wrapped his arms around her, and nestled his face into the crook of her neck.

Jadis reached up with one hand, cupped the back of his head, and looked up at him. "Thank you, baby, they are beautiful!"

He cupped her jaw in his hand and turned her head toward him. He smiled and his mouth fell to hers.

They began looking at the clothes, flipping through them together. "These aren't left over from one of your other girlfriends, are they?" she teased.

"You're jealous!" he joked back.

"Nope!" She laughed.

"For your information, I don't have an ex, and I've never had a girl-friend, just in case you're curious."

Jadis rolled her eyes in jest, turning her attention back to the clothing. Everything was of the highest quality, cut from finest cotton, silk, and satins. Shirts, tank tops, sun dresses, beach attire, and day wear filled the closet from top to bottom. Most of the clothing was casual; the perfect choices for someone who might be living on an island or going on an adventure.

He pulled open a drawer; it was filled with beautiful, lace underwear and matching bras, all folded perfectly into sets. Closing that drawer and opening the next; it had about a dozen bikinis with matching sarongs.

"I can't believe you did all of this. I don't know what to say?"

"You don't need to say anything. The look on your face and that smile says it all. Your happiness is my happiness after all." His eyes were kind and honest.

She almost felt guilty thinking about any form of clothing that might be missing, but it dawned on her that Silas had supplied her with everything except sleep wear.

Being the little mind reader that he was, he answered, "You don't need those when the only thing you'll be wearing to bed is your birthday suit."

Jadis spun around, giggling as she wrapped her arms around his neck and kissed him.

"Seriously, I love all of it. You don't know how much this means to me."

"You don't know how much you mean to me." He gently stroked her cheek. "Now, let's get you dressed. If we don't leave now, you won't be eating until lunch time or later."

They picked out an emerald green bikini, a pair of black, see-through bottoms, and matching crop top.

Jadis dropped the sheet and flung it into his face.

"Keep it up, and I'll throw your ass right back on the bed."

She sauntered over to him coyly. "Is that a threat, vampire?"

"More like a promise," he stated with a low rumble.

He grabbed her face and put his mouth to hers. Jadis placed her hands on his chest, shoved him backward onto the bed, and crept over the top of him, ready for more.

He rolled her over and pinned her arms above her head. "Nice try, but we are going up to get you something to eat." He had a deep, silken tone in his voice as he continued, "We have a lot to discuss, so this— and you will have to wait a little while longer."

He pulled Jadis off the bed and led her out of the stateroom, and she reluctantly followed.

The air was warm, and the sun was bright and glistened off the blue ocean waters. She looked up and there wasn't a single cloud in the sky. She looked around for the island they had recently visited several times and it was nowhere in sight. *Apparently, Silas and I spent a little too much time in the stateroom,* she thought, having missed the fact the yacht had set sail after Silas, Syth, and Agaeus drug them back. The ocean stretched as far as the eye could see.

Silas and Jadis took a seat and were sipping their drinks when Skye, Ivory, Syth, and Agaeus joined them.

Once again, breakfast looks amazing, Jadis thought as she looked at the assortment of fresh fruits, pastries, and eggs, which made her stomach growl.

Silas re-filled Jadis's glass, not letting it go until he'd moved in for a kiss. They played a gentle game of tug-o-war with the champagne-filled flute as he playfully kissed her.

"We hate to interrupt." Coughed Ivory. "Maybe the two of you should take it back to the cabin." She followed up by shooing her hands toward them.

"Not a bad idea," Agaeus replied, looking at Ivory, who was practically sitting in his lap.

Ivory stroked his chin in between her fingers. "Maybe skipping breakfast wouldn't hurt."

Jadis causally glanced at Silas. "Where are we?"

"Headed out to sea," Silas replied, offering nothing else. He rested his arm behind her shoulders and stretched his legs out under the table.

"Out to sea where?" Jadis turned her body, so she was facing him and laid her legs over his lap.

"Anywhere you like, baby." He smiled.

"Don't be coy." She chuckled. "Where are we?" she asked again as she popped a strawberry into her mouth.

"Looks to me like we are in the middle of the ocean," he answered with a cool, slightly mischievous grin. He winked and nodded his head toward the food on the table.

Jadis looked at her sisters. "Were either of you told where we are going?'

"No," they replied in unison."

"These two aren't saying anything more than Silas," Skye replied.

"It isn't as if we can't figure it out ourselves," Jadis said as she winked at Silas.

Skye nodded in agreement. "Exactly right."

Jadis ran her hand down Silas's leg and squeezed his knee. "You can't hide much from us. You know we can play games too, if you'd like."

Silas chuckled. "If you're going to touch me like that, you'd better mean it. Do you remember what happened the last time the three of you played around?" Silas's tone became mischievously serious.

"How could I possibly forget?" Jadis slowly wrapped her lips around a grape and gently sucked on it.

"Later." Silas winked. "If you must know, my brothers and I are going on a reconnaissance mission."

"Are you going to fill us in?" Jadis asked, uncertain if he would even consider it.

"Yes."

She motioned for him to continue. "Well?"

Silas began to tell the story. "A few years ago, rumors surfaced from a couple of other clans. They spoke of a cave hidden in the Valley of the Old Gods containing more than a few ancient Ipheanor relics. They weren't dealing in the lucrative black market, and they certainly weren't tomb raiders. They couldn't care less about the precious antiquities so many mortals relished. They were busy hunting for something altogether different. All of our clans had been experiencing an unusually high level of energy, which was proven in the way we were all witnessing dramatic reenactments of the war from a thousand years ago. The visions all depicted the Valley of the Old Gods in some form; we knew something had managed to escape and hide for all these years. What had escaped managed to not only survive, but to go undetected.

"How the hell did it find me?" Jadis wondered as she continued listening to Silas.

Our brother Dante, along with Bain and a few other wizards, used their skills to decipher the visions until the location in the Sacred Valley was finally pinpointed. The valley consists of endless, arid, hot, rolling sand dunes, but within it lay a hidden oasis. It's ripe with lush vegetation and an abundance of life. The cool waters pour from a natural spring that keeps the fertile oasis alive and well. Our mission was to locate and then destroy whatever resided in the Valley that didn't belong there. The Valley itself is on the west bank of the river, opposite the city of Thones. Unbeknownst to many, the Valley is separated in two. In the East Valley, most of the royal tombs are situated, and in the west is the location of the cave."

Jadis side-eyed Skye and Ivory, having a dreadful feeling creeping up as she continued listening to Silas.

"It wasn't going to be easy to track down a myth that had been hidden for almost thousand years, but if anyone could do it, our clans had a better chance than any. We began our search in the west, based upon the premonitions of a hidden cave with the marking of a High Priest. We were ready, armed, and prepared to do whatever it would take to eliminate the monster whose kind had ravaged the land, pillaged everything in its path, and slaughtered countless Ipheanorians in the process. During the Great War, vampires and witches fared much better. The Baskale and their masters, the Segans, easily began eradicating the mortal population. They were tall, thin-bodied creatures with large heads, black, lifeless eyes, and the hairless skin of reptiles. One scratch of their four-inch talons was lethal. The bacteria alone were enough to infect its victim, often taking hours or even days for the infection to seethe through the victim's body. The Segans are merciless, undeniably rabid, and all too powerful; they needed somewhere new to sustain their kind and clawed thier way to the surface and walked right through the vortexes and into our world. The Segan invasion raged on for about a hundred years or so, becoming a bloodbath for most of the mortal population. The skies filled with smoke, the never-ending stench of death, and the land became barren. The Segans wanted to supplant mortal life, along with all other life forms. They desired to enslave everyone, and even harvest mortals for food. It would have resulted in the complete destruction of the world as we know it, had our ancestors allowed it. If they were to have gained control over Ipheanor, they would have easily migrated across the planet, most of which was uninhabited at the time. There wouldn't have been anything or anyone standing in their way."

Jadis, Skye, and Ivory looked at each other in awe as Silas paused and Agaeus took over the story. "Our ancestors were powerful, lethal, and they too, possessed archaic powers. Nosferatu were a force to be reckoned with; capable of fighting, surviving, and destroying the Segans. The witches, in turn, were almost as powerful, some of whom were the direct descendants of Hecate herself. She, of course, didn't take it lightly that the witches were being targeted. Since the Gods themselves were unable to interfere in the affairs of mortals, it was said Hecate gave a select few the powers she herself possessed. The witches used this to their advantage, as Hecate had wished, managing to fight and survive the attack. The mortals however, didn't stand a chance, and their entire race was nearly wiped out. Only those who were lucky enough to hide or to be protected by various Nosferatu clans or covens survived. Prior to this, there was no indication the Segans were clawing their way from beneath the surface of Ipheanor."

Silas took over again. "The technology needed to make such predictions didn't exist at the time. The Segans began showing up in a seemingly random fashion. At first, the mortals believed it was a due to small earthquakes. The Segans first showed up in uninhabited areas, appearing to be some sort of luminescent, blueish light disappearing into the horizon. This continued for months; the mortals did whatever they could to appease their Gods, whom they thought were angry. They didn't know enough about science or the world in general to question it any further. The Segans concealed themselves until there were enough of them on the surface to emerge from hiding and begin the takeover. The invasion was catastrophic, catching all living creatures, both mortal and immortal, completely off guard.

As Silas paused to take a drink, Jadis spoke, having been shocked by the story. "We have never heard any of this. We heard rumors of course, but this is terrifying."

"I agree," Skye added. "And we are a part of this?"

"It's fine baby. The three of you don't need to worry. We've got this," Silas replied.

"Well, don't stop now," Ivory insisted.

Silas squeezed Jadis's thigh to re-assure her as he continued, "Our ancestors, however, knew it wasn't a few earthquakes and began preparing. After the Segans had arrived, they laid in wait for a short time. Eventually, our grandfathers and great grandfathers attempted to communicate with them, wanting to understand their motives. The Segans however, weren't interested in communicating, especially with our kind, whom they saw as their only threat. Our ancestors didn't have experts in linguistics as we do nowadays, but they did have the knowledge of Nosferatu. This allowed them to communicate in other ways, seeing how they had supernatural abilities. They wanted a non-violent response from the Segans, but again, they weren't interested. The original clan that had made the first attempt to communicate with them were attacked and a handful of them were killed. The remaining members of the clan, including our grandfather Damianos, managed to warn the rest of the clans, who then prepared for war. After much work and preparation, their efforts resulted in the making of a modern-day military. Once Nosferatu and witches banded together, they were unstoppable. Eventually, the clans discovered the weaknesses of the Segans and carried forth the necessary tactics to finish them off." Silas stopped to rest for a moment.

"What happened during the war? Did the original clans and covens survive? Well, obviously, since we are all here, they survived," Jadis said, answering her own question. Not only was the curiosity killing her, but she knew within this story were many of the answers to the questions she and her sisters had for so long.

Silas chuckled as Jadis answered her own question and continued, "My brothers and I were not yet born. It was the year 1020. It would be another three hundred twenty years before we were given life. We were born in the year 1340, and the story has been passed down from generation to generation."

"You've kept this information all these years?" Jadis asked.

"Yes. Our ancestors knew it would be important one day. If we were to forget, and the Segans rose up again, it would be disastrous. We needed to remember; remember the destruction, the capabilities of the Segans, their inherent evil, and most of all, their weakness, Dragon Stone."

"Dragon Stone?" Jadis asked, raising her eyebrows at Silas.

"Yes." He pulled out a small dagger he had tucked into the waistband of his lounge pants. He looked at it before flipping it around, so the razor-sharp blade was against his wrist, the handle facing Jadis.

He motioned it toward her. "Take it."

Jadis took it from his hand.

"It's been carved from the oldest Dragon Stone, found only in the original quarry in Musgacar. "My great-grandfather hand carved it and a powerful Master Wizard created the sorcery surrounding it," Silas explained.

"It's beautiful," Jadis offered. *It was obviously carved with purpose. A lot of thought, energy, and magic went into making it, and not just magic; powerful sorcery is what it is.* She could feel that for certain as she held it in her hand. The color was a swirling mix of black and cream, resembling the skin of a python. She ran her hands over it, feeling its sharpness with her fingers, being careful not to cut herself. It was like nothing she'd ever seen or felt before. After studying it for a few minutes, she went to hand it back to Silas, but he pushed it toward her.

"Keep it. I brought it for you. I have another."

"Are you sure? It's beautiful, don't you want it?"

"No, it's not the only one in existence. We all carry them, just as we always have. We still have a small stash, if you will." Silas winked.

Syth took over the story, holding Skye's hand as he began, "The day they invaded was hot, dry, and the winds were at a standstill. There was something in the air all Nosferatu could sense. Our ancestors lived near the Valley of the Old Gods, which eventually became their stronghold. The desert sand swirled relentlessly that day, even though there wasn't as much as a breeze. The creatures had all taken cover, and nothing stirred except for the red shifting sands. Each vampire felt a surge of urgency, echoing the visions they had shared with witches, High Priests, and Priestesses. By the time they had gathered and were able to put the visions together, it was too late. The Segans had already begun the invasion and thus began the war. Nosferatu, witches, and Ipheanors all took a stand, hiding in the temples and triangular structures you know as Ziggurats. Clans and covens laid in wait within the hidden oasis resting on the edge of the valley, ready to strike. At that time, Nosferatu could only be in the sun for a couple of hours at the most. The witches would send subliminal messages during most of the daylight hours. The Ipheanors were not fairing very well, resulting in them being ruthlessly tortured, and slaughtered. Those who survived were eventually turned into slaves, and later, harvested for their meat. Nosferatu hid in the shadows, studying them, learning from them, and finally, revealing their weaknesses." Syth paused, looking up to see if the girls were still following him.

Silas took over again, knowing what he was about to reveal to Jadis, "Our ancestors could bend the energy of the world around them, blending with the environment to take on its smell and overall energy of the Segans, hiding right under their noses. They also figured out that when the Segans were moving, there was an energetic buzz around them which smelled of rotting flesh. They could be heard, more importantly smelled before being seen." Silas raised his eyebrow at Jadis, waiting for her to really hear what he just said.

After taking a moment to contemplate his words, Jadis realized what he was saying. "Rotting meat? That was the smell around my cabin. Silas, they were there! One of them tried to attack me the night Aiden pulled me from my car."

"No, baby, it was a Baskale, not a Segan. Aiden and his brothers have told us everything. You have nothing to worry about and nothing to fear. We're handling it."

Silas's voice was reassuring, but she couldn't stop the sense of dread washing over her as she looked at Ivory and Skye, who were speechless.

"You really have our attention now," Jadis stated.

Silas continued, "The witches and wizards worked together and were able to seal off the vortex's entrances. Our kind used the mortals as distractions and targets, which sounds heartless, but they had little choice. It was either the mortals or the vampires. The mortals were weak compared to our kind and the witches, which ultimately made them disposable. Without us, they would have all perished, anyway. The day it all came to a head, the desert appeared to be on fire; everyone glared at the scorching hell laying before them. The river on the West bank, now known as the Nakele, had turned dark from the blood of their victims. What was left of the corpses floated aimlessly down the river. The bodies were unrecognizable as they drifted soullessly downstream. Crocodiles fed on the remains, tearing the flesh to pieces, consuming what they could. Occasionally, the crocs would come across the body of a Segan floating in the river, blending in with the other corpses."

"Not to interrupt, but this is a nightmare we want nothing to do with," Ivory stated.

"I couldn't agree more," Skye replied.

"Let him finish. I want to hear this. What was wrong the bodies?" Jadis questioned.

Silas continued, "Our ancestors thought it odd the crocodiles did not consume their bodies. Our great-grandfather, Luscius, became curious, so he waited, watched, and eventually pulled a few of their bodies out. There was something odd about their deaths. A vampire, witch, or even a mortal hadn't killed them. There was a smell, but not the stench of death. The bodies were covered in dust, and it was not a dust that belonged in the valley; it was Dragon Stone. They must have encountered it while digging tunnels beneath the surface of Ipheanor, and it was obvious it had eaten away the flesh. That's when they decided to test it. They set up a plan and captured a few of the Segans. Each time the theory was tested, and a Segan met Dragon Stone, the result was immediate. The lizard-like scales sleuthed off and their flesh burned. With one strike to the chest, they immediately perished. That's how the weapons made of Dragon Stone came about. It was this discovery that eventually turned the war around. Their weakness was finally exposed. It took about a year to fabricate enough tools for all the clans to have access to them. Our ancestors mined only at night, not only to keep themselves out of the sun, but to remain cloaked in the darkness, hidden away from the Segans and their scouts the Baskale. The wizards completed the rituals around every tool, making sure there was nothing that could stop it from killing a Segan, once it penetrated its heart. Our ancestors who practiced sorcery went to the witches who were bestowed with Hecate's powers, to harness the darker forces. They studied the witches' ways, familiarizing themselves with Hecate's magic. This enabled the vampires to become the most powerful wizards to ever exist. Once their own skills had been combined with the Hecate's knowledge, they were unstoppable."

"Your parents, are they still alive?" Jadis asked.

"Yes, very much so," Silas replied with a heartfelt smile. My father's name is Santiago, and my mother's is Luciana. Our grandfather and great-grandfather have since perished, but that is a story for another time; my father also fought in that war, although he was very young."

"Where are they now?" Jadis asked.

"They spend their time traveling wherever the winds or tides take them."

"Do you hear from them at all?" she inquired again, wanting to hear more about his parents.

"Yes, they send word here and there," Silas answered before dropping the subject.

"That's what we have been doing for the last couple of years," Agaeus added. "We have been looking for a Segan we suspect is living and hiding somewhere in the Valley. We've made multiple reconnaissance trips over the years. In addition, we have studied the ancient Ipheanor ceremonial engravings still residing within the ziggurats, the shrouded tombs, and on the corridor walls. Some of which depict the events of the great war, battles, victories, and deaths. Because they had etched the drawings into the solid stone, some colors remained inlaid in the symbols. The Ipheanors' enemies had been conquered with the help of their 'New Gods', the Nosferatu. The High Priests of Ipheanor left behind many inscriptions of their victories, some of which, we knew, had the potential to provide the clues we may someday need. Our team explored every inch of the ziggurats as well, all the while feeling as if we were being watched over by a set of benevolent eyes." Agaeus paused, thinking something over.

Silas remained quiet momentarily, and Jadis could sense he and his brothers were thinking about them. *They no longer see us as weapon in their war. No doubt Silas and his brothers will look out for us at all costs, keeping us out of harm's way.*

Silas cleared his throat, carefully contemplating his words, not wanting his emotions to cloud his judgment.

"Don't stop now. It can't be that bad, whatever it is," Jadis stated.

"I wouldn't be so sure, baby." He lifted her hand and kissed the back of it. "The three of you are the direct descendants of Hecate herself. Your identities were well hidden within the mysterious engravings we found. There was a female adorned in a copper headdress, another donning a headdress of ravens' feathers, and the third wearing a headdress crafted with strands of reddish-brown bark."

Jadis, Skye, and Ivory listened intently, absorbing exactly what Silas was and wasn't telling them and then glanced at each other. "The colors of our hair," Ivory stated.

"Precisely," Silas agreed. "Your stories are written in red paint on the floor of one particular chamber. Everything we had deciphered seemed to point to a mysterious key of three with the abilities to open a vortex. They also depicted Hecate in the engravings, holding two torches and a key. She is known as the Goddess of Witches," Silas explained.

"Yes," Jadis agreed. "We know who and what Hecate is, just as we've always known we are her direct descendants. She is our mother, after all. The Gods granted her rulership over earth, sea, and sky. She guards the cosmic world's soul. Just like us, she is more at home on the fringes, which is why we live in the woods among the plants and animals. We also know that Hecate is the Holder of the Keys which can unlock the gates between realms, essentially the gates of life and death. The entrance to the underworld is known as Hecate's Grove, though she holds equal powers in both realms." Jadis paused, looking to Silas for a reaction.

"Yes, darling," he acknowledged. "The depictions of her and of the three of you were clear. The night we met you in the club, we didn't yet know the witches in the woods were the three of you, nor that you would end up being the keys."

"I don't understand. Why were we in the depictions? We weren't even born?" Skye questioned.

"True, but based on the cosmic signs within the drawings, we knew they were predictions of future events. We suspect Hecate relayed the visions to whomever she deemed worthy? Who knows, but it's the only logical explanation," Syth explained.

"You put it all together by the lagoon that day, didn't you? Why didn't you tell me?" Jadis asked.

"I didn't know how to. I was still in shock. Just being with you again was more than I could bear at that moment. I didn't want to say the wrong thing, ruining the moment. I needed to find the right time to tell you what we knew. I was afraid of scaring you away, or worse, having you taken from me and hidden in the shadows again. However, everything changed for me that day. My mission had been clear for so many years, yet in one afternoon, it took an entirely different direction. You are now my mission—my only mission."

Silas slid a few strands of her hair away from her forehead and pulled her onto his lap.

"You are mine," he whispered. "Nothing else matters. I love you, and in about three weeks, I will show you how much."

Jadis pulled away slightly as she ran her hand down his cheek and smiled. "Before I agree, what else are you hiding from me, vampire?"

Silas continued, "We eventually found what we thought might be the cave from the original visions. It was in the mountainous region of Snaegro, between the Esheaton Sea to the north and the Cospain Sea to the south. If there is a chamber hidden within the mountain, so far, we have been unsuccessful in opening it because of the vortex surrounding it. It's going to take more than the typical amount of sorcery, magic, or Nosferatu technology to penetrate the vortex. Regardless if it's one of the original entrances, or newly formed, it needs to be destroyed."

Jadis knew he was being careful not to upset or to scare her. *"Us!"* she stated telepathically, looking at Skye and Ivory. *"It's going to take the three of us."* She didn't know why she said it telepathically, other than out of sheer habit. She knew Silas and his brothers were listening, anyway.

"We're going to have to fix this," she said, looking directly at Silas. "I'm going to stop you from listening."

"Never." He chuckled. "Not going to happen."

"We'll see about that," she said.

"Yes, we will, my love."

They sat in silence for what seemed like an eternity. Each one of them intently studying the other, trying to judge emotions and reactions, along with what it ultimately might mean for them as individuals. Jadis, Skye, and Ivory yielded the power they needed. However, their potential mates would not put their lives on the line for any reason.

They finished breakfast, having continued with only light conversation. They discussed the mission and what Jadis, Skye, and Ivory's role would be. It seemed as if they would not allow them to accompany them anywhere dangerous, much less to track down a thousand-year-old creature. Jadis tried to argue her point, and they went back and forth for a brief time. However, it became clear a solid decision would have to wait, because Zach was approaching the table.

"Silas, the phone is for you."

Silas planted a kiss on Jadis's forehead. "I'll be back shortly. Don't you go anywhere." He turned back around and gave her a wink and a smile before he and his brothers disappeared once again.

CHAPTER 9

Jadis and her sisters still needed to get their questions answered after having been so rudely interrupted the other night when Silas and his brothers caught them sneaking to the island. They knew they had a meeting which would likely go well into the night, hoping it would keep their attention diverted away from them.

"That was an unexpected story," Skye sighed, as she took another drink.

"No shit!" Ivory replied.

Jadis looked at her sisters, but was lost in her own thoughts. *This is going to be the only chance we have to try again. If Silas thought for one minute I'm planning to leave the yacht, he won't hesitate to lock me up. At least my sisters and I can speak to one another privately without them having any knowledge of it.* They had shifted their communications to another realm. Just one of many tricks they had up their sleeves.

Shortly after Silas, Syth, and Agaeus left, the girls went to the front deck to lie out in the sun while they carefully planned their escape.

Silas was not looking happy when they returned from their meeting. "What's wrong, baby?" Jadis asked as she sat up on one elbow.

"Nothing, darling. We have business to take care of, and we have to leave."

"Leave? I thought you had a meeting?" she asked, looking around. "We're in the middle of the ocean. Where are you going to go?"

That's when she realized the plans she and her sisters had just made were not happening, not unless some other arrangements had been made they weren't aware of. Unless, of course, Silas had known his business was going to take him off the yacht.

Had he planned for this? Jadis thought to herself.

"Oh, my God. You shithead! And the wizard who's been here, that's Dante, your brother? You have been planning this all along."

Silas laughed a loud. "*A shithead*?"

"You knew you had business that was going to take you off this ship. You planned this so we couldn't go anywhere!"

"You are correct, mon chéri. Not only are we in the middle of the ocean, but I'm leaving more than my crew here to keep an eye on you."

Jadis, Skye, and Ivory looked around and noticed six large Nosferatu males looking more like fully armed military guards than a of couple deckhands making their way up to where they were. They each took their places standing at each end of the yacht; two walked to the bow, two more headed to the stern, and one stood on each side of the deck they were on. Jadis immediately stood up, not knowing what to think. *They are not your ordinary warriors,* she told herself as she studied their appearance.

"*What do you think is going to happen?*" Skye and Ivory asked Jadis telepathically.

The three of them stood facing Silas and his brothers in a stand-off of wills. Jadis hadn't yet been able to give her sisters her response before Silas spoke up.

"Aiden and his brothers released custody of you to us," Silas stated unemotionally, as if it were common knowledge.

Jadis squinted her eyes at him. "That was the phone call you accepted earlier?"

"Yes, why are you acting like you're surprised by this? You knew I would not let Aiden and his family resume control of you. I believe I've been pretty damn clear about that all along."

"*Custody*? Am I your prisoner? They don't just *release custody* of me, as you so eloquently put it," she snapped.

"Okay, then how about this; you are in MY care now. Is that better?"

Silas is always so self-assured, she thought to herself. "By the Gods, Silas. No, it's not okay. Who does Aiden think he is, and exactly who do you think you are? Did the conversation I had with him earlier have anything to do with this?"

"Maybe. Apparently, my cousin can be reasonable," he replied. "The call helped, not that he would have had a choice in the matter, regardless."

"*Your cousin*?" The admission shocked her. She had no idea they were all related. "*Reasonable*? My ass! As far as I'm concerned, you and your *reasonable cousin* can both go to hell. This just keeps getting better and better," she snapped. *Leave it to Aiden to pull some shit after I thought we had finally come to an understanding.* She walked away, but Silas grabbed her arm and turned her around to face him.

"Listen, my love. Regardless of how we word it, what matters is you belong to me. If you aren't planning on leaving, what's the big deal?" Silas cocked his head, waiting to hear what she would come up with.

"Maybe we just wanted to go hiking or lay on the beach," she said, trying to act as if she didn't have other plans. She turned and stormed off, leaving Skye and Ivory to do their own bidding with Syth and Agaeus. Jadis headed straight to the stateroom and shut the door behind her.

She turned, only to find Silas at the edge of the bed already. He stepped toward her and grabbed her by the waist.

"*Hiking, lying on the beach*?" he repeated sounding amused.

"Silas, stop." She tried to push him back, to no avail.

"You know you want this." He chuckled, bending over to steal a kiss. He wrapped his arm around her so tightly she couldn't break away.

"Stop, Silas!" She put her hands on his chest and tried to push him away again. "You don't own me, and you can't lock me on your boat, regardless of the situation." *Silas has to be out of his goddamn mind.*

"You are my mate to be, Jadis, so technically I do own you—at least I will."

"Good luck with that," she quipped.

"*Good luck*?" he shot back, cocking one eyebrow up at her. The tips of his canines slid from his gums, and his eyes swirled with excitement.

"You can't be serious right now? I'm in no mood, so no—you're not getting any. Especially right now. This isn't a game, and I'm not a toy you get to pass around, transferring ownership of, now let go."

Jadis felt like his whole body was suffocating her. She was annoyed with the realization he would go to any length to know where she was and what she was doing. It was going to be harder than they had imagined sneaking off the yacht later. It would take a lot of magic to get away from the Breed Warriors now surrounding the boat, not to mention Dante.

Silas did not budge. "I'll let go when I'm damn good and ready."

"I'm serious, let go of me!"

Jadis tried to pull away again, but he held her steady. *Okay, that's not going to work,* she told herself. *But how about this?* She summoned the energy from the surrounding air and chanted the words under her breath. The light hit him dead in the chest, which sent his body about three feet away from her.

He was taken aback at first, even though he gracefully steadied himself. He stood in a half-crouched position, looking like he was ready to pounce. The familiar slits of anger, shown in his eyes, and a low growl slowly rose from deep within his chest.

"Shit!" She turned to run from the room.

"I don't think so," he snarled, as he blocked the door before she even had the chance to turn around.

Damn! Jadis's heart was racing, and her pulse was pounding as she struggled to calm down. She told herself he would not hurt her, but she also couldn't help but notice how dangerous he looked. She knew she crossed the line this time.

"Well, aren't you full of surprises?" he said with two furrowed eyebrows. He pulled her up against his body again and held her hands behind her back in a vice-like grip. He stroked her cheek with his other hand, and she found herself walking backward with him, and not of her own free will. The back of her legs hit the edge of the bed; had he not been holding her so tightly they would have surely buckled beneath her. She tried to protest, but her voice became wedged somewhere between her chest and her mouth.

He lowered his head and the heat of his breath tickled her ear with a wicked whisper. "Do you have something to say, mon chéri?"

He grazed his canines along her neck and wrapped a handful of her hair in his fist. He gently pulled her head back, exposing the throbbing pulse in her neck, all the while keeping her arms pinned behind her with one hand. She could feel his hardened groin pressed against her stomach, his eyes reflecting a burning intensity. As much as she didn't want it to happen, especially when she was trying to remain angry, she couldn't help but to give in, and she struggled to keep her boundaries up. Silas and her body had other ideas, and both anger and desire now coiled within her.

His kiss was hungry as he forced her mouth open, and plunged his tongue against hers. She met him with the same insatiable hunger. She was suddenly on her back on the bed with his body on top of hers. He consumed her, and she melted in his arms. He was like a drug to her, and she craved her next fix.

"These wicked little games you play are such a turn on," he rumbled, as he reached his hand up her shirt and cupped her breast before rubbing his thumb over her nipple. He slipped her swimsuit top off and tossed it, along with his own shirt, to the side of the bed. He lay most of his body weight on her, pressing his chest down against her breasts.

She wrapped her arms around his neck and became lost in his kiss and the way in which his powerful body dominated hers. She forget why they were fighting to begin with. Somehow, when it came to Silas, she was defenseless in his arms.

Every time he dragged the tips of his canines along her neck, it sent chills through her veins, quickening her already racing pulse.

"Don't stop, Silas," she begged. "What could go wrong if you drank from me now?" She knew he wanted to drink from her as badly as she wanted him to.

"A lot could go wrong," he rumbled. He kissed a trail down her neck, sending another wave of desire rushing through her body.

He pulled himself away from the throbbing pulse in her neck.

Jadis was disappointed, but he was right. He had no choice but to control himself when it came to feeding from her.

He spread her legs with his own and rubbed the tip of himself against her core as he carressed and squeezed her thigh.

She was once again ready to take all of him. She moaned into his mouth as he thrust himself inside.

"Damn, you feel so good," he groaned.

"You're so hard," she moaned, as her body rocked in sync with his. She planted her head into the pillows; she couldn't get enough of him.

He growled in response, "I want to crawl right inside of you."

He re-positioned their bodies, allowing him to push his shaft further in.

She began to climax with each hard thrust of his hips; his shaft penetrating deeper and deeper. "Fuck me," she moaned.

He forced his tongue into her mouth again as her body trembled with the release. He then let his orgasm surface and he climaxed with her. "Damn, that hits hard," he whispered.

He rested his forehead gently on her as their chests rose and fell together, their breathing slightly labored. They stayed nestled in each other's arms for a while, not speaking, just enjoying each other's presence.

Silas's gentle voice broke the silence, "I am only doing this for your safety."

"I know, but I'm still annoyed."

"Yes, I can see that. If this is you being annoyed, I'll take it anytime, anywhere, any day," he teased.

Jadis rolled her eyes at him. "You're ridiculous."

There was nothing better than dozing off in his arms, and she found herself more than perturbed when a knock at the door interrupted their peacefulness.

"Silas, it's time," Syth called from the other side. "The raptor is ready."

"Why didn't you just reach out?" Silas asked.

"We've been trying. Apparently, you have other things on your mind because you sure as hell haven't been listening," Syth replied.

"I'm always listening—" Silas began, before stopping mid-sentence. He sat up on one elbow and looked at Jadis. "I didn't hear my brothers'? That's odd, isn't it? Have you been blocking them?"

Jadis shrugged her shoulders. "No, of course not. I have no idea what you're talking about."

"I don't believe you. You can't be trusted at all now, can you?"

"Neither can you nor your cousin, Aiden." She smirked.

"How am I going to trust you and your sisters are not up to something? I can feel it. I smell it." He was now fully on top of her, crushing her body into the bed.

"I don't know. I guess you should stay to make sure."

Jadis grabbed his head and pulled him in for another heated kiss. "Don't leave. I don't want you to go," she whispered.

"I have to, baby. You know I don't have a choice. I'll be back before midnight. Don't you even think about pulling any sneaky shit."

"I wouldn't dream of it," she said sweetly, smiling up at him. She tried to look as innocent as she could, knowing she and her sisters did, in fact, have a plan. However, she suspected Silas was seeing right through her bullshit.

He rolled off her and landed a smack on her ass.

"Dammit," she yelped, laughing through the sting.

Silas chuckled and hopped out of bed to get dressed while Jadis lay there, comfortable and drowsy. She watched her gorgeous vampire's every move. *God, he is perfect.*

"I like how you think." He winked.

He pulled on his black, military-style pants and put a dark grey t-shirt on; it hugged every muscle in his toned chest, biceps, and shoulders. He tucked his shirt in, sat down in the chair across the room from her, pulled on his black military boots, and laced them up.

Once he stood, he reached over and slid a large painting aside which revealed another closet. It looked like a small cache and was full of weapons, guns, blades, swords, and rounds of ammunition. He took out a leather gun belt which had already been partially prepped and strapped it on. He then picked out an automatic Glock G20 from the cabinet and pulled the slide back before slipping it into his side holster. The belt had multiple pouches holding fully loaded magazines, as well as a large combat knife.

She watched as he pulled a vest over his head and strapped it on. He also slipped another knife, much like a large dagger, into the side of his right boot. *Dragon stone. That's tactical gear for someone heading into a battle.*

"Damn, Silas. What is this business of yours, exactly? You are freaking me out now. What you're doing is dangerous, I can feel it. It doesn't take a witch to see the obvious. What if something happens to you?"

Silas walked over to the bed with a sultry look on his face. He lifted her chin and his eyes met hers. "This is just standard protocol, my love. There's no reason to worry. I have one huge reason to return and I'm looking right at her."

"Silas—" she began, before he bent over and placed his perfectly sculpted lips on hers, stopping her from speaking.

"Don't try to distract me. I'm being serious. You look like you're going to war, not to a *standard business* meeting, as you so casually put it."

"Listen darling, we are going to be mated and we will complete the blood bond. If you can trust anything, trust in that. I'm more concerned you might be up to no good. I have a feeling you're hiding something from me. I can sense it. If you try to pull anything stupid while I'm gone, there's going to be hell to pay."

Jadis looked at him, knowing he wasn't wrong. *It's a good thing I'm able to keep those thoughts to myself.* She wrapped the cashmere blanket around her body and stood up. She walked over and snuggled against his chest.

"Don't go, baby. I don't like this one bit. I feel like something bad is going to happen."

He didn't say a word, he just held her and stroked her hair. He bent over and kissed the top of her head. "I have to go, my love."

Jadis held him, refusing to let go. He pulled her arms from around his waist and cupped both of her hands in his.

"I'll be back as soon as I can. When I return, I want to find you right here, naked in this bed, waiting for me. Again, this is the last time I'm going to say it. Don't try whatever it is you're up to, don't even think about it." He paused briefly as he cast her a skeptical stare. "Jadis?"

"Okay," she answered hesitantly. In that moment, she felt like she was betraying him, but she knew she and her sisters needed answers for all of their sakes. "I love you, Silas. I'll be here waiting." *I'm not lying about that.* She had every intention of being back before he even knew she had been gone. She would fill him in later, depending on the circumstances and his mood at the time.

He walked toward the door and stopped momentarily to look back at her. "By the way, don't think I haven't made arrangements to keep you here." He smiled coyly before closing the door behind him, leaving Jadis standing there.

She laid back down on the bed for a minute, contemplating what he had just said. *Arrangements?* Shit!

CHAPTER 10

Silas met up with his brothers on the top deck as they continued loading up the rest of their gear. "I don't trust Jadis at all," Silas stated. "I know the three of them are up to no good in our absence. Jadis is full of schemes, witchery, and rebellion."

"I agree," said Agaeus. "I was getting the same vibe from Ivory."

"As was I," Syth agreed.

They casually glanced at each other as they continued to load the helicopter, knowing the girls were going to try to pull some fuckery.

"There's more than one reason we need to ensure they don't leave. One being I have every intention of taking her as my mate," Silas stated.

"At least we've made arrangements to ensure they don't get off the boat," Syth replied. Silas and Agaeus nodded in agreement.

They looked over at Dante. "You got all that?" Silas asked.

"Yes, loud and clear. You don't have to worry about it. I've got this under control," Dante stated.

"Make sure you do," Silas stated firmly. "If anything happens to Jadis, or her sisters, it's on your head, and I promise it won't be attached to your body for very long."

Dante nodded his head, unfazed by the threat. Even though he knew Silas was talking shit, he was taking his brother's orders seriously. "Don't worry, the spell you asked me to weave earlier has already been in place for hours."

Dante was not just any warrior, he was a Master Wizard; was well-trained in the dark arts, sorcery, spell-casting. He had spent six hundred years studying the craft, along with Aiden's brother, Bain.

Zach, who was piloting the helicopter, came over the headsets. "Ready to go? We need to head out. You can finish whatever business you have with your hellions." He then chuckled into the headset. "Damn, Silas. You have it bad."

Zach was looking back at them as they climbed in, watching Silas as he gave him an unamused glare in response to his subtle jab. Zach turned back around and prepared to take off.

Silas could hear Jadis yell from the stateroom, "Goddammit, Silas! You can't keep me locked in here!"

"Someone's angry right now." Silas chuckled.

"Apparently," Syth replied.

They all laughed, feeling amused with themselves. They looked over at Dante, who stood with one hand on the Glock tucked into the holster hanging from his hip. He waved them off, making the motion of pedals spinning with his hand to letting them know he had it under control.

Back at the command center, Eden, Aiden, Bain, and Lars were getting ready to head out on a separate reconnaissance mission, along with a legion of warriors Eden commanded.

"Everyone's good with the plan, right?" Eden asked.

No one really needed to answer. It was more of a move out command than any sort of question. Just as they were turning to leave, the satellite phone rang. "Zach?" Eden answered.

"Glad you all haven't left yet. Silas and his brothers need you in the valley at 2:00 p.m." Zach stated.

"What's this about? I thought we were running two separate missions?" Eden questioned.

"That was the plan, however they have been located so load up. Silas will reach out momentarily. By the way, Jadis is really angry right now." Zach chuckled, before hanging up.

"What the hell is that all about?" Lars asked.

"Change of plans, brothers. Based on the intel we've been gathering; I have a feeling we're heading into battle. We will hit the armory on the way out. They want us to join their mission, and apparently Jadis is not happy right now." Eden chuckled.

"Silas probably has her in chains." Aiden laughed. "They definitely have their hands full now that she is on their watch." Since she was destined for Silas, to his dismay, Aiden didn't have a choice in the matter.

Jadis got up after lying there for a few minutes trying to absorb what Silas had meant by *having eyes on them*. She put on a pair of jeans, a t-shirt, and boots from the wardrobe Silas had provided for her. She knew it was time to get her sisters and get out while they had the chance. She grabbed the door handle, only to find it didn't turn. *That's weird*. She tried again, and still there was no movement. She swirled her hands, demanding it to open, and it still wouldn't budge. *What the hell?* She placed her hands on the door to feel its energy, realizing someone had placed a reversal spell on it. *It feels strange, almost as if I had done the spell myself, using magic I don't even possess. That son of a bitch!* "Goddammit, Silas! You can't keep me locked in here!" she bellowed from her newfound jail cell.

It took everything the girls had for them to communicate with each other. The energetic barrier that had been cast around them was like nothing they'd ever come across. After a short time and a great deal of effort, they were able to open a portal they kept in order to communicate with each other in the event of a worse-case scenario. They had to get out of their staterooms and off the boat. There was only one way for them to accomplish their task, and they needed the earth itself, not the water currently surrounding them, to grasp the energy from another realm.

"Skye and Ivory, are you there?" Jadis called out for the tenth time.

"Yes, we've got you, finally," responded Skye. *"What the hell did they do?"*

"I'm not sure, but I've never felt anything like it before, not that it matters now. The only thing that does matter is getting out of these rooms and off this yacht. Not only are the warriors prepared, but Dante is one badass wizard," Jadis stated.

"Yes, he is," Skye agreed. *"I say we take care of Dante first. However, the other warriors are just as concerning, there is something more to them than meets the eye."*

"There certainly is," Jadis agreed.

"Dante is going to be a problem first and foremost. He's definitely on to us, and I promise he won't let his guard down for a moment," Ivory stated.

Jadis could hear the nervousness in Ivory's voice as she responded, *"Ohh, he's onto us alright, it's going to take a powerful punch to put him down long enough for us to get into the portal. Hell, we can't even trust he won't feel the portal begin to open. When we do this, we must do it all at once."*

"It scares me we lack the earth's connection and energy seeing how we are surrounded by water. I'm not confident we can do this," Ivory admitted, feeling really nervous.

Jadis looked at one drawer in particular. *"That's not exactly true."*

"What have you got?" Ivory asked.

"My familiars. We all know what is born from the earth returns to the earth after death. How much purer can we get?" She walked over and pulled the three vials out of the dresser drawer.

Skye had no idea Jadis had them with her. *"You have their ashes?"*

"I sure do, so let's get this done. We don't have any time to waste. Skye, I'll let you know when to open the portal. Ivory, you take care of our bodyguards. I will handle Dante. Keep in mind all of this has to be done perfectly the first time, otherwise we are screwed and going nowhere," Jadis added, nervously.

"We are all on the same page, so let's begin," Skye agreed.

They sat in their separate staterooms on the floor, in the middle of the circles they had drawn, energetically. Ivory worked on the bodyguards, Skye worked on the portal itself, and Jadis worked on conjuring up a powerful punch for Dante.

"Skye?" Jadis called out to her.

"I'm here."

"Whatever you do, please don't forget to close the portal behind us," Jadis said as she thought about what it would be like to be chased by Dante. *He would probably give me a heart attack.*

"I've got it," Skye replied.

The entire process was going to take them at least an hour. To travel through a portal, which is essentially a rip or tear in the fabric of reality between space and time, they had to create it. This would allow them to travel instantly between two points. They had to bend space and time to create a door, two doors to be exact, one on either side of the portal itself.

Jadis began by taking a pinch of the ashes from each of the vials, along with the salt she had snagged earlier. She sprinkled it together around the energetic circle surrounding her. She inhaled deeply, grounding her energy and requesting assistance from her deities, whose protection they would need in order to pass through the portal and onto the island.

Jadis had to remain in both dimensions simultaneously. If Dante appeared, she could hit him with their powerful magic, sending her familiars to hold him back. They would then have just enough time to slip into the portal before closing it behind them.

Jadis chanted aloud three separate times. "In this darkest hour, I call upon the sacred power. Three together stand alone, command the unseen to be shown."

A whisper responded, and she could no longer feel the physical part of her body. There was a light ethereal sensation warming her core, surrounding her heart and soul. She floated above her circle, still sitting with her legs crossed and her forearms resting on her knees.

All three of them had now separated their consciousness from their physical bodies. They could connect with each other, joined in thought and soul. They could now see, touch, and speak to each other face-to-face. More importantly, they could chant in unison to make sure they were done with their spells at exactly the same moment.

Jadis began her chant in Lativian, calling upon her familiars first three times. "Producat in canibus aperi portal. Producat in canibus aperi portal. Producat in canibus aperi portal."

Skye began her chant, to open the portal itself. "Aperi portal. Aperi portal. Aperi portal."

Finally, Ivory joined with the third and final chant. Opening the door to the mouth of fire to subdue the bodyguards. "Aperi os tuum ad ostium custodibus corporis domare ignis."

They were all three at the point in each prospective ritual, and it was time for them to take the leap.

Jadis looked at Skye and Ivory. "It's now or never. Everything is ready, the portal, the blow to the bodyguards, and the trap for Dante. We need to count down the final sixty seconds together." They reached out, held hands, and began.

CHAPTER 11

The warriors were up on deck, pacing back and forth, evaluating each of their assigned areas. They scanned the air above them, looking for a bulge or energetic shift which seemed odd or out of place. Each step they took and inspection they made was done with militaristic precision.

Dante went beyond the curtain of reality, ready for any magical or energetic shift emitting from anywhere within the vicinity of the yacht. There wasn't one amongst them that trusted the girls. However, Jadis was the one Dante was especially concerned with. Bain had filled him in regarding how powerful and cunning she was, alerting him to all the reasons not to trust her.

He made his way to each of the stateroom doors, circling around about every twenty minutes or so, listening intently as he continued using his abilities to keep each of the girls sealed in. He was getting somewhat nervous as his senses picked up on a subtle shift in the energy coming from the staterooms. Their silence was deafening. He knew they weren't sitting in their rooms politely behaving themselves. The moment he heard a whisper beyond the veil, he knew something erroneous was about to take place.

He couldn't open the doors to any of the staterooms. It would require dropping the shroud, if ever so slightly, and it would still provide them too much of an opportunity to get out. According to Bain, he had made that mistake once already. He had no choice but to stand outside each door during his rounds. He placed his palm on each one, relying on his abilities to peer beyond the here and now. On the surface, it appeared as if they were each searching for a way out. He found it strange he could see them, yet something still felt amiss.

He made his way back up to the deck to see if anyone else was feeling the slight shift or had heard the whisper. It was the same with all of them; they felt something but couldn't place it. They gathered around Dante.

"They are up to something," Dante stated, trying to get a grasp on what the girls were doing.

"They most definitely are," Paxil agreed. "We all feel it."

"They are not sitting in those rooms, fumbling around. They are most definitely getting ready to make some sort of move, whatever the hell it is," Dante stated

Dante scanned the yacht, trying to get a feel for where the energetic shift was coming from and doing his best to get ahead of the girls. If they got out, Silas would be furious. Jadis and her sisters would pay for their disobedience. That was if they decided to return. He, however, would face the full wrath of his brothers if he failed and something happened to them.

"What now?" Amun asked. "At least you have a fighting chance with Silas since you're his brother. The rest of us might be dead weight, in the literal sense."

"So far, it seems my binding is working. They have yet to break through, and it's already been over an hour. No matter what, at the first sight of something being amiss, I need to know immediately," Dante ordered.

"Milord," they answered simultaneously.

"This is going to be one hell of a long evening." Tomas looked tired of it already. After all, he was a highly trained assassin, not a babysitter.

Dante felt another subtle sift in the energy. *Where the fuck it is coming from?* he wondered. As soon as he had given the command to spread out, the air waned. They looked up to see a swirl of energy, the air above them spinning, shifting, and changing colors. A halo of light began radiating overhead.

"Fuck!" yelled Dante, "It's them. The three of you stay here. Tomas, Paxil, and Maat, get to the fucking staterooms."

Unfortunately, they were too late. The air suddenly split wide open, and a fireball exploded in the middle of them, knocking everyone but Dante back about six feet. They landed in a crouched position, ready to attack. However, Dante threw up his arms, shielding himself from the blast.

The portal opened above their heads, revealing Jadis, Skye, and Ivory in the mouth of it. Dante jumped up with a roar and reached in to grab Jadis.

Jadis jumped back and yelled, "Ite nunc! Ite nunc!"

Her three familiars leapt out from behind her and headed for Dante, who was not at all expecting them. They succeeded in knocking him back just enough for the three of them to shout, "Prope!" slamming the portal shut, leaving Dante fuming on the outside.

"Holy shit!" exclaimed Ivory. "Dante was right there. He almost had you by the arm!"

"I told you, and believe me, after this, he will never let it happen again." Jadis was truly terrified.

They were standing in the portal itself, but they needed to keep moving before Dante broke the veil. Within minutes, they had made it to the small, isolated, uninhabited island. They dropped from the sky and onto the beach where they plopped down and laid on their backs, trying to catch their breath and give their racing hearts a chance to calm.

"Dante looked scary as hell, and angrier than anything I have seen in our lifetime," Jadis stated.

They looked at each other, amazed they'd been able to accomplish what they did.

"I can't believe we did it. I didn't actually think it would work," Skye admitted.

"Neither did I," Ivory added as she placed her hand over her racing heart.

"Did you see the look on Dante's face?" Jadis could not keep from laughing. "You have no idea how much that scared the shit out of me. Can you imagine the place we'd be in right now if we had failed?"

"I don't even want to think about it. Agaeus, Syth, and Silas are seriously going to kill us," Skye stated nervously.

"Please, don't even mention Silas. I wonder if Dante is telling him right now or trying to figure out how to get us before Silas even finds out what we did?" Jadis questioned nervously.

"Ohh, he's trying to get in as we speak. I promise. I saw the look on his face and he is not playing around." Ivory said along with a nervous laugh.

"How long do you think we have before Dante opens the portal back up?" Jadis asked.

Skye shrugged her shoulders. "I don't know?"

"We had better get moving." Jadis was already standing, ready to go.

"Did you feel that?" Ivory asked as she stopped in her tracks.

"That feeling?" Jadis whispered. "I know that feeling." She grabbed Skye and Ivory by the arm and stood still.

"What feeling? Jadis, what is it?" Skye demanded.

"You remember the feeling I told you about? The one I had the night Aiden killed the Baskale?"

"Yes. What are you saying?" Ivory questioned; her face was now as white as newly fallen snow.

"I don't know for sure, but I'm having the same eerie feeling," Jadis replied as she looked around.

They gripped each other's arms tightly and scanned the entire island. Fortunately, they found nothing out of the ordinary and none of the wildlife appeared to be unsettled.

Skye let go and slapped Jadis on the arm. "Cool it! Your paranoia is freaking me the fuck out. Enough of this. There is nothing here, Jadis, and if you keep that paranoid shit up, I'm going to have a fucking panic attack."

"I'm not being paranoid! There is something fucking watching us. I can sense it."

"There's a lot watching us," Ivory snapped. "Do you think Dante is doing something that is allowing him to see us? Maybe that's what you're feeling?"

The hairs on Jadis's body continued to stand on end. "I don't know, maybe?" She replied. Although she wasn't sure at all. "It sounds logical. If there were others, I would assume Aiden and his family, not to mention Silas, would have told me."

"This is all creeping me the hell out. Let's just get this done and get back on that boat. Right now, I'm not so sure this was the best idea." The fear was clear in her tone; Ivory was always easy to spook.

A monkey jumped above their heads, causing the trees to sway, which caused the three of them to scream until they realized their imaginations were getting the better of them.

"There's your Baskale, you idiot!" Skye yelled.

They laughed a loud and took deep, nervous breaths that allowed them to exhale sighs of relief.

"Apparently we are the intruders, Jadis. Come on, we can't waste any more time," Ivory demanded, urging Skye and Jadis to regain their focus.

They headed toward the middle of the island, and although they couldn't have been more than a few blocks into the jungle, the sea had disappeared from view, lost behind a seemingly impenetrable screen of vegetation. They found a cave off to the side of the path they followed. The lush vegetation and fallen rocks, obscured it and they decided to take a peak, out of curiosity.

The stone surrounding the entrance was jagged and uneven. It was cool and damp; the floor littered with jungle debris and fallen rocks. Vines and roots lined the walls and hung from the ceiling. Even though it was small, it was still large enough for the three of them to fit inside if they found the need to hide.

When in unfamiliar territory, always have a back-up plan, Jadis thought.

After a few minutes of exploring the cave, they settled into a clearing not far from the entrance for their ritual to take place.

They needed to find out more about what it meant for the being the Key of Three. Was there something else they were supposed to do? Was Jadis truly at the center of it all? They had a hundred questions, and they hoped Hecate would provide the answers they were seeking. They also wanted to know exactly why she thought it necessary to separate them from their vampires one hundred fifty years ago and then flood them with the memories without warning. They were tormented for years after that night, feeling as if they had lost a period of time so unexpectedly and without explanation. They had never believed the initial reasoning, but they had no choice, It wasn't as if Hecate was a mortal being sleeping in the next room.

They began creating their circle. Time warped within the portal, and it became twisted. In other words, all events would happen simultaneously, yet the periods of time would be different. What would be a few hours for Dante and warriors back on the yacht would be double that for Jadis, Skye, and Ivory on the island. They knew they needed to hurry. If Dante broke through early, he would be right in the middle of their ritual, interrupting the entire process.

Dante was still trying to get into the portal, fuming he was so close and yet so far. He had reached in, only to have Jadis sick her dogs on him. That had certainly not been expected, and the familiars gave the sisters the mere seconds they needed. Dante was now barking orders at the others, dreading the call he was about to have to make.

"I feel for you, milord," Tomas said. "I would not want to be the one to call Silas and let him know the shit his little witch just pulled."

Dante had no words, so he chose not to acknowledge the comment. He was still too busy attempting to open the portal. *Apparently, Jadis is a quick learner*, he thought. *All this time, she has been studying me as much as I have been studying her.* She had used his own binding spell and turned it on him to keep him from sensing the portal. Just as he had done to her when he bound her stateroom door shut.

"Not to interrupt, milord," Paxil said. "Maybe you should make a call to Bain? He might be able to help? He's certainly had his fair share of run-ins with her."

As worked up as Dante was, he knew what Paxil said made sense. He also knew the longer he waited, the more danger Jadis, Skye, and Ivory were in. If anything happened to even one of the girls, it would likely be the death of them. He decided he couldn't hesitate any longer, and he made the call.

They arrived for their meeting in the Valley of the Old Gods just as planned.

Silas greeted Eden first, and grasped his forearm, "Eden, how are you?"

"Good, and you, Silas?" he asked, returning the gesture.

"I'm good. Everyone ready to do this?" Silas asked.

Despite the differences in their lifestyles, Eden and Silas were very close. Both were Lords of their clans and relied on one another for intel, missions, as well as other business that needed to be conducted. Both clans greeted one another and casually spoke amongst themselves while Silas, Aiden, and Eden were all business. They stood together in front of what should have been an oasis, waiting on the clans and covens joining them.

"Eden, did you give Jabari my orders?" Silas inquired, though he was already certain of the answer.

"Yes, they are all up to date and ready to do this," Eden answered.

"Good to know," Silas responded. After a momentary pause, Silas shot Aiden a mischievous grin. "How's Aria?"

"*How's* Jadis? You sure she's patiently waiting for you?" Aiden shot back, knowing she wouldn't be sitting around waiting on him.

Silas ignored the jab. *He isn't wrong after all.*

Aiden had met Aria on one of their missions just a month ago. She lived in the oasis they called Seba; she and her sisters were its keepers, a job that had been handed down from coven to coven since before the Great War had ended. Aria had allowed Aiden and his clan to stay with them during their most recent trips. They, too, were busy gathering information needed to address the Segan believed to live in the valley. They had also filled Aria and her coven in regarding the Baskale. Aria knew the creatures had been looking for another witch. They just didn't know who it might be, at least not until Aiden had told her about Jadis and her sisters. The way Aiden spoke about Jadis didn't sit well with Aria; she had taken more than a liking to Aiden.

The Nosferatu, many of whom had taken a witch as a mate, had also offered their allegiance to Silas and Eden. Altogether, between the vampires, witches, wizards, and healers, there were over a thousand of them, all currently living in the oasis.

Crows began circling above, beginning with just one, until there were six of them. The air ahead of them shimmered and morphed, and everyone lined up behind Aiden, Eden, and Silas.

The oasis formed and slowly appeared in front of them. Normally, one would have expected a tiny green spot being fed by a small, freshwater, underground spring. This oasis, however, grew until it had enveloped the entire group. Every warrior in the valley now stood in the middle of the most lush, fertile landscape they had ever seen. Most of whom had never seen the oasis since they weren't from the valley to begin with.

It was naturally beautiful, giving the appearance of having never been touched by a mortal hand. It was a refuge for the creatures calling it home. Butterflies filled the bushes with fluttering colors. Amphibians took their places amongst the abundance of plants and trees, while fish, reptiles, and crocodiles were the lifeblood of the flowing river. Various birds flew overhead; the crested wood partridge, violet turacos, and the blackest crows flew amongst the trees. This was no small oasis by any means. It stretched on for miles.

Off in the distance, they saw Aria, along with a large group, heading their way. Silas was the first to notice the look on Aiden's face.

"Looks like a little witch got you by the balls," Silas replied.

Aiden looked at Silas with a smirk. "I'm pretty sure you're not one to talk. At least I don't have Aria locked up."

"Touché." Silas chuckled.

Aria looked like Sebanian princess. She was beautiful, with jet-black hair that reached the middle of her back. She wore a faience beaded band around her head that looked as ancient as she did. Her long bangs were partially braided, and pulled back from her forehead, while the rest of her hair fell naturally around her shoulders. Sebanian tattoos lined her body, decorating her arms, chest, and legs. She wore a form-fitting cropped top made of leather and a matching skirt that stopped just short of her knees. The uneven cut of the skirt drew an onlooker's attention to the knee-high, lace-up leather flats adorning her lower legs and feet.

She looks like a warrior princess, no doubt about it, Silas thought.

Two daggers hung from each side of her hips in a nefer beaded belt. A golden bracelet in the shape of a scorpion wrapped around each of her biceps, their heads facing forward.

She approached the group and made her way to Aiden, who walked over to greet her. Everyone fell in line behind Aria's father, Jabari.

"Kayf halakum," Aria said to Aiden, with a smile larger than life.

"Afdal alan," Aiden responded.

He bent down to greet her with a hug. She wrapped her arms around his neck, and he picked her up and moved in for a kiss.

After a moment, Aiden set Aria down, and they joined the rest of the group. In the meantime, Jabari, Lord of the Sebanian clan, was greeting Silas and Eden.

"Ahlan wa sahlan, al nazafat hasharat jusasat dima!" Jabari declared. in his Iphenorian native language, as he turned to welcome Eden and Silas's clans. He stretched his arms outward in their direction as he repeated the phrase in their language. "Our oasis is yours. Please make yourselves at home."

"Are you going to be able to handle business and keep it in your pants?" Silas asked Aiden telepathically.

Aiden snarled back at him, *"I'm not even dignifying that with an answer."*

They were all in the valley for one reason, and one reason only; to take out the remaining Baskales they had finally located. The one that had come after Jadis on more than a few occasions was just one of many. If their calculations were correct, there were precisely fifty-three they were aware of. Most importantly, however, was their mission to destroy the one thousand-year-old legacy of terror.

They knew the hiding place of the Baskale already, having been back-and-forth from the area for the past few years, and each group had gathered as much information as possible and put it all together. Once it was deciphered, they were able to pinpoint and exact location.

As soon as they eliminated the Baskale, which they all hoped would be a relatively simple task, they could then go after the Segan. Based on their intelligence and the information they already had, the Segan should be alone following the destruction of its minions.

They began making their way to the Abal Simpel Temples, which would be the place they would launch their attack. Aria's coven was there to stay at ground level, and form a ring around the area to ensure nothing escaped. They would seal off the entire area in a bubble of sorts, preventing anything from getting in or out. They were all out to destroy the witch-hunting marauders; nothing came after one of their own.

Neither Aria nor anyone in her coven were the direct descendants of Hecate. They were, however, the direct descendants of the original covens. Even so, Aria and her sisters were ancient, and their magic was archaically powerful.

Aria and her sisters were shocked to find out three descendants of Hecate were alive and well. They had only heard rumors and stories many had shared. Aria, however, cared little for Jadis, regardless of who she was, given she had long ago tired of hearing Aiden speak of her.

The oasis disappeared back into the scorching red sands, as if it had never existed. Aiden and Aria walked together, separating themselves a few feet from the rest of the group so they could catch up with one another.

They expected they would have a relatively easy fight on their hands. The Baskale would not be armed; they never were. The Segan, however, carried weapons that were a threat to them all. The Baskale were nothing more than anthropomorphic slaves, doing the Segans' bidding.

A mortal would not stand a chance against them, but to the vampires, they were just an invasive species needing to be eliminated. Though they did not need such a large group to deal with them, Silas, Eden, and Jabari figured it would be the best course of action to have a legion of warriors, given the chance they might come across more than one Segan. They were making good time when Silas's phone suddenly rang. He and his brothers, along with Aiden, Eden, and Jabari, stopped mid-stride and looked at each other.

"This can't be good." Aiden chuckled, knowing who the call was regarding.

"Dante? Why the hell are you calling me, although I have a feeling this is about none other than Jadis?" Silas said.

Everyone on the mission was now intently listening to the call. Agaeus and Syth had joined Silas and stood directly in front of him.

"Jadis," Aiden mouthed to everyone, enjoying Silas's newfound problem. He had to turn away to hide his amusement, as did many of the others who knew the situation all too well.

Eden, sensing exactly what was up, motioned to Aria and Jabari to keep moving along with everyone else. They politely obliged, wanting to refrain from someone else's personal business.

"This is not a good call, Silas. Jadis and her sisters pulled some heavy shit today about an hour after you left the yacht." Dante said.

"Damn that girl!" Silas bellowed. "What am I going to have to do, chain her ass up? Hell, I'm going to do more than that. She has no idea what's coming for her sneaky little ass!"

"Good luck handling Jadis," Bain retorted to no one in particular, as he let go of his laughter. Bain turned to Aiden and Lars. "I think this girl might be the death of him."

Silas heard the off handed comment and snapped his head in their direction. Aiden, Bain, and Lars took heed and stepped a few feet away from Silas, based solely on the look he shot their way.

"Go on. What the hell is she up to now? And if you tell me you don't have eyes on her, I promise I will reach through this fucking phone and snap your neck." Nothing but silence followed.

"Dammit! She's not there, is she?" Silas snarled.

Silas was worried as hell, knowing the danger Jadis and her sisters could be in. Everyone around stepped closer to Silas. Their amusement succumbing to concern.

"No, we don't have eyes on them right now," Dante answered honestly. "But we are doing everything we can. We will have her back on the boat before you return tonight."

"What are you not telling me, brother? Out with it. I want the truth right now," Silas snarled, his voice raucous. Another long pause from Dante followed his words.

"Tell me," Silas demanded.

"I'm not sure how to say this—" Dante stopped there, knowing there wasn't any good way to inform him Jadis and her sisters have disappeared.

"Stop being evasive, Dante, out with it."

"Well, they slipped through a portal and have completely disappeared," Dante rumbled. He thought for sure once the words had escaped his mouth, Silas was really going to reach through the phone. All the warriors standing near Dante took one giant step back in unison, leaving him to deal with Silas alone.

Dante stood frozen, waiting for a response from Silas on the other end of the line.

"Gone? Completely gone? You can't sense her at all? Did you say they slipped through a portal and locked you out?" Silas questioned, sounding one step away from total rage.

Lars was laughing hysterically, repeating aloud the words he'd just heard, "She locked Dante and six warriors out! Sound familiar, Bain—Aiden—Anyone?"

The group didn't know if they should laugh along with Lars or share Silas's concern. Hell, they didn't know how to act right now. In all their years, none of them had ever come across such a formidable non-vampiric female.

"Yes, brother. Again, we are working on it, and we won't stop until we have them back," Dante replied.

Silas reached out and grabbed Lars by the throat and body slammed him onto his back. He snarled in his face and bared his canines; Lars held up his hands in a gesture of submission.

Eden spoke for the first time. "You're on your own, Lars. You deserve his wrath. You know better than to laugh in his face."

"Silas, I would like to talk with Bain," Dante requested.

Silas stood up, pulled Lars to his feet, and tossed him about ten feet away from where he stood before answering Dante. "So now you need Bain, brother? Is that your way of telling me you need backup? You can't hang on to three little witches? Backup—well, isn't that just fucking great. You need backup. What the hell do I need you for if Bain is so much more powerful?"

Bain was already speaking with Dante privately. *"Whatever you need, cousin, you've got it. I've been there and done that with her already."*

"I need her ass back before Silas gets here," Dante said, sounding desperate.

"No problem, we'll get it done." Bain was already looking at Eden.

Eden nodded in response. "We've got this. Go, get that headache back in safe-keeping before we lose Silas."

Bain silently chuckled and rubbed his forehead, waiting for Silas to give him the go ahead.

"So, tell me, Dante, just how are you locked out? It's just a goddamn portal. You should have been able to follow her in instantly, regardless of whatever shit she did. Nothing can stop you from passing through a fucking open portal. You have some serious explaining to do, and you better have a solid fucking reason for them getting anything past you."

"I can go over all of it with you later. Let's just focus on our immediate situation. We have already been trying for about an hour—"

Silas cut him off mid-sentence. "Did you say *an hour*?"

"Look, she had three dogs—" Dante began, before being interrupted again.

"Three dogs? You're telling me you're locked out because of a couple goddamn deceased mutts? That's your explanation?"

It suddenly dawned on Aiden. Jadis had the ashes, and she used them against Dante. *Damn she's good,* he thought. *She's impressive as hell.*

Eden was the only one who dared approach Silas. "I've already given Bain the go ahead. The two of them will have Jadis and her sisters back on the yacht in no time. If you want to go, we will all understand. No one's judging, and we can handle business here. If it were any of our mates, we would feel the same way."

Dante was listening intently to Eden, grateful for the temporary interruption.

Silas took in his words, carefully contemplating his next move. An odd feeling crept up from within. He was a cold-blooded Assassin, yet his heart belonged elsewhere. It was as if charging horses were pulling him in opposite directions, and he found himself caught between opposing needs; the need to annihilate his enemies and the need to find Jadis. Silas couldn't control the emotions he was feeling any more than he could alter the tides. He either had to leave his group here to deal with the Baskales, putting them in greater potential danger, or he had to leave Bain and Dante to tend to the chore of locating Jadis without him. He couldn't stop thinking of the danger she was in.

Silas looked over at Eden. "Your thoughts?" For the first time, Silas was at a loss. The power of a mate was like nothing else.

"I say give Dante and Bain a chance. If they don't have her back in an hour, we all go. We will leave behind Jabari and his clan, along with our warriors. They can handle this. Knowing what I know and based on what I've seen, I think Bain has enough of a grasp on Jadis's abilities the two of them, together, will get her ass back in one piece," Eden stated calmly.

Agaeus and Syth walked away, and headed for the yacht, feeling as torn as Silas. Silas looked at his brothers and ordered them to stay "Hold tight."

"Go," Silas barked toward Bain, hanging up on Dante. He looked at Eden. "Let's get this shit over with quickly. Fifty-three? We can take care of that in no time at all. After which, I'll have a little pain in the ass to contend with."

"That she is. More like a big old pain in the ass," Aiden offered. Silas ignored him as usual.

"Fifty-two," Eden corrected him. "Don't forget the one Aiden killed back at Jadis's cabin a few weeks ago."

CHAPTER 12

Bain suddenly materialized behind Dante. "So you have a little problem named Jadis on your hands?"

Dante turned to face him, looking like he wanted to murder someone. "I have three certain someone's to be exact," Dante corrected. "You have no idea what I'm up against right now."

"Unfortunately, I do, cousin. This is becoming an all-too-familiar occurrence. A couple of insolent little witches will not outdo us. They happened to catch you off guard; Jadis is known for doing that. Don't start thinking you're the first one she's disappeared from or angered, and I'm fairly certain you won't be the last." Bain chuckled, trying to help Dante calm down.

"You don't have to deal with Silas," Dante reminded him, with a look of dread written all over his face.

"No, but I had to deal with Aiden. Is one any easier than the other? Take your pick," Bain said, as he shrugged his shoulders.

Dante waved his hand. "It's not important at this point. Once we get ahold of them, they will be chained to us until Silas, Syth, and Agaeus return. I swear on the name of Nosferatu and all that is immortal. If it weren't for Silas, I'd put her ass over my knee and punish her in so many ways."

"Agreed." Bain chuckled. "I wouldn't mind smacking that ass myself, and in more ways than one."

Dante laughed aloud. "I don't disagree, but we'd better make sure Silas doesn't catch that thought." Dante then drug his finger across his throat.

"So, which one do you want to be chained to anyway?" Dante asked.

"If you're talking about being chained to Jadis, then we'll have to flip a coin. I'll take heads on a double-headed coin. We both know she's bringing discord wherever she travels. I'm understanding Eden's sudden onset of headaches," Bain joked.

Eden and Silas caught up with their group who were heading down the Nakele river, having put the recent phone call aside.

The ancient Ipheanors perceived their territory as comprising of two distinct regions. The first was Hodari, also known as the black land, denoting the fertile area surrounding the Nakele river. The second was Akmet, referred to as the red land, symbolizing the dry desert sands and scorching heat. The river, flowing through the two lands, was the lifeblood of all. They knew the Baskale would be in the red land; it was the perfect place for them to go undetected.

The clans made their way across the valley at lightning speed and stopped at the base of the rocky hills running north and south between the valley and the mountainous region, where the elevation rose abruptly from the Nakele river. The downward-sloping plateau would be the place where they would launch their attack.

"There it is," Jabari pointed at a structure barely visible, rising up just above the Ipheanor's Twin Temples. The temples were two massive rock formations which had originally been carved out of the mountainside.

In the center of the rocky formations stood a small form appearing to be part of the temples themselves.

"Is everyone ready?" Eden asked. "This is it. Once we surround the formation with our legions, we will split into three waves as planned. Do not deviate, understood?"

"Aye, milord," they replied in unison, along with a slight nod.

"Remember," Silas added, "whatever you do, don't look into the light radiating from their core. Some will have it, and some will not. Keep the solar blockers on at all times. If you look, you will be temporarily blinded and an easy target."

They had only heard of the radiant light through stories passed down over nine centuries. Although the warriors themselves had never witnessed it, they were equipped with powerful UV lenses. Once the two groups set out, they had only an hour of daylight remaining before the sun gradually disappeared below the horizon. Aware the Baskale hunted at night and would be inactive until well after their arrival, they held the advantage. Barring any unfortunate surprises, they should successfully accomplish their mission as planned.

Aria and her coven stayed on the outskirts and formed a circle around the formation. They chanted in unison and created an invisible barrier surrounding the entire area.

Eden took his clan north, around the face of the rock, and Silas took his south, while Jabari and his clan would surround the bottom before moving upwards toward Eden and Silas. They would blow the top of the main epicenter, which would send the Baskale scrambling in all directions; theoretically, they would become easy targets. Each clan had assumed their positions, encircling the structure and moving in perfect synchronization, reminiscent of a gyroscope.

Takat walked around the face of a rocky ledge scouting the cliff-side, when a lone Baskale lunged and knocked him to the ground on his back. Takat drove his Dragon Stone dagger deep into the its chest. Before it slumped over in a defeated heap, its piercing screeches would undoubtedly alert the rest of the Baskale to their presence. Takat tossed it aside before swiftly getting back to his feet. Two more appeared out of nowhere, having been alerted by the sounds of the first one they encountered. They attacked Takat, but he and the warriors with him were well-prepared, and easily eliminated the two additional Baskale.

Eden tossed the explosives onto the top of the rock formation while Silas threw his explosive from the other side. Together, they blew the main epicenter wide open. If the Baskale hadn't been fully aware of the warriors' presence beforehand, they were now. As the top blew open, boulders and pieces of metal debris crashed down from every side of the formation while the dust swallowed the clans, and billowing plumes of dark smoke swirled into the atmosphere.

Just as expected, the Baskale emerged, spilling over the top like ants from an anthill.

"Holy shit!" Silas yelled. "There are more than fifty-two! Who the fuck can't count? There's over three hundred of these motherfuckers!"

Every warrior sprinted to the cliffs, jumping, and leaping and they went. The fight became a choreographed dance of destruction.

Dante and Bain spent the next few hours working to open the portal back up. They had to figure out how to untwist the original spell Dante had used against Jadis and her sisters. Dante could have undone his own spell with little effort. However, Jadis made sure it was bound and twisted within theirs. It was tantamount to opening a puzzle box. However, despite their anger towards the girls for the stunts they had pulled, Dante and Bain were beyond impressed.

"Shit! It's working," Dante announced.

"I can feel the energetic shift. They cast their spells in old world Lati-vian. We just need to reverse it, and it should tear open," Bain instructed.

"You have no idea how much I want to get my hands on them," Dante reiterated, not able to quell his anger.

"Oh, I do."

"Be ready, warriors. The moment you see or feel the slightest tear, everyone needs to be ready to rush in, find them, and pull them out. Be prepared for anything, only the Gods know what those little hellions might have waiting for us, or what the fuck they have been up to," Dante ordered. "Make sure we not only open the portal entrance but take full control."

"Aye, milord," they stated in unison as they lined up, ready to leap in and do as instructed.

"Let's do this," Dante stated.

As they wove their own incantation, Dante and Bain attached them-selves to the girl's physical energy before opening the portal and began their incantation, repeating the words in succession three times, "Priori incantatem imperio."

The ground was damp, uneven, and woven with ancient tree roots, lit-tered with new as well as decaying foliage. They brushed it aside, having chosen the place they would create their circle. Jadis picked up a stick and drew a large outer circle, one that would surround the three of them.

She poured a mixture of her familiar's ashes and salt within the border to seal the outer ring. In the middle of the larger circle, they situated dead branches into the shape of a pentagon; in the center of the pentagon, Jadis sketched the intertwined faces of a goat and a bull with a branch. They each reached into their pockets and pulled out various herbs and crystals. They placed those in the center of the animals' faces covered them with a tepee made of small logs.

"That should do it," Jadis stated.

They knelt on the damp ground and chanted repetitiously, "Goddess Eternal to show us the way. We evoke thee, Mother Hecate, from the golden realm. Come. Appear before us, be here with us now. Inde animorum impetus excitetur in nobis Matrem deam Hecate," three times they continued.

They swirled their hands over the pit and the fire flickered and then flared with colorful forked flames leaping into a fiery dance. Dark smoke and glowing orange embers twirled above the flames and rose into the dense canopy. It wasn't long before a swift breeze swirled around the girls. Moments later, hovering above them, was the Witch Goddess herself, Hecate.

"My girls, what 'tis so important you summon me?"

"We have questions, mother," Jadis replied, knowing that calling upon Hecate was a rarity, and she was not very tolerant.

"What are thy questions? I hope you are not bothering me with unimportant matters?"

Jadis got right to the point, "The Three Keys, we are it?"

"Yes, my child, and you need to be prepared. Thy time is near," Hecate spoke, though not fully.

"What are we supposed to do? Is there a reason we are the keys?" Ivory questioned.

"Jadis, I bestowed you with my powers when I created you in my essence. You are now thy last of thy living who carries my magic. I bequeathed to you not riches, but thy spirit of reverence. There could be only one, and you are thy key to defeat thy vulgar savage who rampaged thy lands long ago. 'Tis waiting in hiding; thy battle 'tis nearly upon you. Fifty-three is misguided." Hecate's words seared deep.

"What battle? What do you mean *fifty-three is misguided*?" Jadis asked.

"When thy fight consumes you, you will need thy salve, and others," Hecate instructed. "Do not cower at its feet."

"What is it we are fighting?" Skye asked.

"You will know when thy time has come. Follow your intuition. Jadis, thy threat is upon you first and foremost. Bow to your third eye, for you are being hunted by thy licentious savage. They live without law and order, be wary."

"How do we stop it? Stop them?" Jadis asked again, feeling as if Hecate was speaking in riddles.

"When thy vortex appears to you, I will be waiting. 'Tis all I can offer."

Jadis glanced at Skye and Ivory. "Vortex? You mean the cave's vortex?"

"Yes. You have all adapted well, become masters of your own reality. Rely on your powers, your magic, and thy powers of Nosferatu. Reach deep. You already have thy answers for which you seek. You will know in due course. 'Tis ingrained in each of you. Trust yourselves and see past thy illusions. Use your divine intuition. Do not be fooled, thy universe is fickle. There will come a time when you, Jadis, will be torn between two realms, and you will need to choose. Choose wisely, my dear."

"I don't understand? What do you mean I will have *to choose*?" Jadis was now more confused than ever.

"You will know when thy time comes."

"Wait, what three others?" she demanded.

"Thy three you covet most."

"Silas and his brothers? Why did you take them from us?" *That much we have to know before losing her*, Jadis thought.

"'Tis trivial. You have been reunited. I will grant thy three of you permission under thy next Full Blood Moon to be mated. Now take heed, you are in grave danger, thy jungle hunts you."

The forked flames crackled and spit toward the sky, flashing into a wash of reds and oranges before bellowing into a dark, twisting plume of black smoke rising into the canopy. Hecate was gone, leaving riddles as usual.

"Well, that's always fun. Fifty minutes of preparation for a twenty-minute conversation. Typical," stated Ivory, annoyed, as always, with their mother's evasiveness.

"Anyone else really uncomfortable right now besides me? I think I have more questions than I had before," Jadis admitted.

"Yes. You and me both," Skye answered. "Let's get the hell back to the yacht. I can't believe Dante hasn't arrived yet."

Jadis felt the anxiety and dread of having to face Dante.

"Who are *the others*? *Fifty-three is misguided*? What the hell?" Ivory questioned.

"I don't know. Why can't we ever get a straight answer? It's annoying as hell. If she would just tell us, it would make things so much easier. Although I'm praying the *more than fifty-three* aren't more Baskales I have a terrible feeling, going all the way back to when Aiden and his family wouldn't let me leave. If Aiden killed the only one, then why did they keep me?" Jadis questioned.

Skye answered, "I was thinking the same thing. The feeling you had earlier is really creeping me out now, not to mention what the fuck was that about, *the Jungle is hunting you*? Let's get the hell out of here—and now." Skye was already getting up.

As Jadis walked away, she glanced at the ashes and noticed a small tin laying in the center of the goat's face. *What's this?* She thought. She looked back at Skye and Ivory who were already walking away. She shoved it into the pocket of her jeans and quickly hurried to her sister's side, not wanting to be left alone.

They ran down the path to the entrance of the portal, but they had only made it about halfway when they stopped mid-stride, having felt a sudden chill searing through each of them.

The jungle roared. The monkeys were howling and barking, jumping up and down in the trees, and shaking the branches violently.

"It's a warning. We are being hunted," Jadis whispered. But she had no idea who or what it was. "I feel like I'm about to be bludgeoned to death!"

They stood and looked all around for the looming threat. "A Baskale! Run!" Jadis suddenly yelled.

Out of nowhere, Skye was pulled from behind by her hair. She screamed, having been knocked to the ground on her back with it hovering over her. It was massive, just as Jadis had remembered. She could see its coal-black, round eyes, and searing red corneas. It's body was grotesque, covered in pulsing, slimy scales that gave off a putrid odor. Its skin is a sickly shade of gray, with sharp spines jutting out and oozing a venomous substance. The smell emanating from is a combination of rot and decay.

As it loomed over Skye, brownish, rotten mucus dripped from its torso and every acidic drip burned away at her t-shirt. The rancid stench was nauseating.

Jadis and Ivory ran toward Skye, and they were both knocked back with a swipe of its long, slim, bug-like appendage. Skye and Jadis swirled their fists and sent it flying backward with an energetic blow to its body. They scrambled to their feet and ran further into the jungle.

"If we make it to the portal, the last thing we needed is to provide it with a passageway to us!" Jadis yelled.

They had no idea of its power, or what it was capable of, or how it located them on the island in the first place. Most importantly, they needed a place to hide in order to figure out what to do. They followed the sounds of the animals in the jungle as they ran for their lives. The branches closed in behind them as if the Jungle itself was trying to block its path. The brush grew thicker, but the creature easily crashed through it.

Three leopards appeared before Jadis, Skye, and Ivory as if waiting for them. As soon as the girls were in the leopards' line of sight, they ran.

"Follow them!" Jadis yelled. She, Skye, and Ivory changed direction and followed.

Running frantically, Jadis stumbled over the uneven, root laden ground, losing her balance long enough for the Baskale to grab her. It yanked her back so hard, it lifted her backward off of her feet. It then slammed her face first into the ground with such force it took her a minute to gather her senses.

Hecate said it wanted me; this means it will not kill me? If I stay with it, Ivory and Skye can gather their thoughts, she said to herself as she let it drag her down the path.

Skye and Ivory slowly followed Jadis and the creature. "Jadis, when we say now, get up and run!" Skye demanded.

"Hurry!" Jadis screamed.

They pulled deep from within the earth, summoning all the power they possessed, and hit it mentally. The Baskale roared as it released the grasp it had on Jadis's hair and spun around, thrashing its appendages wildly.

Jadis jumped up and ran like hell. It was once again closing in, but this time, two of the leopards attacked it, one on either side. The Baskale struck them, sending them tumbling through the jungle.

As they continued running, they heard the leopard's roars and the snapping of branches. They made it to the path leading to the cave they had discovered earlier. The sounds of the brush crunching behind them let them know it was giving chase again. The leopards moved swiftly enough to surround it, allowing the girls time to gain some distance. From what they could gather at that moment, it appeared to be easily distracted. It seemed to be more interested in fighting than chasing them. They continued to run to the mouth of the cave, knowing it was the only place they could truly blend in and hide.

The leopards were still circling the creature. One of them leapt onto it from behind and sunk its canines deep into the nape of its neck. The creature flung its appendages wildly, but could not reach behind itself to grab the attacking leopard as it lacked the dexterity of a human. The second and third leopards attacked as well, one from either side. They tore at its throat and ripped off an appendage.

The screeching sound it made was exactly what Jadis had heard the night Aiden had killed the one at her cabin. *That sound,* she thought. It had haunted her ever since she had first heard it.

The girls made it to the cave and hunkered down inside, deciding what to do next. As they crouched together, they heard a horrible roar.

"What are we going to do now?" Skye questioned.

After taking a few moments to catch her breath. Jadis whispered, "Think, we need something!" She was mostly talking to herself aloud when it dawned on her. "What Hecate said—hide!"

"Hide?" Ivory was looking at Jadis like she had lost her goddamn mind. "Hide where? Like behind a fucking rock or how about we just stand behind a tree? How hard did you hit your fucking head back there?"

"Listen, dammit, Silas's story, take on its essence, Hide, blend in, the shelf in the cave— go!" Jadis shoved them both in front of her, when suddenly, she was pulled by her ankle.

With its remaining appendage, the Baskale flung Jadis from the mouth of the cave and sent her plummeting into the trees. Ivory and Skye were now trapped in the cave, with it blocking their only way out.

Jadis was too stunned to move. The blow had knocked the wind out of her and she felt a searing pain radiate across her rib cage. She lay there, trying to muster the energy to get up.

Ivory and Skye quickly chanted. "Per dimidium conscidisti. Per dimidium conscidisti. Per dimidium conscidisti."

The Baskale shook violently, and feverishly twisted its decrepit body. The more they chanted, the more the brownish, rotten substance seeped from its body. It jumped into the air and disappeared within the canopy.

Ivory and Skye ran out of the cave, and after helping Jadis up, they ran back inside, crawled under the ledge, and hid. They lay there, concentrating silently in order to take on its essence as a chameleon does with its surroundings.

Become it, Jadis said to herself. She pulled the small dagger from her waistband and nodded at Skye and Ivory.

"When it comes back, Jadis, strike. You've got to hit it right in the chest," Skye stated.

They chanted in unison in order to blend into the surrounding environment. "Faciesque in, faciesque. Faciesque in, faciesque. Faciesque in, faciesque."

It was as if they had removed the Baskale's own skin and put it on. They heard it rush back into the cave. It let out a deafening roar, tossed rocks, and scratched at the dirt. It knew they were there, but it couldn't see them. It became increasingly angry and volatile, and it slammed its remaining appendage on the rocky shelf above the girls. The blow sent rocks and debris flying throughout the cave and raining down around them.

Jadis jumped up and shoved her dagger directly into its chest. It flung itself around wildly, screeching that ear-piercing sound Jadis had become all too familiar with.

Jadis twisted the blade and it sent her flying into the jagged wall before it fell limp..

"Jadis!" Ivory yelled as she ran to her.

"Are you sure it's dead?" Jadis asked.

The three of them remained motionless, not wanting to take a chance on moving away from it, and weren't about to turn their backs to it until they were sure it was indeed dead.

Ivory and Skye grabbed Jadis's arms and helped her up. "Are you okay?" Skye asked.

"For the most part," Jadis replied.

They then stood in a circle around its lifeless body, lit it on fire, and waited until there was nothing left but ash. They then blew the ash out of the cave into the cool evening air. The girls limped out of the cave, thinking about what had happened and how close to death they had come.

"It's gone. We owe the jungle a big thank you." Jadis cautiously looked around just in case it wasn't the only one there.

"Yes it is and yes we do," Skye agreed.

"The animals are returning to normal," Ivory mumbled.

The energy in the Jungle felt calm once again. Jadis called out and the three leopards appeared out of the dense landscape and cautiously approached them. The girls kneeled down and felt their bodies for injuries, healing whatever wounds they had sustained. The leopards butted foreheads with the girls before they leapt away, disappearing back into the brush.

"I don't know about either of you, but I'm ready to get back to the boat and now," Ivory stated.

"I think I'm going to get a hotel room. I'm not sure I want to see Silas. I guarantee Dante has told him we are missing." Jadis held her ribs; even breathing was becoming painful.

"Hotel it is," Skye agreed. "I don't think any of us want to face our vampires tonight."

They nervously chuckled and limped their way back to the portal's entrance. They heard a noise behind them and started running despite their injuries and the pain. After what they'd been through, they weren't about to take any chances, even if they were running from a falling rock or a bunch of monkeys. Regardless, they felt as if we were being chased again, and Ivory started screaming.

As they ran, they felt themselves being pulled down the path but could not stop the force. They floated just above the ground, feeling powerless to do anything. "What the fuck is happening?" Ivory yelled.

"Dante!" Jadis stated.

Just as they were pulled into the portal's opening, they shouted, "Portal prope ianuam!" Sealing the portal behind them.

CHAPTER 13

Dante and Bain stood on the deck, prepared for the girls to appear while the rest of the warriors lined up behind them.

"We got them!" Dante announced.

"We sure do. Be ready," Bain replied.

The air before them rippled, and slight a tear in the atmosphere appeared. At that moment, the three sisters came flying through the opening and came crashing down onto the deck of the yacht.

"Holy shit!" Tomas yelled.

They had all drawn their weapons and stared at the girls who now lay on the deck in a tangled heap, not knowing what to expect.

The girls gathered themselves together as much as they could. When they looked up, they found six fully armed warriors all aiming their weapons at them, along with the bewildered stares of Dante and Bain.

Jadis looked at Dante. "Hey," was all she said.

They thought they could sneak back into their cabins and hide. It was a big mistake to not plan their return well enough, if at all. It infuriated Jadis that Silas had Dante lock them down, so she focused more on getting out rather than returning.

Jadis looked around again and realized the second wizard was Bain.

"Bain? What the hell are you doing here?" she asked.

Bain knelt down and whispered, "Someone's in trouble." He then stood and stepped back.

"*Hey*? That's all you've got to say?" Dante roared. "And what the hell happened to you? The three of you look like you've been in a goddamn street fight. Fuck, Jadis, what happened to your ribs? I can feel it. You and Skye are bleeding. Ivory is covered in scrapes and bruises. Her clothes are torn—" He stopped mid-sentence, "Skye, are those burn holes in your shirt? What the hell have the three of you been doing? Jadis, if Silas were here right now—" he stopped there and threw his hands up in exacerbation. He pushed his hair back from his forehead with both hands and interlaced his fingers together on the back of his head. He stood motionless, staring at the mess laying on the deck before them.

The girls sat as still as frozen corpses, and the warriors remained standing in a circle around them with a look of shock, as they stared at the girls' disheveled appearance.

The warriors waited for their orders, yet no one spoke. They had re-holstered their weapons, and were no longer pointing them at the girls, but they didn't know what to think.

The smoldering anger underneath the hardened expression on Dante's face terrified the girls.

Dante let go of his head and placed his hands on his hips. Jadis looked at the Glock on his hip and couldn't help but to think about Silas and the danger he may be in, despite the shit they had just been through.

Dante was still trying to figure out his next move and dreading the inevitable phone call he had to make. *At least this time,* he thought, *I can tell Silas the girls are safe and sound.* However, he couldn't help but fear what Silas's reaction might be to the way they looked once he saw that picture. *Shit! Silas is going to lose his mind over this.*

As a last-ditch effort, Jadis looked at Bain for help, but she should have known better.

"You brought this shit on yourself, darling. And now, you get to deal with the consequences. This is going to be very, very entertaining." Bain leaned against the deck railing, crossed his arms and legs, and waited for the show to begin. "By the way," he added, as he looked directly at Jadis, "I'm not leaving."

Even though Jadis wanted to tell him to wipe that smug smile off his face, all she did was sneer at him and squint her eyes.

Dante knelt in front of Jadis and grabbed her jaw.

Shit, that hurts like hell, she thought, but she wasn't about to say a damn word.

Dante moved her head from side to side, taking in all the wounds she'd suffered, including the gash on the side of her face that was still bleeding. He let go of Jadis's jaw with a vast sigh as he continued kneeling in front of her.

Jadis tried to scoot back; she couldn't breathe in his presence. It was as if his anger were suffocating her.

Dante moved to Skye and Ivory, assessing all their injuries, and making sure nothing was life threatening before he made the subliminal call to Silas, Agaeus, and Syth. Their disheveled appearance was not the picture he had hoped to project. *Hell, it might be better to let them shower and put some clean clothes on first.*

"Bad idea," Bain said calmly. "He'll smell it anyway, if he hasn't already. Don't hide anything. They're big girls with big magic. They can handle the brothers."

Jadis felt the direct jab, knowing Bain also knew how afraid she was of seeing Silas.

"Finding this amusing? Don't be an ass, Bain, you have no idea what just happened!"

Bain uncrossed his arms and legs and pushed himself off the railing.

Yep. Keeping my mouth shut would have been the wise thing to do. The way Skye and Ivory glared at her confirmed it.

Skye was terrified. "Jadis, shut up right now," she demanded. "This is a terrible situation, and you're not helping matters. I already feel like a goat in a dragon's lair."

"Have you looked at yourself, my dear girl?" Bain growled, having fully 'turned'.

If he is doing it to intimidate me, it sure as hell is working, Jadis thought.

He knelt down in front of Jadis, and Dante moved to the side to allow Bain to move in closer. He quickly seized her attention. "You, my dear girl, have an extraordinary knack for vanishing. In our world, there are dire consequences for such behavior. Up until now, you have come out relatively unscathed. This time, however, you have taken it too far. You realize you are dealing with Silas rather than Aiden now, right? My God, the three of you look like you have been dragged through purgatory!" he paused briefly. "By the way, what is that smell?"

The girls looked at each other but didn't speak. The last thing Dante and Bain needed to find out was that they had a bit of an altercation with a Baskale and they almost met an untimely death.

Well, Skye and Ivory almost died. I was just going to be kidnapped by a fucking monster, Jadis said to herself.

Bain grabbed Jadis's jaw in his hand and bent his head toward hers. He leaned in and took in the scent. He slid his face up the side of hers, from her neck to her forehead.

"Holy shit! Please tell me it's not what I think it is. Dante," he snarled.

Dante was immediately kneeling in front of Jadis, also having grabbed her jaw in his hand. He smelled her in the same way Bain had, before moving to Skye and Ivory to do the same.

Bain and Dante stood and looked at each other. Something flashed beneath the surface of their frozen expressions at the realization of where the smell had come from.

"They know," Jadis said telepathically.

"Shit!" Skye stated.

Ivory laid her head on her knees, rocking it from side to side. She wrapped her arms tightly around her legs and pulled her knees close to her chest.

Skye turned ashen and covered her face with both hands, and rested her elbows on her knees.

I have one of two choices; vomit or run, Jadis thought. She was so terrified, she impulsively tried to jump over the railing and into the water. She instinctively responded to the looming threat before thinking.

Dante had her wrapped in his arms before she'd made it a foot off the deck. He held her in front of himself as Bain moved in close and stood in her face.

"Well, well, well. It seems someone can't stay put. Whatever are we going to do with her?" Dante asked Bain.

"Not sure yet. I think it's time to talk with Silas, Agaeus, and Syth. We'll let them decide."

"Tell me, my little escapee," Dante snarled, "how did you get away from the Baskale? I assume it's why the three of you look like you've danced with the devil?"

Jadis looked at Skye and Ivory, trying to get them to come up with something, but Dante chimed in, "We can hear you." He raised his eyebrows at Jadis and bared his fangs. "My patience is wearing thin—very thin, in fact."

He still had her wrapped tightly in one arm while the warriors surrounded Skye and Ivory. Not one of took their eyes off of the girls.

Bain stood next to Dante, clearly in support of what Dante was about to say and or do.

"Speak now, Jadis, and not one false word. You've got two seconds to explain before I take the information myself. Do you understand what I'm saying?" Dante warned.

Jadis didn't know where to begin. She again looked at Ivory and Skye for help, but Bain grabbed her face and turned it back toward himself and Dante.

"Do not look at your sisters. We would like to hear this directly from you, dear girl." Bain was expecting nothing less than a smart-ass remark as he waited for her to answer him.

If I reveal the truth, I'm up shit's creek, she thought.

"Something about *shit's creek*?" Bain relayed aloud to Dante.

"We only want the truth, and by the way, you can no longer keep us out of your thoughts," Dante informed her.

This just keeps getting better and better, she thought. She could tell Skye was about to cry, and she started chuckling out of sheer nervousness, and the thought of either of her sisters crying. She couldn't help herself.

Skye and Ivory had the same reaction when they heard Jadis chuckle in Bain's and Dante's face.

At least they can keep their faces covered to hide their giggling. I, of course, am not so lucky being in my current position, Jadis thought.

"I see you find this amusing?" Dante snarled. Jadis's reaction didn't sit well with him, and he picked her up and carried her to Silas's office to take the information he wanted. "I am tired of your fuckery!"

Yep, she thought. *He's had enough.* She tried to break free, to no avail. "I'm sorry. I didn't mean to laugh. It just came out." Jadis did her best to sound sincere.

"As will the information—the hard way." Dante was also being sincere as he continued to carry her away, with Bain following closely behind.

Bain turned to the warriors, who were guarding Skye and Ivory. "If those two so much as move, chain them, and use the ones we gave you," he ordered.

"Aye, milord. They won't move." Tomas looked at Skye and Ivory, asking, "You won't move now, will you, lass?" They looked back at him and shook their heads no.

Dante tossed Jadis onto the chair in the office, placed both hands on either armrest, and leaned her so far back she thought she was going to tip over backward. Bain tossed Dante a wet hand towel from the office sink and sat on the corner of the desk with his arms crossed.

Dante handed the towel to Jadis, which she barely reached for. "Now wipe both the blood and the laughter from your face."

The smell of the thick, crimson liquid dripping down her face was causing reactions in Dante's body he was struggling to control. He stood fixated on the throbbing pulse in her throat.

Bain knew how Dante might react, which was just one of many reasons he stayed around. However, he enjoyed the situation entirely too much.

Jadis caught a feeling Bain wanted her to keep trying to push her luck with Dante for his own entertainment.

"Dante," Bain called, in order to pull his fixation away from her throat.

"Speak now," Dante demanded, only inches from her face.

"Okay Dante. Calm down. I don't know where to start or what to say." Jadis raised her eyebrows, not knowing where to begin.

"Start at the beginning. How about that?" he snarled.

"Seriously? The beginning—like all of it?" She wasn't trying to be a smart ass; it was just such a long story.

"Are kidding me?" He looked at Bain as he took his hands off the arms of the chair, letting Jadis fly forward; she barely caught herself.

"Is she always this difficult? I need some goddamn answers. I'm the one who has to call Silas!"

Bain rubbed his temples. "From what I've seen so far, yes, she is."

Dante turned back to Jadis, and the look on his face told her to speak and now.

"Fine!" she snapped. "But it was your dumb ass who locked us up in the first place, remember that?"

Dante cocked his head, and his eyes swirled with anger.

Jadis realized if she was going to save her own ass, insulting Dante was not the best idea.

Bain subtly covered his mouth, trying to hide the laughter brewing up. He couldn't get over the fact Jadis had just called Dante a dumb ass. *This girl must have a serious death wish,* he thought.

Based solely on how Dante tilted his head at her remark, she took a deep breath and tried to begin from the start. "We had to get some answers. You had locked us up so tight we didn't have a choice but to do what we did. Everyone knows my sisters and I are the keys, yet you all think you can keep the truth from us until you're ready to talk about it." She went on and explained a bit more, though not in great detail. She hoped it was enough to satisfy them. "We only planned on being gone for a couple of hours, but things took a turn for the worse as we tried to make our way back."

Dante motioned his hand toward her, "Continue, the smell on you is from a Baskale—yes? It found you?"

"Yes, but we killed it, so really, it's all good." Jadis started to get up, but Bain then stood.

He and Dante each put a hand on either of her shoulders and held her in the chair. They stared at each other in disbelief.

Jadis was trying to hear what they were saying. However, they were blocking her out. Their expressions alone were enough to make her feel as though she was about to end up in the gallows.

"So just like that, the three of you killed a Baskale? No big deal?" Dante questioned, being facetious.

"Well, sort of, yes. I mean, it didn't happen right away. It took us a minute. Really, we are all fine, so can I go?" Jadis was stumbling for words; nothing came out the way she had intended.

Dante and Bain squeezed her shoulders and closed their eyes. Suddenly, a nauseating wave of energy hit her, and she felt a searing, stabbing pain shooting through her head before everything blurred. As she faded in and out of consciousness, she assumed they were taking all the information she had failed to provide.

They wanted to see every detail of the entire day. Once they finished, all Jadis could make out was them saying to each other how bad the situation they had put themselves in had been.

Dante had to carry Jadis back out to the deck. He laid her on one of the leather benches before he looked at Ivory. "She's next."

"Next for what? My ass!" Ivory slapped Dante's hand, but he grabbed her up off the deck and carried her into the office with Bain. There was no more time for playing around, and Skye was next.

Once they took all they needed from the girls, Dante decided it was time they made the psychic call to Silas. "They have to know they may be facing more Baskales than expected."

"Let's do it," Bain agreed. "Everyone needs to know all of it. We can't leave out one minor detail. How those three are even still alive, I'll never know."

Eden's clan began slaughtering Baskale after Baskale. The creatures spilled out from the main epicenter and frantically scrambled down the side of the formation, their awkward bodies crashing into each other and the warriors.

One of which attacked from behind, lunging for Eden. It knocked him forward while two more attacked from either side. Eden spun around and slid backward. He swiveled his sword and landed a deadly blow with his blade to the Baskales on either side of him, spinning from one to the other. He then spun around again and swiftly beheaded the one attacking him from behind.

Another came toward him, and he swiftly lunged forward, thrusting his sword ahead. He pierced its chest just as another lunged. Eden dodged to the side in one fluid move. The Baskale swiveled in his direction, but Eden moved fiercely around its back, striking with deadly force. He was a master swordsman and he manipulated the sword effortlessly; it was a bloodstained instrument of justice.

His clan continued the assault and the more Baskale they defeated at the top, the fewer the warriors in the center would have to deal with, and even less at the bottom. The Baskale continued to move down the rocky formation in droves.

Silas and his group could take them out easily once he figured out how to mind-bend them. The only downside was he had to be in close, too close for comfort. Given he had had no practice in mind-bending the creatures, he had to put himself in the direct line of fire. Once positioned in the center of two or three, he could force them to turn on each other, which allowed the other warriors to strike multiple targets at once.

Each time they killed particular Baskale, the luminescent light radiated outward like electrical bolts of energy.

"Turn them against each other! Once they are distracted, take them out!" Silas shouted out the order to his clan.

"Got it," Syth answered, as he slit another one open from nape to neck.

"Oh shit!" Agaeus shouted as he dodged two more and struck them down.

Zach went tumbling backward down the formation, when a group of Baskale lunged at him at once. One attacked him head-on, slicing his face, while another slit his thigh. Zach was able to fend them off until three other warriors rushed to his side. One of them grabbed Zach, pulling him from beneath the pile of Baskale.

Another warrior slit the neck of one of the oncoming creatures; its head rolled off its shoulders as its body slumped to the saturated, blood-stained ground.

"You upright, Zach?" Kane called out.

"Aye, already healing. Merci, brother!" Zach replied as he wiped the blood from his face. He suddenly shoved Kane to the side and drove his blade into the chest of a Baskale approaching Kane from behind.

Seemingly out of nowhere, another burst out from the center of the rock, throwing itself at Silas, who swiftly evaded the attack. He grabbed the Baskale by the throat and the center of its chest split open; a light radiated outward along with two bug-like appendages, reaching out for him. Silas reached into the back of his belt and pulled out a larger Dragon Stone dagger; and plunged it into the middle of its chest cavity, causing it to slump over with a mind-numbing screech. He withdrew his hand and forearm from the grotesque wound and tossed the body out of his way before taking out three more in one swift spinning move.

Out of his peripheral vision, Syth, who was fighting next to Silas, noticed two more approaching from behind. He spun around and brought his sword across one of their necks, recoiled his blade and plunged into the other's chest. "I got your back, brother."

Dante suddenly interrupted Silas's thoughts. *"I have the girls, but you need to know there are more than fifty-three Baskale. You're heading into a nest!"*

"Too late. We already figured that out. Jadis, is she okay?"

"She's fine."

"That's a huge relief, but I don't have time to speak right now. We're a bit tied up."

"Be careful, brother."

"Always. Syth Agaeus, you hear that?"

"Yes," they replied in unison.

Agaeus felt a tremendous sense of relief. *"Let's get this shit done. I need to see Ivory for myself,"* he said telepathically.

Eden felt the relief wash over Silas and his brothers. *"At least* they're are safe. *Too bad we didn't get the heads up on the nest earlier!"*

"It doesn't matter now, let's move. I need to get my hands on Jadis." Regardless of the shit she pulled, he was completely relived Dante had her.

The girls woke up, and they were on the middle deck of the boat with searing migraines and the warriors surrounding them.

Dante and Bain had laid them down on the plush furniture, providing a softer place for them to recover.

At least they put us in the shade, Jadis thought. She had expected to wake up in the middle of the deck, in the same place they had originally crash landed. Jadis assumed the conversation with Silas, Agaeus, and Syth was painful, but before she had finished her thought, Dante and Bain appeared.

Dante approached Jadis. "I see you're awake?"

Yep, this is it, she thought. *It's our final moment before being forced to walk the plank.* Skye and Ivory scooted as close to Jadis as they could get.

"I'm thinking more like shark bait," Dante replied as he looked at Bain, who shrugged his shoulders.

Jadis forgot about that little tidbit of information; they were no longer communicating privately, on any level.

"How are the headaches, girls? We tried to do this the easy way. You can also forget about self-healing; it's not happening either. There are three Nosferatu Assassins who are fit to be tied and want to see you just as you are," Dante stated.

"*Fit to be tied*? I would say more like furious." Bain chuckled.

They continued looking at each other, making jokes at the girls' expense. Once they turned their attention back to them, Bain looked at Jadis. "Have you ever seen a mate whose patience has been tested and tried?"

None of the girls spoke, they just stared at Dante and Bain with their arms crossed with one another's.

"One word comes to mind; Mortem," Dante stated. He looked at Bain and then back at the girls and laughed.

"I think I'd rather be shark bait," Bain replied, laughing as well.

"What the hell is Mortem?" Jadis asked Skye and Ivory silently; well tried to anyway. Skye and Ivory shook their heads, not knowing what *Mortem* meant, either.

"We may have underestimated the three of you, but the three of you have mistakenly misjudged us," Dante said, as he pointed his finger at each of them.

I feel like a child that's been caught sneaking out, Jadis thought.

"In essence, that's pretty much what we did," Skye replied.

Dante continued to correct them, "We have been doing this for—I don't know, what—about six hundred plus years? The three of you are one hundred and seventy-three, tops. Is that about right, Bain?"

Dante is clearly trying to point out that we are not only weak, but just babies compared to the two of them, Jadis thought.

"Yes, but I think fifteen might be more fitting, given your behavior lately, Jadis," Bain said, addressing her directly.

This is getting seriously annoying, she thought. Everywhere they tried to go with their thoughts, Dante and Bain were there to intervene.

"See those pretty little anklets you're each wearing? Consider this house arrest," Dante said.

They looked down at their ankles, noticing the bracelets for the first time. They had awakened with what felt like hangovers from hell, all the while being guarded by six fully armed warriors. All of this had been followed by a one-sided conversation the three of them had tired of long ago. They hadn't even noticed the anklets until Dante pointed them out.

Jadis studied the anklet and noticed the writing on them was from another place and time altogether. There were symbols etched into each one of them she didn't understand. *They have forged these using powerful sorcery. Dante and Bain look all too proud of themselves. Our situation is not headed in a good direction,* Jadis thought

"Not for you anyway, but it's headed in the perfect direction for us," Dante chimed in.

Jadis quickly tired of Dante and Bain taunting them, but she didn't get the chance to open her mouth before Dante was hovering directly over her, mere inches from her face. He placed his finger over her lips and pushed her backward onto the chaise lounge. Ivory and Skye quickly slid over, leaving Jadis to Dante.

"I can and will place one of those over your pretty little mouth if needed," Dante snarled.

Jadis placed her palms on his chest, trying to hold him back. However, he grabbed her wrists and pinned them above her head.

She heard Bain chuckling, but she dared not speak again; they had been rendered speechless.

My sisters and I have been through way too much today. We are scared of what we have seen, scared of all that transpired in the jungle, and scared we came far too close to losing our lives. If we think this situation with Dante and Bain are bad, I can't imagine what it will be like to explain ourselves to Silas, Syth, and Agaeus, Jadis thought.

"Get up," Dante demanded.

Dante and Bain escorted Jadis, Skye, and Ivory to their staterooms. Dante stopped and ordered the warriors to take their designated positions.

He then turned to address the girls. "This is how it's going to be until our brothers' return. The three of you will stay in your designated staterooms. There will be two guards for each of you. Ivory and Skye, the two of you will share a room. Jadis, you will be in your room alone."

"Why am I alone?" Jadis asked.

"What Silas wants, Silas gets. Anymore stupid questions? Now move," Dante ordered.

Ivory and Skye moved immediately and were escorted to their rooms by four warriors. Jadis moved slower, feeling the pain that had set in hours ago.

"Not so fast." Bain placed a hand on her shoulder and held her in place. He pulled a coin out of his pocket. "Heads or tails? Your call, Dante."

"Heads!"

Bain flipped the coin, and it landed on tails. He tossed the coin at Dante. "She's all yours." Bain chuckled.

Jadis made her way into the stateroom while two guards stood on either side of the door. She walked in, and as she turned to close the door, but Dante held it open with the palm of his hand. "You can't be trusted, so I'll be staying until Silas returns."

"You've got to be kidding me. You are not staying in here, Dante!"

"The hell if I won't," Dante rumbled. "We have our orders, and you are as far from being trustworthy as anyone could get."

"Well, if your little anklet is so amazing, what do you need to be here for?" she snarked, realizing she was poking the bear.

"After everything that has happened, are you seriously trying to bait me right now?"

Bain telepathically broke into Dante's argument with Jadis. *"I am so glad I won the coin toss. Enjoy the rest of your night."* He chuckled, feeling relieved. *"These two are like a couple of tamed little kittens."*

"Yes, and I have the mouth of the tiger to contend with," Dante grumbled, as he looked at Jadis.

"I know that feeling all too well. I'm going to need a drink later, if Silas doesn't have your head on a stake," Bain joked.

"I'm going to need the entire bottle after a few hours of babysitting Jadis."

Jadis picked up some of her belongings and headed to the shower. She no longer wanted to entertain them or add to their amusement. Dante suddenly snagged the belongings out of her hand.

"What the hell are you doing? Give me my shit!"

"Sorry darling, whatever you need is already in the bathroom, anything else you can do without."

Is this really happening? She tried to grab for her clothes, but Dante was too quick. He tossed them onto the table on the other side of the room. Jadis stepped forward and gave him a hard shove.

He grabbed her hands, spun her around, and held her tightly against his body. "If it weren't for Silas, I would punish you for that," he snarled. "We can do this for the next few hours if you want, or you can get your dirty little ass in the shower to try to soothe those aches and pains. Those ribs don't look so good, and you won't be healing yourself anytime soon. You seem to have forgotten."

"What do you mean?" She asked.

He released his grip and pointed to her ankle, and she failed to come up with a response. Instead, she walked away and shut the bathroom door behind her. She stood under the hot water for forty minutes; it felt amazing until a sudden rush of Deja vu engulfed her. *I feel like I'm back in the guest bathroom at Aiden's the night I tried to run from him. Shit, at this point I would prefer Eden and Aiden to Dante any day. What have I gotten myself into now? And Silas? I really don't want to think about that confrontation.*

Jadis got out of the shower with the towel wrapped around her and sat on the toilet lid; it hurt too much to stand. She tried to dry off her hair as best she could with another towel. She looked over her body and noticed the bruising was becoming quite apparent. They were especially noticeable around her ribs. She was also thinking about what to say to

Silas that might help to calm him down. *Shit, I don't even know him well enough to know where to begin.*

She finished towel drying her hair and got dressed in the matching satin shorts and tank top that had been laid out for her.

The boat rocked back and forth, which made it hard for her to keep her balance in her physical condition. She stepped out of the bathroom, hoping Dante had been joking around earlier, but there he was, completely relaxed in the chair, with a highball glass in his hand, and full decanter on the table.

"There's something for you to eat and a drink on the table, along with a couple of pills for your pain. I assume you're hungry?" he stated as he motioned toward the table with his glass.

Jadis wasn't the least bit hungry and it was the last thing she was thinking about. She sat down at the table opposite Dante and swallowed the pills without speaking.

Dante casually filled both of their glasses again and stared at her, thinking about how she looked sitting in nothing more than a silk top and a pair of matching shorts.

She pushed the plate aside and pulled one knee up to her chest to alleviate some of the discomfort.

"What, no smartass remarks?" He smirked.

"Why? You looking to start a fight?"

"Haven't you had enough fighting for one day? Don't you ever get tired? Shit, you make me tired just listening to you." He chuckled.

"You're such a funny wizard," she retorted, as she held her glass up to him as if she was giving him a cheer. They finished their drinks, and Dante filled them back up.

"If you're trying to get me drunk and take advantage of me, Silas might not like it," she said in jest.

Dante choked on his drink and laughed aloud. "Right now, I believe you are the only one who has to worry about what Silas doesn't like. You don't know our brother like we do. We've walked side by side our entires lives. You have no idea who you're up against or just how angry he is right now. Hell, I'm even afraid for you, to be honest."

"Why don't you enlighten me then, Mr. Know-It-All?"

"There's not enough time to *enlighten* you about Silas. Hell, it'd take a week for you to understand who and what you have enraged. I don't believe you understand the power of the bond he has with you. We do not take it lightly, nor do we take it lightly when our mate, or soon-to-be mate, such as in your case, puts herself in harm's way. You have pulled every trick in the book and then some, and that was just today. Look at yourself, you're a goddamn mess. The bruising is everywhere, your ribs are cracked, and you look like you've had the shit beat out of you. Need I continue? You've been challenging the poor bastard since the night the two of you met. Let's not forget, I've known about you since day one and have been closer than you think."

Dante continued from there, reminding her of her altercations with Bain and his brothers, and Aiden in particular, while she stayed at the mansion.

"Yes, you have been. Cheers to that." She lifted her glass in another fake salute. The most concerning part of his entire lecture was the one word that stood out the most. *What! What—I have enraged.* The question was running wild in her mind. Dante chuckled, to her annoyance, knowing he had heard every thought.

He pushed the plate toward her. "At least eat some bread. The last thing I need right now is for Silas to come home to find you drunk, or worse yet, passed out. You're already going to have plenty to contend with. All I know is that I would not want to be you."

Just as Jadis picked at the bread, the boat lunged again. She grabbed a hold of the table and the motion scared her to death. For the first time, she was glad to have Dante there with her. She was still jumpy after their little altercation today, and she didn't realize how much she was trembling.

Dante glanced at Jadis and did a mental check-in with Bain. *"All good, Bain?"*

"Yes, the girls are asleep. How's it going with Jadis?"

"How is it ever going with Jadis? Are you sure that was nothing more than a wave we just felt?" Dante wanted to ensure that nothing else had gotten into the portal.

"Yes, I checked it out myself. It's nothing more than a storm on the horizon. It's been heading our way for a while now. It's going to be a big one, you should buckle your little pain in the ass down. The last thing she needs is another bruise for Silas to look at. Why don't you put her out for a while? It seems she's making you nervous. Hell, doesn't she ever sleep?" Bain chuckled.

"You heard Silas too, and he was very clear about what we were or were not allowed to do with them. More specifically with Jadis."

"You enjoy yourself. By my count, we only have a couple of hours left before they get back, pending things continue to go as planned," Bain stated, still feeling relieved he was not the one in charge of watching Jadis for more than one reason.

"At least yours are asleep." Though he joked with Bain, Dante had truly been watching out for her. There was an undeniable pull he felt toward Jadis, and she had quickly become more to him than an assignment, against his better judgement.

Jadis was still trembling as she placed her hand on the table to keep her balance. Dante placed his hand on top of hers. "It's just a storm, nothing more," he offered.

His touch was reassuring, and she didn't pull her hand from under his. After a moment, he slid his hand off hers and poured a couple more drinks.

As the storm picked up, the boat lunged, and the wind howled outside the windows, sending the waves crashing against the hull.

"It's going to sink, isn't it? We're all going to drown or be eaten by sharks, aren't we? And with these anklets you have us strapped in, we are powerless to do anything about it," Jadis barked.

"Jadis, relax—the ship will not sink. We have the most skilled captain and crew around; none better can be found. They are not mortal, if that tells you anything. We are going to be fine." Dante was trying his best to reassure her.

"Take it off. If something happens to the boat, I need to be—" He cut her off before she could finish her sentence.

"First off, the anklet is staying put. Second, if the boat starts to sink, any of us are perfectly capable of getting you to safety." He again pushed the bread plate toward her. "Finish it. Don't make me force it down your throat," he added, followed by a wink.

"Oh, please," she said, challenging him, simply because he was annoying her.

"You really want to try me right now, in the shape you're in? Not to mention, Silas has entrusted me with your care. I will do whatever it takes, so don't push your luck, darling."

Jadis rolled her eyes at him.

The sudden motion of the boat careening from side to side caused her to hit her ribs against the arm of the chair and she winced in pain.

"Ahh, shit." Dante got up, walked over to her chair, and scooted it back. He picked her up and walked across that rocking boat like it was sitting on still waters.

He pulled the covers back and gently sat her on the bed and propped a couple pillows behind her back. He reached out, and her highball glass was in his hand. He again placed the plate of half-eaten bread in her lap.

If Silas has the power to turn Dante and Bain into personal nannies, then I'm really screwed, she thought.

"Yes, *you are screwed,* and we are not *personal nannies,* by the way," he said, sounding amused. He pulled a chair closer to the bed and took a seat. He casually rested his feet on the edge of the bed and crossed his legs.

"You're thoroughly enjoying this, aren't you?" She knew he was reveling at the thought of her having to face Silas later.

"You have no idea how much. I know what's in store for you." Dante was still chuckling.

There is more than one storm on the horizon, she thought. *I'll take drowning in the ocean over dealing with Silas.*

"I agree, I would too," Dante replied.

"Stop that! Enough is enough, It's been a long day, if you haven't noticed."

"Look, what you don't understand is Silas looked for you for one hundred fifty years. He has come and gone as he pleased for all that time, leaving a very long trail of heartache and woe. It's you, Jadis, it has always been you. He has finally found some peace, though I'd be lying if I called you peaceful." He chuckled. "But he is genuinely happy to have you back. He loves you like no other, and there you go and almost get yourself killed. Do you understand what he would do if someone laid a finger on you, much less killed you? Yet, you go off, risking your own life. How do you expect him to react?"

"I don't know. It's not like I did it on purpose, Dante. I wasn't out to get myself killed. I needed answers."

"You don't understand what he is going to do to you, do you? You stupid, stupid girl."

"And you're a *stupid, stupid* nanny with an anklet," she retorted.

He laughed aloud and poured himself another drink."Seriously ? You're actually the one with the anklet."

As the clans continued annihilating Baskale after Baskale, the only thing standing out against the veil of darkness was the acidic blood, glowing like burning embers across the valley. Even the putrid smoke rising from the ground beneath dead, was nauseating, overwhelming, and strong enough to sting their eyes. The ground was slick with the blood and innards of the fallen creatures, making it difficult to not slip on the body fluids underfoot.

Jabari had ordered his clan to continue moving up and around the formation. Being the bottom group, they were faring well and could span out. His clan continued to move further toward the top to assist the two other clans when three Basklae burst from within a rock. They lunged toward him and surrounded him. Jabari jumped straight upward before firing down at them. Three consecutive shots rang out, followed by the sound of the Baskales' screeches as each Dragon Stone bullets found their target. As the bullets penetrated their bodies, the tip of the bullet released its shards, exploding within its victim's body.

Jabari spotted the hole in the rock and made his way to it. When he peered in, he noticed the opening led to the center of a structure.

He psychically reached out to Eden and Silas. *"I've got something. You might want to come take a look."*

Silas and Eden materialized beside him. Whatever it was, it must have been at least one thousand-years old. They gathered a group and headed in, leaving the rest of the warriors to tend to the outside.

"Aiden, we're going in. See to the outside," Eden ordered.

"You got it," Aiden replied as he plunged his sword into another Baskale's chest before spinning around and efficiently decapitating an-other. He lunged forward and landed a well-placed front kick to another, sending it flying backward and into another pack. Its body knocked two more over, allowing the surrounding warriors to eliminate them as they clumsily scrambled to their feet.

Jabari had multiple weapons strapped to belts, along with numerous fully loaded magazines. "Heads up," Jabari stated as he tossed Silas and Eden a couple of the magazines. "These work like magic!"

Silas ordered a couple dozen of his own Mortem warriors to accom-pany them. "Keep an eye out, I have a feeling there's something in there."

"Aye, milord," Sigurd stated.

They made their way into the structure and the air became thick and heavy with a pungent, rotten smell. A slime-like substance oozed down the smooth interior walls, and the floor sounded like a metal grate be-neath their combat boots as they walked. As they moved further into the darkness, they headed in opposite directions. The structure was shaped like a triangle, and they wanted to cover as much of the area as they could. They planned to meet in the west corner before making their way down to the bottom.

They searched multiple levels at once in order to head off any possible threat. The structure was not large, so they were able to check every exit leading off the main corridors. The small compartments lining the corridors did not appear to be rooms; they were cages.

Eden spoke, breaking the silence, "These are cages. Is anyone seeing anything indicating it's something else?"

"No," Silas answered, "I'm getting the same feeling. Seal each one shut as you pass," he instructed.

"Jabari, what are you seeing?" Eden asked telepathically.

"It appears to be the same all the way down. There is a thick mist hovering below. I have a feeling something is down there. Everyone needs to be prepared." Jabari moved with a sense of readiness and checked to make sure his magazines were still in place.

Had it not been for their supernatural hearing abilities, the structure would have been too soundproof for them to hear the incessant screeches of the creatures and the battle raging outside.

The further down they went, the wider it became. Jabari's group stopped at the fourth level, waiting on Silas and Eden's group so they could search it together. It didn't take long for them to make their way down, sealing every door, pod, or vent.

The remaining four levels didn't appear to have been used as a holding area, as they were significantly different. Pipes of all sorts ran down the smooth walls, and what appeared to be foreign equipment filled various compartments. Stairways were at either end of the triangular corridor, allowing easy access to the lower levels. Each new level opened into large rooms they assumed would be working areas or command centers. It all became more elaborate the further down they went. Different geometric shapes and designs had been built on top of one another on the walls using various materials and three-dimensional structures.

The three groups spread out, continuing to check the last areas of the structure. It became an open concept of sorts; one could stand on the fourth level and view downward into the others. The floors were no longer grated, but smooth, except for the raised, three-dimensional structures.

The mist on the bottom of the structure quietly hovered above the floor and moved as serene as water. As they made their way to the bottom, the mist moved with them, swirling around their legs and moving away from them as they walked before closing in behind them.

The bottom of the container was cool and clammy, but the most noticeable thing about it was the pungent, foul-smelling stench that differed from the of the rest of the structure.

Jabari and his group made their way down to the second level, which appeared to be the main operation area. They studied it in detail, feeling the controls, the foreign equipment, and taking mental pictures, noting whatever might be significant.

After taking a little time to assess it, and deciding what to do, Eden spoke up, "I say we blow it up."

"I agree, we have no idea what this is, and I'm not about to leave it and find out later. Unless my mind deceives me this appears to be some sort of air vent?" Silas replied and he ran his hand over a large pipe that disappeared beneath the bottom of the structure.

Jabari came to a nerve-racking realization. "This shit has been right under our nose for centuries. They've been pumping in fresh air all this time and have been able to come and go undetected." He kneeled down and swept his fingers across the solid floor and then held his hand out. "Fresh dirt."

"The structures beneath us must be covering their entrances," Silas said.

They paused mid-stride as their heightened senses all picked up on something scurrying around them, but from where they could not tell.

They continued to walk together in pairs, some walking backward and some walking forward, in order to monitor all directions. The corridors were tight for such tall, muscular beings. It had been built for something that could easily scurry about. If any of them became trapped in the corridors, it would be one hell of a tight fight.

"Anything?" Eden asked.

"Yes," Silas replied. "We are being watched, so keep your heads up, and I mean now!"

Just then, one of the triangular, three-dimensional structures blew from the wall above, moving like some sort of ejectable door. The sounds of the heavy metal crashing to the ground radiated off the walls with a deafening bang, and echoed throughout the entire ship.

About thirty smaller bug-like creatures began swarming from its opening, not unlike an interrupted nest of baby spiders. The creatures scurried in every direction, lunging and leaping from within the walls.

Sigurd reached out, snatching one of them in mid-air. He plunged his sword through its chest and sent it flying into a control panel. He then spun the sword, crouched down, and drove his blade into the chest of another bug, attempting to attack him from behind.

The bugs continued to rain down on them, and fighting was taking place on three separate levels.

Eden was attacked by multiple bugs scurrying from a door that had blown open directly in front of him. He kicked the door and sent it crashing into the wall, smashing another bug-like creature. He evaded their attacks by spinning, ducking, and leaping away.

A metal structure blew from the bottom of the structure at Silas's feet. The bugs spilled up and out of the hole. He landed a few deadly blows with his sword before leaping into the air.

Loud pops rang out, one after another, in quick succession, which was followed by the deafening screeching of injured bugs reverberating off the metal walls.

Eden, Silas, and Jabari emptied what remained of their magazines, deciding it was too closed in to continue the physical fight. However, they also had to evade the bullets ricocheting off the metal; the shards of dragon stone were as dangerous as the bugs.

"Better to kill quickly when fighting in such confined quarters!" Jabari yelled as he shot the last one between its eyes.

"Warn the others, a blast is coming!" Silas yelled out as he pulled out the charges and explosives Eden had given him.

He and Eden tossed a few of the charges to Jabari and instructed him to hit the upper levels. Once they had finished setting all the explosives in place, and dropping a few into the holes, they met in the center, where they had originally entered the structure.

Jabari spoke mentally to everyone fighting outside. *"Aria, are you and your coven ready?"* he asked, making sure Aria's bubble would protect those on the outside.

"We're ready, Father. Do what you need to do."

"Everyone, out," Silas ordered.

As Aiden looked up, Eden, Jabari, and Silas appeared from the entrance of the structure, followed by their warrior's.

The entire legion made their way to the outer edge of the bubble; killing the last of the Baskales' along the way. Shortly after they crouched down, ready to watch the explosion. The entire structure erupted into chaos, unleashing a torrent of metal, rock, and dirt that soared across the valley. A colossal mushroom cloud emerged in the aftermath of the explosion, which shook the ground beneath them. The blinding brilliance of the blast transformed the surrounding desert into a mesmerizing kaleidoscope of vibrant hues.

As the smoke settled, they stood up and cheered. All things considered it had gone off without a hitch. Each Baskale now lay before them in a vast graveyard for the unburied. They stood and took it all in for a moment; body after body lay dismembered, bleeding, and disemboweled under the gentle glow of the crimson moon.

Eden, Silas, and Jabari made sure they accounted for everyone, assessed the injured, and the bodies of their fallen warriors would be properly attended to in the oasis.

Many Nosferatu were wounded and had lacerations from the talons of the Basklales. The injuries, however, weren't life threatening. The wounds weren't severe enough they wouldn't be able to heal, since they didn't carry the deadly bacteria the Segans did.

"This is going to be one hell of a cleanup effort." Lars laughed.

He and Aiden grasped each other's forearms and patted each other on the shoulder.

"Fantastic job, brothers." Eden walked up and greeted them in the same manner. "By the way, the cleanup is going to be the responsibility of the two of you," he ordered, as he looked at Lars and Aiden.

"What the hell? Why us?" Lars questioned.

"Well, you thought it funny, so I figured you wouldn't mind cleaning up the mess. As for Aiden, there's a little princess he might want to spend some time with, so he can use it as his excuse to stay."

Silas laughed aloud when he saw the look that crossed Aiden's face.

"I believe you need to be heading home to relieve your babysitters," Aiden said, as he smirked at Silas.

"Don't test me, cousin. I wouldn't want to embarrass you in front of a certain little someone," Silas added, winking at Aria.

"Go, Silas, your work here is done. We will take care of the rest." Eden grasped Silas's forearm with one hand and placed his other hand on his shoulder.

"I have an insulant little bruja waiting for me," Silas grumbled. Even a hard night's battle couldn't erase the effect or hold Jadis had on him.

Silas placed a hand on Eden's shoulder, returning the affection. "Eden, this would not have gone so smoothly without you, as usual. We will always be grateful, as we always have been. Let us know if you need anything, cousin. I need to get home. If anything goes awry, we'll be back."

"We've got this, Silas. Go."

"Silas, come to the oasis and clean up. You look a mess, and you reek of death." Aria chuckled. "If you're heading home to your girl like this, you're likely not going to get much of a welcome."

Aiden looked at Aria, ignoring Silas, but making sure he heard the following comment, "I'm not so sure this is a welcome home, sweetie, kind of situation."

The rest of the family laughed at Silas's expense, knowing the inside information.

"Low samaht, inta bitigi," Aria said, motioning Silas, Syth, and Agaeus toward the oasis. "Any matter of home needs to be handled properly. You cannot go home looking and smelling like this." She waved her hand up and down his soiled, blood-soaked body, speaking with a mix of ancient Iphenorian and English.

"Go, Silas. Our home is your home," Jabari offered. "I insist, and I will not take no for an answer. My daughter will escort you. My clan and I will stay and help clean up the mess."

Silas took Jabari by the forearm and placed a hand on his shoulder. "We owe you a debt of gratitude."

"Say nothing more. We have known each other for far too long, and you don't owe us anything. This war is the responsibility of all clans, my friend," Jabari stated sincerely.

Silas nodded as he and his brothers followed Aria back to the oasis to wash off the stench of war and death.

Eden turned to Silas once again, "There is just one thing, Silas."

"Whatever you need, you've got it."

"Think you could keep that headache of yours to yourself for a while? Or better yet, a long while?"

"I'll do my best," Silas replied with a slight chuckle.

"I have one more question," Lars said.

"What is it now?" Eden asked, annoyed.

"Any way can we watch the homecoming?" Laughter once again rang out from all of them.

"I would do it if it wasn't Silas we were talking about. Let's finish up here. I want to get home myself, some of us have a real welcome home awaiting us." Eden chuckled.

"Well, I'll be damned. Your sense of humor has returned, Eden," Aiden joked.

Silas and his brothers made their way back with Aria. They cleaned up in one of the old temples, which had been updated with all the modern conveniences. Silas had to admit the hot shower felt amazing. It also gave him some time to pull himself together. Hell, he couldn't stand the smell of himself, so it certainly wouldn't have helped to return home that way. Aria and her sisters took care of cleaning their gear and clothing, and before long, they were ready to return home.

CHAPTER 14

D ante sat back, thinking about the storm that was in full force. *It's going to be a long, rough night,* he thought.

Jadis struggled to keep her balance as she sat on the bed with her legs crossed. "You going to stare at me all night?" she asked, sounding annoyed.

"Maybe you should lie down and get some sleep. You're exhausting me," Dante replied.

"*Maybe* you should leave." She smirked.

"Not a chance in hell," he stated.

"You're so annoying, I've put up with you for hours now," Jadis replied with an over-exaggerated eye roll.

Dante chuckled as he looked at Jadis. He finished another drink and lowered his arm with his glass still in hand. He moved it around in little circles, clinking the ice cubes against the glass.

"Why are you looking at me like that?"

Dante stood up. "I thought you could use another drink. Is the storm making you nervous?" He filled their glasses a quarter of the way.

Jadis took a few sips while she watched Dante walk to the door and casually lean against it.

"You're lying. I can see it all over your face. What gives? Fess up." Jadis motioned her hand toward him, waiting for a response before asking again, "Are you going to answer me or not?"

"Your boyfriend's back." He laughed. Silas had let him know he would be there in five minutes.

Jadis dropped her glass on the floor and instinctively jumped up. She ran for the door, but Dante blocked her only exit. "Nope! Not leaving."

Jadis bounced his body and landed on the floor. Dante continued to stand in front of the door with one hand casually resting on his Glock as he waived his drink at her with the other. "Nowhere to run, and nowhere to hide," he stated, sounding more than amused.

It took Jadis a moment for her to gather herself off the floor. She slowly made it back onto her knees and she looked up to find Dante was still laughing at her. She swirled her hand when he interrupted her.

"Nope, we've fixed that too."

The boat lunged to the side, and she tumbled onto the floor again. *Shit, I'm more scared now than I had been while being attacked by the Baskale,* she thought. She scrambled to her feet and ran to hide in the bathroom, locking the door behind her.

"Really, Jadis? You think the door is going to save you, much less stop Silas? You might as well put a sheet over your head."

She hated being Dante's source of amusement, but she had to admit he was right. *What the hell am I thinking? I can at least face him and take it like a man.*

"I'd stay in the bathroom if I were you. I wouldn't suggest you *man up* to Silas tonight."

"Shut up!" She yelled from the bathroom. She didn't hear the door open, but she heard Dante and Silas greeting one another.

"Brother, thank you for getting her back here," Silas stated as he grasped Dante's forearm.

"No need to thank me. I'm glad she's here and in one piece."

Dante knew Silas was in no mood for conversation, so he handed him a full glass and left.

Dante spoke to Bain telepathically, *"You need that drink?"*

"Hell, yes. Syth just dragged Skye to their room and Agaeus is with Ivory. I'll meet you in the stateroom below."

Jadis heard Silas's footsteps as he walked toward the bathroom.

"So you're in the mood for yet another game of cat and mouse, I see?" He let out a deep chested growl that sent a stampede of shivers throughout her body.

"Here, kitty, kitty, kitty," Silas called out, toying with her.

Fuck me! Just the tone of his voice alone is more menacing than his words.

She was sitting on the edge of the tub, feeling like an idiot. She couldn't make her body move in order to open the door and face him. She heard him walk across the room and fill his glass. *Good,* she thought. *Maybe he's not as angry as I thought.* The next thing she knew, he was in the bathroom, standing in front of her.

"You have no idea just how angry I am!" he roared.

He reached out and snagged her by both arms and picked her up off the edge of the tub; her feet were no longer touching the ground. She let out a yelp when she found herself face to face with the most terrifying vampire she had ever laid eyes on. Silas no longer had four canines. There were eight. A smaller one next to each of the larger ones had dropped from his gums. She was so fixated on the double set of canines; she hadn't noticed she was now kneeling on the bed, still in his grasp. *Other than anger, Silas is completely devoid of emotion.* In that moment, all the blood drained from her face.

"Baby, I can explain. I—I—" she stuttered.

He put his finger over her mouth, and snarled. "Shh—not one fucking word."

Her heart flip-flopped and fell into her stomach. *I'm in trouble, big trouble. Big, big trouble.*

"I said, not one more fucking word. Not even in that suborn head of yours."

Yep! This is it. I'm going to die right here, right now. I've pushed Silas too far.

"I won't tell you again," he snarled.

Silas stood at the edge of the bed, staring at her with his angry, cat-like slits of swirling, heated colors. She had seen him turn, but never in anger, and not like this. She watched as his expression switched from relief to rage and back again.

She was still kneeling on the bed, looking at him, when he motioned for her to stand up. She did so quickly, and he took one step back and motioned her forward with his finger. Jadis took a second step forward, and he held up his hand.

With a flick of his wrist, her shorts and tank top were floating down onto the floor at her feet. He walked in a slow circle around her, and she knew he was assessing her injuries, looking for anything that might be serious.

Jadis covered herself with her hands as best as she could. She was suddenly feeling completely exposed. All she wanted to do was crawl under the covers and disappear. She was sure he would notice her cracked ribs first, along with the multitude of bruises. *And the gash on my face is also quite visible. Shit! Don't think,* she told herself.

Dante and Bain hadn't tried to cover up the injuries. They'd just stopped the bleeding and left me as is, so Silas could see everything for himself, she seethed, unable to stop thinking. *Bastards! Dante and Bain could have fixed all of this, or at least let me do it myself!*

A low growl rose from his chest. "Unlike you, they follow directions, my dear," he snarled into her ear from behind.

She about jumped out of her skin, having forgotten all about the little golden anklet. *I really need to stop thinking. Stop thinking, stop thinking.*

"I am very curious. What goes on in that stubborn fucking head of yours?"

He motioned for her to get back on the bed. He didn't have to tell her twice. She jumped into the bed and covered herself with the sheets before the lunging of the boat almost knocked her off. She bent her knees up to her chest, clinging to the duvet.

Silas slowly stalked toward her and crawled onto the bed and knelt over her. "You have quite a few injuries, but I still want to ring that skinny little neck of yours," he snarled, with his canines in full view. "Should I mention the Baskale you put yourself in front of as well, or should we leave that one alone for the moment?"

His coolness was even more frightening than the anger. At least if he was yelling at me, I'd have had a better idea of where I stood. At the moment, I have no idea what to expect. All I want is to be anywhere but here.

He wrapped her hair in his fist and pulled her head back, exposing her throbbing pulse. He did nothing but stare before speaking. "I fucking own you. All of you. You will never disobey me again."

She felt a tear fall from the corner of her eye, and it slowly trickled down her cheek. Scared to death didn't describe the fear she felt in this moment. She was no longer looking into the familiar eyes of her vampire.

Suddenly, Silas stood up from the bed. He flicked his wrist, and a chain appeared around her ankle. It didn't feel heavy, but it was anchored to the floor. It was Silas's way of letting her know she wouldn't be going anywhere.

"Do not be mistaken, mon chéri. I am not the lover you wanted. I am the monster you need. You have pushed your luck too far this time. Don't go anywhere," he said expressionlessly. "I'll be back to deal with you."

He walked out of the stateroom, not bothering to open the door, leaving her chained up.

What the fuck was that? Not even Hecate's wrath had ever scared her like this, and she had angered her on more than one occasion. Her hands wouldn't stop trembling and the tears were now flowing down her face. She was also concerned he had called himself a monster. *What in the hell did he mean, calling himself a monster? He just left me sitting here?* She flopped onto her back with her leg chained to the floor. She didn't want to cry, but she didn't have the energy to fight it. She rolled over and sobbed into her pillow.

"Today has certainly been an adventure." Dante chuckled.

"I almost feel bad for Jadis right now—almost." Bain laughed as he motioned to the steward to bring another bottle to the table.

"Jadis is exhausting. Do you think after she and Silas are mated, she'll settle down?" Dante asked.

"Not a chance in hell. She's going to have the poor bastard running in circles." Bain laughed.

They cocked their heads as a cool feeling washed over them. They turned to look toward the door and Silas stepped over the threshold, looking mad as a hatter. Dante and Bain looked at each other, confused.

"Holy shit, he killed her," Bain said telepathically.

They stood immediately, but Silas motioned for them to take a seat and they cautiously did so.

"Is everything okay, Silas? Is Jadis doing okay?" Dante asked, with an expression of both curiosity and worry.

Bain's expression matched that of Dante as he gave him a quick side-eyed glance. *"Silas must need something, and something big. I bet he's here to ask us to resurrect her."*

"We're going to have to perform a necromancy ceremony. Holy shit," Dante stated.

"I did not kill the poor girl. Remember those chains I had you conjure today? Well, she's currently wearing one, along with the anklet."

They dared not laugh. As hard as it was, they choked it down.

The steward walked over and set a drink on the table in front of Silas. He picked it up, finished it, and motioned for the bottle.

Neither Dante nor Bain spoke as they waited on Silas. They didn't dare speak up when they hadn't yet figured out why he was there with them instead of in the stateroom ripping Jadis a new one.

"I know you're both wondering why I'm here with you and not handling Jadis, but I just can't deal with her right now," he confessed.

The expressions on Dante's and Bain's faces said it all. Never in the past six hundred plus years had they seen Silas unsure of what to do. He was the Lord of their clan, the eldest of their family, and a master planner. He was one to think through every detail and to make decisions with deliberate precision. He was an Assassin at heart who didn't hesitate to kill and found enjoyment in the act. Yet, here he sat, drink in hand, unable to determine what to do with his mate to be. He had finally met his match in every way. Jadis met him toe to toe, which was an unfamiliar feeling for him. Anyone else that had ever met Silas in such a way was long ago dead and buried. Jadis had not only tested and tried his patience, but ran over them. He was completely out of his element.

"I just want to snap her skinny little neck," Silas admitted, feeling utterly exasperated. "She's a goddamn mess, and she almost got herself and her sisters killed today. She even outwitted you, Dante, not to mention the fact she put herself face to face with a goddamn Baskale. Not only did she survive, she killed the son of a bitch. How is that even possible? I can't figure out how the three of them are still alive. In all honesty, they should be meeting their Gods right now." He looked at Dante and Bain as if they had the answers.

"We know, brother, we've been dealing with her all day. Believe me, we feel for you. You should have seen her ass when we pulled her out of the portal. I know we showed you, but I don't think I did the picture justice. It was one of those moments in which you had to be there. You should have seen the look of shock and horror on their faces after they came crashing down on the deck. Jadis looked as nervous as a pregnant nun in a convent!" Dante laughed aloud.

"I can only imagine," Silas replied with a slight chuckle.

"I've had to spend the last nine hours babysitting her, and that was all it took to get me to the point of exhaustion," Dante admitted. "This is far from my first run-in with that girl, yet she never ceases to amaze or surprise me. I wonder if there's anything she wouldn't try to pull. I've got to hand it to you, Silas, taking her on as a mate is going to be a lifetime of headaches."

"*If vampires could get them*," Bain chuckled, mocking Eden.

Dante tilted his glass. "Cheers to that."

"I knew she was willful, but I don't remember it being to this extent. Thinking back on all of it, though, I recall an incident in the woods by her cabin on the night we met. I made an offhanded remark, and she tossed a log at my head from the woodpile on her porch," Silas added, feeling somewhat amused by the memory.

"How does that not surprise me?" Bain replied.

"She has grown extremely powerful over the last one hundred fifty years, not to mention so goddamn headstrong." Silas was back to being frustrated.

"You can say that again," Bain agreed.

"What are you going to do?" Dante asked.

Confusion crept over Silas. "I don't know. I want to scoop her up in my arms, heal her, and take all her pain away. She's still scared to death from all that happened today and could use some comfort. At the same time, I want to hear her panting and moaning beneath me. I'm so goddamn angry," Silas snarled.

"Damn, you have it bad for that girl." Dante said. *Silas really is at a loss.* "You have always been a glutton for punishment, brother, but this is on a whole other level. I would love to tell you what to do, but from my own dealings with her, I don't have any answers for you either. I am at as much of a loss as you are. I suppose you could always turn her. At least she'd have to obey you." He chuckled.

"Can you imagine Jadis as a vampire? You may be command her, but everyone around her would be in dire straits. Hell, she'd probably drain everyone. You think the Segans killed the living? We'd all be dining on rats," Bain joked, with a hearty laugh.

"I absolutely agree. I think I'll stick with her as she is now. I came close—too close. I was a mere second away turning her. That's why I'm here. I don't need to create any more problems for myself than I already have." Silas swirled his glass around in his hand before setting it onto the table.

Dante and Bain side-eyed each other and then looked at Silas, but said nothing.

"What to do, what to do? If I would have turned her, I would have lost her as sure as the sun sets." He paused momentarily. "I have to deal with her eventually, so it may as well be now." He finished his drink, stood, and disappeared from the stateroom.

"I feel sorry for your brother. Unfortunately, I'm enjoying all of this a bit too much," Bain admitted.

"You and me both. Silas is at his wit's end." Dante thought about Silas's situation. "I wouldn't know what to do with her either, you?"

"It depends. If I let my dick do the talking, I would throw her ass on her back in a minute. If I let my brains do the talking, I would permanently chain her." Bain smirked.

"My sentiments exactly. Dealing with her today made it difficult for me to keep it in my pants. Hell, being in the stateroom with her was worse. All her shenanigans today were a bit of a turn on to me too, if I'm being honest. On top of it all, I had to sit with her for hours while she had nothing more on than a silk top and shorts." Dante remembering exactly how she had looked; especially her hard, pink nipples that were barely visible through the silken top.

"Well, since we are being honest, I took a peek when we checked in with each other. I can only imagine the self-control it must have taken to be in there with her, but you have no idea how happy I was you lost the coin toss."

"Tell me, how the hell did Aiden spend weeks in her bed and not take her ass?" Dante was truly curious about how Aiden kept his shit together in bed with her.

"I had to add a layer of protection. We knew he could never hold back on his own will. I also added a little something to Jadis, thankfully.

Knowing what I know now, she probably could have enticed him to do anything she wanted," Bain admitted.

"That explains a lot. It's clear he has feelings for her that run pretty deep."

"Since day one. Watch how he looks at her; he's in love with her. I'm sure he's using Aria as a distraction."

"She's a hell of a distraction." Dante chuckled.

"That she is. Here's to Silas never finding out about this, and to those perfect tits." Dante tilted his glass to Bain.

"Cheers to that." Bain laughed, tilting his glass in response. "We take this to our grave, Dante, otherwise we may end up there early."

"Agreed. I'd hate to miss out on this show, anyway. I believe it's just getting started." Dante stated as he tossed back another full glass.

Silas stood at the edge of the bed, watching Jadis sleep. *She looks as innocent as a kitten lying there,* he thought.

Her beautiful mahogany hair flowed down around her shoulders and onto the pillow. She looked so peaceful, so innocent. He didn't want to wake her. Jadis had snuck in and stolen his heart like a thief in the night. He had no doubt he was absolutely, irrevocably in love with her. He couldn't stand the sight of her bruises, the cut on her face, and the thought of how painful the cracked ribs must be. As angry as he was, he was more relieved she was alive and well, and sleeping peacefully in his bed. All he could do was to slip into the bed next to her. He wrapped her tightly in his arms without waking her.

It was above her; the saliva dripping onto her face and searing her skin. She was broken and alone in the dark with no way out and she had no one to help. The Baskale took her to a Segan and tossed her in front of it like a bleeding carcass. It was hideous, tall, and skinny. It gaped at her with depraved, spider-black, angular eyes; soulless and lifeless, nothing but inherent evil. It snatched her up by her throat and tossed her onto the table. She was on her back and was being strapped down; the smell was revoltingly nauseating. She could barely see, and was unable to move; death was trying to claim her soul, and it wanted what she had, her archaic powers. It pressed its hands to her head and squeezed. She yelled, and tried to fight it off, but it had her pinned down like an iron coffin nail.

"Jadis, stop. It's me, baby, you're having a nightmare." Silas was lying next to her, rubbing her arm, as he propped himself up on his elbow, trying to calm her down.

"Silas, you don't understand," she mumbled. "It wants me. Just me. The Segar is coming for me because it wants what I possess."

"Calm, my love, it was just a nightmare. You're safe, I've got you."

He lay down on his side and pulled her into him, enveloping her body in his. He felt her wince from the pain of her broken ribs and let out a deep sigh.

Her back was to him, and he had his arms and legs wrapped around her. She never felt safer than she did in Silas's arms. She tried to scoot closer to him, and he held her tighter.

"I don't think it was just a dream, baby. I think it was a vision."

"Shhh—sleep, my love." He turned her head toward him and kissed her. That was the last thing she remembered; other than the fact she was once again looking into the familiar eyes of her vampire.

They slept until late afternoon the following day. When Jadis woke up, she was still wrapped up in Silas's arms. She cautiously moved, afraid of the pain, but nothing hurt at all. She felt for the cut on her face, and it had healed. She ran her hand across her ribs and they felt fine too.

"I healed you last night, in case you're wondering," Silas admitted.

"Why? I mean thank you, but I thought you were going to kill me last night."

"For a second, I almost went too far. That's why I left. I needed to clear my head, so I sat with Dante and Bain for a bit. I almost turned you. I didn't think I could stop myself had I stayed in the room."

"I'm really sorry, baby. I can't even imagine what they told you."

"They didn't have to tell me anything. They had been projecting the entire altercation to me, we watched it all."

"All?" she was afraid to ask.

"Yes, all of it—every last infuriating minute. You will wear the anklet until further notice, by the way."

She moved her foot. *At least the chain is gone. I'll argue the anklet later, perhaps in a couple of days, but now is definitely not the time.*

"There will be no *arguing* at all, not even a day or two from now. This is non-negotiable."

"Silas, I'm really sorry. I didn't mean for any of that to happen. I really didn't. Please don't be mad at me," she begged as she stroked his cheek.

"Mon chéri, I am still mad. However, we are all impressed with your abilities. However, saying we're a bit tired of them is an understatement."

Silas moved the hair off her forehead and ran his fingers along some of the wavy strands. He held his head propped in his hand as they lay on their sides, facing each other.

"This is how it's going to be until further notice. You will not be leaving my side; not to eat, to sunbathe, or to take a stroll around the yacht. You will be attached to my hip, and I mean that in the literal sense. You won't stray more than a few feet from me. If I have so much as a phone call and need to leave, you will be chained to both Dante and Bain."

"Dante and Bain, both of them at once? Hell no, I surely won't," she objected cautiously, very cautiously.

"What part don't you understand? And I can assure you, Dante and Bain can follow orders. Unlike you, my love," Silas rumbled.

"I mean, we're on a boat, so how far can I go? I said I wouldn't do anything again, and I meant it," she practically begged him once again to reconsider.

"I've seen exactly how far you can go, and it ceases today. You won't be straying anywhere alone for a while, if ever again. Oh, there's one more thing I should mention to you. As far as Skye and Ivory are concerned, my brothers have decided it's best to keep the three of you separated, and I can't agree more." Silas raised an eyebrow, waiting for her to protest.

"Keep us apart? Where are Skye and Ivory? You can't keep me from my sisters."

"I assure you I can, I will, and I have. You don't need to worry. They are safer with my brothers, anyway. The three of you seem to bring more trouble in your directions than anyone/anything else does. Plus, it's not like you're alone. You'll have Dante and Bain to keep you company." After a brief pause, he spoke again. "What? No words, no thoughts? It's not possible for you to be speechless and thoughtless."

"You're thoroughly enjoying yourself, aren't you?" She playfully slapped his stomach, and he grabbed her hand.

"Actually, I am. I feel at peace for the first time in weeks. We have found a way to clip your wings, at least for the moment." He waited momentarily again before speaking, "What, no thoughts, my dear?"

"We? By we, you mean you, Dante, and Bain?" She plopped back on the pillows and rubbed her face. *It isn't even worth trying to argue with him. Hell, I brought this on myself, after all. I knew that fucking with Silas wasn't a good idea.*

"You absolutely *brought this on yourself*, and you're just now realizing *fucking with me* is a bad idea?" Silas asked.

"Okay fine. Keep me prisoner, but at least get out of my head. I can't believe you are so proud of yourself right now."

"Maybe at some point, but not right now. It seems if I give you an inch, you jump through a portal."

"So, tell me, were you ever going to let on to the fact you have eight canines?" She chuckled.

"I didn't want it to scare you, and it takes a special kind of provocation for them to appear."

He rolled over and pinned her on her back, held her hands above her head, and looked down at her.

"For now, not only do I own you, every delicate, infuriating inch of you, but I have your thoughts as well. I— we—will never make the mistake of underestimating you again. Now that we have that cleared up, let's talk about the little slap," he said, arching an eyebrow.

He bent down, and his lips fell to hers. He moved his mouth to her neck and whispered in her ear, "Let's get to it."

Silas moved one of his legs between hers and pushed them apart. He dragged his canines down the vein on her neck, all four of them this time now that he was no longer keeping them a secret.

Jadis's pulse quickened, and the feeling of the cool tips as they scraped her skin sent shivers up her spine.

He slid his hand up her thigh and pulled her leg a bit higher. He was slowly rocking back and forth between her legs, rubbing his hardened erection against her nub, setting her body on fire.

Damn, how I want him, she thought.

His hand made its way up her waist and across her ribs. He cupped her breast and rubbed his thumb over the hard, pink bud.

He let go of her arms and shoved some of the pillows onto the floor. She wrapped her arms around his neck and reveled in his touch and the way his heavy body consumed hers.

He grabbed a fist full of her hair, pulled her head back, and took her mouth to his; the soft warmth of his tongue finding hers.

Her moans were desperate, which only retched up his arousal and his need to dominate her—to fuck her.

"Ahh, mon chéri. You never disappoint." He groaned.

"And neither do you. Now take it."

He pulled away, dragging his canines along her neck again and slid his tongue across her throat, desiring nothing more than to sink them deep into her soft flesh. Instead, he chose the safer option, and began trailing gentle kisses down her neck before moving to her breast and suckling her nipple, teasing it with his tongue.

"I want to fuck you so hard." He groaned, as he slid his hand further down. His fingers finding their way into the warmth between her legs.

"Silas," she arched her back, her body begging for more.

He rubbed her nub with his thumb and slowly slid his fingers in and out of her body as he licked and nipped his way down her stomach.

Her body quivered beneath his touch. "I need you inside me."

He moved far enough down to place his face between her legs. He pushed her knees aside, spreading them further apart, and swirled his tongue around her sex. He looked up briefly. "I want you begging."

"Silas," she moaned, as her sex throbbed beneath his lips. He continued sucking and teasing her with his tongue and penetrating her with his fingers. She grabbed a fistful of his hair in one hand and bunched the sheet in the other.

With each taste, each twirl of his tongue, her body began to tremble.

"Oh my god—shit," she said, with a raspy, breathless whisper. The climax rose, and her body convulsed. He remained in place and continued to tease her body.

"Now I'm going to give you what you want," he rumbled.

He moved up from between her legs and stopped to suckle her perfect bud again. His mouth fell to hers, and with a hard thrust, he was deep inside of her.

"Exactly what I needed," he growled into the heat of her mouth.

He forcefully rocked back and forth, not holding back. He wanted to feel both her pleasure and her pain.

Silas was being rough, and it was painful, but she didn't care. She wanted it; she wanted it rough, and she wanted Silas.

The way her hip's moved matched his, and the tightness of her body enveloping his shaft brought about his orgasm.

He snarled with his release, and she let out a guttural groan as the waves of pleasure surged through them both.

Silas fell on top of her, and could feel her heart beating against his chest, matching the rhythm of his own.

As heir breathing calmed, he slowly pulled out and laid on top of her. Both of them enjoying the peace and calm between them once again.

She kissed his neck and whispered, "I love you, vampire."

He looked down at her. "And I you, mon chéri. Never forget it. You are mine and you will never stray again. Say it, I want to hear it."

"I am yours. I always will be. There is nothing I want more than to stay like this, here with you, forever in your arms and in your heart."

"You have caged my heart for one hundred fifty years." He rolled over, pulled her close, and rested one arm behind his head while he used his other hand to play with her hair.

"That feels good," she whispered.

"You must be hungry. We should get you some dinner. I was told you didn't eat last night."

Of course, he was told I didn't eat, she thought, rolling her eyes again. She felt Silas chuckle under his breath. "Silas, stop it. But since you asked, yes, I'm hungry."

"Enough said." Silas sat up, rolled over the top of her, and once again squished her into the bed.

"Silas, I can't breathe." She giggled.

"I like the way you feel beneath my body. Maybe I'll stay like this, and you can eat a late dinner," he teased.

"Get off!" she laughed as she pushed him; he pushed back, and they ended up wrestling between the sheets.

Silas finally rolled out of bed, letting Jadis breathe again. "Get dressed, my love." He tossed her a pile of clothes he had laid out.

She had no idea when that had happened. She didn't remember seeing them there. Nonetheless, she got up and walked to the bathroom to get ready. As she turned to shut the door, Silas was standing there.

"Not so fast." He held the door open with the palm of his hand.

"What are you doing?"

"That little romp in the hay changed nothing. I'll give you your privacy in the bathroom, but if I sense anything suspicious at all, you will lose that privilege as well. I assume you'd like to keep it since it's the only one you have until we leave for the Valley of the Old Gods in a few weeks?"

A few weeks? Silas is definitely asserting his control over me now, she thought as she stood there in silence. Not only was he holding the door, but he had taken her clothes from her as well. "You will also get dressed out here."

He chuckled as her mouth dropped open. "You can close that pretty little mouth of yours. This is the way it is until I decide otherwise."

He walked away, leaving her alone in the bathroom. *Don't think, don't think, don't think,* she thought, and then she heard him laugh aloud. She came out a few minutes later and dressed. Silas was sitting in the chair at the table with a drink, waiting for her.

"Take your time. Dante and Bain will wait," he said, knowing how she would react.

She swung around to face him. "What did you say? What do you mean *Dante and Bain are waiting*?"

"You heard me. Dante and Bain will join us for all activities outside the bedroom," he stated with a smug smile.

She plopped onto the bed and leaned back on her hands. "There's no way this is happening. I'm not leaving then."

Silas remained sitting in his chair, casually sipping his whiskey. "My love, where do I begin? Are we back to this again?"

She raised her eyebrows in protest. "What do you mean *back to this*, it seems that's become your favorite statement?"

"We can do things the easy way, which means you follow directions, or we can do it your way, which tends to be the hard way. You can either walk on your own, or I can, and I will, carry you."

She quietly sat there, contemplating her choices, or lack thereof.

"So be it."

The next thing she knew, Silas picked her up, tossed her over his shoulder, and carried her out of the stateroom.

"Holy shit. Put me down, Silas! I'll walk on my own. You can't keep doing this!"

"You took too long to make a decision, so I made one for you."

Out of the hornet's nest and into the lion's den, she thought.

"You guessed it about right, my love. *Into the lion's den* it is. The only difference is that it's on the middle deck," he said, mocking her.

"Silas, do not carry me out there, put me the hell down!" She smacked him on the ass as she hung over his shoulder.

"I like the way you think."

He carried her all the way, and as he appeared with her over his shoulder, a burst of laughter came from Dante and Bain. Silas walked up to the table and set her down. He then pulled out a chair for her and waited for her to take a seat.

Joining my captors. Great, she thought.

"Well? I assume I'll be making all the decisions from now on?" Silas put his hand on her shoulder before gently pushing her down into the chair. He took a seat next to her and handed her a drink.

"Well, I'll be damned. Jadis is being forced to do something," Dante chided. "Who would've ever thought?"

"And she's speechless," Bain added.

Jadis had no choice but to sit there, listening to them laugh at her expense. *I suppose I sort of deserve it after all I put them through.* She looked over and noticed two other boats off in the distance. *I wonder if Skye and Ivory are on one or both of them.* She thought about how much better things would be if the three of them were at least together.

"Both," Silas answered, to her annoyance.

"We separated the two of them as well. Syth and Agaeus have made sure they each have their own set of bodyguards as a precaution. Fortunately for you, we are yours," Bain said.

Jadis scowled at Silas. "So they are still reading my thoughts as well? I think you're taking things too far."

In unison, the three of them answered, "We are *taking things too far*?"

She was still glaring at Silas, doing her best to ignore Dante and Bain.

"Yes. They can hear your thoughts. So I'd be careful what you think about—outside the bedroom." Silas winked. He casually motioned his hand, and the steward brought her dinner.

I now have all three of them at the table, keeping a watch on me and listening to my every thought. Not to mention they never eat. She thought as she pushed her plate aside, having lost her appetite with the awkwardness.

"No, we eat. We just have a different appetite," Bain replied in jest.

"We'd be happy to dine with you if you don't mind a few guests bleeding at the table," Dante joked as he tilted his head and waited for her to respond.

Silas also laughed as he pushed her plate back in front of her. "Eat, Jadis."

"*Eat* this." She playfully tossed a piece of bread at him. She knew he would catch it but she didn't realize it would send the three of them into hysterics. *That's fine. I can sit here all night and ignore them. No big deal.*

"And how are you going to do that, dear girl? You can't even keep us out of your head," Dante retorted.

Jadis followed up by tossing a piece of bread at his face as well. *I am obviously their entertainment for the night. They are going to make sure they put me in my place. This is going to be a very long and annoying lock down,* she told herself.

CHAPTER 15

S ilas and Jadis were in their stateroom getting ready for their return trip to the Valley of the Old Gods. Jadis pulled out a pair of jeans and a t-shirt and tossed it onto the bed.

"You can't go dressed like that," he stated.

"What's wrong with it?" She asked. *Apparently, what I picked out isn't appropriate attire?*

Jadis watched as Silas pulled out an outfit he deemed appropriate, as well as the necessary weapons. He laid out a pair of dark grey cargo pants, a light grey tight-fitting t-shirt, black combat boots, and a military belt. She sat on the bed, watching in amusement as he meticulously picked through her closet.

Silas turned to Jadis and tossed the items onto the bed. "I assume you know how to use this?" he quesitoned as he set a smaller Glock on the bed."

"Of course."

"Then get dressed, baby, we're on a tight schedule."

"So serious," Jadis replied jokingly.

She stood up after checking out all the clothes he had tossed her way. She put on the cargo pants, the t-shirt, the boots, and the belt. She then pulled the slide back to see if the Glock was chambered. Once she finished, she looked over at Silas, and realized they matched perfectly.

Silas watched her checking her Glock and nodded. "Good girl."

Jadis was fully amused as she studied their appearance. "Really? You bought me a matching outfit? Isn't that what I'm supposed to do?"

"Funny girl." He grabbed her by the belt and pulled her into him. "If you look like me, everyone will know you're mine if something happens or we get separated," he said, as if it were common knowledge.

"Is this some sort of Nosferatu code?" She chuckled. "When people look at us, they'll immediately know I'm off limits as long as our outfits match?"

"Come here, and yes, if you must know, I would hate to have to remind someone I own you."

"You are ridiculous, Silas."

"I am, huh?" he answered playfully. "Well, I'd rather be making you laugh than fighting with you, so I'll take it."

He grabbed her face with one hand and stole a little tongue. She jumped up and wrapped her legs around his waist and her arms around his neck.

"You sure we need to leave right now?" she whispered in his ear. She then slid her tongue up his neck and nipped his ear lobe.

He set her back down and pointed at the chair, and did his best to ignore her sexual advances. "You forgot some things," he stated.

Jadis looked over at the items still sitting on the chair. "You're kidding me, right?" She laughed again and began picking through the items. There were pads, a helmet, sunglasses, more pads, and a vest. "I'm supposed to look like I belong to the bomb squad? This is a no." She tossed the helmet aside. "Nope, I'm not wearing this either," she said as she tossed the knee pads, padded vest, and shin guards back into the chair.

She picked up the sunglasses and put them on. "These are cute, I'll keep them. They look just like yours."

"You will wear all of it," Silas demanded.

"Umm, no I will not." She put her hand on her hips and stood her ground.

"Jadis, aren't you tired of playing around? Can you be serious for once? I need you to be protected. You're not Nosferatu, and if you don't have access to your powers for some reason, you cannot heal yourself. The pads will protect you, if for some reason you come in contact with their blood, so it doesn't matter what you think they look like."

Silas looks annoyed again. Go figure. "The pads are stupid. How am I going to die? By bumping my shin without a pad? Not to mention, I will die of a heat stroke wearing all that shit."

"I don't have time for this. Put it on. And it's self-cooling," he added correcting her.

"No, I will not waiver, Silas."

"I will *not waiver* either." He grabbed the vest and pulled it over her head before strapping her in. It was the size of a t-shirt, only stronger and slightly thicker.

She looked at Silas's vest and and it really didn't stand out or look uncomfortable. "Fine, I'll wear the vest but that's it."

He stepped back and looked at her as she stood by the edge of the bed.

"Stop looking at me. You're staring at me because I look stupid."

"On the contrary, mon chéri, you look amazing." He was suddenly chest to chest with her and had a hold of her vest.

"I have to admit, you look pretty goddamn hot adorned in all your gear," she said, as she looked him up and down, taking in the delicious sight. "I bet I can get those off of you pretty quick." She grabbed his vest and stood on her tiptoes to kiss him.

"I bet I can get you naked faster," he replied.

It only took seconds before Silas had her naked in bed again. He peered deep into her eyes, as he lay on top of her with a serious expression. "I need you to do exactly as I say today. Do you understand? I can't imagine living the rest of my life without your naked body beneath mine."

After he spoke, she noticed a look of worry wash over him. "I promise, I will do whatever you say, for today anyway," she joked.

"Jadis—" he began when she interrupted him.

"Yes. I promise. I will listen to everything you say, and I will not stray from you." She tried her best to reassure him.

"This is not a joke. It will be extremely dangerous, but especially for you."

His words sent an all too familiar wave of chills up her spine, and she felt his sense of dread. "I get it, I have no intention of leaving your side. I can assure you I have no desire to face those things alone again."

His mouth fell to hers as he shoved her legs apart and thrust himself inside her tight, wet core.

It took about ten minutes for them to get dressed after they had finished. They did their best to hurry, thinking the rest of his crew had likely been waiting for them for at least forty-five minutes by now.

"Just one more thing." He flicked his wrist and the golden anklet appeared in his hand. He made a point of holding it up in front of her face before tucking it safely into one of the inside pockets of his vest.

"If I feel one ounce of fuckery from you, I will put it back on as quickly as I took it off." He didn't wait for a response from her. "Let's go, baby."

They made their way up to the deck, where the rest of the group was already preparing to leave. Skye and Ivory were also waiting to greet Jadis when they reached the top deck.

"Holy shit!" Jadis exclaimed, excited to be reunited with her sisters. She hurried over, and the three of them embraced. It was the first time they had been together in two weeks.

Silas watched them, looking less than enthused with their reunion. Jadis knew he wanted nothing more than to keep them separated.

Silas stepped toward them. "The three of you need to get one thing straight. You will do exactly as we say. Is that in any way unclear?"

Silas's word of warning seared through Skye and Ivory like an icy chill, and they quickly nodded in agreement, looking to Agaeus and Syth for help.

"Don't look at us. We are all on the same page," Syth replied. Jadis, Skye, and Ivory nodded once again.

Dante and Bain were just a small distance away, chuckling with one another and glancing in Jadis's direction, and more than once. She glared at them, but all she got in response was a wink from Dante.

Yep, they're up to something once again, she thought. There was just something in the way the two of them looked at her that made her feel self-conscious.

"By the way, it's about time the two of you showed up. Your tardiness lately is irritating," Agaeus scolded, looking directly at Silas as he tossed a duffle bag into the helicopter.

Silas cocked his head at Agaeus. "Since when has anyone other than me decided when we leave?" He raised an eyebrow at his brother in a challenging manner.

Agaeus kept his mouth shut; he knew better than to challenge his brother. Silas would have no problem putting Agaeus in his place, regardless of whomever else was around.

The rest of the group continued getting ready, ignoring the brothers baiting each other. Two more helicopters had landed on the yachts anchored not far from theirs.

Jadis, Skye, and Ivory tried their best to use this time to catch up with one another. They disregarded the fact multiple sets of ears were tuning in to every word they spoke.

They all arrived at the Valley of the Old Gods just after noon. The arid, sweeping sands were all they could see for miles on end. The rays of the sun beat down relentlessly, and the heat was almost suffocating. The desert was barren; there wasn't a single bush or tree in sight that would provide any type of shade or relief from the scorching heat. Though the terrain was harsh, it was not without life. The animals inhabiting the area somehow thrived in the harshest of conditions. Ahead in the distance, they could see scorpions scurrying across the sand, along with snakes slithering down the sandy dunes, leaving sideways tracks which were casually swept away with the hot, arid breeze. The desert was a melting pot of life and death, each surviving off the other.

This was it; the place of a war long forgotten, Jadis thought, as she looked around.

Silas, Eden, and Jabari had decided to meet on the outskirts of the hidden oasis. Their final destination was the mountainous region of Solei.

Jadis turned around to see another clan appearing off in the distance, and Silas stood unwavering at her side, just as he said he would.

The moment Jadis spotted Aiden heading their way, she ran to him. She leapt into his arms and he caught her, spinning her in circles as he held her tightly. Aiden was as happy to see Jadis as she was him.

Agaeus and Syth stood on either side of Silas, each with one hand on shoulders.

"Easy, brother. You knew this reunion was going to take place, and this would more than likely be the outcome," Agaeus calmly reminded him.

Silas cocked his head to the side. To see Jadis in the arms of another, much less Aiden, felt like a powerful serpent slowly wrapping itself around his body, restricting his breath; the air around him felt devoid of oxygen.

Jadis knew her greeting Aiden didn't sit well with Silas, but she didn't care, she was truly happy to see him.

Aiden set her down and placed his hands on either side of her face. She in return rested her hands on his forearms and their foreheads met.

"You still smell like jasmine," Aiden said with a smile.

"You still smell like an idiot," she joked, causing them both to laugh.

He held her out in front of him. "You look amazing. It is so good to see you in person. You have no idea how worried we all were about you." He pulled her in for another tight embrace and his scent was exactly as she'd remembered, and she savored it.

"It's good to see you too, Aiden." She was grinning from ear to ear as she hugged him back.

Silas had had enough. He materialized next to them and pulled Jadis against his body.

"Reunion's over. You've said your hellos, Aiden, now take your hands off her."

"I see you haven't locked the poor bastard up?" Aiden replied to Jadis in a joking manner.

Jadis couldn't help but to chuckle along with Aiden.

Silas stood silently. The animosity he had toward Aiden right now was like acid, and his stare was burning, potent, and deadly. Jadis wrapped her arms tightly around his waist, trying to reassure him she was his and only his.

Jadis looked over and saw another witch appear off in the distance as the oasis grew and slowly engulfed them all. *She looks like an Ipheanorian princess. She is stunning, no doubt about it.* Jadis thought.

Aiden and Jadis were still barely making small talk when Aria's voice broke the tension as she reached them.

"This is her?" Aria asked with a slight huff as she glared at Jadis.

She has about the same look on her face as Silas had on his. Except Silas, of course, is a thousand times more intimidating and could back up any look with one deadly blow, Jadis thought. She couldn't help but to feel a ping of jealously knowing she and Aiden were together.

As Jadis spoke, Aria's eyes pierced into hers like daggers. "I assume you're none other than Aria?" Jadis offered.

"I am, not that it's any of your business," she replied smugly.

"Jealous much?" Jadis asked.

At the same time, Silas and Aiden were back to bating one another.

"She's mine. Never touch her like that again. Understand? I only let this happen for Jadis's sake, but trust me when I say it's the last time," Silas warned again.

Aiden, always up for a good fight, stepped closer to Silas. "I believe Jadis is perfectly capable of making her own decisions." Before he had finished his sentence, however, Silas pushed his shoulders back; a rumble of warning rising from his chest.

"When it comes to Jadis, she is none of your concern," he snarled.

"Ohh, she is my concern," Aiden replied sternly.

Silas and Aiden were now in a half crouched position, ready to fight, having fully 'turned'.

"You have anything else to say?" Silas questioned, waiting for Aiden to challenge him.

The rest of the scene looked like two platoons lining up behind their own Commanders. This was not the fight anyone was expecting, they weren't there to fight each other. They were there for one reason and one reason only, killing the Sagan.

Eden's concern the brewing animosity between Aiden and Silas would rear its ugly head was coming to fruition. He had hoped if anything occurred, everyone else would step up and help separate the two, rather than let a potential war start amongst their clans. To his relief, he saw some of the others doing exactly that. *At least some of them are exercising common sense,* he thought.

Agaeus and Syth each took hold of Silas's shoulders; their warriors lined up behind them. Lars had already taken hold of Aiden when Eden joined him, as did their warriors.

With all the attention on the fight about to ensue between Silas and Aiden, no one noticed the altercation brewing between Jadis and Aria.

As multiple warriors from each side stepped in to intervene between Silas and Aiden, Jadis realized she was left to deal the bitch named Aria.

"You look like a little girl playing warrior princess," Jadis chided smugly.

Aria laughed in her face. "Warrior princess? I expected more from you too, based on what Aiden told me. You're nothing more than a wannabe Nosferatu soldier." Aria laughed. "Trying to look just like your mate, as if its soo intimidating."

"Don't try me, Aria. I will cut you down without breaking a sweat," she rumbled.

Aria pulled two daggers from her sides and spun them around. "You think so?"

Skye and Ivory rushed over and stood behind Jadis, while Aria's sisters, rushed over and stood behind her.

Jadis and Aria walked in a slow circle around each other, taking one slow, choreographed step at a time as they continued to exchange words.

Based on the ferocity of Aria's vent, it is clear she sees me as nothing more than a threat where Aiden is concerned, Jadis thought, being more amused than afraid. "You better bring more than your little crack knives, you jealous bitch!"

"Jealous bitch? Those are fighting words, Jadis. I'd be careful if I were you," she warned, as if she were faking to be calm.

Ivory, Skye, Akela, and Messit stared at each other waiting for the other to make a move. As they stood there, it was clear this fight was not between them. Unless, of course, one of them got involved.

"Is your sister always like this?" Messit asked, breaking the tension and relaxing her stance.

"When provoked. Is yours?" Skye replied, as she too relaxed.

Akela and Messit glanced at each other and began chuckling. "Yes, she is."

Ivory and Skye joined in on their amusement and they stood side by side fully amused as they watched their sisters.

Jadis continued taunting Aria, "The way you throw yourself at Aiden, drooling at his feet, is pitiful." As she kept her eyes fixed on Aria, she overheard Eden telling Silas and Aiden to settle their bullshit at a later time.

They had no choice but to hold his commands in the highest regard. Aria and Jadis, however, didn't pay any attention to what was taking place between Silas and Aiden.

Jabari and his clan, also being part of the mission, stood nearby to take it all in and enjoy the show playing out in front of them. *Not just one fight but two.* He chuckled to himself. He couldn't remember the last time he was this entertained as he watched his daughter stepping up for another fight.

"Your presence is like that of a botfly. It's time to put an end to your incessant buzzing," Aria seethed.

Just as they lunged for each other, Lars materialized in the middle of them and stretched one arm out toward Aria and the other toward Jadis.

Shit! thought Lars. *I wasn't expecting this fight.*

"Hello? Aiden—Silas? You have bigger problems than yourselves right now!"

"Move Lars!" Jadis demanded as she stepped around him, trying to get to Aria.

Lars reached for her arm. However, she ducked and dodged his grasp. Now that she wasn't wearing the anklet, she had her powers back. But as she lunged at Aria, she felt herself being swept off her feet and realized she was in Silas's arms.

Aiden grabbed Aria and pulled her back, genuinely afraid of what Jadis might do to her.

Aiden and Silas looked at one another. "This is far from over," Silas rumbled.

"I will watch out for Jadis, even if I have to step over you," Aiden snarled.

"We'll see about that."

Silas carried Jadis away from Aria and Aiden before addressing her and the situation. "What the hell are you doing?" he asked, looking at her, a bit confused.

"She called me a bitch and came at me first with some jealous bull-shit."

"What is wrong with you? Did you not notice that she had a couple of daggers with her? Do I need to remind you again I still have the anklet?" Silas was only half joking.

"Of course I noticed her little crack knives, and the anklet is a non-issue. You won't slap it on me here." She knew it would take much more than a confrontation with Aria for Silas to render her powerless in their current situation.

"*Little crack knives*? Jadis, I can assure you I will slap that anklet on." Silas raised his voice, but at the same time he looked more entertained than angry, since he was smiling coyly. "That's my girl, taking no shit or prisoners. However, this is more proof I need you to stay with me."

"You were busy, were you not? Plus, she started the bullshit. I was just going to finish it."

Aria, whom Jadis assumed was having a similar conversation with Aiden, heard her from a distance.

"Finish it? You would be on the losing end, bitch!" Aria shouted as she looked around Aiden, who still had a tight grip on her.

"Oh please, little princess," Jadis yelled back. "Exactly what are you going to do?"

Silas turned Jadis around and walked her further away; he was now laughing.

"My God, you're a turn on when you're fighting. If we didn't have such a big audience right now, I would throw your ass down and fuck the hell out of you."

"I swear sex is all you ever think about."

"When it comes to you, hell yes." He winked.

Jadis rolled her eyes in response, but Silas's amusement made her chuckle. *At least he has my back.*

"You can't go around killing or beating the shit out of everyone that annoys you or you don't like for whatever reason," he added, now looking at her somewhat seriously.

"That's rich coming from you. Isn't that the flame calling the spark dangerous?"

"Sometimes the shit that comes out of your mouth." Silas laughed.

Eden was fed up with all the drama, and he called everyone to gather around. The three separate clans all listened in.

"That's it! No more bullshit! I hope everyone is listening. Jadis, Aria, Aiden, and Silas, the four of you are done. Damn. I expected nothing less from Silas and Aiden but Jadis? What the hell were you thinking? Scratch that. What the hell was I thinking? Jadis, I shouldn't expect anything less from you either, I know better by now."

"Just finishing what the bitch started." Jadis wasn't purposefully smarting off to Eden, especially in front of everyone.

"You can't finish shit," Aria retorted.

"Enough!" Eden demanded once again. It was obvious he was at his wit's end. "The four of you can finish whatever bullshit this is some other time, on your own time. Right now, I need everyone to focus on the mission. Distractions will get someone killed, and I'm not having it. Silas, if you can't keep your shit together, I will take charge."

Eden then turned his attention to Jadis. "Jadis, that goes for you too. There is a time and place for everything, but right now is not the time nor the place for this shit. Holy hell, I'm feeling a familiar headache coming on."

Of course he's looking right at me, she thought, doing her best to ignore the snarky remark as well as him rubbing his temples.

"Covens and clans, you all do as I say. Have I made myself clear enough?" Eden stopped speaking, scanning everyone's faces to check for understanding.

Jadis backed into Silas, and he wrapped his arms tightly around her. After all this time, Eden could still scare her when he got down to business. *There is a force to be reckoned with lying beneath his astute surface. Whatever it is, is no joke, and neither is Eden,* she thought. "I think someone needs an aspirin," Jadis quietly said. However, you can't quietly say anything around their kind. Unfortunately, everyone heard her sarcastic comment and watched as Eden snapped his head in her direction. Jadis could feel the tension radiating off him.

Everyone else in the group turned away from Eden as their laughter was getting the best of them.

Silas spun Jadis around to get her out of Eden's line of sight. "I cannot believe you said that. Are you trying to get yourself killed again? You have a serious death wish, baby."

"It's just that he's always so serious. Apparently, this isn't the first headache I've given him, *if vampires can even get them.*"

"I'm not even going to ask." Silas continued moving further away from Eden.

"If that's all, it's time for all of us to get to work," Eden ordered. "We need to refocus on the reason we've all come together; to locate and destroy whatever has hidden itself in the valley for the last nine hundred years."

Intention replaced the looks of amusement many had had on their faces, as they listened to every word and instruction Eden and Silas gave. They all committed the plan to memory. They knew who was responsible for each step along the way, as well as what to do in the case of being separated from the others.

"Girls, are you ready? Jadis, I assume you can behave yourself for the time being and focus your attention solely on the task ahead?" Eden scolded.

Jadis narrowed her eyes at him as he continued to berate her. Silas looked down and winked at her, letting her know Eden's scolding her wasn't a big deal.

Jadis winked back, deciding ignoring Eden was for the best, with the little prompt from Silas, of course.

"Aye, milord," they all answered in one way or another.

Silas squeezed Jadis's hand, trying to give her some reassurance. He felt her fear and nervousness growing as things became serious. He was aware of the entire conversation she had with Hecate and knew how uneasy it was making her as she carefully replayed Hecate's warning over and over in her mind.

"I'll be right here." Silas kissed the back of her hand and stepped away, if ever so slightly.

Skye, Ivory, and Jadis formed a circle along with Aria, Akela, and Messit. Aria and Jadis put their issues aside for the time being. They stretched their hands out to their sides and touched each other's fingertips. They closed their eyes and took a deep breath, absorbing the energy from the world around them.

They moved into a self-induced trance and created an energetic-mirror that would allow Dante and Bain to see what they saw. Eden and Silas agreed it would be best for Dante and Bain to follow their vision, not wanting to miss anything no matter how insignificant it may seem to the girls.

As soon as Dante and Bain psychically let the girls know they held the vision, the girls began their incantation.

"In this earth, where we stand, digging our roots deep in the sand, fill us with the strength of immortal sight."

"In hac terra, in qua stamus, radices altas in arena fodientes. Reple nos virtute immortalium aspectus. In hac terra, in qua stamus, radices altas in arena fodientes. Reple nos virtute immortalium aspectus.

The girls looked beyond the vale, with one sight, one mind, one energy. They scanned the landscape in unison, moving forth with the scurrying scorpions, as they stared sightlessly into the darkness, relying on the devoid stratum between Earth and air. They followed the scorpions as they scurried across the scorching sands, rippling like water before they disappeared deep into the sandy tide. The darkness softly waned, and a thick, grey fog swirled and churned with the shifting sands. A hole slowly took shape having been buried deep beneath the shapeless, drifting red tide. The twisted mixture of fog and sand followed the scorpions as they disappeared.

The scorpions led the girls to the entrance as they scurried down the smooth walls with stingers curled. They then felt something foreign, evil, and unwanted. Whatever was hiding had been hibernating in a cave, lying in wait just as suspected. They went deeper into the pit that had been bored straight down into the earth. The walls were obsidian and seamless; there would be no escape should one fall victim to the hole. There was also a corridor leading to a hidden chamber at the bottom. Something suddenly engulfed the girls in a chilling blackness. They were being beckoned by a foreign entity into the unknown void. A heinous sound echoed throughout the corridor, the adjacent chamber, and vibrated off the entrapping obsidian walls.

"It's somewhere in the vicinity," Jadis whispered.

All eyes were now on the girls, as everyone stood silently waiting for Dante and Bain to relay their visions.

"Careful, Jadis," Dante whispered psychically, also having heard the chilling sounds.

She could feel his presence close in behind her; somehow Dante had tethered himself to her, and she was more than grateful to feel his presence.

They watched as another waning image took shape. It seemed to be a cave that had nothing to do with the obsidian pit, along with three figures scrounging around.

An inauspicious feeling crept up Jadis's spine, and without warning, a looming pull began to effortlessly drag her from the circle. She tried to fight back, but with the self-induced trance, her energy was tied into the rest of the girls.

Whatever it was, Jadis was being sucked into the filth of its indifference. *Shit! It's been waiting for me,* she thought.

Her body slipped from the circle in between time and space, and she was being trapped in between the two realms. It was as if a necromancy ceremony was being performed. Only instead of resurrecting her from death, it was pulling her from life and into the snare of its deception.

"Jadis!" yelled Ivory and Skye as they grasped her hand, having felt her being pulled from them.

"Dante!" Jadis screamed. She suddenly did a face plant on the ground, hitting her head hard enough she couldn't see anythingg but speckles. Something had grabbed her foot from behind and began pulling her down the corridor. She clawed at the sandy ground, trying to stop it from taking her. She then flipped her body over, pulled her Glock out, and kicked at it with her free foot, before firing. All the while screaming for Dante. "Dante!"

"Jadis!" Dante called out.

The girls rushed after her but were hit with a powerful punch, which sent them crashing into the solid obsidian walls.

Dante grabbed Jadis and she swung her fist around blindly, trying to fight the invisible threat.

Dante grabbed her arms, took her Glock, and tucked it into the back of his pants; he then wrapped her body tightly in his. "It's okay, darling. It's me, Dante. I've got you," he said as pulled her out energetically.

Once they were out of the void, Dante handed her over to Silas, who held her steady. "Baby, look at me."

It was hard to get a grasp on reality since they hadn't fully come out of their trance after having the incantation ceremony ended so abruptly.

"I've got you," Silas said softly, holding her tight in his arms. Her confusion subsided, and she wrapped her arms around him.

"Silas, just like I said, it was waiting for me," she whispered.

"Shh, baby. You didn't think I would let you go in alone now, did you?" His tone was calm and reassuring. "That's why I had Dante attach himself to you."

"Dante, where is he?" Jadis asked, keeping her face buried in Silas's neck.

"I'm right here, darling," Dante replied as he rubbed her back.

When she looked up from the crook of Silas's neck, Dante and Bain were kneeling next to them.

"Dante, had you not been there—" Jadis began.

He interrupted her, "Ahh—come now, darling. I thought Silas made himself clear over the last couple weeks you were to be chained to us indefinitely," he said, with a nervous laugh. He then gently wiped the blood away that was seeping from her nose.

Jadis chuckled, and smiled at them.

Syth, Agaeus, and Aiden had were holding Skye, Ivory, and Aria who were also disoriented and still coming to.

"Holy shit," Eden stated. "Jadis, are you okay?"

"I'm okay, physically anyway."

Eden walked around to all the girls, making sure they were okay. The entire group stood in stunned silence, gaping at the six girls, but especially Jadis.

"It's coming for her," they said, quietly amongst themselves.

Silas lifted her chin. "Are you sure you're okay, my love?"

"Yes really, I'm fine. It just scared the hell out me. It's never easy being ripped from a trance like that." However, she was still trying to collect herself.

Silas ran his fingers down her nose. "It's not broken."

Jadis reached up and felt it. "The side of my face took the majority of the blow."

Silas gently turner her head from side to side making sure there wasn't anything serious.

"Silas, I'm fine." Jadis smiled.

"At least now there is no question about its existence," Eden said.

"Yes, but we also saw the cave it's waiting in. It's not in the pit where we were looking," Jadis explained.

"It's a Segan?" Aiden asked.

"Yes," Bain replied.

"Just one problem though, I don't think there is one Segan, I think there are three," Jadis added.

"What do you mean, *three*?" Silas asked.

"I don't know. Hecate always talks in riddles, as you now know. She kept saying three, but we had three leopards, we have the three of you, we have three witches, so right now your guess is as good as mine."

"Maybe It's us, Jadis, The Three Keys?" Ivory questioned, as she looked up at Agaeus.

Agaeus nodded. "It's a logical explanation."

The chills crept over Jadis's body once again. "I really don't know."

Silas stood up with her and looked deep into her eyes. "We don't work based on guesstimates. Now that we know it's here, I think it would be best for us to send the *three* of you home. I don't like this at all."

Agaeus and Syth had the same daunting feeling.

"Agreed. We need to get them out of here," Agaeus stated.

"No, Silas," Jadis stated gently as she pulled away. "We're not going anywhere. You know as well as we do you can't do this alone." She waived her hand toward the girls. "We were given the powers to manipulate the vortex, least you forget."

"I'm not risking your life. After what just happened, forget it." Silas was clearly in no mood for another argument.

"You don't have a choice, Silas. It's not just up to you, and we are not leaving. My sisters and I were sent here by Hecate. You know this. You don't defy the gods, Silas."

"*Least you forget*, they are not our gods. Therefore, I am not *defying* them," Silas retorted as he cocked his head at her. "Nosferatu is ruled only by Nosferatu."

Skye and Ivory were standing in front of Syth and Agaeus. "We're not leaving," Skye stated.

"We want to see this through. We were sent by our mother for a reason," Ivory added.

"Dante and Bain cannot ask Hecate for assistance," Jadis shot back. "This is as much our fight as it is yours, and I think you forget, vampire, our ancestors survived the war as well. What? Are you going to call upon

Hecate to open the vortex?" Jadis asked as she raised her eyebrows in defiance.

"I don't need Hecate's assistance when it comes to you. I will decide your fate, not your mother."

"Is that so?"

"It is *so*."

Again, all Jadis could do was roll her eyes and wait to see what Silas would ultimately decide.

Everyone else remained silent, waiting to hear what was going to be decided. When it came to Jadis, Ivory, and Skye, their fate would be at the discretion of Silas and his brothers. No one was about to get involved in the standoff between them.

After an awkward silence, Aiden spoke up, "She's not wrong, Silas."

Aria spoke next, backing Aiden, "As much I hate to admit it, we need them." Aria's tone had softened a tad toward Jadis after what had just happened and she gave her a subtle smile, along with the jab.

Jadis obliged her peace offering with a soft smile of her own.

Silas, however, stood still and eyed Aria, reminding her to watch herself.

He then changed his expression, looking at Jadis with genuine concern. "Jadis, you haven't followed directions very well, if at all. If you so much as wander a foot away from me, I will have your ass on the helicopter headed home at a moment's notice. And don't forget, you'll also be wearing the anklet as well."

"Got it." Jadis stood on her tiptoes, grabbed his head, and placed her forehead on his. "Everything will be fine as long as you're by my side. I have no desire to stray an inch from you."

Dante held out her Glock and winked. "You might want this back."

Jadis looked at him with an enduring smile. "Thanks, Dante."

"Alright then, time to head out," Eden announced.

By the time they made their way to the cave, it was late in the afternoon and dusk was not far away. The vampires had no trouble seeing in the dark, but the girls would have to rely on magic. Regardless, Jadis had no intention of leaving Silas's side. And after what happened, she practically clung to him.

When it was time, Dante and Bain began the ritual and discretely weakened the entrance to the cave. It would take a world of knowledge they possessed in order to conjure a powerful enough spell to make this happen. Jadis, Skye, and Ivory would be the ones responsible for summoning Hecate to untwist the vortex, allowing Dante and Bain to open it fully, while Aria and her sisters would weave an energetic binding spell into Jadis and her sisters.

Dante and Bain reached out for their arcane power source, while Jadis, Skye, and Ivory stood behind them and waited until it was their time.

Dante and Bain began, three times they chanted, "Descendit, summi-to ut imperium."

Aria and her coven then began their incantation, and they, too, chant-ed three times. "Patentibus, retego, aperi, aperti."

Jadis, Skye, and Ivory followed with their own incantation, one that had been bestowed upon Jadis by Hecate. Three times they chanted, "Et ego invocabo Hecate."

Once again, Dante attached himself to Jadis. It wasn't long before there was a rattling of stone upon stone, and the entrance began to open. What began as an innocuous crack in the air, gradually morphed into a swirling vortex of ethereal colors, spinning like a whirlpool. Once it consumed the cave's entrance, all that remained was a faint outline, barely discernible amidst the ethereal haze.

Just as she had said she would be, Hecate was waiting. Jadis followed with a chant of her own in order to appease her generosity. "Gratias ago deorum."

Bain and Dante stayed in place and once the entrance opened, they took control of the powerful magic with their sorcery.

"Stay here," Silas ordered.

"What? Out here alone?" Jadis questioned.

"I will have a few warriors on guard. You don't need to be in the cave," he stated matter-of-factly.

"Silas—" Jadis began.

He interrupted her and held up his hand. "No arguments."

"I hate to interfere, but the vortex is also a gateway to a realm of darkness and chaos. If they remain out here and we lose whatever connection Jadis has, the consequences can be dire, Dante explained.

"Aren't you controlling the entrance?" Silas asked, angrily.

"Yes, but it's complex. In simple terms, our sorcery and their magic are intertwined," Bain replied.

"Silas, you know as well as I do mother specifically warned us to choose." She paused momentarily as it dawned on her; *should you choose wrong, the vortex will be sealed permanently.* "Silas?" Jadis stated, feeling even more concerned. "What if I don't make the right choice? Will it seal us all in?"

"Well hell," Silas mumbled under his breath.

"Silas?" Eden questioned.

"Fuck it," Silas sighed as he stared at Jadis. "Let's get this shit done."

They made their way in and remained divided into the three clans, as was often the case. Bain joined Eden and his group. They would be the first to enter. Silas's group would enter next, along with Dante, Jadis, Skye, Ivory and Aria. Jabari and his clan, along with Aria's sisters, were the last group to enter. Each group stopped through the vortex and as they made their way further into the cave, Jadis ran her hands along the walls, feeling the writings that had been carved so long ago. The further they walked through the passages, the more familiar it became. Jadis was once again reliving a distant memory, a dream. *The visions I've seen for so many months before Aiden killed the Baskale on my porch that night are becoming clear.*

"It's here. I can feel it, but there is something else," Jadis whispered as she continued to psychically read the writings. She touched the walls with one hand and clung to Silas's forearm with the other.

Bain answered, "I agree, there is something else. We need everyone to be ready."

They continued to move forward until they had made it about a quarter of a mile in. Silas walked directly behind Jadis and held onto her shoulder, to her relief. Jadis stopped briefly when she felt an intense, throbbing sensation in her head.

"What's wrong?" Silas asked, as her turned Jadis around so she was facing him. "Tell me, baby, what is it?"

Not only could she not speak, but she struggled to stand. Something unknown was pulling her with a power she did not recognize. *Whatever this is, it's fucking evil!* she thought to herself.

Silas announced telepathically, *"I'm taking her out."*

Jadis barely got the words out. "No. It's a vision. But it's nothing like I've ever had before. Something is trying to pull me to it." She tried to reassure Silas she would be okay so he wouldn't drag her out.

"You're leaving," Silas demanded.

"No! Skye, Ivory, Aria, come here. Are you feeling it?" Jadis asked.

"No, what is it, Jadis? Tell us so we can help," Skye replied.

"Take my hands," Jadis stated calmly.

They did so right away. As they came together, the vision grew; one key, not three.

"Aria, are you getting any of this?" Jadis asked.

"Just bits and pieces. This is not good, Jadis. This is evil and old, from before the days of the Ipheanors. It's you, Jadis, and it's not just the Segar. There is also something/someone else pulling you."

Silas was about to pull Jadis out of the cave, but she stood her ground. "Silas, calm." She placed her hand on his cheek. "It was only a vision, but it knows we are here. We cannot leave now, we're too close."

"I'm far from okay with this. I have a bad feeling about it all, and I don't like this one goddamn bit," he snarled. *"Eden?"* Silas called his name telepathically without following up with an actual question.

"I don't know, Silas. It's your call," he answered, without needing a question. *"I don't feel good about this either."*

"Well, shit!" is all Silas said, his confusion apparent.

"Let's just go, baby. We're already here and there are about thirty of you right now," Jadis argued.

"It's against my better judgment, but we can't stand here arguing all night," Silas said, still not confident in his decision. *"Eden, hold up. We're going the rest of the way together."*

Their groups merged, and the familiar stench overtook all of them. It permeated every inch of the cave. Jadis, Skye, and Ivory side-eyed each other, afraid to face whatever it was.

Before them stood the entrance of an enormous cavern located within the cave. Jadis scanned the area again, feeling overwhelmed by its size, depth, and darkness. *It's down there somewhere,* Jadis thought.

A large rumble grew from below the cave's floor. *An earthquake?* Jadis thought. *No. This is something more.*

The ground was shaking, and the noise was like extended thunder, but the vibrations were coming from deep within the cave.

"Get back, Jadis!" Silas grabbed her forearm, but she was yanked back, as the rocks came tumbling down, the eruption ended up separating Jadis, Skye, Ivory, and Aria from everyone else.

The stench of rotting flesh grew fouler each dreadful second they lay trapped beneath the pile. The sounds of rocks and boulders being tossed aside caused debris to rain down on them. Once the sounds subsided, Jadis no longer felt her sisters or Aria. She was alone, lying amidst a pile of rock. She swirled the surrounding energy and shoved the rocks aside, freeing herself from the stony grave. It took a moment to gather her senses before standing up. The dust was heavy in her lungs, and it was making it difficult for her to breathe. She choked and coughed with each shallow breath, and could taste the blood running down the side of her mouth. She wiped it away with her thumb, and felt around trying to see how badly she'd been cut. In her disoriented state of mind, she began panicking. She was terrified about what had happened to everyone else, but she was more concerned about whatever it was that tossed the rocks around and took her sisters and Aria; Its energy differed from the Baskales.

The words *divide and conquer,* crossed her mind. *Of course, I'm all alone, go fucking figure!* She suddenly heard the clans calling out their names from the other side of the cave in.

"Jadis!" Silas yelled. "What the hell happened?" he roared. "How did she get pulled from my grasp?"

"We all know it wasn't a fucking earthquake," Dante stated angrily. "It used another form of powerful sorcery and it has them. I'm still connected, but I can't pull her through a solid barrier." He looked to Aria's sisters. "Are you getting anything from them?"

"Yes, and we have been divided on purpose," Akela answered.

Akela and Messit did all they could to connect with Aria, but all they were receiving was an empty, dark void; they had been cut off.

Messit and Akela stared at each other with the same dreadful thought. *"Aria, Skye, and Ivory are disposable,"* Akela whispered.

Silas landed a powerful blow to the rock, but nothing happened. He then landed an explosive front kick multiple times, but it stood, as if forged in iron. "I should have broke through by now," he lashed out. "Hell, I barely made an imprint in the fucking rock!"

Every one of them was scrambling, trying frantically to break through. It had their mates; it had the power to separate them, and it had the power to prevent them from tearing down the rocky barrier.

"It's harnessing its energy from something else. That's why we haven't been able to breach it. It's a wave of energy from the old world. I can feel a slight pulsing sensation," Bain announced.

Bain and Dante simultaneously harnessed their powers in response to subtle blue pulsing light they picked up on. They could combust, transform, and manipulate matter on a molecular level and they would break through the rock one way or another.

"They won't last long against the Segar. It's ancient, powerful, and it seems the energy it's harnessing is more powerful than the girls combined," Silas rumbled.

They faced the rock wall together, anxiously waiting for Dante and Bain to break through.

"Once we get in, it's all ours," Silas snarled, as he looked at Agaeus, Syth, and Aiden, who nodded in agreement.

"There won't be anything left of it but pieces of their corpses when we're done," Syth stated.

CHAPTER 16

"*Ivory, Skye, Aria. Can you hear me?*" Jadis called out telepathically, but didn't get a response. She knew right away they weren't within the immediate area. She needed to calm her racing thoughts. *Shh*—she told herself, *listen—think—feel.* She tried to remember everything Hecate had said to her.

The cold, musty damp air seeped in from deeper within the cavern bringing about a chill. She reached up and only a couple of claustrophobic feet separated her head from the ceiling.

She cautiously made her way further in and the cave opened once again. Jagged stalagmites rose from the ground, and stalactites pierced down from the ceiling. Water was seeping down through the bedrock, dripping off the tips of the stalactites, forming acidic pools of water beneath them. Standing in the pitch black, she created an energetic prism to see what she couldn't with her naked eyes. Although she was petrified, she knew she needed to do something other than stand there waiting for Silas.

I have one of two choices right now. I can try to break through the rock, which would let Silas and the others in, or I can move the other way and go after my sisters and Aria. The only choice I have is to go after them.

She glanced around and then looked back the pile of boulders. Option one would take far too long, and truthfully, she knew she could never penetrate the rocks and boulders. *Hell, if Dante and Bain haven't broken through by now, what makes me think I can do better?* She did not yield the powers they had combined, not even close.

She could feel the energetic barrier separating herself and the clans, and it was completely foreign. She wasn't sure how much time her sisters and Aria might have now that they were in the clutches of whatever had taken them. She made her way a few feet back, placed her palms on the pile of rock, and reached out. *"Silas?"*

Silas responded immediately. *"Holy shit, Jadis, are you okay, baby?"*

"I think so, but it has Skye, Ivory, and Aria. I have to go after them, or this thing is going to kill them," she replied.

"No! Don't do it. It's using them as bait. We are working on it from this side. You know Bain and Dante will not let us down, don't you move. It's only a matter of minutes and we'll be there with you." He waited momentarily for her to respond. *"Jadis? Are you listening to me?"* Silas demanded.

"I love you, Silas. I had to let you know I was okay, but I have to go after them before they run out of time. I can feel their energy waning. Just hurry and get in here. I need—Silas, I need to move! Something else is closing in on me." She felt a spike in adrenaline as the surrounding energy shifted and another presence approached her. She placed her back against the wall and removed her Glock from the holster on her hip.

"Jadis, don't do it. You can't stand against it alone. It's too powerful, and you know it. Wait for me!"

"Silas, I have to go. Something else is here!" She aimed at the shadow approaching her and fired at whatever/whoever it was closing in on her.

"Jadis? What else is in there?"

They all heard the rapid fire of her Glock, which sent a wave of dread through them all.

"Dante, Bain, you need to do it now. Something/someone else is in there using her sister's as bait and she's going after them." Silas landed a well-placed front kick to the barrier, which sent small amounts of debris scattering from beneath his boot.

"Of course she is. When has she ever listened to us?" Dante's comment came from both a place of respect and endearment. No matter how many times she had frustrated the hell out of him, he secretly held an unrequited love for her. The undesired feelings were the eye of his own storm.

Each panicked, frantic step Jadis took felt tortuous knowing she was heading toward, the beast who had been haunting her, hunting her. Not only that, but something else was stalking closely behind. She was shuffling her feet as quick as she could, trying not to trip. She followed the cavern's uneven walls with her palm. It was absolute silence except for the sounds of her shallow, raspy breaths, the shuffling of her footsteps, and the beating of her heart drumming in her ears. She felt the presence close in behind her and as she spun around and aimed, someone snatched the barrel, twisted downward, and pulled it from her grip. "What do want? Who the fuck are you?" Jadis yelled.

She gasped for breath, ducked, and shielded her face as a flock of winged creatures suddenly flew past her. She wished nothing more than to be invisible to all that lurked somewhere nearby and held deathly still for a moment as they swept across the ceiling as if they were flying away from something. Their screeches and shrieks numbed her ears and only increased her anxiety.

That smell? She thought. *It's familiar, but it's not the smell of rotting flesh that always accompanied the Baskale. Nosferatu!* She hoped with everything in her it was Silas, even though she knew it wasn't.

Just as she began walking again, the atmosphere changed before her, and she jumped back. However, it was too late. A hard blow radiated across her cheek, followed by a thick fog slowly enveloping her mind; she felt as if she was dangling from the hangman's noose.

Jadis didn't know how long it had been before she regained consciousness, but when she did, she was being dragged by her foot further into the cavern. The jagged rocks tore at her clothes and skin as she was drug across the harsh, uneven floor. The creature's savage talons gripping her ankle.

It didn't appear to be that tall; maybe 6', she thought as she stared at it. It was skinny in stature and both its hands and feet appeared to be too large for the rest of its body. It looked sick, and its large, dark greyish scales, similar to that of a lizard, were covered in mucus. Some of its skin hung from its body, sloughing off in some areas, dry and crusty in others.

Its talons sank deep into her skin and a burning sensation seared throughout her foot and ankle. It peered back at her, and its sardonic eyes were a deep, black and suffused with red. It continued dragging her with it until they reached the far edge of the cavern.

After being tossed aside, Jadis could barely make out the silhouettes of her sisters and Aria where they lay on the cold, hard floor of a smaller cavern. They were injured and she could see the faint outline of bruising around their faces, which were partially masked with blood. Had they not been energetically connected she would have thought they were dead.

"Are you guys okay?" Jadis asked telepathically.

Ivory and Aria showed subtle signs of movement, and it relieved Jadis to know they were conscious.

"*Yes,*"Ivory answered. *"I'm okay, but I think my arm is broken. We are going to have to get out of here another way. I'm not sure I can put up much of a fight—physically,"*she muttered.

"I'm okay. Although, I'm losing enough blood out of my thigh to feed everyone." Aria tried to make light of the current situation rather than focusing on the fact death was enveloping them. Aria subtly removed a leather strap from her waist and wound it around her thigh to slow the bleeding.

"Skye?" Ivory called out to her a couple of times before hearing her moan from the corner.

*"I'm not sure how I am,"*Skye muttered. *"Are the three of you okay?"*

"*Yes, sort of,"*Ivory, Aria, and Jadis answered in some fashion.

*"Did any of you catch the scent of another Nosferatu?"*Jadis asked.

Ivory thought for a moment. *"Yes, now that you mention it."*

"Someone took my gun, I think it was him."

"What would another vampire be doing in here with the Segans?" Aria quesioned.

*"Your guess is as good as mine,"*Jadis answered.

*"What are we going to do?"*Skye asked to no one in particular.

They were planning their exit strategy, but dared not move a muscle. They lay there playing dead, hoping it would buy them some time.

Jadis subtly tried to pull a large rock from beneath her, that was pressing into rips. But the moment she moved she felt her body rise from the ground before bouncing off the cave's wall. She hadn't seen or heard any signs of its presence before she was thrown across the cave. After tumbling to the ground, she rolled over to Ivory, hoping whatever heaved her into the wall wouldn't notice. The pain radiated throughout her body, and her head was throbbing worse than ever. The warm moist liquid ran down her face, just above her eye, and the blood and debris blurred her vision.

She heard a warm voice call out to her, *"Root yourself in thy present, in this moment, sight, and sound. Beg not of physical connections. Harness thy energy around you and call upon thy* ancestors. *Blend in. Become what is hunting you."*

Hecate! she thought.

"Jadis, what is it?" Skye asked.

"I've got it. Aria, are you listening?" Jadis asked.

"Yes. Get to the point, Jadis!" Aria replied, sounding as frustrated and terrified as the rest of them.

"We need to cast a spell, and we need to do it now. Follow along, call to the Old-World Gods."

"What?" Ivory asked.

"I don't have time to explain," Jadis snapped. *"Dammit, just do what I say. We don't have the power to hide right now. We need their help."*

"I knew you were crazy the minute I laid eyes on you. The Old World Gods have been devoid to us for centuries!" Aria snapped.

"Bitch, do what I say!" Jadis snapped back. *"Something's wrong. It's as if I'm being poisoned."* The nauseous pressure felt like it was ripping at the pit of her stomach.

"Jadis, what is it?" Ivory asked.

"It's talons, the bacteria they warned us about," Jadis said in a panic.

"Then we need to do this now. You're will not die, Jadis, just hang on," Aria said.

Together, they chanted, *"Rex Tremendae Majestatis. Qui Salvandos Salvas Gratis. Salve me, fons Pietatis."*

They were concealing their physical nature from the Segar and could feel a powerful energetic shift, as if someone was adding a layer of protection. They did their best to blend in with the cavern's environment. Jadis, Skye, and Ivory had done this once before, not so long ago, and it had served them well. That creature, however, did not possess the power of the Segar, and Jadis had no knowledge of what it was that had tossed her into the wall moments ago. However, she knew was it wasn't the Segar.

The girls moved in the shadows and shifted with the dead air. They had to do whatever they could to conceal themselves long enough for their clans to find them. They had not only their captor to deal with, but two more Segars who had appeared from other passages.

They faded into the environment, and they took on the Segar's smell. The Segars circled the cavern in search of them; they tossed rocks aside, scratched at the ground, and snarled words between them in a foreign dialect; their voices raucous.

It wasn't long before Jadis was found. She struggled to control the energy; her physical presence morphed and waned enough the creatures were able to catch a glimpse of her. One of them grabbed her and pulled her effortlessly from the floor. Skye and Ivory were able to conceal themselves and moved in front of the Segar who held Jadis, in an effort to distract it.

Aria had also blended in and limped to its side.

With a gut-wrenching roar, dead, rotting air spewing out of its mouth as it reached up, pulled its appendage back, and blindly swung in Ivory and Skye's direction, lashing out at the invisible threat it could only sense.

"Now!" Skye stated.

She Ivory, and Aria hit the two Segars aproaching from the side with a powerful blast; their bodies hit the wall and bounced off. The Segar holding Jadis spun around and headed down one of the corridors. The other two gathered themselves up; one of whom disappeared down another corridor. The other one stood staring in the girls direction as if it sensed them. It swung its arm and nearly connected with Skye who ducked out of the way.

As a wave of energy washed over Jadis, she heard the thunderous sound of boulders and rocks echoing off in the distance. She felt a breeze of fresh air and knew Silas and the rest of their clans had gotten in, however, she was already being drug away.

They rushed in, crouched down defensively and drew their weapons, as they briefly assessed the situation before attacking.

Agaeus and Syth shoved Ivory and Skye behind them, having sensed them immediately. Aiden pulled Aria behind him and was shocked when he smelled the amount of blood seeping from the gash in her thigh.

"Where's Jadis?" Silas demanded.

"It took her!" Skye yelled.

Silas inhaled deeply and pointed toward one of the many corridors. "I got her. They went that way." He and Dante took off down the corridor and headed in her direction, with the others following closely behind.

Ivory grabbed Agaeus's arm. "One ran down the cavern that way," she pointed, "another went that way," she said, pointing toward another passageway.

"Jabari, go after the Segar with your clan. The rest stay here with me. When this piece of shit is dead on the floor, split up and find Silas and Jabari," Eden ordered.

Eden and his group surrounded the Segar, and it stood before them in the center of the cavern. It was wild and strong, but crazed; its body weak from so many years of impenetrable isolation. Even so, it was a formidable opponent.

The Segar grabbed what appeared to be an ancient bow and arrow leaning aginst cave's wall. It pulled the arrow back and aimed at Zach. As old as the bow looked, the arrowhead, was crafted from some type of a luminous bluish glass, and was softly pulsing against the thick veil of darkness. Zach turned his body and knocked the arrow to the side with his sword.

Eden, Syth, and Agaeus moved the girls behind them and a few of the other warrior's pulled them back and surrounded them, while Eden, Syth, and Agaeus surrounded the Segar.

Jabari's squad ran after their Segar and chased the creature deep into the cavern. There was a thunderous rumble and rocks tumbled down around them. This time, however, they moved effortlessly to avoid the falling rocks. The Segar spun around, faced the warriors, and released multiple arrows. They were able to track the bluish colored tips and either struck them down or dodged them as they surrounded the creature, and cornered it.

The Segar lashed out at them with its long, decaying appendages, attempting to strike at anything within its vicinity. It lunged for Soyan, who slipped to the side evading the blow and swung his sword with precision as he moved; one of the Segar's appendages fell to the ground.

Soyan kept the wounded creature distracted, allowing Jabari to move in. Jabari leapt over the top of it in one swift movement and landed behind it. He then thrust his sword into its back, while Zach thrust is into it's chest.

The creature lashed out with its remaining appendage, but Zach recoiled his blade and its appendage fell to the ground.

Jabari pulled his sword from its body, gripped it with both hands and swung. As Jabari pushed it's body forward with his foot, the Segar's head hit the ground and rolled foward.

Zach stopped it with his foot and rolled it back toward it's body. "I believe this one is dead.

"Burn the body and head for Silas," Jabari ordered.

Silas, Dante, and their warrior's were in close pursuit of the one who had taken Jadis. Silas could see the shadow moving before them and they swiftly had it surrounded. Jadis, however, was nowhere to be seen.

Silas could feel her and smell her, yet it was as if she had disappeared. Silas gave strict orders not to kill the Segan until he had a hold of Jadis.

He began using his mind-bending abilities on the creature. It went wild, stumbling and lashing out in every direction, at every warrior, and sometimes at nothing at all; it then tilted its head, stared at Silas, and stood frozen in place.

"Show me where is she," Silas demanded as he began pulling its thoughts.

After the Segar tossed Jadis to the side of the cavern in order to face its enemies closing in behind, she created a mirage around her with all the energy she could summon. Once Silas was there, the need for revenge consumed her.

If I can kill it myself, then I can take its memories and know exactly what *they want with me,* she thought.

Jadis launched herself between the creature and Silas. She landed on the ground in a crouched position, slowly rose up, and stood face to face with the sickening beast.

Just as Silas was about to extract all information he needed from the creature there was a loud thump, and something else was standing in between him and the creature. Silas spun his sword, ready to strike, only to realize it was Jadis.

"You're mine! Tell me—show me everything," Jadis raged as she flipped her dagger at an angle, pressed the sharp blade against the Segar's throat, and slid it through the scales and flesh with little effort. Thick, putrid blood spewed from the grievous wound. Jadis then plunged the tip of the blade into its chest. She slammed her palm on its forehead and began pulling the images. The Segar lashed out, and the force of the blow sent Jadis spiraling backward, mere seconds before Dante severed its appendage. It then let out a guttural roar, which sounded more like gurgling before its lifeless body slumped to the ground.

Silas leapt across the cavern and caught Jadis. As her body went limp in his arms, he dropped to his knees, and cradled her. As she lay across his lap, he could hear the raspy shallowness of her breathing.

Jadis's head spun with the visions she took from it and the nausea welled up in the pit of her stomach. The pain was becoming intolerable as the toxins seared through her veins like a stampede of fire ants.

"Jadis? I told you not to leave my side," Silas whispered.

Eden stood next to Silas, and placed his hand on his shoulder.

"We need to get her out of here. The air is stale," he said with a heavy heart.

Silas immediately carried her out of the cave and into the cool, dark night.

Jadis felt Silas pick her up, but the bacteria from the Segar's talons had been seeping into her body through every puncture point.

I'm dying, she thought.

"Look at me, my love," Silas said.

Jadis tried to focus on him, but her vision was blurry, having been saturated with blood and dust. He continued to hold her in his arms, but all she could feel was her body going numb. She reached up and cupped his face in her hand.

"I love you with all my heart, vampire—" she whispered.

Silas slit his wrist and held it out. "Take my blood, baby."

She wrapped a hand around the back of his wrist and swallowed. She took what she could before her head rolled back and the world around her faded from dawn to dusk.

"Noo!" Silas bellowed. "Jadis—come back to me. Come on, baby, I can't lose you, not like this!" He rocked her in his arms with Bain, Eden, Aiden, and Dante at his side. "What were you thinking going after them alone? You stupid, stupid girl," he cried out.

He stroked her face, and wiped her hair away from the gash above her eye. "You should have waited for me, goddammit. You knew I would be there," he rumbled.

He arched his head back, and with a raging fury, he let out a gut-wrenching roar. The sky became eerily dark, and turbulent and unforgiving black clouds formed. Thunder cracked, and lightning split the night sky above them.

"Please, baby—say something. I'm not giving up on you. Not here, not now, not ever."

Everyone standing around felt the pangs of sorrow, guilt, and anger as they watched Silas, who appeared broken as he knelt on the ground with Jadis in his arms.

"If she dies, Silas will never be the same," Syth said to Agaeus, silently.

"She has brought the assassin has to his knees," Agaeus mumbled.

"Give her to me," Dante demanded respectfully, with Bain at his side. "If you don't do this now, we will lose her."

Silas, in a moment of sheer despair, lashed out at his brother as he tried to touch her. Silas snarled, "Get the fuck back, brother. I won't tell you again." The inferno of emotion was more than his mind could handle.

Dante held both hands up in front of him. "Brother, we can heal her. You need to trust us. A few drops of your blood aren't enough. Bain and I would never do anything to harm her, and you know this. You have entrusted her to us before, and more than ever, we need you to trust us now—her life depends on it. Time is fading quickly, and so is Jadis."

Eden was the only one who dared step forward. He walked up behind Silas, knelt down, and put his hand on his shoulder.

"Trust them, cousin. They mean her no harm. Let them take her."

"Come on, brother," Dante gently urged as reached for Jadis again. To his surprise, Silas allowed him to take her from his arms.

Silas handed Jadis over to Dante and they disappeared into the darkness.

CHAPTER 17

Jadis opened her eyes and looked around to see where she was. The excruciating pain she had felt earlier had calmed. She was in bed, lying between the burgundy satin sheets. She heard the familiar sound of the curtains gently rustling from the warm ocean breeze and the doors leading to the private balcony in their stateroom were open.

Silas was sitting in a chair next to their bed when Jadis woke up. "Well hello, mon chéri. You're awake. It's about Goddamn time."

"Hi baby." Jadis smiled and reached for his face.

He leaned down onto the bed with both elbows. He then cupped her hands in his and gently kissed her knuckles before resting his forehead on them.

"Where are Skye, Ivory, and Aria? Are they okay?"

Silas lifted his head ever so slightly. "They are fine. Everyone is just fine. For a moment, I thought I'd lost you," he whispered, as he hung his head.

Jadis could see the dread, sadness, and anger written all over his face. "How long?"

"Three days, love. The first day was touch and go. Dante and Bain never left your side. I owe them everything. They saved your life."

"Your blood saved my life," she said softly.

"How do you know, baby? You were barely breathing."

"I was watching you, without your blood—" she paused, "I was so far gone, so far from my body, while you held me in your arms. I called to you, but you weren't there. You didn't answer me."

"I couldn't reach you either. You were hovering in between light and dark. All I could do was hold you in my arms and try to take away your pain. You know there's nothing I wouldn't have done to hear your voice again, or to see you look at me with those mesmerizing eyes." He winked, with a soft smile.

"I would never leave you. You have promised me a lifetime, and I have every intention of taking you up on your offer." She stroked his face before he bent over and took her mouth to his. He kissed her with such emotion, you would have thought she had died and been resurrected.

"The Segar?" she asked.

"Dead thanks to the dagger you kept with you."

"Did you know the day you gave it to me I was going to need it?" she asked, knowing how calculating Silas always was.

"There was an undeniable pull, and I knew it would protect you, save you. How or when I had no idea," he admitted. "Had I known back then this was going to happen, I would have done many things differently." Silas's tone was serious, tormented.

There was a soft knock on the stateroom door. "I think you have a few visitors who have been anxiously waiting for you to wake up. Come in," he announced.

"Well hello there," Aiden stated, as he led an entourage into the room. Skye and Ivory ran over and hugged her tightly as the tears ran down their faces.

"Jadis, it's good to see you awake," Agaeus smiled.

"You scared us for a moment there," Syth added.

"Thank you, and I'm okay," Jadis replied to Syth and Agaeus.

"My god—we thought we had lost you!" Ivory cried. They nervously messed with her hair and adjusted her covers and pillows. Jadis waved her hands at them dismissively.

"Stop. Really, I'm okay. I was so worried about the both of you. It's such a relief to see you're okay."

Jadis, Skye, and Ivory chatted for about ten minutes when Jadis recalled something she had noticed while in the cave. "Did the two of you happen to see the other vampire after I was drug away?"

"No," Skye replied, looking at Ivory for confirmation.

"Me either, things were so crazy we didn't give it much thought at the time," Ivory said.

"That's weird," Jadis said as she looked at Silas for an answer.

Silas, who had remained silent to that point, bent over and gently laid a kiss on her forehead, ignoring her comment. "You have no idea how good it is to see you awake, my love; we are going to throw one hell of a party as soon as you're feeling up to it."

Everyone seemed to have forgotten she mentioned another vampire, so she let it go as well. "I don't know about anyone else, but I could definitely use a drink or two," Jadis added, avoiding the apparent non-issue of the other vampire.

"You and me both." Skye chuckled, also dropping the subject.

Every move Silas's brothers made seemed purposeful and precise, showing only the utmost respect to Silas. Jadis thought it was strange to see them behaving so cautiously. She got the sense that they were afraid of him. *It is odd, very odd.*

The mood Silas had been in for the last three days was one everyone feared. No one wanted to say or do anything that would set him off.

Anyone who might have contact with him, or with Jadis, had been forewarned. No one dared snap his icy chill.

Silas sat quietly, heavy in thought, while Jadis and her sisters chatted. *Watching her almost die in my arms about pushed me over the edge.* He had been pinned to the wall by a force stronger and darker than himself; insanity had been licking his face. *The only thing keeping me from total despair was the sound of her breathing. Though shallow at times, she was still breathing.* Silas stopped thinking back for a moment and looked at Agaeus and Syth.

"Come, let's give them some time," Agaeus suggested. "We'll come back later." They knew Silas was asking them to leave.

Skye and Ivory hugged Jadis again before making their way out. As they left, Aiden moved from the doorway and looked at Silas for permission to approach. Silas nodded, reluctantly.

Aiden bent over and cautiously kissed the top of her head. "You know what a pain in the ass you are, right?" He chuckled, trying to keep it lighthearted.

"Well, from what I've seen, you've taken on an even bigger pain in the ass. I believe her name is Aria?" Jadis joked.

"Jadis, there will never be a bigger pain in the ass than you. I don't think anyone on this yacht would disagree with me." He chuckled again as he sat on the edge of the bed and reached for her hand, giving it a firm squeeze.

Jadis immediately picked up on his anguish and a deeper thought, he kept to himself. *He also thought he was going to lose me.* He leaned over and gave her an endearing hug. It wasn't welcomed by Silas, but it reminded Jadis how much she and Aiden meant to each other. *Our friendship is priceless, one I truly treasure.*

She reached over and gently squeezed Silas's hand. *"Relax, vampire,"* she whispered telepathically. *"Always so jealous,"* she added, along with a wink and an enduring smile.

Aiden took heed of Silas's warning, which was apparent by the look on his face. He obliged and stood up without hesitation. "There's always time to catch up. I hear there's a party being planned. Someone said something about needing a couple of drinks?" Aiden added.

"Apparently, should I send an invitation?"

From the doorway, a voice answered Jadis's question, "As long as you make it a plus one."

Aiden turned toward the door and reached his hand out to Aria.

"I see you had your own little *crack knife* back at the cave?" Aria joked. She walked over and gave Jadis a hug. "It's really good to see you up. It seems we still have some unfinished business. I would have hated to see you take the easy way out by dying." She glanced at Silas realizing she should have thought before speaking.

"Won't be much to settle, but if you insist, I'm happy to oblige." Jadis chuckled.

Jadis and Aria began laughing at the stupidity of it all. They didn't really know why they were fighting to begin with, other than Aria not liking Jadis's relationship with Aiden. However, none of that mattered at this point.

"Look, Jadis, we owe you. You're the only reason any of us made it out alive. Had it not been for you, I know for a fact I would not be standing here today. Thank you for all you've done for us."

Jadis waved her hand at her. "You don't need to thank me, Aria. I almost got all of you killed because it was me it was after. I should have known better, or at least paid closer attention to my instincts." Jadis winced a little as she tried to re-adjust herself in the bed.

Aiden had been watching Silas the entire time and knew it was time to go. "Let's go, baby, they need some time alone. Jadis just woke up, and she needs her rest." He winked at Jadis, took Aria by the hand, and led her out of the stateroom.

Before closing the door behind her, Aria looked back. "Jadis, our covens are one. Anything you need, whatever it may be, you've got it. There are no exceptions."

Jadis smiled back. "Thank you, and if you ever need anything we'll be there."

"Are you okay, my love?" Silas asked as he sat on the bed next to her and pulled her into his arms. "There is going to be pain. We could help initially, but we can't take it all away. The bacteria invading your body is foreign to us. It took a lot to not only keep you alive, but to offset the infection. Which reminds me, there's someone else I need to thank."

Silas looked at the door as Eden entered. Jadis would have sat straight up if it hadn't been so difficult to move. She anxiously waited for the scolding to begin. *Here we go,* she thought.

For the first time, Silas stood. He walked to Eden and grasped his forearm and they gave each other a brief hug. Jadis was a bit taken aback by the closeness she felt between the two of them. *Neither of them has been the lovey-dovey sort toward anyone else. Maddie and I being the exceptions of course,* she thought.

They walked back to Jadis, and Eden stood on one side of the bed while Silas took his seat on the other side.

"Guess what, baby girl?" Eden asked, as he pulled a chair over and took a seat.

Jadis raised her eyebrows in a questioning manner without speaking.

Eden looked at Silas. "Damn, I thought you said she was okay?"

Silas chuckled for the first time. "She's fine. Sort of," Silas replied with a wink in her direction.

"No words? Who the hell would have thought? Had I not seen it for myself, I wouldn't have believed it." Eden waved his hand. "It's okay. I understand you've been through a lot. You don't have to speak. It's actually pleasant."

Eden's sense of humor shocked her. "Wow, you actually have a sense of humor. *Who would have thought? Had I not seen it for myself, I wouldn't have believed it.*"

The three of them laughed, but Jadis held her ribs and her breath. She noticed the look of worry move across their faces. She also noticed how they continued to glance at one another, as if there was something they were not telling her. For now, she played it off, figuring she'd somehow get it out of Silas later.

"I'm fine, really," she said to them, dismissing their concern and trying to hide her discomfort.

"Like I was saying, guess what I discovered based on my dealings with you?" Eden probed.

"I have no idea?"

Jadis looked at Silas, who was looking at her with a coy smile. He held up his hands. "Don't look at me, I have no idea either."

Jadis looked back at Eden. "Well? What?"

"It's called a migraine and guess what else? Vampires get them after all." He and Silas laughed aloud.

"Seriously? I think you found a sense of humor; I believe it's what you refer to as a migraine," she teased back.

"On a more serious note, there are no words to express how happy I am, how happy we all are, you are going to be fine. Maddie and Chloe have been worried sick ever since they heard about it all."

Jadis again caught that weird side-eyed glance between Eden and Silas. They were also saying something to each other telepathically while blocking her.

"As for the little party everyone's talking about, count us all in. The girls will be ecstatic. I'll leave you two alone now. You need your rest. You've been to hell and back, literally."

Eden stood and returned the chair to its proper place. He walked over to Jadis and placed a kiss on her forehead, which she found odd. Eden also hadn't had to ask permission to approach her as all the others had. *It's becoming clear something is really wrong,* she thought. Between the glances back and forth along with their silence, she thought she must either be dying, or hell had frozen over. Eden's kiss confirmed it.

After Eden left and closed the door behind him, Silas settled in behind Jadis on the bed. She scooted into him, rested her head on his chest, and laid her arm across his stomach. Silas played with her hair and held her as tightly as he could without causing her any pain.

"It's so good to have you back, my love. You scared the hell out of me. Don't ever do that again." His statement was followed by a kiss. Silas rolled onto his side and wrapped her legs within his.

He propped up on his elbow and looked down at her. "Are you feeling okay?"

"I'm fine. I was thinking about the way you and Eden kept looking at each other. I get the feeling there's something the two of you aren't telling me. Am I dying?"

"Mon chéri, you worry too much. We are just concerned about you. You cannot possibly realize what it took to bring you back to me. You nearly died, but no, love, you are not going to die. I don't want to go into detail right now. All that matters is you are safe and here in our bed, talking with me. Nothing is more important. I will tell you everything, let's just be in the moment. I can't explain how I am feeling. I don't think you understand how much I love you. Had I lost you, it would have been the end for me. I would have given up all my days for one more minute with you." Silas's expression was heavy.

"I'll never leave. I feel the same about you." She reached around to the back of his head and pulled his mouth to hers. He rested gently next to Jadis until she fell back asleep in his arms, his body covering hers.

When she woke again, Silas was still there. He had one arm wrapped around her, and the other was behind his head. Dante and Bain sat at the table on the other side of the stateroom.

"Hey baby," Silas said as soon as her eyes opened. "Did you sleep well?"

"I don't know? I keep having these strange, lucid dreams. But other than that, I guess I slept fine. I feel strange though. I don't know—I suppose I'm just tired."

"What do you mean you feel strange?" Silas asked.

Jadis looked over at Dante and Bain, who were sitting casually enough, but she could tell they were not there for a friendly visit.

"Have you two left at all?" she asked. *It appears as if they are looking at Silas for permission to answer, or for Silas to answer for them.* She wasn't quite sure.

"No," Silas answered. "I asked them to stay. Your body is still fighting the infection. They are here as a precaution." He then changed the subject. "You should try to eat something."

"I guess we should tell her." Dante chuckled.

"Tell me what?"

"We've decided you're a bit much to handle, so the two of us will also be permanently at your side. It wasn't so bad the last time, was it?" He followed his statement with a wink and heartfelt smile.

Bain stood up. "Seriously though, I'll get you something to eat. You need some food to help you regain your strength."

Jadis knew they were joking around to avoid her real question. She glared at them, knowing they were lying to her. *That's okay,* she thought. *I'll let them dodge my questions for now. I'm too tired to deal with it anyway, and I'm probably better off not knowing what is wrong with me. It is logical that Silas would order them to stick around if I were hurt. Ordering them to stay in the stateroom with us? Nope!* She knew there was something big they were keeping from her, and that was disturbing.

There was a lot of casual conversation in between her falling in and out of sleep the rest of the day. The three of them never left her side, nor did anyone bother to disturb them.

"Silas," Jadis said, feeling herself about to doze off again.

"What is it, my love?" he answered, rubbing her cheek.

"Your shirt is itching my back." Silas pulled his shirt off and settled in next to her.

"Much better," she replied lazily

.

CHAPTER 18

Jadis was looking through a foreign set of eyes. She was having another terrible nightmare. Which, unfortunately, was one of many. Each time she woke up, she was jumpy and out of sorts. This time, however, she felt evil. As if she were an executioner looking for her next victim. She scanned the room with blurred vision, finding that even her perception was distorted. Objects seemed to bend and twist into some sort of strange configurations. She looked down and could see the bed, yet she was not there. She was robotically scanning the room as if she was using some type of intellect rather than her own eyesight.

She hovered just below the ceiling, looking down at everyone in the room. Silas, Dante, and Bain were surrounding her from below. They were speaking to one another but she couldn't make out what they were saying.

Dante and Bain were handing each other instruments, and Silas appeared to be giving them orders. The three of them lunged at her, which was the last thing she remembered. The same process happened three times. As far as she knew, her recollection had become as fuzzy as her mind.

The following day, Jadis woke, but something felt off.

"How are you feeling? You had a rough night and were in and out of it," Silas said.

"The nightmares are plaguing me." She was groggy and felt worse than she did yesterday. She looked at Silas. "I know something is wrong with me. I can feel it. Tell me what's happening. Please."

"Nothing is happening to you. Like we said, you have been to hell and back. The infection is taking a while to leave your system. You'll have good days and bad days, good moments and tough ones, but it's normal."

Silas looked sincere enough, but she knew he was trying to calm her nerves. She desperately wanted to believe him, but struggled to do so. "That look you gave Eden yesterday, along with the way you, Dante, and Bain keep looking at each other now, is making me smell bullshit! That was not a normal nightmare last night. It really happened, didn't it?" She tried to sit up, but she needed help from Silas. "Oh shit! I am dying, aren't I? I'm dying and you're refusing to tell me! The three of you are here to burn my body after I'm dead," she emphatically declared.

"We are not here to burn your body." Silas chuckled.

She could tell Dante and Bain found her comment humorous as well, but they didn't laugh.

She suddenly moved onto her knees on the bed. She hadn't been able to sit up on her own just minutes earlier, but she sure moved effortlessly this time. *What the hell?*

"Listen, baby." Silas moved behind her and rubbed her shoulders. "I promise you are not dying."

"Liar!" she shouted as she turned toward Silas and knocked his hands off her shoulders. She had lost all mental restraint as soon as the odd sense of sight she'd experienced during her so-called nightmare returned.

Dante and Bain moved in behind her, and appeared to have been ready; ready for what she did not know.

They moved in unison, and once again, they were doing much more than checking on her. Jadis felt a prick on her shoulder.

Silas stuck me with a syringe? She thought, as she tried her best to knock it out of his hand. However, whatever it was took effect immediately.

Silas laid Jadis back down in bed while Dante and Bain stood at the edge.

"There's a storm on the horizon," Jadis mumbled, her words and the tone sounded demonic. Silas stood in shock.

"She's changing fast, too fast," Silas stated, sounding desperate. Once again, he could not control what was happening to her.

Eden had arrived that morning, but stayed out of the stateroom while she was awake, not wanting her to be any more suspicious than she already was.

"So how long do you think it will keep her out this time?" Silas asked.

"I'm not sure. It's hour by hour at this point. At first, we were getting four or five at a time, now we're getting two at best," Dante answered.

Silas turned to Eden, who had entered as soon as she was out. "Have you discovered anything more about the bacteria taking over her body? It seems to be turning her. Did you see her reaction?"

"I did, and I don't like it either." Eden responded. "We've been running labs since day one. I have put together the best team possible. They have and will continue to work around the clock. The only new information we have from the most recent blood draw is that her cells and whatever it is in her system seem to be merging. It's trying to take over her body. It's treating her like she's its host. The foreign bacteria are inserting their genetic material into hers. It's already taken over some of her functions, which is causing her anger, the lashing out, and the changes in her voice." Eden stared at Jadis carefully going over all if it in his head.

Dante was also standing in contemplation. "What about her eyes? There is something bizarre that doesn't fit."

Bain was rubbing his chin. "I agree, but we can't do anything about it. Not right now, anyway. When she is sleeping, or awake and lucid, they're normal. It's only when she changes we see the difference. Don't forget, we cannot use our powers on her physically, no matter how bad it gets. I told you there is something else in there trying to obtain information from us. I've felt it reach into me more than once already."

"What Bain says is true. It's tried to attach itself to me as well. I felt it when I reached in to help Jadis the first night," Dante admitted.

Eden placed a firm hand on Silas's shoulder. "Silas, we will stop you if need be. Don't make us have to go there."

"I haven't forgotten. The orders stand. Should I 'turn', you know what it will take to stop me. Sigurd and a few other Mortem warriors are prepared to intervene."

"We know." Eden patted Silas on the shoulder, trying his best to comfort him.

Silas paced the room, deep in thought. He couldn't physically help her, none of them could, and that was the worst feeling in the world. He was at a loss, not knowing what to do, but damned if he was going to let whatever it was take Jadis from him again. If he could just heal her, this would all be over, and he couldn't stop reminding himself. He felt as helpless as a fish flopping on the sand.

When Jadis woke, everyone was looking at a tablet and discussing whatever was on it. Eden was now in the room as well. Silas looked up and saw Jadis trying to open her eyes, and he immediately moved to her bedside. As soon as he did, Eden, Dante, and Bain focused their attention on her.

She noticed that none of them so much as blinked, and they looked like they were prepared for something to happen. Eden slowly set the tablet down onto the table.

She felt worse than ever. The nausea never left her, and her head pounded like someone was beating a drum inside of it.

"Darling, how do you feel?" Silas bent over and kissed her forehead before gently laying the back of his hand across it.

Jadis slapped his hand away, catching him off guard. *Well, that was clearly not the reaction he or anyone else in the room had been expecting, myself included*, she thought.

"Silas! I'm dying, aren't I?" she moaned, barely able to speak.

"No baby, you are not dying. I will no more lose you than the night sky loses the moon."

"And if the moon should fall, then what?" she whispered.

Silas gently kissed her lips. "Then I will be there to catch it."

"Silas," she groaned; the pain so intense all she could do was curl up in a ball. "Make it stop!" she pleaded and grasped his shirt in her fist, trying to keep him close.

She could feel Silas's calm state of mind, before she growled in response to Dante, Bain, and Eden's presence. She let go of Silas's shirt and rolled onto her back, before arching her back and bunching the sheets up in her fists. Jadis struggled to recognize the sound of her own moans.

"Oh, hell. I'm fucking possessed!" she cried.

She heard the cool, soothing voice of Silas reach out to her, "You are not possessed, baby. I told you, you are sick. Rest assured we are all working on it, just hold on a little longer, my love."

Dante studied her eyes and then looked at Silas and Bain. "I want to see something. Hold her body and her head still, and give her one injection."

Silas and Bain did as asked. Once they had her secured and injected, Dante clenched the top of her head in one hand, held up one finger, and then, slowly, he moved it from one side of her face to the other. Her gaze remained fixed on him, but there were another pair of irises, reddish-orange and bloodshot, lurking behind them, tracking the movements of his finger as they slipped out from behind Jadis'.

"Oh, shit," he mumbled telepathically.

She sat straight up on the bed and scanned the room with her distorted, vision before she felt another prick.

Silas and Bain looked at Dante for an explanation.

"There is something possessing her," Dante answered.

"It's also mutating, becoming more resistant to the medications and sedatives we have been using," Bain replied.

"Oh, fuck me," Silas stated as he stared at Jadis.

Dante rubbed his face with his hand. "We can't use anything stronger, either. Her body won't be able to handle it, physically."

Jadis suddenly shot up from the bed in some sort of catatonic state once again, and hovered above the stateroom. She was looking down at all of them as she had done before. She was in a half-crouched position, similar to the position the Segar had been in before it readied itself to attack everyone in the cavern the night she killed it.

It had taken over enough now to control her. They took their positions, waiting on Silas's command as they studied her as much as she studied them. They were now in a standoff; they didn't know what she might do, but they would not make the first move.

She roared down at Silas, who was the first in her line of sight. She lunged and Silas ducked, spun around, and grabbed her from behind. She swung around with such fury she was now face to face with him.

"Jadis, it's me. Come on, baby, fight! This isn't you. Take control. Come on, Jadis," Silas urged.

She snarled in response, and looked like she was ready to put him to bed with a shovel. Silas was just one more obstacle in their way. He moved in a slow circle, trying to get her to follow him so she would have her back turned to Dante, Bain, and Eden.

Jadis blinked her eyes and heard a familiar tone calling out in the back of her head. As distant as it sounded, she tried to listen through the fog that was her mind.

"*Come on, baby. Follow my voice,*" she heard. She grabbed her head, trying to get whatever it was out of her mind.

"*That's it. You can do this,*" the voice said. "*Keep fighting. I'm right here. Fight!*"

Silas was still slowly circling her, and she let out another gut-wrenching roar in response to his presence. Her eyes went black as coal, and Silas knew he was no longer looking at Jadis. He was looking at the Segar, and it was looking at him from behind her eyes. Silas moved slowly, keeping her eyes fixated on him, and watched as her body followed his movements.

"Now!" Silas yelled.

Jadis's body suddenly crashed through the wall and into the small passageway leading up to the deck, with them giving chase. As she appeared on the deck, she was ambushed by a dozen warriors all prepared to stop the monster from taking her. She snarled, crouched down, and began walking in a slow, choreographed circle, as if looking for an escape route.

Dante and Bain stood in front of her, their hands raised as if conceding, and took a few, slow steps toward her. She snarled in response, and met them step for step. Silas, Eden, and Sigurd, discretely positioned themselves behind her. Once she stepped toward Dante and Bain, they lunged and pinned her to the deck.

Jadis looked up, only to realize she was outside. She stared at the white clouds moving serenely against the azure-blue sky. As the world slowly faded, she could clearly remember what she saw after the Segar left her mind; the distressed expression on Silas's face.

Jadis had been having nightmares non-stop throughout the night. Her body ached, and she had vomited more than once. She no longer had control over herself, her thoughts, or her body. It seemed she couldn't break the sleep paralysis. She could see the room and Silas looking down at her, yet each time she opened her eyes, she was paralyzed. She didn't know how long this went on, but when she woke up, nothing had changed. She winced, and the tears ran down her eyes when she tried to roll over.

"Don't move, I've got you, baby, just lay still," Silas said.

He moved her around and placed her in what he thought would be a more comfortable position. Jadis didn't speak; she grabbed his forearm and squeezed it as if he was her lifeline. She knew he felt every ounce of her pain and fear. She saw him look at the others in the room as they all sat quietly around the bed in their perfectly positioned chairs.

Silas handed her a glass of water. "Drink baby, even if it's just a sip."

She tried to take the glass from him and noticed the IV in her arm. She looked at it for a moment, as if to study it, though she wasn't sure why. She didn't give a shit about it at the moment, but nonetheless, she felt herself making a mental note. She was also studying everyone in the room, as if it was the first time she'd laid eyes on them.

"Silas, you have to tell me what's happening," she muttered.

"You're going to be fine, my love," he assured her. "Just try to relax. I will never let anything happen to you. I promise you. If you choose to believe nothing else, you can believe that."

Jadis took the glass from Silas, and the minute the sip of water hit her stomach, she reeled from the pain and dropped the glass onto the floor. She curled up in a ball, and a low growl rose from her chest once again; this time it was aimed at Dante.

Dante stood ready for whatever was coming at him. She fell back on the bed and her breathing became labored.

Jadis could hear faint voices chatting around her. Silas was calling out orders and they were trying to calm him down.

"Silas, we are doing everything we can. We can't heal her. You know it's attached itself. If you go in her head, you're going to give it everything it needs from us," Dante chided.

Silas knew what they were saying was logical, but when it came right down to it, this was about Jadis. As far as he was concerned, all bets were off.

The lucid dreams were becoming worse, more vivid and more violent. She thought at one point she had tried to kill Eden. She opened her eyes and without conscious thought, she crawled across the bed toward Silas.

"Come on, baby," she cooed.

He looked at her as if she'd lost her goddamn mind. Her only thought was, *since when does Silas not want me?*

He met her on the bed, knelt on one knee, and placed a hand on her shoulder.

"Jadis, it's not you. Listen to me. Don't let it control you, get it out of your head."

"Ahhh—baby, control me?" She tilted her head to the side. "You control me, don't you?"

She grasped his hand and tried to remove it from her shoulder, to no avail. She stopped crawling toward him, rose up on both knees, and met him eye to eye. She rested her hands on either side of his face. "Baby, let's do this. Come on," she begged.

Silas did all he could to not allow his rage to consume him. He could see Jadis in front of him, yet he knew it wasn't her looking at him.

"Listen to my voice. You've fought this for days. I know you're in there, Jadis. Hear my voice and then follow it back to me," he instructed.

Jadis heard Silas calling for her, though barely. He was becoming nothing more than a distant whisper now.

"How about you follow me to bed, baby," it said, "I know that's what you want." She ran her cheek down his and snarled in his ear.

Silas pulled back immediately in shock; her voice had sounded like his. She then dragged her own fingernail across her neck and leaned back, tempting him to drink from her as the blood slowly ran down her throat, turning her white t-shirt crimson.

Silas nodded to Dante, who put her out with more sedatives.

"Goddamn, she sounds like me," Silas snarled.

"This is bad, and continuously sedating her is dangerous. Watching her cut herself is a clear sign she's in real trouble." Dante stood calmly, trying to be unemotional, for Silas's sake.

Silas looked at Jadis as she lay on the bed, noticing new bruises on top of the older ones. He sighed and laid a hand on her forehead. "I'm coming, baby." He immediately felt something trying to pull his thoughts.

Jadis woke, if only for a moment. "Silas?"

"I'm right here, darling," he said, stroking her cheek.

"What's happening to me?" *What a dumb question,* she thought, answering herself in the only way that was needed. "It has me, doesn't it?" She grabbed a hold of his forearm. "The Segar, it's consuming me—I—I can feel it."

She tried to lick her lips, they were dry and chapped. Her mouth was parched, and her throat was so sore speaking felt as if she was swallowing shards of glass. She had never felt as weak as she did at that moment.

"Take a sip, baby." Silas held the glass to her mouth. This time it wasn't water, but something else. It didn't hit her stomach as hard as the water had, and she could take a few sips and hold it down.

"Tell me, darling, can you feel anything? What does it want? Can you see anything or hear anything? Anything at all is important, no matter how minor you think it is," Silas questioned.

"If it takes me over, I'll be lost to you. They will kill me when I get the sepulture opened."

They looked at her and then glanced at each other, with the same overwhelming feeling of urgency.

"It's happening again. Be ready," Dante ordered.

"You thought we brought the fight to your door. What you didn't know was that it was already within your walls!" the thing within Jadis blurted out, still transfixed with Silas.

"Whatever you do, stay out of my head. All of you, do nothing. It—a trap—I'm—trap!" Jadis exclaimed, taking back control if only for a brief moment; her words discordant and broken.

Her back arched up off the bed. She snarled and began moving off the bed, like a siren in search of a sailor. She put one leg on the floor, followed by the other. She made her way around the bed toward Silas, attempting to seduce him again.

Jadis stood facing Silas. "Come on, baby. I'm right here, take me. You know you want this."

Jadis grabbed her shirt and tore the V-neck apart, bearing the tops of her breasts. She ran her newly grown fingernail across her collarbone, making another large gash in another failed attempt to get Silas to feed from her.

Silas was ready to protect her with life and limb. He fought the urge to attack physically, for any strike to it would be a strike to Jadis; he would end up killing her. He needed another approach, since physically there was nothing he could do.

"I know you can hear me," Silas snarled at the Segar. "You want me? I'm right here. Come and get me!"

"Ohh vampire. I don't want to fight you. I want to fuck you. Isn't there a difference?" it snarled crudely.

Dante moved in with a needle and Jadis swung around to knock it out of his hand. Dante was quicker, but the sedative had no effect on her.

"So you want to play too?" She seductively moved in Dante's direction.

"I think I can open my legs for more than one of you," it snarled.

Silas grabbed her shoulder and spun her back around. "Look at me, you fucking mutant! You will never have her," Silas raged.

"Oh, I think I already have her, vampire. That is what she calls you?" it questioned, using Jadis's words against them.

She looked down, ripped the IV out of her forearm, and tossed it across the room. "That's better." She moved in a circle, one leg crossing the other in a half-crouched position, and a set of canines dropped from her gums.

"Holy fuck!" Dante and Bain replied in unison, telepathically. Not wanting to give the creature any satisfaction.

"It's not physically possible," Eden stated.

They looked at each other in shock; her body had morphed and taken on the physical essence and appearance of a vampire.

"Maybe you'll like her better like this? How about a little vampire to tempt your cock?" She reached up and cupped both of her breasts in her hands. "Don't you like what you see yet?" she snarled, sounding exactly like Silas again. "You disappoint me, vampire. She should pay for that!" There was a loud pop and Jadis screamed before falling to the floor in a heap.

Jadis reached for her forearm and held it with her other hand, realizing the Segar controlling her had broken it. She wailed in response.

"Jadis!" Silas yelled, as he gathered her up in his arms. He laid her back on the bed and his innate reaction was to fix her arm himself. It took Sigurd, and three warriors who had been standing outside the stateroom to not only hold him back, but to talk him out of healing her.

Dante had also jumped in between Silas and Jadis. "No Silas! This is exactly what it wants! Jadis warned you. It's what she knows is true."

"Get the fuck out of my way, Dante. I'm not telling you again," Silas snarled. He flung Dante's hand off his shoulder; while his men pulled him back.

"Silas, get your shit together!" Eden demanded. "You are not helping Jadis right now!"

Jadis could hear the altercation all around her. "Silas—I can't do this anymore," she cried. "If this goes any further, I'd rather burn." She barely get the words out of her mouth.

Silas's canines receded and he quickly pulled himself together in order to tend to Jadis. "Don't go there, baby. Trust me, trust us. We will not let this filth take you."

"Promise me, Silas. Put me on the stake and release me to mother. Don't let it take me. I can't die like this. My sisters will know what to do," she begged.

"Hang on, darling. You are not going to die, and no one is burning anyone at the stake." Silas held her in his arms, doing anything he could to soothe her without using his powers.

"I can't take it anymore," she cried.

"You're going to be okay; I promise you," he said calmly.

This went on for two days and Jadis was no longer with them in any fashion other than physically. She moved in and out of consciousness and had been broken from the inside out as the Segar taunted them relentlessly. Aside from Jadis, the biggest problem they had to contend with was Silas.

"We've got to do something, or we're going to lose Silas," Dante said to Bain and Eden telepathically.

"He needs a break—" Eden began, before Jadis spoke again.

"Lock her down in her gilded cage," it sneered.

Jadis was once again standing in the middle of the room, arms halfway stretched out to her sides. "Let's play!" it said with a throaty voice. "What should we do to this little bitch today?" The Segar now appeared to them in a more mortal way each time Jadis reared up.

"She will not be locked in here much longer. Soon you will release her to us, or you will watch me break her limb from limb, one piece at a time."

The more it continued hurting Jadis, the more it struck and hurt her body and seethed disgusting words from her mouth, the more it all took its toll on Silas. He slit his wrist and stared at Jadis as his blood dripped onto the floor at his feet. Sigurd and another Warrior stood ready to intervene, while Dante and Bain did all they could to reason with him.

They tried to take him out of the room altogether so he could think and breathe.

Silas knew healing her would be a huge, undoable mistake, yet he struggled to remain rational. The Segar was taunting him with his failures, and he was falling prey.

Eden placed his hand on Silas's shoulder. "Let's get out of here for a minute. You need to get some air and take a break."

Dante nodded. "We've got her, Silas."

Just as Silas and Eden stepped away, it spoke again.

"Oh no vampire, you will not leave. We are just getting started. I like to watch you suffer, but you should know this is only the beginning. Let's call it payback for the life of the three you took," it seethed.

There were six pops, one right after another, as it broke Jadis's ribs. They all cringed inside, feeling every bit of her pain as if they had taken it on themselves. The monstrosity roared with laughter.

Jadis heard its demonic voice from inside of her, laughing as she fell to the floor.

Silas felt a cold chill rise up his back and he turned around. He then felt a soft breeze on the nape of his neck as if someone let out a breath of air. "Jadis possesses thy panacea," the voice whispered.

Silas glanced eveyone in the room. "Did anyone else hear that?"

They looked at each other, and then back at Silas. "No, what did you hear?" Eden asked.

Silas *looked at Jadis and then spoke telepathically, not wanting the Segar to hear. "Clear as day someone just said Jadis has the cure."*

"What the hell are you talking about?" Eden asked.

"Jadis has something in her possession. Tear this fucking room apart," Silas said.

It only took them a few minutes before Silas found a small, round tin, wrapped in a black cloth in one of her wardrobe drawers. The tin looked as if it has been burned and as Silas wiped the black ash off the lid; etched across the top was a sigil.

"Let me see that," Dante requested.

Silas handed it to him, and Dante removed the top. Within it was a runny, salve-like substance. He studied the top of the tin. *"I think its a sigil for panacea?"* he said telepathically.

"That's what the voice whispered," Silas stated.

"This has to be it," Bain agreed.

The excitement they felt was short-lived, as Jadis's body rose up again. "Vampire, it's almost time." Jadis grabbed her shirt and ripped the front of it the rest of the way open, holding each half in her outstretched arms, baring her breasts.

"You like this, don't you?" sneered the Segar. "She is our prophecy. We will not kill this filth right away. She will be taken to the underworld of Ipheanor with us. We will use her body, torture her. Fuck her. Is that what you call it?" it threatened, with a sardonic laugh. It then spoke directly to Silas. "Nosferatu, release her now or the consequences will be dire."

Jadis's skin burned and seared like a piece of meat over an open fire; the smell rose from her skin, and her stomach turned black with deep burns before otherworldly symbols appeared, etched into her chest and stomach.

Each blow to Jadis was a blow to Silas, both mentally and physically. If she was going to suffer, so would he. Silas would not let her carry that much pain alone. He reached out enough to feel it all for himself, taking in every break, blow, gash, and bruise. They were able to subdue her once again. This time, however, they had a plan and were working with more than just the sedative.

CHAPTER 19

A vague voice called her name; each time she heard the voice call out, it grew further and further out of her grasp. The ground beneath her feet gave way with each step. The decaying vegetation barely visible, vanishing into the dismal landscape. She felt as if she was trying to run through a murky bog; with each step denied, she was pulled back to the gluttonous ground. The suction under her feet made it difficult to pick up one foot at a time, rendering her helpless to gain any momentum. The more effort she exerted, the more her body fought against her. She looked all around to see where the voice was coming from but the only sound was that of her own footsteps, neither slow nor quick. She did not know where she was but one thing was certain; she was in a place that seemed old and otherworldly; a place of death and decay.

Unable gain any momentum she dropped onto her knees feeling alone, helpless, and exhausted. Just as she was about to give up, she heard the faintest of voices calling out in subdued, muffled tones, echoing from all directions.

The girls had slipped into the veil Dante and Bain helped them create and stood in a circle, finger tip to finger tip.

"This place is dangerous," Skye stated as she looked down and saw nothing but the gliding, featureless fog. There was a familiar stench that wafted through the air, searing her nostrils; rotting flesh. Nebulous waves of mist drifted aimlessly across the vastness of the obscure wasteland, engulfing her and the girls.

"Exactly why we need to get to Jadis now," Ivory stated. "Let's do this."

Jadis glanced around and the voices grew with intensity, and as they became louder, she recognized the voices of Skye and Ivory. Although they were there in her mind, she could not see them.

"Fight Jadis. Take us with you into the place of shadows. We are here. Let us help you. Come to us, sister—fight!"

Jadis instantly knew they were performing a ceremony, only they weren't alone. There seemed to be an entire coven with them, all of whom were chanting in unison. She then heard Aria's voice and stood up.

"Come on, Jadis. Let us in," Aria urged.

"I don't have the strength to do this anymore. You've got to help me," Jadis begged.

"We've got you," Ivory replied.

"I'm letting go. Don't let me slip back!"

Against the blackened landscape, a circle of flames appeared. The girls moved in and merged with Jadis energetically. They hoped together, they would be stronger than the Segar possessing her.

As Jadis drifted into the center of the forked flames, the coven gathered around the fire, creating a protective barrier. Back in the stateroom, Dante and Bain were adding their own sorcery to the ritual from Jadis's bedside.

Skye, Ivory, and Aria met Jadis in the center of the ring of fire, and with outstretched arms and their palms facing upward they surrounded her and began their incantation. "Creatures of evil far and wide from this spell you cannot hide in this body no longer will you dwell!"

"Creaturae de malum procul et wid de haec incantatio vos potes corium. Hoc corporis vos autem nullus iam habito!" they continued.

Jadis could see them as if they were all together in the organic realm. The four of them reached out and grasped each other's forearms.

In order to give the girls as much time as possible the coven began a chant to summon the sands of Ipheanor, which would conceal them behind an archaic veil of protection. "Nastadei alramal misr! Nastadei alramal misr! Nastadei alramal misr!" The sands rose up and swirled around them, hiding them within the eye of the storm.

Skye nodded. "Talk to us, Jadis. Show us. Let us see what you are seeing. Let us see what has ahold of you. Once the flames burn out, the Segar will be able to attach to all of us if we are still in your mind."

Jadis relaxed, let down her barriers, opened mind, and let them all in. For the first time, it became visible to her. It wasn't just a bacterium she had been infected with; it was the Segar itself. It had implanted itself within her to merge them into one being.

The seed inside the bacteria had been growing like the roots of a plant, spreading throughout her entire body by attaching itself to her cells; it was some sort of nanotechnology. It was a miniscule, living creature, capable of learning and manipulating Jadis on a molecular level. The Segars were using Jadis as a type of informational, organic entity. All she had seen in the catatonic fits, the Segars had seen with her. The technology they used to control her was unparalleled by anything they had seen.

"I need at least five minutes," Jadis said.

"We will do what we can, and you don't have five more minutes. Get in and get out!" Aria stated.

They continued their ceremony as Jadis went searching for answers herself. She used the Segars sight to look back at the them as they invaded her mind and body, and she found what she was looking for. There was something hidden. It was sacred, powerful, and deadly. It was a technological weapon they could use to control the vortex and return to upper part of the world. This had been a part of their plan all along, right up to the moment the Segars were killed in the cave.

The Segars had used her to gather information on the vampires, which would explain why they weren't healing her. They knew it was taking information and power from anyone and anything reaching into her, which is how it had quickly become accustomed to the drugs being used to sedate her. They planned on using her to open the sepulture. It had been sealed during the Original War and had remained sealed ever since. Only a direct descendant of the Gods could either open it or destroy it. This was the reason the Baskale had taken her to the Segar that night; they needed her alive. After which, she was disposable.

"Are you getting this?" Jadis asked.

"Yes, we've got it and you were right all along, It's you they wanted," Ivory agreed.

Suddenly she heard Aria yell, "Get out!"

Jadis did so right away, and as she let go, the bonfire exploded. It sent cinders, smoke, and ash spewing into the air, along with Skye, Ivory, and Aria.

It was only a brief period of time, but the coven was able to merge with Jadis long enough for Dante and Bain to get all they needed.

Dante, Bain, and Eden stayed in the stateroom with Silas and Jadis, and for the first time in a week, she was sleeping peacefully.

They learned all they needed from the visions Jadis, her sisters, and Aria had provided. They recognized the technology that had been found with Jadis's vision. It was the same technology they had discovered in the structure before having destroyed it. They had been cognizant enough to know the information they had mentally catalogued while in the structure would eventually unlock a trove of undiscovered secrets, yet they did not know at the time how valuable the information would be.

They sat at the table with a drink and spoke quietly, going over every detail of the events. Of course, they remained prepared with a dozen filled needles and Silas's men, as a precaution.

Eden set his tablet down. "It seems to be working, but we won't know for sure until Jadis awakens. I have to hand it to the girls they sure know their shit."

"Cheers to that," Dante and Bain replied.

The only exception to the positive vibe in the room was Silas. That time would come when Jadis—all of her was back with him.

"We know she somehow took the Segar's knowledge when she killed it in the cave. Do you think she knew what she was doing?' Bain asked the group.

"I don't know?" Dante replied.

"Does anyone ever know what Jadis is thinking until it's too late?" Eden chuckled.

Silas leaned back in his chair, looking as casual as ever. He stretched one leg out, and the other was halfway bent. He rested his arms on the armrests of the chair and swirled the half-full glass in one hand. He refrained from uttering a single word; he kept his eyes fixed on Jadis.

"She's going to be okay, Silas," Dante offered, as the rest of the group continued analyzing the data that was being projected in 3D images rising above each of their screens.

"What makes you so sure?" Silas rumbled, taking a drink.

Eden responded to Silas with a more definitive answer, "The formula is working; all the data is here. Her body is fighting; every blood sample we have taken in the past four hours has shown positive results. The amount of blood you initially gave her increased the strength of her cells a thousand times over. Her white cells are working to eradicate the infection. The salve has also eaten away the Segar's implant; destroying it one miniscule amount at a time. Jadis's cells are in the later phases of healing now."

Silas stared at Eden and took another drink before replying, "I hope you're right, cousin."

Jadis could make out familiar voices, but she couldn't shake off the grogginess no matter how hard she tried. She could barely make out Silas's face as he softly spoke to her.

"Hi, my love," he said as he stroked her face.

"Hecate said I would have to make a choice. I chose you." The room blurred like oil caught in the rain before she drifted away.

The boat lurched and rolled to the side, scaring Jadis awake. She jumped and cried out in terror. The room was eerily quiet, and Silas, Dante, Eden, and Bain slowly set their glasses and tablets down.

They look like they are ready to besiege me, she thought.

Silas remained at her bedside, and as she turned to him, he leaned toward her and cupped her hand in his. The energy in the room was heavy, and the tension was as thick as thieves.

"Where have you been? I called for you a thousand times." Her throat was so dry it hurt to speak.

"I promise I have not left your side, and I never will," Silas assured her, his voice even and calming. "We have all been right here the entire time." He cupped her face in his hands and kissed her. "You have been heavily sedated for days, but we have stopped them." Silas smiled, a real, sincere smile.

Jadis started crying and licked her chapped, burning lips. The skin was peeling off and her battered body was burned and broken in so many places she couldn't move of her own free will. She glanced at her body and it looked like she had just crawled out of a grave.

"I've been somewhere else for a very long time," she whispered.

"You were lost to us for a while, darling," Silas sighed, knowing he had already taken her memories so he could stop the demons that would try to come back and haunt her later. There was a hell residing in him, where they would remain locked away; he would not let her relive any of it.

"You're lying to me. My sisters and Aria, were they here? I thought I saw them too."

"Rest, love, there will be plenty of time to explain everything to you." He carefully sat on the bed next to her. "Be still, my love," he stated softly.

"I don't believe you, vampire," she replied in a raspy whisper. She rubbed his face with her hand and struggled to do so. "You have a funny way of not telling me the truth." She tried to smile, but even that hurt.

Silas bent over and gently kissed her forehead. She was freezing cold, and her body shivered as the tears slowly trickling down her face turned into sobbing cries; her mind conceding to the torment.

She leaned into Silas's chest, and he picked her up in his arms and headed to the shower. He held her under the hot water, washing her hair and her body as gently as he could. Every touch caused her to wince with pain. All he wanted was to take her pain away, and he knew she needed more from him than a shower. They wouldn't be able to take a chance healing her until they were sure the Segar was out of her head.

Silas stepped out of the shower and sat her on the edge of the tub. He wrapped her in a towel before kneeling in front of her. He slid his hands along her hair, pulling the water down through the long strands, as he dried her hair with nothing more than his touch.

Jadis sat quietly, rubbing her face. She was focused on trying to refrain from crying any more than she already had been. The shower and Silas's touch did however, feel amazing.

He lifted her chin to meet his gaze before softly kissing her lips. He picked her up and carried her to the stateroom, and laid her in bed between the soft satin sheets. He slid in next to her and held her body as close to his as he could. He then tossed the towel he had wrapped her in onto the floor.

"Just one more thing, my love." Silas pulled her face close to his, bit his lip and rubbed the blood across her lips with his tongue, healing them immediately.

Silas is truly the anchor in the storm that has become my life.

"The sheets are green? Hunter green?" she mumbled.

"I thought we should redecorate. These reminded me of the colors of the jungle you love so much. By the way, you have no idea how happy I am you chose me." He kissed her again, and she fell back to sleep.

Silas had asked Dante and Bain to change everything while he cleaned her up.

Jadis woke up two days later. As usual, Silas's voice was the first thing she heard.

"It's good to see you awake, darling." Silas smiled, but she could see the concern in his eyes.

She looked at Dante, Bain, and Eden, assessing them one at a time. *Aiden's here? They seemed to have similar expressions,* she thought.

She moved with caution, trying to sit up against Silas's body, but she barely had the strength to move herself. Of course, Silas was there to help her.

She finally felt as if the fog had lifted from her mind. *Thank God I am no longer seeing myself running through the murky black bog. I am here for real this time. I am back in both my body and my mind. Whatever they have done has worked,* she thought.

"You all are up to something. I can smell it. I wonder, who's going to fess up first? I already knew why Dante and Bain were here. After all, they are my nannies," she joked.

As they chuckled the tension in the room disappeared with it.

Jadis looked at Eden. "What are you doing here? I thought I gave you migraines?"

"I found a pill for them." Eden winked, along with a sigh of relief.

"Aiden?" What are you doing here? Does Aria know where you're at?" Jadis winked.

"No. I told her I went to the movies." Aiden chuckled.

Jadis almost laughed but her ribs were still broken. Although they were acting casual enough something was off. It's *apparent not one of them trusts me right now,* she thought.

Dante walked over and gave her a kiss on the cheek and a gentle hug. "You have no idea how good it is to see you awake and healing." He smiled warmly.

"What did I do now? Tell me, dammit, I can handle whatever it is. Well? I'm waiting?" As she looked amongst them, she assumed they were waiting for Silas to answer. So she looked back at him. "Silas, what did I do?"

As the boat rolled to the side again, a spike of fear and adrenaline surged through her. Silas kept her from rolling off the bed and she snuggled into him as tightly as she could, and he wrapped her firmly in his arms.

"There's a storm on the horizon. They will be coming. We are all as good as dead if we don't destroy it," she mumbled. The tension returned and she felt Silas nod to Dante.

"Darling, I'm going to give you another round of antibiotics."

Dante smiled sincerely, but there is something he isn't letting onto, she told herself. *No one is going to tell me anything tonight, and I certainly don't have the energy to question them any further.*

Jadis watched as the flashes of lightning lit up the room through the glass doors, and the thunder cracked outside. She listened to the rain beat against the sides of the yacht, and she felt as if the ocean itself, or maybe something else, wanted to swallow them up. "Silas, you know I can't sleep like this," she mumbled.

He was under the covers, wrapping her in his half naked body immediately. Her last thought was, *Antibiotics, my ass. Dante sedated me again.*

Dante, Bain, Eden, and now Aiden stayed busy monitoring Jadis and tending to her injuries. They had more than one IV, each dripping vital nutrients and Silas's blood into her veins. They were able to use the salve she created to stop the Segar's control; she was healing.

It took another week for Jadis's body to recover, not to mention her mind. She had constant nightmares, each time jumping awake and lashing out at nothing. Silas was always at her side; his loyalty was beyond measure. She was still groggy, and her body moved sluggishly, but she truly felt better.

"Is everything okay?" Silas asked, stroking her hair.

"Yes, I was thinking about everything that has happened over the last couple of weeks. I keep dreaming about it, but I don't remember anything once I wake up. I recall flashes of being tortured and broken, but then the memories dissipate like fog. Sleeping feels dangerous."

"It will take some time," Silas reminded her once again. *He sounds like a broken record. Hell, what else could he say?* she thought.

"Just know you will not have to bear this alone."

I know what he keeps telling me, but how could I truly believe it was a nightmare when I still feel the presence while awake? She thought to herself.

She rolled over to face him. She was still sore, but the majority of the pain was gone. Jadis also noticed she and Silas were alone for the first time in over a week.

"Do you know how much I appreciate everything you have done for me? Not to mention how much Dante, Bain, and Eden have helped. You all saved my life. I don't know how to thank them for staying here with me through all of this."

"They know how grateful we are. I've made it more than clear to each one of them. I will repay them in kind. There is nothing any of us wouldn't do for our family." He bent over and kissed her. "Jadis," he said, leaning in again. "I can't explain what it means to be looking at you right now and staring into those hypnotic eyes. By the way, don't think I've forgotten. I will take you as my mate in about a week." He smiled.

"You bet your ass you will be," she said with a sassy tone. She grabbed the back of his head and pulled him down into a long, much-needed kiss. He pulled her closer and wrapped his legs around hers. "I want you," she whispered.

"And I you," he whispered back.

His body enveloped her, and the warmth washed over her like a wave, unfurling all of her senses. She wrapped her arms under his and around his back before she slid her hand down. She gripped his perfect ass and pulled him further between her legs.

He slid his hand behind her head and claimed her mouth. She pushed her tongue past his fully extended canines, and they met in a desperate, long-awaited reunion.

His touch is exactly what I need. I need to feel him, to make love to him, and to be desired by him. She needed all of him. Every stroke of his touch brought her body back to life.

"You already have all of me," Silas whispered. "You feel amazing, by the way. You know how badly I want you?" His voice raspy with need as he kissed her more passionately.

She knew Silas needed to feel her as much as she needed to feel him. Despite his passion and desire, he was gentle with her body, and she knew he feared the possibility of hurting her.

"I'm okay, baby. I need you. I need this," Jadis said softly.

He pulled her thigh up over his waist and gently settled himself further between her legs, rubbing his tip against her wet, impatient core. He bent his knee to hold up her thigh, and she wrapped her leg around his back.

He rocked back and forth as he moved his hand up her thigh and over her hip. He then ran his fingers across her ribs, touching ever so lightly.

Silas's touch was so gentle it almost tickled. He caressed her breast and teased her nipple with his thumb, and she squirmed beneath him, needing him inside of her.

"Silas," she whispered.

"You taste amazing," he groaned. He slithered his tongue down her neck and dragged his canines across her throat. He hovered over her throbbing pulse for a moment before pulling back.

She moaned with every touch, every kiss, every breath. "Jesus, you feel amazing."

She glided her hands over his shoulders, down his arms and around his back, feeling his muscles flex and ripple with every move he made. He was strong and powerful, yet his touch was so gentle it only increased the anticipation of his dominance. She began trailing her tongue over his throat and gently bit his neck just above his vein.

"Keep that up, mon chéri, and I might not be able to stop myself," he rumbled. As he pushed her legs further apart, he gently slid himself into her core.

She arched in response and wrapped her legs tighter around his waist, matching the rhythm of his hips with hers. She cupped his ass with her hand and pulled him further in; he moved slowly and cautiously.

He is being careful, too careful, she thought.

"I'm okay, Silas," she assured him, again. "Just do me like you do, and give it to me," she moaned. She ran her tongue along his ear lobe sending a shock-wave of desire through his body.

"I don't want to hurt you," he whispered.

She pulled his head back and looked into his eyes. "Silas, I need this. Stop holding back. I need a pain I'll actually enjoy," she said with a wink and a desperate smile.

He studied her momentarily. "You don't have to tell me again." He parted her lips and took full control.

He repositioned her body under his and gave a hard shove. She flung her head back into the pillow and moaned with each powerful thrust.

She couldn't believe how amazing he felt. "That's more like it." She relished the pleasure she felt between her legs as his erection stretched her battered body.

"You feel incredible too," he responded as he dragged his canines across her throat again. "I can't wait until I can taste you, drink from you, and take you all in. I want your blood rushing over my tongue and down my throat. Say it, Jadis."

"I belong to you, Silas," she replied with a breathless groan.

He forced Jadis's arms above her head, pinning them to the bed before plunging his shaft deeper.

She couldn't take any more; the sensation brought her ecstasy to the surface and her climax throbbed from the inside out. Her head was reeling from the familiar feeling; one only Silas could bring.

"Holy shit," she groaned.

He felt her release and moved more aggressively; rocking with even greater force. He let out a low, throaty groan, allowing his cum to flow into her body.

"Sicut cum quis magis puto non possum venire," he moaned.

They fell together, wrapped in each other's arms, his head resting next to hers. After a few minutes, she lifted his face to look into his eyes and smiled.

"What did you just say?" She chuckled.

"Just when I think I can't come any harder," he replied, with a slightly breathless chuckle.

She laughed aloud.

"I love you like no other, Jadis. There has never been anyone for me but you. I was so afraid I was going to lose you. I would have ended it all. I would have put myself to the sword had you left me."

She stroked his face, seeing the love he felt for her reflecting in his eyes. "I have loved you since the night in the cabin. It has and always will be you, and I haven't been with another since that night. I love you more than you will ever know. You might put yourself to the sword, but if anything happened to you? I would burn myself on a stake."

Silas let out hearty laugh. "Mon chéri, no one will be putting themselves to the sword or the stake."

"I never want to leave this bed," she said, pulling him in closer.

"I feel the same way, baby." Silas said it sincerely, yet she could hear the reflection in his voice telling her something was bothering him.

"What's wrong, baby?"

"Nothing, my love. Rest, you need your sleep."

"You should know better than that. I want to know, and I want to know right now. I can feel the thoughts weighing on you."

He rolled over, pulled her close, and enveloped her body with his.

"It's business, darling. You know we have to finish what we've started. I don't want you going. It's not safe. It never has been. This situation will never be repeated, on the life blood of Nosferatu. I will never put you in harm's way again. We will have to figure something else out. You are going to stay right here."

Silas was dead set on it. Jadis rolled her eyes, thinking how history had a way of repeating itself.

"Roll your eyes at me again and see what happens." Silas chuckled.

"I'll let the others do the arguing on my behalf," she joked.

She laughed to herself at the thought of them trying to convince Silas to take her with them to finish the job.

"Keep laughing, and I might have to lock you up again," Silas joked, though she could tell he was considering it. "No one else will handle any decisions when it comes to you." He smacked her ass, causing her to let out another giggle and a yelp.

"We'll see." She wasn't about to argue with him. She didn't have the energy, and all she wanted to do was fall asleep in his arms.

A couple of days later, Jadis was up and able to get out of bed on her own. Silas decided it was safe to heal her the rest of the way, and so he did. Things had also calmed down on the yacht. Everyone settled back into a normal routine, and Jadis was more than grateful to have the attention on something other than herself.

They had been planning and preparing for their return trip to the Valley to address their unfinished business. It took Eden, Dante, Bain, and Jabari to convince Silas to agree on letting Jadis join them. Dante and Bain assured him she would not be in harm's way, and they acknowledged they needed her powers, Hecate's powers. Without them, the trip might end up being a waste of everyone's time.

After everything they had all been through, Silas didn't want her so much as leaving the yacht, much less going back to the Valley having just recovered. "I'm not comfortable with this," Silas stated.

"Neither am I, and I don't want to be there, but I know if we don't destroy the sepulture now, we may lose our chance forever. If that happens, there is every reason to believe they will come for me again, and that is more terrifying than anything else," Jadis stated.

Silas pulled her close and wrapped his arms around her. He then nodded at the Eden, agreeing to let her accompany them. "I want to make one thing very clear, everyone will follow very strict guidelines concerning Jadis and her protection. Dante, Bain you along with a few of my warrior's will accompany her at all times, with no exceptions."

Everyone agreed one way or another.

CHAPTER 20

Eden and Aiden had already run a preliminary threat assessment using artificial intelligence to analyze the contents of the sepulture and the biological data, which included bacterial samples collected from Jadis. Opening the sepulture would reveal all that had been hidden in the Segars' arsenal, as well as any potential threats they may have missed. Guided by the scorpions in the vision obtained from the girls, Dante and Bain provided Jabari a precise location in order to send a team out to survey the area. Although the sink hole didn't house the sepulture itself, they discovered a lengthy tunnel leading east towards the base of the triangular structure. It was believed to be the secret passageway that would lead them to the elusive chamber they had all been searching for. Jabari's clan members, responsible for overseeing the data mining, discovered the technology the Segars had been using. With this information, Dante, Bain, and Jabari created a substance they hoped would destroy the contents of the sepulture, after which they would take complete control of the vortex.

As a final assessment, they scanned the chamber from every direction, generating a complete picture within minutes. As the high-resolution holograms rose above their tablets, they did not detect any potential threat that may have been missed. However, they did capture the infrared movements of twelve Segars, who had been using the tunnel to enter and exit through the triangular structures without being detected. They returned to the valley hoping this would be the final confrontation. Despite the setbacks they had encountered before, they remained hopeful this time would unfold smoothly. They met up with Jabari and discussed the location of the large sink hole just outside of one of the smaller triangular structures. It lay beneath nine hundred years-worth of blowing desert sands. It was covered by black granite and sealed shut, hiding whatever lay within it. The clan members and warriors lined up and awaited their orders from Silas, Eden, and Jabari.

Silas, Dante, and Bain stood with Jadis and it wasn't long before three fully armed warriors Jadis didn't recognize materialized beside them. Dante gently squeezed her hand, noticing the look of trepidation on her face. "They're not so bad once you get to know them." He winked.

Jadis looked up at him and smiled. "I think I'm good."

From what little Silas told Jadis, the warriors were dark, lethal, and the most elite of their kind. They lived beyond the shadows and their special forces training spanned over eight hundred years; their legion was created as a result of the war. Nosferatu referred to them as Mortem, meaning death. four hundred years ago, Silas had become their commander.

Jadis was not allowed to go into the sinkhole in search of the sepulture, and she was fine with it. She had no desire to be anywhere near the Segars. Her contribution would take place when the warriors carried the sepulture outside and brought it to her.

The anxiety and unrelenting fear grew as the tormenting thoughts besieged her mind, and she couldn't stop her hands from trembling. The remnants of the possession still weighed heavy, and they continued haunting her. Even though she couldn't recall most of it, the adrenaline pumped through her body as if it were telling her to run.

"Don't worry, mon chéri, I've got you." Silas pulled her into his arms and hugged her tightly, trying his best to comfort her.

He looked to his Lieutenant, Sigurd, who immediately responded, "We will protect Jadis with our lives, milord."

Jadis side-eyed the warriors, and she would have crawled into a hole given the chance.

Sigurd glanced in her direction and nodded. *I believe my shadow just went into hiding,* she thought.

"I'll be back. You stay put. Sigurd will remain here with you, and even though Dante and Bain will be with us, they will have your ethereal back."

"Where the hell are you going? This wasn't part of the plan. You were to let the others search for the sepulture and bring it to us. You were to remain right by my side!"

She tried to fight the fear along with the relentless feeling something bad was going to happen. After all, this was the first time he had left her side in weeks.

"Be still, baby. I wouldn't leave you if I didn't trust my men completely and without question. I have unfinished business. Don't you move from this spot." He kissed her lips, and she grabbed at his shirt, trying to keep from leaving.

"No, Silas. Please don't leave me."

Silas felt her anguish and looked at Dante, who nodded and surrounded her in an energetic tranquil embrace.

Silas held both her fists cupped in his hands and he gently released her grip from his shirt. He grabbed the back of her head, placed his mouth on hers, and she felt herself relax.

"I'll be back in no time at all, hang tight." With those words, Silas slipped out of her grip.

As he walked away, she felt the warriors move in around her. However, she didn't look in their direction. She watched Silas head for the sinkhole.

"It'll be okay, Jadis," Aria said softly as she walked over and wrapped an arm around her. "By the way, who the fuck are the warriors?"

Jadis looked at her and simply shrugged her shoulders. "They scare you too?"

"Fuck yes, look at them."

"I'm good." Jadis chuckled as she reached for Aria's forearm and held on.

Dante and Bain lifted the top from the sinkhole. It slowly rose and slide to the side, revealing the opening for a moment before the dust and sand swallowed the entrance in a brown, swirling plume.

"You ready?" Silas asked.

"I've got it. Toss it in and I'll guide it toward our targets," Dante replied.

Silas looked back at Jadis and winked before he tossed an explosive made of dragon stone into the sink hole. They ducked near the edge as it blew; the ground rumbled beneath their feet and dark swirls of dust and debris spewed from the sinkhole. The team hovered above the opening momentarily, letting the dust settle before dropping in.

The dust rose around their boots as they landed at the bottom with a heavy thud, sending thousands of insects with black, hard shells scurrying in every direction. They had been feeding on the remnants of the bodies the Segars had tossed aside and ended up trapped within its slick, vertical obsidian walls. Not a single scratch or imperfection could be seen or felt.

Bain covered his mouth and nose. "Ah damn. That fucking smell!"

Dante took a few steps near the pit. "No shit! Check out all the bodies."

Silas, Eden, and Aiden studied the remains. "Well, this would certainly confirm the Ipheanor's whispers about their people simply vanishing into the mouth of the twin peaks," Eden replied.

The stories passed down through generations recounted how individuals vanished under the cloak of darkness, whisked away by enigmatic beings that materialize from the depths of shadows. Apparently, the Segars had been disposing of the bodies there for centuries, based on the number of decaying corpses lying piled one on top of another in a pit near the base of the circular wall.

With each step they took, the insects crunched beneath the heavy weight of their boots. Despite the putrid stench of the rotting corpses, they detected a faint trace of another scent; they shot each other a curious glance.

"Nosferatu," Silas rumbled.

"The same scent we picked up on in the cave," Eden agreed.

"Once we're done here we need to find out who he is and what his involvement in all of this is," Silas stated.

"Heads up," Dante interjected.

Four badly wounded Segars emerged from the tunnel just beyond where they stood.

Silas drew his sword and dodged the oncoming Segars. "Who wants the one on the right?" They each moved swiftly, evading the approaching threats.

Eden moved with precision toward it. "I'll take it."

Aiden moved to the side of Eden and his target. "I'll take the other."

Dante moved next to Bain, both of whom drew their swords as well. "Bain and I have the other two."

Eden was the first to take hold of a wounded Segar. He grabbed it by its throat, and it tried lashing out. The brownish, acidic substance spewed from its grotesque chest wounds caused by the explosive. He then stared into its blackened eyes. "I know you can see us, so let's show you what we to do to our enemies." He pulled out his dagger and spun it around in his hand. He then plunged the blade into its abdomen multiple times; it's deafening screeches echoing off the circular walls. He then slammed its body onto the dirt floor. *A quick death would be too humane for any one of these monsters,* he thought. *It needs to suffer.* "What shall we do now?" he asked the Segar as if he was talking to someone else. "What do you think, Silas?"

"Let its death be painful and slow," Silas answered.

"Sounds good to me." Eden pulled out another blade from behind his back. This one was larger and longer than his dagger. He drove it through its body and pinned it to the ground; leaving it to suffer until death took over.

Silas stepped in front of its half-dead body and looked into its eyes one more time. "We're just getting started," he spoke to the one on the other side.

Aiden spun his sword and sliced off the appendages of the one he held in place. It let out a mind-numbing screech as the fluids flowed from its body and onto the ground at his feet. "I don't want you to die quickly. That wouldn't be any fun."

"Place it with Edens," Silas sated.

Aiden pulled a long knife, hanging attached to his thigh, and drove it through its chest. He then slammed it onto it's back next to Eden's victim and pinned it down as well.

Silas stepped in the middle of the two flailing creatures and watched as they struggled for a breath, their movements sluggish.

Dante and Bain had the remaining two injured Segars in a powerful hold, keeping them suspended in mid-air. The creatures tried to lash out at but their attempts were futile.

"What should we do with these two?" Dante asked Bain.

Bain looked at Dante. "I'm not sure? Pain is all that comes to my mind."

Silas spoke up, "Didn't it get inside of Jadis? You know, using her from the inside out. Hurting her from the inside out." Silas continued as he circled the two Segars, suspended in the air. Their screeches of desperation music to his ears.

"I do believe it did," Bain verified.

"How about we show them how it felt to her? Let's turn things up a notch or two. Sometimes it takes a monster to fight a monster," Silas said.

Out of respect for Jadis, and all those things had put her through, Dante and Bain began to chant to disintegrate them from the inside out. "Liquescimus uri intus de. Liquescimus uri intus de. Liquescimus uri intus de."

Dante conjured up two bamboo poles that slowly rose from the ground in the center of the room. They allowed the suspended Segars' bodies to fall onto the pointed ends of the bamboo, piercing their thighs. Their heavy bodies slowly slid down the poles until the tips protruded from the crook in their necks. As they melted from the inside out, slowly, their flailing appendages became listless.

Dante circled them, "I think that should do it."

"Looks good to me." Silas chuckled.

Silas's men followed him through the passageway as they headed for the chamber. They easily took out four more Segars, who were beheaded by two of the Mortem warriors. Dante and Bain scorched each body as they passed by, leaving nothing behind but ash. They made their way into the hidden chamber through the hole in the wall, Silas created with a few well-placed kicks. The few remaining Segars attacked as soon as they entered the chamber.

Every move Silas made looked like it had been beautifully choreographed, every strike skillfully executed. He leapt, spun, and turned with lightning-quick speed. Silas's physical prowess was like none other, and he was brutally efficient.

He ordered everyone back, wanting the remaining four Segars to be his and his alone. He remembered every bruise, scratch, cut, and broken bone they had inflicted on Jadis. He recalled every nasty word they called her, and the threats to use her body for their pleasure.

Silas jumped from one wall to another before landing on the back of his first victim. He planted a foot on the back of its head and drove its face into the sandy floor. He let the creature choke on the sand and dust as it fought for a breath. He then shoved his hand into its back and pulled. He held up the long strand of vertebrae and as it swayed back and forth, the fluids splattered across the Segar's body and the dirt floor. "Shit smells putrid," Silas stated as he tossed it aside. He then picked another target.

There was a loud thump in front of the second one and, without warning, all four of its limbs were severed. Silas jumped back when its body hit the ground, doing his best to avoid the blood gushing out from the gaping wounds. "I don't suppose you'll be running off," Silas chuckled as he watched it squirming like a helpless slug, screeching in pain.

His Mortem, in the meantime, had cornered the other two; once Silas nodded, they released one of them. It lashed out in circles, with raised talons, attempting to strike at anything and everyone. Silas materialized in front of it, and using his mind being abilities and forced it to stand still. He plunged his dagger into its midsection, and twisted the blade. He then spun his wrist in circles, slowly extracting its innards, one slow twist at a time. With each spin of his hand, it's innards splashed onto the floor at its feet. Everyone watched as the Segar fell on top of its own acidic entrails.

"I still hear it breathing, but it won't be for long," Silas said to no one in particular.

He spun his sword, severing the arms of the last Segar. He then reached out, grabbed it by its throat, and squeezed, leaving it gasping for breath beneath his unforgiving grasp. He looked into its eyes, and saw the Segar peering back at him. It was seething in its diabolical, soulless hatred. Silas spoke to it for what he had hoped would be the last time.

"Welcome to the new world of gods and monsters. Only we are the gods, and you are the monsters. Unfortunately for you, I am not a benevolent god," Silas snarled.

The Segar on the other side spoke to him from another place. "We have a surprise for you, Nosferatu," it threatened.

"I'll be waiting," Silas nodded, as he gripped its head between his hands. He then spun its head and as a loud pop rang out, he let it fall to the ground. "I think we got the point across."

He and along with the rest of his group laughed, and gripped forearms.

Aiden stepped forward and gave Silas a of couple hard pats on the shoulder. "I believe we did."

Silas returned the gesture and gave Aiden a slight nod.

"Grab the sepulture. We are finished here. Seal the chamber and the sinkhole behind us. Burn the dead, as well as the semi-living. Leave no trace behind. Dante, on our way up, do a cleansing spell. I don't want Jadis to see or smell anything that could potentially trigger her memories," Silas stated.

"Will do, brother. What do you want to smell like?" Dante chuckled.

"How about Jasmine?" Silas replied sarcastically.

"But of course." Dante rolled his eyes, a little something he had picked up from Jadis.

An hour and a half later, they appeared from the sinkhole, to Jadis's relief. However, in her anxiety ridden state of mind, it had felt like days. The moment she saw Silas, a wave of relief fell over her.

Silas walked over and wrapped his arms around her. "I told you I'd be back shortly, my love."

Jadis didn't have the words to express the relief she felt, she just hugged him tightly.

After a brief moment he pulled away and patted her butt. "There it is, baby. Do your thing."

Jadis made her way to the sepulture and ran her hand over the top, pushing the sand to the side. She let it slide off the edges, watching as it gently drifted onto the ground at her feet, awaiting all that would be revealed. All the knowledge she had taken from the Segar was at the forefront of her mind. She knew exactly what they wanted, and she knew what they expected to find inside. She took a moment to assess the sepulture as she continued walking in a circle around it. She closed her eyes, feeling the engravings and seeing flashes of memories from days long gone. She read the inscriptions, and the visions faded in and out like black and white silent movies playing from an ancient film reel.

She didn't want any more reminders of the Segars and their destruction, so she tried to stay focused on the visions. She saw the Segars during the war nine-hundred years ago. They were right where she now stood, loading their weapons. They knew they were losing to the vampires and the witches; it was only a matter of time before they were defeated. They wanted to ensure their survival and their return. Jadis watched as the Segars removed a body wrapped in linen from the sepulture before they destroyed it. In its place, they put their own sealed arsenal. There were a dozen Segars in there working, setting the device, and then sealing the heavy, obsidian lid shut. The slow, pulsing, blue light residing within a sealed container was the most dangerous of all the items.

The descendants, whom Hecate had bestowed her powers to, along with a few Master Wizards, sealed the sepulture sometime after the war ended, which prevented the Segars from accessing the contents inside. After which, to ensure it was never to be found again they performed a ritual and wiped the memories of anyone having contact with it, leaving it hidden and forgotten. For within the foreboding-looking sepulture was a weapon that could unleash a war no-one wanted to see repeated.

The clans worked together to create an aqueous substance that once poured into the sepulture, would consume the container laying within it. Its molecular structure cold scatter light, so when the device blew inside the sepulture, the solvent would absorb most of the contents' harmful rays. What it did not absorb would be stopped by the shield Dante, Bain, and a handful other of wizards from Seba, had created using their arcane powers. Once the shield was placed over the sepulture it would create a wall of protection from any of the harmful rays of light that would escape the substance.

Dante stepped next to Jadis and smiled. "We're ready, darling, are you?" he asked, as he rubbed her back and pulled her into him.

She wrapped her arms around his waist. "As ready as I'll ever be," she replied nervously. She had one more spell to cast on the object itself in order to break the hold the original witches had placed upon it.

Dante let go of Jadis, reached for the container, and Eden handed it over.

Jadis began the Litha Ritual of Light and Shadow. "As above, so below. As within, so without," she said, before she began carving out the sacred place between the worlds: their world and the Segar's world.

Dante and Bain joined Jadis, and they opened the gates to the four elemental realms. They evoked Jadis's deities to join them on consecrated ground, acknowledging the existence and partnership of all involved and currently being called upon.

Together, Jadis, Dante, and Bain swept their hands beneath them to scoop up the underworld.

Jadis began another incantation. "Thee I invoke, the born less one. Thee that didst create the darkness and light. Come with the serpent's heart."

At the same time, Dante and Bain harnessed their own energy and sorcery. "Te invoco, unum ad born less. Te, qui talem creare lucem et tenebras. Veni serpentes corde."

As they chanted, they swirled their hands over the top of the sepulture, and walked clockwise around it. The lid shook and trembled, and the sand poured over the edges, creating a gentle cloud of dust that partially consumed the three of them.

Their ritual was tantamount to spinning a nut off a bolt. With each circle they completed over the top of the sepulture, the lid slowly rose. With each inch it rose, mist puffed out from underneath it, revealing the pulsing blue light. The gentle sound of humming became louder, and the sounds rose and fell in unison with each pulse of the light itself. Dante and Bain then moved the lid to the side and placed it on the ground.

Once opened, they peered in. The container itself was a three-foot-long tube and about twelve inches in width. The outside of the container had three layers of various elements holing in the swirling, bluish liquid. It appeared to be made from a kind of clear metal and other organic minerals unlike anything from their world.

Bain reached in and pulled out the ancient scrolls, as well as the weapons that lay hidden with-in it, and handed it over to Eden.

Once Bain retrieved all the contents, Dante poured the luminescent liquid into the sepulture. It enveloped the tube and immediately ate away the casing, layer by layer. They needed to replace the lid and seal it shut before it came into contact with the light.

Aiden, Eden, and Jabari placed the lid back on the sepulture and stepped back.

Dante, Bain, and Jadis moved their hands counterclockwise over the top to re-seal it. The ground trembled beneath their feet and the sepulture shook and bounced on the ground.

"Dante, I want Jadis away from there right now." As Silas said it, he was already reaching for her arm.

Bain and Dante lifted the energetic shield and placed it over the sepulture.

"Get back!" Dante yelled.

The group moved as far back as possible, and Silas covered Jadis's body with his as he knelt down, tucking her in close.

With a loud rumble, it exploded, sending shards of obsidian in every direction. The searing heat and radiating light burst from the container like a tempest of lightning. The jagged tendrils of shimmering, multi-colored light defied the swirling plume of dust and debris ensnared within in the confines of the translucent shield.

Once the dust and smoke settled; the last of the Baskales, the last of the Segars living above the underworld, and the contents of the sepulture had been destroyed.

Cheers, and hollers filled the air around them as the clan members and covens held up their shields and weapons. This was the last battle and the ultimate defeat of the Segars. All they had hoped to destroy and conquer had now been put to death.

Silas, Eden, Aiden, Dante, Bain, and Jadis stood listening to the cheers filling the air. Silas turned his attention to Jadis, scooped her up in his arms, and spun in in a circle. She wrapped her arms and legs around him and a sense of relief washed over them.

It was over, and Jadis was safe. Silas couldn't have held her any closer if he'd tried. He had one hand on the back of her head and his other arm wrapped tightly around her body. He pulled his head back and looked into her eyes.

"You did it." He smiled.

Jadis could hear the joy and pride in his voice. "You did it. All of you were the ones who killed them, and I am so grateful they are gone. I can even feel it, baby. The area is clear." She planted a hard kiss on his lips.

The heaviness once shrouding the desert had lifted. The air felt lighter, cleaner, and brighter, and the tidal waves of dread and torment had passed, bringing the calm that eventually followed every storm.

Everyone around them continued to celebrate, congratulate, and thank one another. However, Silas's Mortem warriors had already disappeared back into the shadows after having acknowledged Silas with a nod of their heads.

Jabari walked over to where Silas and Eden were grouped together with their family. "Your clans are to be congratulated!"

Silas set Jadis down and turned toward Jabari. Jabari grabbed Silas's forearm and placed a hand on his shoulder. "This would not have been possible without you," he said to Silas directly before looking at Jadis.

"Jadis, we owe you a debt of gratitude as well." He let go of Silas and pulled her in for a warm hug. He then took a step back and held her hands in front of him. "You nearly lost your life to these monstrosities, and for you to come here and do what you did is to be commended. You have the heart of a true warrior."

It honored Jadis to hear those words from him.

Jabari turned to greet and thank Eden, Dante, Bain, and Aiden in the same manner.

Jadis watched and listened quietly. Silas stood behind her with his arms wrapped around her shoulders and chest, and she held onto his forearms as they waited for Jabari to address the entire group.

"The conflict was brief compared to what it could have been. As you all know, it has been years in the making. Today we came up against a formidable enemy, yet we have achieved victory! The lives of those lost in battle will not be forgotten!"

Jabari turned to face Silas and Eden before he continued, "Silas, Eden, for as long as the planets continue to move in their orbits, all clans shall be forever in your family's debt. This battle will not perish from the memories of Nosferatu or covens. It will be one legends are made of."

Jabari turned and faced the rest of the warriors. "This is a time for a grand celebration. Come, everyone, to the oasis. Tonight, we celebrate! Witches, you shall have a feast fit for the gods themselves. May the drinks and blood flow freely. Let us feed!" Jabari shouted with laughter and good cheer in his voice.

As the others headed in the oasis's direction, Jabari turned to Silas and Jadis. "Are the two of you going to join the festivities?"

Silas looked over at Jadis grinning from ear to ear. "No," Silas answered.

"Jadis and I need some alone time. She's been through a lot lately, and that's putting it mildly." Silas bent over and gently kissed her lips. She cupped his cheeks in her hands and placed her forehead on his. "I have some big plans for her in a few days," he stated.

All Jadis thought about was how lucky she is; *Silas is mine.*

"I understand. I also hear there is a little party being planned?" Jabari joked. "I assume I can expect an invite?" He raised a questioning eyebrow.

"Yes, of course. You are most definitely invited," Jadis replied sincerely.

"Good, good. I will look forward to it. By then, the two of you will be mated, yes? We shall have a great deal to celebrate."

Another voice broke in, "I assume Aiden's invite is still a plus one—yes?"

Jadis looked over and Aiden and Aria were making her way toward them.

"Seriously, you're still harping on that, are you? I assume if Aiden wanted you there, he would have invited you himself, no?" Jadis joked, before winking at Aiden, who held Aria's hand in his.

"Leaving so soon? You mean to tell me you're not joining in on the festivities? You must be tired from your little possession. I thought you'd be able to handle it better than that. Honestly, I expected more from you." Aria laughed.

"I expected more, too. Begging for an invitation is a bit desperate, don't you think?" Jadis joked.

Aria walked over and embraced Jadis tightly, "Until we meet again, sister." Aria squeezed Jadis's hand as she walked back to Aiden.

"I look forward to it," Jadis replied with all sincerity.

Aiden walked over and picked Jadis up in his arms. "I am truly happy to see you back at it. You look amazing, by the way. All healed, I see?" He squeezed her a bit tighter before setting her back down. He reached for Silas's forearm, "Take care of our girl."

Silas acknowledged him with a slight nod.

Dante and Bain had also made their way back to Jadis and Silas. They looked to Silas, waiting to see if they were needing to head back to the yacht with them. Silas nodded, letting them know they needed to join the others at the oasis for the celebration.

"There are no words for you, Jadis." Dante picked her up and hugged her tight. "You are truly one of a kind."

"I want to thank you again. I appreciate all you have done for me. More than you will ever know."

"I know, darling." He set her down and kissed the back of her hand before he backed away. "I'm going to leave you to my brother now. I'm sure he has his own party planned for tonight. By the way, I left the chains there," he joked.

As soon as he kissed her hand, Jadis noticed something flashing in his eyes, but she wasn't sure what to think about it. *Strange,* is all she thought.

"Party for two?" Bain interrupted. He followed suit of the others and gave Jadis a warm embrace. "Try to give Silas at least one night of peace and quiet. Think you can manage?" he asked in jest.

He gently cupped the sides of her face in his hands, and she held his forearms and smiled kindly. "You know how much I appreciate all you have done for me?"

"I do." He winked.

He walked to Silas and gave him a hard pat on the shoulder. "Good luck, cousin, you know who to call if she pulls any fuckery."

"You are all so funny. Still laughing at my expense?" she teased.

"Well hell. I wouldn't exactly call it amusing." Eden walked over and interrupted them. "Silas, do me a favor."

"Sure, what?" Silas asked.

"You only have two days. Two!" he reminded him. "Do you think you can keep her ass in line and out of trouble for forty-eight hours? I don't think there's enough pills to go around anymore. I believe more than one vampire has found out what a migraine is." He laughed.

Jadis rolled her eyes as usual, although this time it was with endearment for Eden.

"I think I've got this," Silas assured him in a joking manner. "I have forgotten nothing." He reached into his vest, pulled out the golden anklet, and it spun like a gyroscope on his palm.

Jadis stood speechless while everyone laughed along with Silas's unusual sense of humor.

Silas picked Jadis up, threw her over his shoulder, and landed a hard slap to her ass. She let out a yelp, along with a giggle, and slapped him back. "Put me down!"

"Never!" He stated.

CHAPTER 21

Silas lifted his head and looked down at Jadis for permission, and her heart skipped a beat with the nervous anticipation.

"Yes," she whispered.

He bent down, and she leaned her head back, tilting it to the side to give him full access. As she turned her head, she could see the swirling calypso red colors slowly overtaking the bright, silvery moon as the light gently glistened through the rustling curtains.

The hard prick of his bite into her vein seared through her body. He moaned with each pull as her blood filled his mouth. Jadis felt like she was drowning beneath him as he settled his body between her legs and fed.

Once he had taken enough to complete the bond, Silas licked the eight punctures on her neck with the tip of his tongue, immediately healing them. "You taste even sweeter than you smell. Your blood—it's different, it's powerful. Holy shit, I wasn't expecting that." It took him by surprise, having her unexpected energy coursing through his veins. Feeding from Jadis was intoxicating; it felt like he had waited a lifetime to take a mate.

He needed her, and with a hard thrust, he was inside of his mate; her tightness enveloping his hardened shaft. Tonight, he would not be gentle. He was claiming what was his under the swirling Blood Moon.

She moaned beneath him and gasped for a breath as he shoved his hips forward with such force, she had to put her hand on the headboard in order to keep her head from knocking into it.

They both let out a moan-filled chuckle as Silas re-positioned their bodies. He used one of his nails to slit a small opening just under his jaw and across his vein. "Drink, mon chéri."

She licked the blood seeping from the thin gash, before wrapping her lips around it; the warm liquid spilled over her tongue. She could feel a powerful, dark energy searing through her veins. *It tastes like Silas smells— musky—old worldly. Amazing,* she thought.

Every pull of his blood she took drove him into a desperate need, and he struggled to remain still long enough for her to finish feeding from him. He kneaded her breast in one hand and continued rocking back and forth as much as he could without breaking the bond she had on his neck.

As his blood coursed through her veins, she felt as if she was in a trance. Something within her changed and her body ached. The sounds from the world outside grew in intensity and rang in her ears. Her senses lit up as if they'd been in a deep slumber her entire existence. Every nerve ending came to life, bringing about an arousal like nothing she had ever felt before. She could feel Silas's desire as much as she felt her own.

"Mmm." She was in such a daze she couldn't speak. Her sudden thirst caught them both off guard when she wrapped her mouth around the cut and drank again.

"Not too much, love. Just enough," he moaned. A lusty growl escaped his throat, all he wanted was to come inside his mate.

She felt the hunger he had held onto for so long, his life flowing through her body like a distant story. With each swallow, she saw everything in a quick succession of flickering glimpses. She saw hundreds of years of a life well lived, Silas's life. She finally saw all she needed to see, and she understood and fully embraced the love he had for her. It was overwhelming, and she wanted and needed more.

He may be known as Mortem to the clans, but to me, he will only ever be known as my beloved vampire, she said to herself.

"Enough, baby," Silas gently pulled away from her.

She let out a deep, hungry sigh. "Silas, I wasn't done."

"Just enough for now. Your body needs to adjust," he whispered.

He kissed her with greater abandon, as the taste of his own blood on her tongue only ramped up his desire to possess her in every way. He needed her as much as the sun does the moon, or the ocean needs the tides. He responded with another hard shove, driving as far in as he could get.

She lifted her hips to meet his and wrapped one leg further up around his waist. She groaned with every harsh assault. The tremor within her shattered as her body released the painful orgasm; she felt his orgasm release with hers.

"Together, baby. Together in every way," he growled.

She grabbed the hair on the back of his head and pulled his forehead to her as the tremors continued to rock her body with the powerful release.

He looked down into her face, pulled her head to the side, and sunk his canines into her soft flesh once again. He needed one more taste with his release. *Just one more mouthful of her succulent blood.*

They completed their bond under the glowing rays of the Full Blood Moon. Nothing and no one would ever separate them again; they were bonded as one. They lay in bed, folded in each other's arms, in that perfect house by the lagoon he had built for her. They now had a home together, but best of all, they were mated.

Silas is every bit mine; I own his body, soul, and mind, she thought.

He responded, "Jadis, you have always owned all of me. I have been yours since the night I first laid eyes on you."

She stroked his face and gently laid another kiss on his lips. "I love you, vampire."

"And I you, mate." He rolled over, and they fell asleep in each other's arms, while the bond between them became unbreakable.

They slept until late the next morning, which ended up being exactly what she needed. It had taken her most of the night for her body to finish accepting Silas's blood. Everything in her had changed; her strength, her mind, and her abilities all grew stronger. The change hadn't been painful, but it had certainly been uncomfortable.

Silas held her and talked her through all of it. She could feel his compassion and his excitement. He enjoyed every second of her becoming his blood-bonded mate, and he watched and waited with bated anticipation. There was no greater honor for Nosferatu than an original accepting the bond.

The bond is taking longer than usual and seems to be more dramatic, physically. Of course, nothing with Jadis ever goes as planned, Silas thought.

Jadis laid there with her back to his stomach and he wrapped his arms around her. She let out a subtle moan and moved her body closer to his and kissed his forearm.

"Good morning, my love." Silas kissed the side of her face and stroked her hair. "How are you feeling?"

"Amazing."

Jadis rolled over and looked at him and his eyes went wide. Her eyes had become the cat-like slits only Nosferatu possessed. The color of his amber eyes were now mixed with her brown-green hues; she also had his sheer black irises. They were an exact replica of his own.

He had never seen a mate take her mate's physical form, even after having been turned. He gawked at her, reveling in the curious change.

"Why are you staring at me like that?" She had felt no physical change, however her eyesight had become much keener, and she could see the smallest of details. She glanced around and stared at random objects across the room. Each time she focused on one of them, she could see it clear as day. It was as if she had a set of built-in binoculars.

"Is everything okay?" He didn't answer. "Silas! Stop staring at me like that. What's wrong?"

"Nothing, baby. It's just—your eyes? They're a replica of mine, and you look as if you are Nosferatu." He sat up, and leaned further over her as he continued to stare down at her, studying her unexpected appearance.

"What? What do you mean Nosferatu? I have your eyes? I can definitely see better. Is that what you're talking about?" she questioned, being confused.

"No, baby. You HAVE my eyes."

"What the hell?" She got up and ran to the other side of the room. When she looked in the mirror, hanging above the bureau, she could hardly believe the change she saw in herself.

As sure as shit, I have Silas's eyes. They are no longer hers whatsoever. "Holy hell. Did I actually turn?" She spun around and with lightning quick speed, she was kneeling on the bed, and looking into Silas's face.

Her speed and prowess also caught both of them off guard. *I have always moved well, but not like this.* Then it suddenly dawned on her. "Silas!" she exclaimed. She grabbed his face with both of her hands and stared into his eyes; she found herself looking into her own eyes.

"What?" Silas asked, looking even more confused.

"Go look!" She shoved him out of the bed. "You have my eyes as well. Our colors have mixed." She continued to shove him in the mirror's direction, causing him to laugh.

Silas casually walked over to the mirror and stood in utter disbelief. He placed both hands on either side of the antique bureau, leaned forward, and stared at himself.

"Well, I'll be damned!" His chuckling grew into laughter as he studied his new look, taking in every detail.

"What the hell? Our eyes are identical," he reiterated, as the realization of what happened sank in.

Jadis stood at his side watching him. "Why are you laughing? Is this normal?"

"No, baby, definitely not. I have never seen this happen. As far as I know, I don't think any of us ever have. I've only heard whispers of such a thing, but nothing more. All-be-it the gods, Jadis. Leave it to you to turn and then partially change me on top of it." His laughter grew when he turned his head and looked at her.

"Silas, it's not funny!"

As he stared at Jadis, he was immediately turned on. The desire seared through his body like a blazing fire.

He picked her up, rushed to the bed, threw her onto her back, and crawled over the top of her.

"I want you again right now. My god, Jadis, you are stunning. Those eyes, my eyes. Everyone will surely know just by looking at you I own all that you are."

"I am yours. So what are you waiting for? Take me."

She was as turned on as he was, and she could feel their shared emotional and physical connections. He grabbed a fist-full of her hair and pulled her head back. He took one more glance before shoving his tongue into her mouth.

He had tasted amazing, and her thirst grew once again. She wanted to drink more of him. Every touch of his sent tingles radiating throughout her body, and she growled at him.

Having heard how Jadis growl was enough to put him over the edge. He shoved her legs apart with his knees, and with a hard thrust, he was inside of her again.

With each claiming, devouring need, he shoved harder, and she moaned and/or growled. She wasn't sure of her own sounds, but she was sure Silas picked up on it. She turned her head to the side as an offering.

He slid his face up the side of hers and breathed in her scent before focusing on the soft tempo of her pulse.

The bite stung, hurt even, but the painful sensation brought about a wave of euphoria she had never felt.

This time he drank his fill, knowing her blood would regenerate as quickly as his own. He also didn't have to seal the punctures; they healed as quickly as he released her throat. "Damn," he muttered.

He resumed kissing her, and she felt a strange sensation coming from her mouth. He must have felt it as well by the way in which he pulled back and stared at her again. She grabbed a fist-full of his hair and pulled his head back, exposing his throat.

"My turn," she snarled.

She latched onto his throat and sunk her canines deep into his pulsing vein. The feeling of her biting him with her own canines, along with his blood flowing over her tongue, was too much for either of them. They climaxed together as she continued to take as much of his blood as she wanted.

He gently pulled her head back, and she released her grasp; his eyes became as wide as a cat's in the dark and he let out a roar of laughter.

"What now?" She chuckled.

"I'll be dammed!" Silas could barely speak through his laughter.

"What?"

"Mon chéri, you have eight canines."

"Like yours?"

"Exactly like mine. You never cease to entertain or shock me, my dear."

He lay on top of her with his face slightly above hers. He stared into her eyes as she stared back into his. He felt her canines with the tip of his finger. "Holy shit, they're beautiful."

"You taste amazing. Dark, like the earth—the old world, I can't really explain it." Her voice sounded more like a lion's purr than a human's voice and they realized even it had fully changed.

"I can't get over this." Silas looked absolutely mesmerized. "You're more stunning than ever. I can't look away from those eyes. They have me transfixed. You are Nosferatu flesh and blood."

It suddenly hit her like a boulder to the head, "Just like you?" She was now concerned. "Mortem?" That brought about more than a chuckle.

"No baby," he said. "You are not Mortem, but then again, with you, anything's possible. I think we'll have to figure that one out as we go."

She slapped his chest, and her new abilities landed the slap this time. "That's not funny." As his laughter grew, she too cracked up. "I swear to the gods, Silas."

"You swear what to the gods?" he questioned as he flipped her onto her stomach, his body pinning her to the bed. "That little slap will be repaid in kind."

She tried to free her arms, but he had them pinned behind her back. She may have turned and become partially Silas, but she had not surpassed his strength.

He put his mouth to her ear and rumbled, "Next time you *swear to the gods* you should swear on Nosferatu instead. Your maker—me," he joked.

"You're ridiculous, vampire." She laughed, trying to get free.

He held her steady before slapping her ass; which forced her to yelp. He flipped her back over and pinned her arms above her head. He straddled her and looked as if he was studying her new looks in greater detail. He kept her pinned to the bed, contemplating the changes that had happened to them, but especially to Jadis.

"I'm okay? Right?" she asked.

After so much craziness, including multiple near-death experiences, she was still paranoid. She was fortunate to be able to turn to Silas for constant reassurance, and he was always happy to oblige. He was patient, kind, and loving. He did all he could to make her feel safe and secure.

"You are better than okay, baby, and have I mentioned lately that you are mine? Say it. I want to hear you say it with your new voice—with my voice."

"I am yours, vampire. Or shall I call you Mortem?" She chuckled.

She pulled his head to hers and took his tongue, while Silas re-positioned their bodies and they laid wrapped in each other's arms.

She knew that life couldn't possibly be any better for her than it was at that moment. Silas interrupted her thoughts when he began laughing to himself before laughing aloud.

"What's so funny now, vampire?"

"I should be calling you that now," Silas joked.

"Maybe? Apparently you turned me," she joked back.

"I promise, I did not turn you as you think. This is one more example of classic Jadis—you doing shit on your own."

She smacked his stomach, and he batted her hand away as his laughter grew.

"Why are you laughing like that?" She tried to be serious, but she'd already begun to laugh with him.

"I was just thinking, can you imagine what everyone is going to say when they find out you are part or whole Nosferatu? Hell. I don't even know how far it extends yet or what combination of things you are exactly. Finding out is going to be quite an adventure for us."

"Really? *An adventure?*"

"From what I've witnessed thus far, that's probably an understatement. With you, I've learned to expect the unexpected."

He let out an amused growl, and she responded with an eye roll.

"Who should we tell first?" she asked, sending them both into hysterics.

"Just wait until they see you. Eden is going to lose his shit." Silas was laughing so hard he was holding his stomach. "I think we should pull all the family together during the party and tell them at once. The reactions on their faces will speak for themselves. Hey guys! Guess what—Jadis is Nosferatu!"

She had never seen Silas laugh so hard. The way he was reacting made her laugh to the point she was crying when a soft knock at the door interrupted them.

Who could that be? she thought, as she wiped the tears of laughter from her face.

"I almost forgot. It's a little mating present I have for you."

Silas grinned from ear to ear. He gave her a hard peck on the lips as he got up.

What more could he possibly do?

He had already had a beautiful house built for them on the same island where the yacht was anchored days after they had met, and the place where they had first made love after being reunited. It was tucked away into the volcanic rock and stunning island landscape, disturbing as little of the natural beauty as possible. Its floor to ceiling windows allowed the light to penetrate the entire home, not to mention providing them with a panoramic view of the surrounding jungle. It was also only a five-minute walk to the lagoon that meant so much to the two of them. Every detail was precise, planned, and calculated. Just like Silas

Jadis sat up and watched him walk over to the bedroom door. When he opened it, Zach appeared, holding something that filled his arms.

She grinned from ear to ear with excitement, "Silas. What is it?"

Silas turned around, and he had a puppy tucked under each of his arms. He carried them over and gently sat them in her lap. Two Dire Wolf puppies turned their adorable faces toward her.

"By the gods, they are beautiful!"

Jadis took Silas's face in her hands and kissed him before wrapping her arms around his neck, squeezing as tightly as she could. *He can't possibly understand how much these puppies mean to me.*

"I know, mon chéri. I know how much you have missed your old pups. I have felt your longing and the love you had for them. I know these two cannot replace them, but hopefully this will fill the void in your heart."

They laid there, playing with their perfect, beautiful pups. Silas held one of them up in the air; he was talking to it and chuckling. "I think we will call this one Magnus, Mag for short." He looked at Jadis for approval.

"Yes. I love it. And we'll call this one Liminal, Limi for short."

"Perfect," he purred before leaning over to kiss her again.

Continue reading with

The Legend of Mortem Book 2 | Bound in Darkness

* 9 7 9 8 9 8 8 5 7 6 8 2 2 *